The Space Between

Also by Rachel Billington

ALL THINGS NICE
THE BIG DIPPER
LILACS OUT OF THE DEADLAND
COCK ROBIN
BEAUTIFUL
A PAINTER DEVIL
A WOMAN'S AGE
THE GARISH DAY
OCCASION OF SIN
LOVING ATTITUDES
THEO AND MATILDA
BODILY HARM
MAGIC AND FATE
TIGER SKY
A WOMAN'S LIFE

For Children

ROSANNA AND THE WIZARD-ROBOT
STAR-TIME
THE FIRST CHRISTMAS
THE FIRST EASTER
THE FIRST MIRACLE
THE LIFE OF JESUS
THE LIFE OF SAINT FRANCIS
FAR OUT!

Non-Fiction

THE FAMILY YEAR
THE GREAT UMBILICAL: MOTHER, DAUGHTER, MOTHER
CHAPTERS OF GOLD: THE LIFE OF MARY IN MOZAICS

The Space Between

Rachel Billington

ORION

To Kevin

First published in Great Britain in 2004 by Orion,
an imprint of the Orion Publishing Group Ltd.

Copyright © Rachel Billington 2004

The moral right of Rachel Billington to be identified as
the author of this work has been asserted in accordance
with the Copyright, Designs and Patents Act of 1988.

A CIP catalogue record for this book is
available from the British Library.

ISBN 0 75284 692 2 (hardback)

Typeset by Deltatype Ltd,
Birkenhead, Merseyside

Set in Monotype Garamond

Printed in Great Britain by
Clays Ltd, St Ives plc

All the characters in this book are fictitious,
and any resemblance to actual persons living or dead
is purely coincidental.

The Orion Publishing Group Ltd
Orion House
Upper Saint Martin's Lane
London, WC2H 9EA

Chapter One

Saturday

Alice Lightfoot hadn't planned to be naked when the postman arrived. Although not a particularly self-conscious woman, she did draw the line at exposing her body to a relative stranger. It crossed her mind, as she saw him staring through the kitchen window and an open door to herself, lying on a sheepskin rug, that it would have been better if he had been a complete stranger.

How much of her could he see? She hastened to look away for fear of catching the information in his eye. A twinkle, perhaps, or worse, the cold glint of disapproval. It was tempting to jump up and run out of his eyeline. But that would mean exposing more of herself and, anyway, she couldn't do anything in a hurry because the baby would have to be removed first.

Alice wasn't alone. Curled up in the foetal position, as if about to return to the womb – the wrong womb, as it happened – was Alice's granddaughter, Lily.

If the postman is here, thought Alice, it must be seven, which means they had slept together for hours. She'd got up to give Lily her bottle at four thirty, taken off her nappy to change her and decided on a brief cuddle, a moment of delicious skin-to-skin contact. It had been dark outside, a little lamp casting a mellow glow in the room. Her nakedness – she hated a nightdress in bed and there was no one else in the cottage – was perfectly natural. Richard would have said she should have pulled the curtains. I am not a freak.

She could call out to the postman, she thought, but then heard a gruff, embarrassed voice: 'You can sign for it later.'

'Thanks.' He was gone. She heard his van go up the lane.

Relieved, Alice was just about to ease Lily sideways when she felt a warm wetness trickle rapidly down her stomach and between her legs.

'Oh, Lily! How could you?' The baby's eyes were open and gleeful. She even gave a fat chortle. She was a plump baby, smooth head covered with soft down. According to her mother, she slept through every night and played or slept through every day. So far the night information had been false. Lily hadn't settled until after midnight and had woken soon after four. Perhaps she was missing her mother.

'You're going to share a bath with Grandma, my wicked princess.'

Grandma, Alice thought, as she walked through to the bathroom, was a very odd word when applied to one as young as herself. Their generations were so close. Florence, now Florrie, had been born when she was just twenty-one and Lily when Florrie was nineteen.

Alice placed Lily on the changing-mat and stared at her own body in the mirror. For a redhead she tanned easily and was always surprised by how white her breasts and buttocks remained. She twisted round to get a different angle. She supposed she had been shocked by the poor postman's unwillingly prying eyes because no man had seen her naked since Richard's death.

She leant over to turn on the taps and felt her breasts swing. She was glad they were big enough to do that. She imagined hands coming up to hold them, perhaps squeezing the nipples a little. Immediately, she felt a slight and unexpected tingling between her legs. She put a hand there and felt the damp of Lily's urine.

It seemed extraordinary that, after three years of hardly considering sex, she was now aroused – not much, certainly, but enough to make it clear that, in the right circumstances, she might become interested.

'Come on, darling.' She turned off the taps and lifted the baby into her arms. But as she stepped into the bath, she realised that her intention to splash about in innocent delight with her granddaughter had been tainted by her resurrected sexuality. The boundaries had blurred and become dangerous. What if Florrie came back, as she would at any moment from her honest job of stacking shelves in the local supermarket?

Hastily, Alice set Lily down and wrapped herself in a towel. Lily would have a conventional bath and they'd eat boiled eggs for breakfast and she'd behave like a proper grandmother. Alice sighed. A grandmother and a widow.

'It was absolutely horrendous! Fellow workers vile! Boxes filled with jars. Worse than a nightmare!' Florrie burst into the kitchen, her hair newly bleached and standing up in little knots over her head.

'It was very brave of you,' said Alice, and thought that if you went ahead with a plan to be a single mother, as Florrie had, your destiny was sure to include horrendous job experiences.

'Luckily,' continued Florrie, kissing Lily as she stuffed the toaster with bread, 'tonight I've got a job picking mushrooms. Peace. Calm. Listen to the mushrooms grow et cetera.'

'Good,' lied Alice, wondering at what point she could introduce the subject of Lily's bad night behaviour. 'I'm exhausted,' she said, as a lead-in.

'I'm exhausted,' yawned Florrie, at exactly the same time but louder than her mother. 'I'll get in a few hours' kip and be right back on duty. Isn't it lucky Lily's such a dream baby?' Smiling contentedly, she left the room.

Alice tried to recall Richard's often repeated estimate of their daughter's character. Had it been 'the most selfish, self-centred, self-regarding person in England'? Or 'in the world'? At the time she'd hotly defended Florrie, citing the difficulties of being virtually an only child in London – her brother chose to patronise some absurd all-male school in the north, her father worked from very early morning to very late evening, and her mother worked as much as she could. This had made Florrie precociously independent, Alice had argued, so that she knew her own mind and was capable of organising things to get her own way.

'Selfish,' Richard had repeated, inexorable, as always.

Alice had been forced to reel out a longer defence, about how strong Florrie was, how well prepared to thrive in a world where the weak went to the wall. One evening, she now remembered, she'd even upped the stakes to a boast. 'You mark my words, she'll become a captain of industry and give you a heart-attack.'

Richard did have a heart-attack. And since presumably it was decreed by fate, one could count it lucky that he had been taken ill in court just two months before Florrie, ever decisive, made the decision not to take her A levels, and about a year before she announced she was pregnant, father not relevant.

Not that I mind any of this in principle, thought Alice. She went over and lifted Lily out of the high chair. I just don't want to be left holding the baby.

'Mama, Mama,' gurgled Lily, trying to pull strands of Alice's hair.

'No.' The hair was firmly removed. 'I am *not* your mama. I'm an independent spirit who's on temporary duty in this little cottage on loan to your mama, while I enjoy the hard and satisfying grind of a working woman in my flat in London.'

'Mama, Mama,' laughed Lily.

'Whatever are you going on about?' Florrie stood at the door: a childish expression of attack was evidently the best form of defence.

'I'm just trying to explain to your daughter the realities of family life.' Alice noticed Florrie looked tired – young and pretty and tired. 'You go and have a rest, darling. Lily and I will enjoy the garden.'

The garden was small, a patch of grass surrounded by flower-beds overflowing with the sort of flowers that take care of themselves. Theirs was a wild independence that Alice admired: clumps of white daisies, rosemary, lavender, tangled up with straggling old-fashioned roses and a few ancient wallflowers that survived from one year to the next. 'Look.' She bent down with Lily to point out a Red Admiral alighted on a spike of lavender.

Beyond the lawn the garden became even less kempt, the unmown grass overhung by three small, aged apple trees. Alice carefully placed Lily's pram under one and put her into it. She sat on a deck-chair nearby and listened to the baby's protesting cry die away. She wanted to make herself a cup of coffee but the peace, hardly interrupted by birdsong and the steady hum of insects, held her there. This was why she'd bought the cottage, she remembered.

'Mum! It's lunch-time and Lily hasn't even got a clean bottle. You've just left them there on the side and now she'll wake up and scream.'

Dazed, Alice looked up at her reproachful daughter. 'I must have fallen asleep.'

Later, Alice and Florrie sat on a rug under one of the apple trees eating a salad Alice had made. Florrie's bare legs stuck out into the sun. They were beautifully slim with the unmarked perfection of youthful skin. Lily lay nearby waving her hands at the shadows made by the leaves over her head.

'This is a bit of an idyll,' said Alice, and was surprised by her ironic tone. Surely it was an idyll. Three generations in summery contentment, the snakes subdued or gone away. She stood up and stepped over her daughter's legs. 'I'm going to open a bottle of wine.'

Florrie looked up lazily but said nothing.

Alice walked into the cottage and found some wine in the fridge. She'd made their supper at the same time as their lunch, a chicken pasta salad waiting in a pretty painted bowl, which only needed fresh tarragon added at the last minute. Quiet hours stretched ahead in which she could relish being a good grandmother.

'I'd prefer a beer, if you've got one,' called Florrie, from the garden.

'No, I have not!' How could she be so angry, even though she'd said it quietly through gritted teeth? She slammed the drawer from which she'd taken the corkscrew.

'No beer, darling,' said Alice, re-entering the garden. 'You'll have to make do with wine.'

Chapter Two

Sunday

Alice listened for her steps on the pavement, but there was no sound, no hard evidence of her existence. She could have been a ghost floating along these warm, busy streets, with no one knowing or caring about her presence. Yet she had left the country earlier than usual today because she had longed to be in London.

Her flat was on the second floor of a mansion block in Kensington. The building was constructed of scarlet bricks, whose colour was intensified by the sunset flooding its western angles. The block stood on three sides of a paved courtyard edged with urns bearing gloomy shrubs. When Richard had proposed to her, standing just about where she was now at the end of another late July day, she had rejected him on the grounds that her hair clashed with 'all that hideous brick'. What had he said? 'Then I'll move.' But, of course, he hadn't. Richard had loved the flat. She loved their little cottage, bought in the last five years of their marriage.

Alice sighed, shifted her bag on her shoulder and looked up to the west-facing window of the flat. She'd always needed to trace it along, beyond two flats at its left, one with dreadful pink geraniums on its balcony, the other with a row of round balls of clipped privet, then hers – or rather *his* – the balcony flanked by the pyramidal bay trees he had bought. Despite her efforts, they refused to die.

The white curtains were drawn back but beams of sun struck the two long panes of glass directly, making them glossy black and reflective. For some reason, Alice continued to stare, picturing the heavy furniture inside, which easily dominated her own pale cushions and throws, introduced over the years.

Concentrated on her own imaginings, it took her a moment to

6

appreciate that the sun had moved, allowing a section of glass to become semi-transparent. Someone was inside the room.

Her heart skipped. No one should be there. Florrie was at the cottage; she had Peter's key. Could it be the porter? But the porter wouldn't flutter. The glass doors to the balcony must be open a crack and a breeze was catching the intruder's clothes. A woman in a dress with loose sleeves or wearing a light shawl who, she felt quite convinced, was staring out at her.

Hurriedly, Alice opened the gate to the courtyard and let herself into the hallway. The reception desk was unattended but by the time she reached it the porter, putting on his hat hastily, had appeared from some inner recess.

'Quick, Joe, there's a burglar in my flat!' He didn't move so she took his arm. 'You don't have to be frightened. It's just a woman.'

Mumbling something about guns, he disappeared, then emerged armed with a canister of pepper spray. He followed her in an aura of servile unwillingness. He was always like this on Sunday. He had once informed Alice there were too many bags returning from weekends in the country requiring a strong arm. Well, she required a strong arm now.

They went up in the lift and hurried past one flat to her own front door. It was closed, tranquil, secure. Alice unlocked it and gingerly entered, then, rethought. 'You go first!'

Joe became more enthusiastic. He held up his canister triumphantly.

Alice nodded impatiently. They proceeded across the hallway with its shiny parquet flooring. A corridor led to right and left, the living room straight ahead. She indicated the open door. His canister pointed, Joe trod silently on to the thick carpet. Only a streak of orange sunset came through the window but it was easy to see that the room was empty and undisturbed.

'She was by the window.' They went to it – closed, Alice noticed – and stepped on to the balcony. Nothing.

'I'll check the bedrooms.' He went off quite cheerily now, obviously certain the burglar was the product of her imagination. He would like that, Alice thought. All men enjoyed the idea of a hysterical female.

She stood dreamily on the balcony, as if the fearful raising of her heartbeat over the last few minutes had dropped her into a calmer place than before. She supposed the movement had been a combination of shadow and the light curtain fluttering as if it were a woman's dress. The window had never been open.

The streets were emptier than before. A couple came out of the launderette opposite, and a group of three or four were going into the pub a little further down the road. It had outside space, which would soon be crowded and noisy. Sometimes Alice sat on her balcony and people-watched.

In the road directly below, a Volvo estate drew up. Children and dogs spilled out, followed by the Hunter parents. The Hunters kept swearing they were going to buy a house but somehow still squashed into the flat beneath hers. She was about to turn away – watching the Hunters argue about who was going to carry what was no fun – when a woman wearing a dress came into her eyeline. She had evidently left the flats and now approached the Hunters' debouch. As Alice began to be nervously interested, the woman spoke to Mrs Hunter, who stopped lecturing her son long enough to give her a beaming smile and even call something after her. Clearly a friend, thought Alice, and hardly bothered to watch as the woman strolled away down the street opposite.

'All clear, Mrs Lightfoot. No intruders today.'

Alice stepped back into the room. Joe now looked disappointed, as if he had been thwarted of pepper-spraying fun. 'Good. You'd better get back downstairs, then.' He hovered, waiting, doubtless, for a fiver. 'The Hunters are back with piles of baggage.' She took a small revenge as she handed over the note.

Alice sat on one of the large leather sofas. The sun had gone from the room now but the day had been hot enough for her to enjoy the cool breeze blowing from the door to the balcony. She would never like the flat, but this had become a good moment, the being left on her own. She had learnt to enjoy it a little watchfully, though, for after a while, the good moment changed to loneliness.

This evening she felt happy. She enjoyed the knowledge that she could behave in any way she liked. She could take off her trousers and sit comfortably in her knickers and T-shirt without causing desirous expectations or disapproval. Richard had often compli-mented her on her thighs. They were long, slim and unpuckered by the pull of subcutaneous fat. Just genetic luck, presumably, although it wasn't easy to check out her inheritance since her mother, an only child, had died when she was three and her father, still alive, had always refused to talk about her. But Alice knew she had the same auburn hair as her mother had had, so it seemed reasonable to assume she had her thighs too.

She stood up. The next procedure, when she was alone for an evening, was to think about food. Put a little shape into the hours. But instead she sat down again, crossed her legs and looked at her calves and ankles. They were not as satisfactory as her thighs. Not fat but definitely straight. Had her mother's legs been straight? Her father's were too sinewy in that particularly masculine way for her to draw any deductions.

Alice smiled at her absurdity. Why this sudden interest in her body? Yesterday it had been nakedness and the beginnings of sexual arousal; today an examination of her legs. Would she soon be experimenting with hair colour and going on faddish diets? Was it out of mourning and into self? Was her reluctance to take responsibility for darling Lily a sign that she wished to *revert* instead of going forward with the mature wisdom – Alice smiled again – of a middle-aged woman? Perhaps she would take this question to her Cruse counsellor, who was still there for crisis moments. Perhaps, on the other hand, she wouldn't. Perhaps she wouldn't feel like seeing him ever again, with his encouraging talk of one day at a time.

Alice stood up again and stretched. She suspected that these thoughts should be expressed to someone, probably Mitzi, who had made a stab at the role of sympathetic confidante since Richard's death even though her own marriage had been falling apart.

Slowly and reluctantly, Alice went down the snugly carpeted corridor to her study, a neatly ordered room, once Richard's, with fitted bookshelves, filing cabinets and a smart new computer. In this room she became the successful journalist and interviewer whose copy appeared weekly in the magazine section of a national newspaper.

The study door opened with a little whisper as the wood brushed along the carpet. Alice, concentrating on the computer, gasped as the sound reached her consciousness. Someone *was* inside the flat.

Had the woman been hiding in a cupboard all the time she'd been studying Sir Brendan Costa's history, life and work?

'Hi, Mum.'

Alice turned round from the computer screen, which shone with a many-coloured diagram of Sir Brendan's latest takeover. 'How did you get in? I thought you gave me back your key!' There was the edge of a squeal in her usually low voice. Relaxing, she watched Peter's face, like her own in its foxy colouring but otherwise quite unlike, with its long, bony seriousness.

'I lost it. But now I've found it. You are jumpy this evening.'

'But you didn't come here this afternoon?'

'No. Jennie was with me.' He smiled.

Alice thought it the proud smile of a young man who had made love and was both irritated by and glad for him. 'Come to Mum for supper, have you?' She walked towards him, her toes curling into the carpet.

'It's too late for that. I've come for a bath. My boiler's broken.'

They hugged. 'Make yourself at home, darling.' The door to the second bathroom closed, and soon steam and music were trickling through the edges.

Alice wandered restlessly around the flat, trying to look objectively at what it offered. It was very large for one person, the wide living room with the tall windows on to the balcony and on either side one big room, one smaller and a bathroom. It had been quite big enough to house Richard, herself, Peter and Florence – as she had been. Exquisite little Florence with her dark mass of hair and pointed face. Alice's face and Richard's colouring.

She sat on the bed in what had been Florrie's bedroom. It was piled with unironed clothes and an open ironing-board.

Then she got up and wandered to the other side of the flat, switching on lights as she went. The night outside was cooler and darker now; she could hear the noise from the pub drinkers quite clearly, friendly rather than disturbing. Alice liked people. The only room she didn't use was the one where she and Richard had slept. The old-fashioned overhead light that Richard had refused to remove bounced off the heavy mahogany bed, dressing-table, chair and cupboards – all inherited from his mother. Here was the bed in which Peter and Florrie had been conceived. No, that wasn't quite right. Florrie had happened on a holiday in Paxos. Hot nights with the baby Peter in a cot beside them.

The idea that Richard had also been conceived in this shiny mahogany frame had always rather depressed her. At least he hadn't died in it. He'd died in court, with the words, 'Your Honour is mistaken.'

Peter came into the room. He'd put on shorts and a T-shirt but his face was pink and his red hair, veering towards orange – which hers thankfully avoided – was wet and tufty.

'There's something I want to show you.' Alice took him to the cupboard. She slid open the heavy doors. 'I kept just the suits. I mean, a dark suit is a dark suit and you're about the same height.' She watched Peter put his hand forward as if to touch, then withdraw it. 'Your father liked expensive suits,' added Alice. 'It'll save you a mint.' She thought she sounded as if she was trying to persuade him, whereas really she didn't mind at all. She'd removed her own clothes to the bedroom next door where she slept. As Peter said nothing, she shut the cupboard again. 'Anyway, there they are.'

'Why don't you sleep here?' Peter was looking round the room as if this was the first time her abandonment of it had struck him.

'Just didn't feel like it.'

'It's a bit of a waste.' He seemed to be estimating the room's size, the windows in two walls.

'That's what I thought about the clothes.'

Peter hesitated. 'Are you lonely?'

Alice looked startled. Peter never asked questions like that. They were hardly close enough, even if they were mother and son. It must be the sight of his father's clothes. Or perhaps Jennie was turning him into a different person. They began to walk to the living room. 'No, darling. Not really.'

'I could come back here. Live with you.' He'd blurted it out. His face went pinker.

'Absolutely not,' Alice exclaimed, louder than she meant too. Before she could feel guilty, she caught the relief on Peter's face.

They entered the living room and Alice's eyes went immediately to the white curtains blowing inwards quite vigorously now. Should she tell Peter about the woman at the window? The non-woman. Was it a sign of loneliness to create a woman lying in wait for her?

'Such a strange thing happened to me this afternoon...' She began the story but as she told it – quite amusingly, she thought, with descriptions of Joe's pepper spray – she saw that Peter was hardly interested. He had reassured himself about her state of mind and now he wanted to return to his own life.

When she finished, he laughed. 'It was probably your *doppelgänger*. What colour was her hair?'

Alice let him go then. As he collected his things, she went out to the balcony again. After a few minutes, he called out,' I'm off!' She went to say goodbye, but the door banged before she reached it so she returned to the balcony. He emerged quite soon and Alice was surprised to see that, as well as the bag he'd arrived with, he had something over this arm.

''Bye, Peter.'

He looked up, waved briefly, then hurried away, head down, as if guilty. It was almost a run and she clocked then that he was carrying a couple of Richard's suits over his arm. She could see the hanger poking out of the black bag he'd put over them either as disguise or protection. How odd of him. How sensitive.

Alice walked slowly to the large empty bedroom and opened the cupboard. Yes, there was a space. Perhaps he had even taken three suits. Maybe she should reassure him that she, too, was moving beyond his father's death.

Chapter Three

Monday

Sir Brendan Costa looked questioningly at Alice, his hot blue eyes shooting attention and energy over the wide desk. She had thought him ugly and predictable up to this minute but suddenly she saw she had been quite wrong.

'Do you always look so bored when you conduct an interview?'

She would have to give him an answer but it mustn't contain the smallest element of flirtation. She had resolved that that should never be her way. 'You're mistaking concentration for boredom, I think.'

'So I'm blinding you with figures, am I?' He laid his rather pudgy fingers on the empty desk so that the one ring he wore was well displayed. It was on his wedding finger but, according to press clippings – that is, gossip columns – he was presently unmarried, having been divorced three times. She would ask him about it towards the end of the interview.

'I would hate to misrepresent your point of view.'

'Good. Good. Have you ever worked in business?'

Alice uncrossed and recrossed her legs. Despite her no-flirting rule, she almost invariably wore a skirt. It gave her one superiority over her subjects: *they* couldn't wear a skirt. Or, at least, not in public. Today she was wearing a cream linen suit. Her best. She must answer Sir Brendan's question. Pauses were a good way of keeping the subject on his toes but, if too prolonged, risked irritability.

'Never. No.' Should she be more forthcoming? He had just finished a twenty-minute monologue, explaining the reasons behind the takeover of a company that produced up-market kitchen fittings, which was interesting because his core business had always been in property. He couldn't be truly curious, despite those blue, rather small eyes.

'The English middle classes have always despised business, although very happy to live off the proceeds. What did your father do?'

'He was a doctor. A GP. Quite humble.' She didn't mind telling him that.

'Very respectable. And your husband?' This was an unacceptable question. She should deny him, but she found herself saying, 'He was a lawyer.'

The answer seemed to please him. He smiled and drummed his fingers on the desk. 'Don't you want to ask about my family? Interviewers are usually intrigued.'

'Father Italian immigrant, mother Irish immigrant.' She read from her pad. 'Met in Liverpool 1920. Five children – two sons, three daughters. The eldest son killed in action, Second World War. Parents and two daughters killed in bombing raid.' Alice stopped. What was she doing? Just because this man had made millions, married (and divorced) three times, and had a reputation for toughness verging on brutality, she must not assume he was inhuman.

Alice looked up with a sensitive, apologetic expression on her face, and was horrified to see Sir Brendan's eyes full of tears.

He produced a large red spotted handkerchief. 'Don't worry,' he said. 'I weep easily. It's the Italian side of my inheritance. The Irish are tough as old boots.' He blew his nose lustily. 'As you who know everything know already, I was only a baby in the war. The deaths left a mark on my soul but not on my memory. I was brought up by my much older sister. A fiendish woman who made me what I am.'

'I'm sorry,' said Alice, feebly.

A flash of irritation crossed Sir Brendan's face, and he looked at his watch. 'Free for an early lunch, are you?'

'But . . .' Alice, already unnerved, felt out of control. Could she write about his tears? He had forbidden a tape-recorder and she looked rather hopelessly at her pad, filled with shorthand detailing the reason for his takeover.

'Yes. Tell Gudgeon I'll catch up with him this afternoon.' Alice realised he was ordering his secretary to cancel his lunch date. 'Let's go.' He was standing beside her, a big man, twice the width of

Richard who, although six foot, maintained the reedy form of the non-athlete, which was an understatement. He had been 'bookish' – she thought of the word affectionately. And many, many years older than her, even older than Sir Brendan. How odd to be thinking of him now. She never thought of him when she was working.

'Thank you. How very kind.' Formality, that was the thing. But he was hurrying her past two secretaries, towards the lift, down the marbled entrance hall. Clasping her notepad to her breast, she asked, 'Are we still on the record?'

He stopped for a moment, eyed her with a mixture of reproach and humour. 'Do journalists ever go off the record?' Then he was bustling her into a chauffeur-driven car with its engine running. It was, Alice noticed, deliciously cooled. Since he seemed to feel no need for speech, she settled back and tried to remember her unasked questions.

'That's right.' He looked at her approvingly, 'There's a time for everything. Conversation is best undertaken across a corner table with a bottle of Puligny Montrachet *premier cru* and a fillet of steamed sea bass.'

Alice smiled at what she assumed was self-parody and shivered. The car was almost too cool. She understood he was the sort of man who liked to compartmentalise and keep each compartment under his control. And now, she told herself, he had kidnapped her for an hour or two.

Mitzi and Alice lay on their backs, each on one of the big sofas set at right angles in Alice's living room. Mitzi, who was tall and angular with black, straight-cut hair and a small rosebud mouth, painted vermilion, was dressed in tights and a leotard top as if for dancing or an exercise class.

'What a day!' Alice yawned and stretched.

'But was he attractive?' Mitzi rolled over so she could gauge Alice's reaction.

She had always been nosy, Alice thought tolerantly. 'That's not the point.' She watched Mitzi make a disbelieving face. 'The point was – is – I needed an article, not to be given a slap-up lunch at the Ritz and told all about his horrible sister, who locked him under the stairs as if he were a prototype Harry Potter.'

'Perhaps he made it up?'

Alice ignored this. 'Actually, it was quite fascinating but I could hardly scribble away through lunch so I'll have to rely on memory, and when I did slip in an important question—'

'What sort of question?' interrupted Mitzi.

'Like, was it true that he was planning to lay off a thousand workers at this company he's bought – he either ignored it or said, 'All in good time,' and then, of course, he was suddenly in a stupendous hurry and we were back in the icy car and he was delivered to his office and I was brought here.'

'So he knows where you live.' Mitzi put her legs in the air and executed a few desultory turns of the ankle.

'Where I've been desperately trying to knock out something before my memory files it under "not to be retrieved".'

'Just tell it how it was, baby. No one cares about lay-offs.' Mitzi sat up. 'So now you're too tired to come to *our regular Monday exercise class*?' Mitzi underlined the words with heavy irony.

'Be fair, Mitzi. I deliver my piece on Tuesday. Monday was always going to be panic time. It just happens to suit you because it's your day out.'

Mitzi was staring at her mockingly. 'I hope you're not going to change, darling.'

'Whatever do you mean?' Alice was tired – too much wine at lunch, too many hours afterwards staring at the computer. She didn't need to be harassed by her best friend.

'Become more like the rest of us – irritable, demanding, selfish, highlighting the "I" in life.'

'Sometimes I forget you're a copywriter.' Alice, who had half sat up, collapsed back again. 'I guess I've never been good at saying, "No".'

'Anyway, I'm off to sweat out my impurities.' At the door, Mitzi stopped. 'Am I dreaming or did we talk only about you? I knew things were a-changing. Hey, what about swapping Thursday for Monday?'

Alice flapped a hand. 'You know I go to Brighton on Thursdays.'

'And the weekends are for Florrie and the baby. For a wealthy widow, you sure do keep yourself out of trouble.'

After Mitzi had banged the front door with her usual energy Alice continued to lie dozily. It was as warm as the evening before and the same light breeze was moving the white curtains. When Sir

Brendan's chauffeur had dropped her outside the flats this afternoon, she had stood on the pavement for a while, unwilling to make the transition from the wide, bright, noisy world to her dim, cool privacy. It was an unusual feeling for her and, as she had the day before, she looked up at her windows. The curtains remained curtains.

'Has Mum gone?'

Alice had quite forgotten Mitzi's son, Greg, who was often left behind after school to enjoy Alice's computer.

'Just now. Do you want a sandwich?' He was ten years old, with Mitzi's darkness but none of her angularity. His round black eyes gave him a baby-bird appeal.

'That'd be great. Got any peanut butter?'

'I'll look.' Alice tried to remember if Peter had ever seemed so vulnerable. She thought not. Perhaps Greg's was the doubtful air of the child of recently divorced parents.

She found peanut butter at the back of the kitchen cupboard. It probably dated back to when Peter had lived in the flat, over a year ago now. Just as he had begged to go to boarding-school at the age of seven, he had moved out of the flat as soon as he left university and signed up with a law firm to pay for the next stage of his law training.

Alice carried in the sandwich and put it beside Greg, who was far too busy negotiating his racing car round a precipitous hairpin bend to notice. Peter had entered this same kind of boyish oblivion, she remembered, in which people were made to feel extraneous. She found herself picturing his recent exit from the flat, Richard's suits, in their bin-bag shrouds, folded over his arm, as he hurried away, head ducked and guilty. She must discuss the psychology of it with Mitzi. Did Peter feel that by taking the suits, he was killing his father again? Mitzi loved that sort of conversation.

'You've got to finish in five,' said Alice. 'I need to take over.'

In exactly five minutes – he had not been oblivious after all – Greg appeared in the living room, munching his sandwich. He ambled over to the balcony windows. 'Whew!' He made a whistling sound of admiration and stepped outside.

'What?'

'It's a Bentley Azure. Worth two hundred and fifty thousand pounds. With a chauffeur too. I guess I'll be off.' He left with surprising speed, too quick for Alice to point out his backpack. She ran after him, using the lift as he'd taken the stairs, arriving in Reception just as Greg dashed through the doors.

The chauffeur stood at the desk with an air of importance. In one hand he held his cap, in the other an envelope he was giving to the porter. 'Urgent, for Alice Lightfoot.'

The porter, unimpressed, indicated Alice. 'That's her.'

Losing none of his dignity, the chauffeur, who had already driven Alice twice that day, handed over the letter for a second time.

'Thanks.' Alice ran after Greg. She was cross to feel she was blushing – like a silly schoolgirl, she thought. Although probably no schoolgirl, even a redhead, blushed these days. 'Greg!' She needn't have hurried. He was standing a foot from the car, transfixed. He took his bag without comment.

'Like it, do you?' The chauffeur had caught them up. Whether by accident or design he looked like his master, Alice thought: tall, stocky, with the possibility of quick action only if absolutely necessary.

'Wicked,' mumbled Greg, and asked some question Alice didn't catch. She was staring at the envelope. She just hoped Sir Brendan wasn't trying to spike her interview. Tomorrow was her deadline and there was no time to do anyone else, even if she'd had an alternative lined up. She had a couple filed for emergencies but it wouldn't do her reputation with the editor much good. He was excited by getting Sir Brendan, who generally refused interviews.

Vaguely, Alice noticed that the pompous chauffeur was in lively conversation with Greg.

'Wow. Yes!' He had the door to the car open.

'I'll give your son a quick spin, madam.'

They were gone before Alice could respond. She opened the envelope.

> *Dear Ms Lightfoot,*
>
> *My secretary has just pointed out I have two tickets for a charity dinner Wednesday evening and only myself to use them. I would be so honoured if you would accompany me. Please forgive the last-minute nature of this invitation and take pity on my friendless state. Harry will wait for an answer.*
>
> *Yours, Brendan (Costa).*

*

Alice was so relieved that she nearly threw the letter into a nearby bin. Of course she wouldn't go, on too many grounds, the most important being that she must have her piece published without any strings, like charity dinners, attached. That was conceited of him, she thought, not to lay out the attractions of the evening. Clearly he believed he was lure enough. Well, he wasn't. Anyway, she was already booked to see *Die Frau ohne Schatten* with Jonathan.

When the car returned, Alice had borrowed paper from the porter and written a note:

Dear Sir Brendan, Of course I forgive you for the late invitation. I already owe you thanks for a most delicious lunch. Sadly, I have a long-standing engagement to go to the opera tomorrow evening . . .

Alice was pleased with her note. It was gracious, she felt, yet suitably formal. She had also said no. When Mitzi returned from her exercise class, she would have to ask her why it was such a relief to say no to Sir Brendan.

'Because you are attracted to him.' Mitzi, muffled in scarves despite the heat – she believed one must never cool down too quickly after violent exercise – had no doubts.

'Couldn't it be because I don't find him attractive, in fact quite the opposite, but he's the sort of man who's likely to jump on any woman he has under his control?'

'You fancy him.'

Alice laughed. 'So speaks the oracle. Anyway, I'm going to the opera with Jonathan Wouk.'

'Woof-Woof.' Mitzi responded automatically with the nickname given him by the children to mimic the barking sound of his voice.

'Not any more.' Alice smiled. 'He's far too grand.'

'Jonathan, or Woof-Woof, it must be the first Wednesday in the month.'

'It is,' agreed Alice, without shame. Richard had taught her the usefulness of routine in the greater cause of freedom, or words similar. 'Now, go away, dear oracle, and take your son. I've got to final-edit my interview.'

Chapter Four

Tuesday

Alice had always liked to deliver her copy in person. It gave her a reason to go into the office and check out the gossip. She had been favoured by the paper's editor (known to his employees as the Master) for ten years now but what if times should change, he should die, be wooed away to another paper for an even vaster salary or, conversely, be sacked by the owner who might himself change? And what if his successor didn't favour her? She'd started the job as a challenge to herself but now she needed it for all sorts of reasons, including money.

So, every week she ignored her email and took in a printout, plus disk. It was another routine and occasionally she got to have lunch with the Master. More often, over the last few years, she had lunch with Guy, sometimes Guy and one or two other people from the office but more often just Guy.

'How dashing you look!'

Guy Vernon was presently editor of the Saturday magazine for which she wrote her interview. He was also very close to the Master, which gave him other unspecified tasks. Alice had a desk not far from his, which she almost never used. He had always been there, always keen to flatter and chat. Just lately their lunches had become almost a standing date.

Alice looked down at herself. She had dressed in a more dashing fashion than usual, ice-blue bell-bottomed trousers and a white-cotton knit top with white hoop earrings.

'Very fifties,' added Guy. 'Are we going to the the Monkey's Tail or the Admiral's Telescope?'

'We don't remember the fifties,' commented Alice, as they walked out to yet another day of brilliant sunshine. Guy's age was never clear to her, when she thought of it. He was one of those perfectly nice-looking men whose lack of notable features make them physically anonymous. If asked to describe Guy out of his presence, Alice would probably have said he was tallish, with brownish eyes and hair – or perhaps, on the other hand, they were bluish and greyish. She might then have recalled he had a nice voice and liked to surprise her with garish ties. They'd never met outside the newspaper and the lunch hour, except on rare occasions – such as the department's Christmas party.

Alice knew Guy wasn't married because he'd once mentioned it, but she had no idea if he lived with a partner of either sex or an aged mother, or, indeed, where he lived. This was beginning to feel odd.

'So, how did you find Sir Brendan?'

They had settled at a table outside the Roasted Quail – their third choice of meeting-place. The brick wall at their back reflected the heat like an oven and the rather dirty table was crowded with others employed by their newspaper. But Alice was happy, even triumphant. She had delivered another piece. She lived to fight another week. 'He took me to lunch. At the Ritz.'

'And made a pass?'

One of Guy's characteristics was an ability to ask just the right questions so that Alice felt stimulated but not pressured. On this occasion, he'd got it wrong. Alice frowned irritably. 'Of course not.' She decided not to mention his invitation to the charity dinner. 'Frankly, I don't know why people are so interested in him.' This was a straight lie. She saw exactly why people were interested in him and she'd referred to it in her article, which Guy would read. Ambition. Power. Money. Certainly ... but also the gift of intimacy. What was it he'd called her?' 'A Botticelli crossed with a Schiele.' How could he have known that before she had married, her room had been plastered with reproductions from exactly these two apparently contradictory painters?

'So you didn't find him dangerous?'

'Dangerous? What do you mean? Heavens, it's hot here. And filthy.' She wiped her hand across the table. 'Can't we find somewhere cooler? We could buy sandwiches and go to that bit of park by the river.'

Guy smiled, 'I've a much better idea. Let's take our sandwiches *on* the river. Catch a boat from St Catherine's Dock.'

For an uneasy moment, Alice felt as if something had jolted uncomfortably but the sensation passed quickly and she felt filled with energy. 'Brilliant. I've absolutely nothing to do all afternoon.'

'And the paper can manage without me for once.'

Despite the heat they walked fast, as if their decision to change direction must be implemented in military style. After a quarter of an hour, they reached the pier and Guy, acting without consultation, bought both tickets. They found seats on the front deck of the boat, already quite full with tourists of various nationalities, and opened their sandwiches.

Alice looked at hers with distaste. She had a real aversion to tuna.

'Sorry.' Guy swapped it for his, which was ham.

'You can't like tuna?'

'Eating tuna makes me think I'm a brave fisherman with only a sou'wester between me and the gale, force nine.'

'Do you go on boats, then – I mean real boats?' Alice lay back against the bench, with the sun warming the back of her head and shoulders.

'I sail.' He had answered so briefly that she hardly heard. She felt the engines starting up under them and a new trail of Japanese tourists filled the remaining benches. Alice was glad she wouldn't be able to understand what they were saying. She could drift. The boat left the pier and took up course in the river. They were going upstream to the Houses of Parliament, if they wanted.

'You're falling asleep.' Guy's voice was only slightly accusing.

Alice opened her eyes and ate one of her sandwiches. 'I'll feed the other to the ducks.'

'There aren't any ducks.'

'Swans, then. Where do you sail to?'

'Last month we crossed the Channel and carried on down to La Rochelle. King James sent his lover, the Duke of Buckingham, there to relieve the Hugenots. It was a disaster, and Buckingham was assassinated before he could try again.'

As Guy talked on about this small French town, Alice closed her eyes again and thought that Guy's voice was the most characteristic part of him. It was deep and melodious, and produced properly researched information without being boring.

'You're not listening to a word.' His hand was on her bare arm.

'I can still hear with my eyes shut. I was wondering if you'd needed your sou'wester for the trip.'

'The weather was calm. Too calm.'

'A painted ship upon a painted ocean.'

'Exactly.' His hand, which had not left her arm, now lifted briefly and took hers. At the same time, above their heads, a loud microphone voice began to describe passing buildings.

The hand holding Alice's was firm and friendly. The combination of sunny somnolence and the loud explanatory voice somehow made it easier not to snatch hers away. Nevertheless it was disturbing. No one held her hand, these days. Or, if it came to that, had done so for many years past. If Richard had died slowly – of cancer, perhaps – then she would certainly have held his hand, but the suddenness of his death had made impossible any last hours, or months, even, of tenderness. Yet she had held his hand once.

'Oh, God!' Alice pulled away her hand abruptly. She had been taken to see Richard's body in the hospital where they had tried vainly to resuscitate him. He was quite obviously dead. Always a pale man, he had turned almost green. She had stared, too shocked to do more, when a nurse, presumably convinced of her helpfulness, had indicated she could touch Richard's hand and then, as she had not reacted, taken hers and placed it in his.

'As bad as that.'

Alice turned to Guy with surprise. Lost in the memories of that dreadful day, she had almost forgotten him. 'The last time I held hands,' she looked at him earnestly, 'was with Richard's corpse. His fingers were so cold and stiff, like wax. The feeling stayed with me for ages. I'm sorry. I was rude.' Without thinking very hard, she leant forward and kissed his cheek. '*Your* hand was nice.'

'To our right you can see the Tower of London, including Traitor's Gate . . .' continued the massive voice.

Guy was staring at her. 'You never talk much about your husband's death.'

'You don't talk about much outside work either,' countered Alice.

'No.'

He didn't enlarge. They both sat back against their benches. The silence was still comfortable. They passed St Paul's, surrounded

23

now by modern structures. 'The symbol of survival in the Second World War . . .' the voice informed them, in reverential tones.

The sun became cooler and the boat's speed stirred up a pleasant breeze. The voice came less often and the Japanese, who had posed for each other at the front of the boat, settled down on their benches and exhibited the more usual quiet exhaustion of the city tourist. Alice, too, fell quiet again. The two handholding incidents, both immediate and remembered, slipped away on the smooth river ahead, the monotonous pulse of the ship's engine.

'So, who've you got lined up for next week?'

'I've only just delivered.' They had returned to their old terms.

'Someone crossed my desk this morning.' Guy often came up with good ideas for Alice's subjects. 'He's a deep-sea diver. Actually, he's a kind of friend of mine.'

Alice turned to Guy. She saw now that he had ruddy skin, unusually healthy for someone who spent his entire week in an office, and that his eyes were hazel behind their glasses and that his hair was the kind of brown that lightens in the summer. In fact, he did look like someone who went sailing or, at least, spent time outdoors in healthy pursuits.

'Why ever would I want to interview a deep-sea diver?'

'He's got a bee in his bonnet. He's determined to found a diving school for the under-twenty-ones. Only one condition. They have to have spent at least six months in detention. Prison. I'm surprised you haven't read about him.'

Alice thought she had. As Guy told her more, between pauses to allow the booming voice to have his say, 'On our left is the South Bank arts and theatre complex including the National Theatre, the Queen Elizabeth Hall and the Hayward Gallery . . .'

'I'll fax you some cuttings,' continued Guy, apparently not noticing her silence. 'It would be something different for you.'

Now they were closing on Westminster Bridge and the Houses of Parliament. The sun, slanting across the river, gilded the buildings into an old master. Had Constable painted London? Alice asked herself vaguely, but she could only recall blue-tinged Impressionist paintings, not this gold-brown.

'Nearly there.'

'I wish we weren't.' She spoke impulsively but knew it was true. It was fresh on the river: the hot stone city would coruscate and enervate. More than that, she wasn't ready to pick up the reins of life.

'We could take the boat back again.' Guy smiled. He looked at his watch. 'Although I can't say I feel ready for the office.'

'What time is it?' Alice was desultory. The boat was slowing, the engines churning the water under them. The Japanese were already queuing to leave the deck. Alice thought how good-looking they were, how well dressed and orderly. The voice had stopped blasting information. Their journey was over. 'Come for tea in my flat,' she said. 'You've never seen it, have you?'

Alice glanced upwards at the windows, but that morning she had tied back the white curtains.

'Posh,' commented Guy.

'Richard's taste.'

In the lift, they came close together, their faces reflected doubly in the mirrored lining.

'You've caught the sun.' Guy seemed surprised.

'So have you, actually.'

'You should wear a hat.' For a moment Alice thought he was going to touch her face, but they had arrived at the second floor and the lift doors opened automatically.

The living room was once again filled with late-afternoon sun. She broke through a barrier of dust idling on sunbeams and flung open the balcony windows. It was odd to see Guy there. He seemed perfectly at ease, however, choosing the sofa nearest the window and stretching out his legs.

'I'll make some tea.' As she left, she saw him lean forward to pick up a magazine, something Florrie had bought, *Elle* or *Marie Claire*. Had she talked about her children to Guy? She couldn't remember.

When she returned with a jug of iced tea, the glassy cubes making patterns as they melted the amber liquid, he sprang up to help her.

'Where did you get your manners?'

'My father. He was in the army. He used to jostle my mother to get on the outside of the pavement.'

Alice had assumed he was a classless London journalist but an army background gave him solidity. Quite likely he had gone to public school. The thought depressed Alice. They had got on so well without knowing much about each other.

They sat side by side on the sofa as they had on the boat. Guy talked amusingly about his father. Now dead, he had been an eccentric, the high point of whose life had come after his retirement – forcible retirement, Guy emphasised – when he'd set up a school in India. Eventually it had moved, with many of its shivering pupils, to North Wales where they were forced to go on icy treks, led by Guy's father. Tragically, one of the unfortunate boys died of hypothermia or something similar. 'And my mother persuaded him to close down. Or perhaps the authorities did, in return for no prosecution. Luckily I was away at a slightly safer school and never knew the details. They tried to breed pigs after that. And then they both died, one after the other, rather suddenly. At the time it made little impact on me. But we had been separated so much. And they were both so crazy.'

And you're not crazy at all, thought Alice, pleased with him again.

When he took her hand, she made no objection. 'Dear Alice. So clever. So pretty. So independent.'

'Am I?' She was not sure she felt it. First, there had been her father, absolutely dominant, then Richard, then the children, and Lily. Even now, when Richard had gone, there was her father, demanding, it was true, no more than a Thursday visit to his nursing home in Brighton, but there. Very much there.

'I suppose my job makes me seem independent,' she conceded, wondering, as she spoke, why she didn't *feel* it.

'You know, this flat is overawing. I'd never imagine you living in such a well-appointed place.'

'I told you. Richard bought it.' Alice heard her voice sharp and quick.

'Sorry. That tea was inspired.' He put the glass on the table and leant towards her. She could smell sweat faintly, not unpleasant at all, and found herself wondering whether he was going to kiss her, and if he did, would she let him?

Instead he stroked her arm. 'You don't freckle much for a redhead.' He touched the little round bone at her wrist. 'But your forearm here,' he touched again, 'is quite pink.' His tone was friendly rather than seductive but Alice found her body responding in an alarmingly affirmative way.

'Can I kiss you?'

Why did he have to ask?

He kissed her. Even then, Alice continued thinking how odd this all was.

Guy looked at her with his bright hazel eyes behind their spectacles.

'Do you always kiss with your glasses on?' she asked.

'I was carried away.' He smiled.

Richard's love-making had been much more serious. 'Until now I hadn't even noticed you wore them.'

'I don't all the time. I should go.' Guy stood up suddenly. 'I'll fax that stuff to you.' He seemed to be expecting a response.

'Yes. Thanks.' She wouldn't get up. So the kiss had been in the spirit of friendliness, reflection only of a sunny afternoon on a boat.

'I think there's someone outside your door.'

Alice pulled herself together. He was right. A baby was crying, a full-throttle sound that must have been going on for some time. Perhaps that was why Guy had stopped kissing her. 'It must be my daughter's baby. With my daughter, of course.'

'You're not a grandmother?'

'Surely I told you?' But maybe she hadn't.

Alice opened the door. Florrie fell in, with the bawling Lily strapped to her back. Despite these impedimenta, she looked, at least to her mother's eyes, heartbreakingly beautiful. Bubbly blonde curls dangled over her blue eyes and pouty red lips. Her neck was as slim and white as a teapot spout.

'What were you up to, Mum? We've been standing here for hours and hours . . .' Florrie, who had a rather raucous voice, easily rose above Lily who had become somewhat more muted.

'Darling!' Alice tried hard to look welcoming. She could feel the effort twisting her face into a grimace. She wanted to say, 'You're living in the country. I've lent you my beautiful cottage. Whatever are you doing on my patch?'

'I'm off.' Guy, apparently of no interest to Florrie who was emptying herself and her baby on to the floor, side-stepped them, giving Alice a cheery wave.

Alice watched him leave and noticed, standing in the corridor, a stringy young man wearing a deferential expression above his T-shirt and jeans. Inside the flat, Florrie had shouted: 'Baz!'

'I'm Baz,' said the youth, under Alice's enquiring gaze.

Chapter Five

Wednesday

Since Richard's death, Alice had identified Wednesday as her favourite day of the week. It was a day of relative freedom when, although she must start sleuthing her new subject – she lived in hope that she would get one in the bag before the last-minute Monday – she was not yet panicking. Usually she had lunch with Mitzi. And looked forward to an evening out, every so often with Jonathan. It was *her* day.

'Mum,' wailed Florrie, 'if you don't help me with Lily, I'll never get off.'

Alice went along to the bathroom. On her way she met Baz, who nodded at her without speaking as if to show his humility and gratitude. Alice was not impressed. Baz, who was or was not Florrie's boyfriend but certainly wasn't Lily's father, had got into trouble over, Florrie had insisted, the *tiniest* amount of an illegal substance and was due in court that morning. It seemed he had moved into the cottage the moment she, Alice, had left it.

'Good morning,' said Alice. 'I hope you slept well.' This was cruel. She had never seen anyone look more exhausted. His eyes were half closed by the puffy bags above and below, and his skin was grey with reddish blotches. He was wearing the grubby T-shirt and jeans of the evening before. He would not make a good impression on the judge.

In the bathroom, Florrie was struggling to dress Lily and herself at the same time. 'Leave her,' commanded Alice, 'and go and put Baz into one of Daddy's suits. A lightweight one, given it's going to be another boiling day.'

'Mum. You're so thoughtful. So grown-up. D'you know how I love you?' She was off. Soon afterwards the door banged.

Alice looked down at Lily, who'd made herself naked again and was energetically chewing the corner of a flannel. 'We'll get on very well, Lily, if you take the point that I'm your grandmother.'

Drooling milk, for Florrie had been feeding her a bottle up to the last minute, Lily bared toothless gums in a knowingly adorable smile.

At midday Alice cancelled Mitzi, who protested vociferously: 'I don't expect you've noticed I'm a busy woman. There are clients desperate to secure my food-eating services . . .'

Alice laughed. 'Come here, then. You can remind yourself about babies.'

'I *love* babies.'

Alice laughed again. Mitzi had hated being the mother of a small baby, although Greg broke her heart daily now. 'We'll just reschedule, darling.'

At five o'clock, Alice was wondering whether Florrie and Baz would ever return. Perhaps they had eloped, although that seemed far too energetic a concept for Baz. Florrie had assured her they were planning to take a train straight back to the cottage after the hearing and picking up Lily so that she, Alice, would have time to prepare for her opera date.

Surely Baz would not disappear in Richard's suit? Alice left Lily snoozing in her basket, then went along and looked, as she had yesterday, at her husband's clothes. It was strange that, after nearly three years hanging quietly in the wardrobe, they had been raided twice in a week.

She sat on the bed, then lay down. The room was stuffy but, apart from the suits, it had lost all sense of male presence. When Richard had been alive, there was an alarm on his left side, usually set for an early hour. There was also, at night, a pair of reading glasses, some pills – the wrong ones for his condition, as it had turned out – *The Economist*, the *New Yorker*, the *Law Reform* magazine, the *Spectator*, a box of tissues because his nose tended to drip, and the book he was reading. When he died, he had ten pages to go of Paul Johnson's *Offshore Islands*.

Why should this jerk her heartstrings? It was the pathos, she supposed, of there being so few pages before he would have encompassed his nation's history. Richard had been very British.

Alice looked at his clock. She decided to shower and prepare for her evening, whatever Florrie's plans. Jonathan was picking her up in a taxi at six thirty.

At six o'clock, Alice sat cool and fresh in the living room. She wore a lilac silk dress with heavy scarlet beads round her neck and scarlet sandals. The pinkness produced by her boat trip with Guy had already turned a satisfactory gold and, despite an irritating frizziness to her hair caused by the heat, which had now turned humid, she felt pleased with her appearance.

On one side of her lay a stack of faxes received from Guy about his deep-sea diver. On the other was Lily, apparently only interested in catching sunbeams although it was nearly time for her bottle. Alice looked at the severely knotted white curtains with approval.

The doorbell buzzed loudly. So they had made it just in time. Alice went to the door while Lily emitted anticipatory squawks behind her back.

'A chauffeur brought this. He's waiting.' The porter looked nosy, which was his right, thought Alice, forgivingly. But where were Florrie and Baz? She tore open the envelope. 'Dear Ms Lightfoot, I was passing and couldn't resist sending up this note. May I disturb you for a moment?'

Alice felt bewildered. What did he mean? The porter took it upon himself to elucidate. 'He wants to come in, that's what the chauffeur's expecting.'

Alice found herself smiling. It was such an unexpected proposition in one way but so in character. Sir Brendan didn't accept 'No'. If she wouldn't accompany him to dinner, he would call in and have her company, if only for a few minutes. His timing was perfect. 'Send him up,' she pronounced blithely, as if ordering a Chinese takeaway.

Sir Brendan's presence in Alice's flat was quite a shock. He walked round making charming comments about the décor, which did not disguise the predatory prowl. For some reason he wanted her. Alice's heart fluttered in a chicken-in-the-coop way.

The one decoration in the room on which Sir Brendan didn't

comment was the baby. Dear Lily. Alice looked at her fondly and smiled. He must, surely, think Lily was her daughter.

'You're off to the opera, then, leaving me to face the longueurs of a terrible dinner that I would pay a fortune to avoid. As a matter of fact, I've already paid a fortune, which makes it doubly unfair I have to go. I set myself two of these events a year. They seem to come round once a week.' He took a step or two closer to Alice. 'Do you have time for a drink? There is something I want to ask you.'

Alice glanced at her watch. 'I can't go anywhere till the babysitter comes.'

'Quite.' Without glancing at Lily, Sir Brendan, not an elegant man but strong and determined, strode to the front door, which he opened with a flourish. Outside stood the chauffeur holding a tray on which bubbled two glasses of champagne.

Alice giggled weakly. Was this how rich men really behaved or was it all parody? A glass was placed in her hand. 'Cheers!' He touched her glass and his small bright eyes caught hers. 'I'm never afraid of being absurd,' he said. 'It's one of my strengths. Never hang back from the stupid question. Always be hot rather than cool – except when you're cold.'

'I could have put that in my interview,' complained Alice, although she couldn't help accompanying the words with what she feared was a bewitching smile. She sat down and crossed her legs.

'But it's too late?' He took a place beside her.

'Oh, yes.' She was demure now. That was *her* province, outside his control.

He looked at his watch, obviously planning his question, but before he could speak, Lily let out a loud yell. Sir Brendan leapt to his feet.

'Oh, it's not you. She's hungry, I'm afraid.' Rather reluctantly, Alice picked up Lily and placed her against her shoulder, then continued to sip her champagne.

'Quite a chaperone.' Sir Brendan remained standing. 'I have a house in Gloucestershire. A beautiful house, where I entertain.' He seemed surprised by his own information and looking for approval. Alice nodded obligingly.

'I have a weekend coming up soon that you might find amusing,' he continued, and added, in a half-modest, half-proud way, a list of very interesting people – at least, famous people, journalists, writers, actors and a banker or two.

'It must be a big house.'

'It is. Built in the Patrick Gwynne style. So, you'll come?' He seemed in a hurry now to get an answer and depart. Perhaps it was the effect of Lily who had started a continuous light complaint, prelude to something stronger.

'Thank you.' She handed him her empty glass. 'I'll let your office know.'

He didn't press her, but turned as he reached the door. 'And you have a son, too?'

'Oh, yes.' After all, she did have a son, if not the ten-year-old Greg assumed by the chauffeur. Surely she couldn't be expected to take someone as alien to her life as Sir Brendan Costa *seriously*?

'Of course they're invited too.'

When he had left, Alice couldn't resist watching his departure from the balcony and therefore witnessed the arrival of Florrie, Baz and, with his taxi behind him, Jonathan.

They were standing on the pavement, Florrie waving her hands, in full flow, although Alice couldn't make out the words, Jonathan looking impatient, and Baz nattily turned out in Richard's second-best summer suit yet retaining a hangdog crumpled air.

In a moment, Brendan appeared, champagne glasses bulging out of his pockets, and headed as directly as he could for his shining Bentley. Alice found herself almost laughing at the absurdity of it all and didn't bother to wonder why her spirits were so high. 'Jonathan!' she called, as the chauffeur slid his car smoothly from the kerb. 'I'll come down!'

'Mummy!' screeched Florrie. 'Baz got off on a technicality. We're flying!'

Jonathan made it clear that he had not been amused by the chaos on the pavement: Lily screaming for her mother, Baz apparently planning to remove his borrowed suit on the spot, Florrie remembering at the last minute she had no key to the flat. (Thank goodness, thought Alice, briefly, before handing over hers.)

'I feel like I've sprung you,' he commented, as their taxi shot through a London still bright with summer sun and crowded with people.

Alice sighed with a touch of theatricality. She felt sprung, happy. 'Tell me about *Die Frau ohne Schatten*,' she commanded. It was a ritual. He always gave her useful information if the opera was new to her and, afterwards, she gave him her unschooled opinion on the music, libretto, set and orchestra.

'You must understand . . .' began Jonathan, which made Alice look at him reprovingly, although she said nothing: she did not have to understand anything. As he described the Vienna of 1919, in which the opera had had its première, she pulled down the window and let the wind blow the hair away from her neck. It was amazing how hot it still was at nearly seven. She thought for a moment of Guy on the boat, his healthy seaman's skin, then glanced at Jonathan. He was much more obviously good-looking than Guy – or Brendan, who was really quite ugly. Although his once thick dark hair was now mostly grey and thinning on the top, he had a high, intelligent forehead, strong, regular features, and must shave twice a day because, although so dark, there was only a repressed shadow – most unfashionable – which showed he lacked confidence or was a traditionalist. Of course, she knew it was the latter. He had been Richard's best friend at an old-fashioned public school, saved by Richard's support from too much bullying because his mother was Jewish. Alice never thought of him as Jewish but she knew this schoolboy history because Richard had told her once and added, 'That's why he wants to be such a success.' And she had objected, 'But you want to be a success and you're not Jewish?' Richard hadn't continued the conversation.

'I hope we're not going to be late.' Jonathan looked at his watch and then at their driver, who was on his mobile.

'Oh, so do I!' said Alice, with feeling. She loved arriving at the opera house and standing in that great new emporium with a glass of champagne in her hand. Almost guiltily, she remembered the earlier glass with Brendan. It was ridiculous that, like a child, she felt a duty to enjoy the treats provided by Jonathan. Yet he made her feel quite childish. Or perhaps that was the way she wanted it.

'Why are you smiling?' he asked, and it was a relief that he had been diverted from a row with the driver – Jonathan was drawn towards rows over unimportant matters – who had missed two green lights by his dilatory approach.

'No reason. Carefree, I suppose.'

'Carefree,' Jonathan repeated. After his wife had died, following a long drawn-out battle with cancer, he had confessed that none of her suffering had come as a surprise. 'Human existence is essentially flawed. Happiness is a rare accident, the opposite the norm.'

'I enjoy our opera evenings.'

'Oh, yes.' She could see he was pleased by this but worrying again about their late arrival. Apart from his wife's death, his gloomy attitude wasn't justified by the path of his own life. According to Richard, Jonathan's marriage had arisen more of convenience than passionate love. He had earned money enough as a QC to buy a house in Kensington where, having no children, he lived in some grandeur, with a housekeeper in the basement.

'Good,' announced Jonathan, as their driver put away his mobile and made speedy deviations around Covent Garden. '*Nous sommes arrivés.*'

Alice's carefree mood lasted through Strauss's story of the Empress, half spirit, half human, on a journey in search of her missing shadow. Unless she found it, her beloved husband, the Emperor, would be turned to stone. The opera was very long, three acts, each lasting over an hour with twenty-minute intervals between. But Alice didn't mind: the music, with its swooping chords, swept her up into a vague sense of raised emotion. The bass-baritone, Barak, the story's honourable human, even reminded her a little of Jonathan.

'I'm so glad it ended happily,' sighed Alice, as they came out on to the pavement. The air was still meltingly warm around them.

'It's a pleasant surprise,' agreed Jonathan. 'Have you the strength for dinner? I did book.'

'Oh, yes.'

He pulled her arm through his as they walked to the Ivy. Surely he hadn't done that before?

As always, Jonathan had an excellent table where they could watch from a cosy corner the comings and goings of London's rich and famous, although Jonathan hardly seemed in the mood for this. 'Just one course, I think.' Since they had sat down, he had been almost brusque, certainly preoccupied.

'Are you involved in an interesting case?' asked Alice, tenderly, after their order had been conveyed. It was good to have such a long-lasting friendship.

'I can't go on like this, Alice!'

'What? What?' Had she said or done something to upset him?

'You must have guessed. I'm madly in love with you. I have been for years, since before Joyce died. For ever, probably.' His usually sallow face was filled with colour, his usually steady hands were shaking, his usually calm eyes were shooting darts. Flames of desire.

The suddenness of this utterly confounded Alice. Of course she hadn't guessed. Why, he was good old Jonathan who had a problem with enjoying life! Fleetingly, she considered the strangeness of this week, which had seen Guy kiss her, a multi-millionaire she barely knew follow her to her flat, and now her late husband's oldest friend up in flames.

'Say something! Say anything . . .'

Could she point out the waiter standing patiently with a bread basket? But Jonathan had noticed him, at last, snatched a large roll with a distracted air, and plunged it into his pocket.

With horror, Alice felt her face trying to break into a smile or even a laugh. She must *control*. 'Dearest Woof W– Jonathan. You're my oldest friend—'

'No. No.'

A new waiter, arriving with substitute cutlery, ignored this eccentricity and, politely removing Jonathan's elbow, relaid the table.

'I knew you'd talk about friendship. How can you?' His voice rose. 'Can't you see I'm burning with lust?'

Alice became aware of two women at the next-door table who were darting her looks of interest tinged with envy. 'Ssh, Jonathan. We can talk about it later.'

'Talk!'

'Talk.' Alice closed her lips like a trap. She supposed she was a little flattered to have produced such strong emotion in someone she'd classed as a cold fish. But, on the other hand, it had chased away her carefree mood

'You're just so beautiful.' Jonathan sighed. 'But I promise not to embarrass you further. Of course you wouldn't care for me . . .'

'Ssh,' said Alice again, as his voice threatened to rise. 'Look, here comes our wine.'

In the taxi on their way back to her flat, Alice congratulated herself warily on her quelling tactics. Jonathan sat back in his corner and, if his eyes were more hooded and his hands still trembled a little, she could ignore that. It was sad that she must restrain her rejoicing on such a beautiful night but, above all, she must retain their friendship and restore his dignity.

They arrived at the flat. Alice was a little anxious when he paid off the taxi. But, he explained, gruffly, 'I need the walk home.'

'It was a wonderful evening,' began Alice, hopefully, although she knew he always insisted on seeing her to the door of her flat.

It was nearly one o'clock and the evening porter had gone, locking his cubicle. They went up in the lift. Jonathan was pale again, his expression unreadable.

They stood outside her door in the corridor, which smelt strongly of someone's spiced dinner. 'My neighbour loves Thai chicken noodles,' said Alice, rummaging in her handbag for the key. 'Oh, no!'

'Alice, my dear, what is it?' He was far too concerned.

Alice took a step away, but there was no avoiding the facts. 'Florrie took my key.'

'She's probably still there. Try the bell.'

Alice began to panic. Florrie and Jonathan – *and* she hardly had a lead for her next interview. 'She was going back to the cottage, I'm sure.'

'There was a light on. I saw it from below. I even imagined a woman's figure at the window.'

'A woman's figure?' Could this be true? She had been too intent on sending waves of repression to look upwards.

Jonathan rang the bell once, and then again.

'You'll wake the neighbours.'

'Serve them right for making nasty smells.'

Alice saw that Jonathan had returned to his brisk, sensible self and was filled with gratitude. He rang again and then suggested, 'If she has gone, wouldn't she leave the key somewhere?' He bent and lifted the mat. '*Voilà!*'

They were inside the flat before Alice realised that Jonathan was still with her and she could hardly kick him out when he had saved her from a night on the streets. 'How about a cup of tea?'

'Thank you.' He followed her into the kitchen and sat on a chair by the wall. The kitchen was brightly lit and Alice feared his eyes were growing in fierceness as they watched her. 'You needn't be so nervous. I'm not going to jump on you.' He took the mug from her and led the way to the living room. Alice blushed guiltily, but didn't relax a jot. She knew he would jump on her. It was in the air. A man of his age (she'd been to his sixtieth birthday party in his chambers) would reckon, consciously or unconsciously, that such moments of intimacy don't come often.

They drank their tea as quickly as possible. Alice felt the hot liquid burn her throat. She longed to check her emails and go to bed. She couldn't even blame Florrie for all this: the key had been under the mat.

'I must go.' He stood and stared down at Alice, curled up against the cushions. 'May I kiss you? Then I'll go.'

'You always kiss me goodbye.' Knowing she should stand and end this farce, Alice turned her cheek towards him.

'Oh, darling! Darling!' There it was, as expected, all his dignity gone as he pressed himself on top of her. At least he could not find her lips.

I must be firm, thought Alice, for both our sakes.

'Jonathan,' she hissed, 'the time has come for you to go – *now*!' It worked. He was on his feet and, wordless, blundering for the door.

The outside door slammed. He had gone.

Chapter Six

Thursday

Four hours' sleep is not enough. Alice sat on the edge of her bed and looked at her feet. They, at least, were familiar, although perhaps a little more prehensile than yesterday. Her head, which she now bent to her knees, was still lost to a dream in which she swam twenty fathoms deep in a black-green sea. Last night's crop of emails had included one from Guy who, as well as sending faxes about his diver friend, Blue Carroway, the philanthropic treasure-seeker, had passed on addresses of useful websites. Instead of learning about the diver, she had become transfixed by images of an underwater world.

Alice took off her nightdress and smoothed her thighs against the bed. She mustn't miss her customary train to Brighton and, perhaps, if her father was not too demanding, she could make time for a swim. It was the sixth hot day in a row. It seemed sensible not to think too clearly about last night's adventure with Jonathan.

'I'm so glad, darling. So very, very glad. Florrie, can you hear me?' Alice held her mobile close to her ear but the train had entered a tunnel. When they re-emerged, she dialled again.

'You do understand we're not an item, Ma?'

'Of course, darling,' enthused Alice, who had no idea what to believe about someone as unconvincing as Baz.

'He thinks he may be gay but life has been so complicated he's had no real time to work out his true sexual orientation.'

'Is he listening to this?'

Florrie gave a tolerant laugh. 'He's in the garden. Weeding or planting. He has a real thing about nature. I can see them now, Lily on the rug under the shade of the apple tree, trying to catch the shadows as usual – thank shit there's a breeze today – and Baz imitating Mellors, naked to the waist . . .'

It was a pleasant surprise that Florrie's expensive school had left her with a few remnants of Eng. Lit., but the train went into another tunnel before she'd finished her sentence. When she could hear Florrie's voice again she was half-way through an explanation of some woman's appearance in her life.

'I was cut off,' said Alice. 'Whatever's that noise in the background?'

'I was just telling you. It's the Hoover. She's cleaning the house for us. I can't tell you what a difference—'

'But darling, who is *she*? And who's paying?'

'No one's paying.' Florrie sounded impatient. 'I told you . . .'

'I was cut off.'

'She just appeared out of the blue. Like a fairy godmother. She said her priest had told her to make reparation for some sin or other and that was why she's cleaning and washing and babysitting.'

'But how do you know she's not a burglar or worse?'

'She's too old and kind and classy. With a bit of a foreign accent. Actually, she's hopeless with the Hoover – Baz and she spent ages in contemplation before they could get it to work – but she loves that long feather duster. And she adores Lily.'

Staring abstractedly out of the window, Alice noticed another bridge coming up and decided this would be the final cut-off point. 'Let's talk later, darling.' She was nearly in Brighton: the bright reflection of the sea and the usual necessity for stiffening her sinews before meeting her father.

'I'm afraid he's a little more than usually confused, disturbed.' Sister Mary Rose, large and pretty behind gold spectacles, gave Alice a sympathetic pat on the shoulder. They had known each other for eight years, ever since Dr Featherstone had moved from his own house to this nursing home. 'He's looking forward to his lunch with you.'

Alice went down the nicely carpeted corridor and walked up the stairs to the first floor. At the end there was a square window, through which she could see and hear a seagull wheeling and calling. It was often the same – perhaps some juicy rubbish had been dumped below. She could never avoid contrasting the gull's wild freedom with the ancient captured beast that was her father.

'Daddy! What are you doing?' He was bent down by his bed, trying, it seemed, to climb under it. It was a disconcerting sight, his long ankles and feet protruding bonily out of his skimpy pyjamas. She rushed to help him. 'You don't want to fall, do you?'

He hung on grimly to the bed, which proved that he was surprisingly strong. 'She might be under there. Catch my drift? Under the bed.' He let go with one hand and waved it in the direction of the floor. His body swung dangerously, despite Alice's efforts. She must get help. She used one hand to reach for the bell and, to her horror, felt her father slide from her grasp.

'Daddy!' He lay on the floor, like a broken ramrod.

'Nothing there. Well, that's something.' His voice was not of someone in pain but of a man reasonably pleased with himself.

It took two nurses to get him back into bed and by then the lunch had appeared, a steaming unseasonable stew that either Alice or a nurse must feed to the aged doctor.

It was always like this, thought Alice. She came to bring daughterly comfort, positive news from her family and the outside world, and found herself dragged into and submerged by the incomprehensible dramas of his own life. Who was the woman not, thankfully, under the bed? Presumably this was what Mary Rose had meant by him being more confused.

Discomforted by the stuffy heat of the room, the smell of the stew and her father's greedy inability to swallow cleanly, both irritating and tragic in such a commanding man, Alice sat back tiredly in her chair.

Her father, on the other hand, had gained even more energy. She suspected that he had had a pre-luncheon whisky. 'You should have seen her. Wild. Out of control. Harpy. Witch. Strumpet.' His words tumbled out, filled with muddle and venom and, perhaps, fear.

'Who, Daddy? What woman?'

He paused, and a sly, secretive expression came over his face. 'In through the window. Out through the door. If she thinks she's a ghost, she doesn't know me. I can see her, all right?'

Alice watched him as he continued in crazy vein. Clearly he was not going to explain, if explanation were possible. Gradually the shrillness and strength gave way to garbled mutterings, 'If she thinks she can pull my toes . . . whispering in my ear . . . breath like silk . . . fingers like worms . . .' His eyes were closing.

Alice went to find a nurse. 'He's ready for his nap.' Then she went downstairs to see Sister Mary Rose.

Again she got that sympathetic pat. 'Cup of tea?'

'No. Thank you. What is all this? I mean, has a woman visited my father?'

'Well, if so, she didn't sign the visitors' book.'

'And the outside door's locked?'

'Of course.' Mary Rose pulled a file closer. Both of them knew that, in very hot weather, the door was often propped open for half an hour or so. 'I did warn you. Your father's more muddled.'

Alice gave up. 'I'm going for a swim. I'll be back by three thirty.'

The sun was high and hot on the promenade but there were not too many people about. Where were all the ice-cream-eating tourists? Perhaps they were on the pier, playing shrill games in darkened rooms.

The sun was pressing hard on her bare arms. She opened her bag, took out her towel and threw it round her shoulders. The beach pebbles would be scorching hot. She rummaged again in her bag, took out a crumpled linen hat and pulled it low on her head. That was better.

Slowly, Alice walked towards the steps that led down to the beach. As a child, she had prided herself on knowing everything about the sea, the tides, what washed up out of the sea and what came down from the town. The house where she and her father lived and he had his surgery was in Hove, but only a short walk from the front. With no mother and a busy GP father, who was often out or otherwise engaged, she could slip away to check out the playground she'd had since she was a baby. In fact, the shingle was her earliest memory: the noise as large adult feet rubbed the pebbles against one another, the colour and the way she could never find an exact pair. One hot Sunday when she was about six, she'd spent the entire day trying to match them. She'd collected two or three dozen and brought them home but they weren't the same and, when they dried, looked dull. Her father, who'd never seemed to worry about her independence even at such a early age, had suggested putting them in a glass bottle with water, but she'd decided they'd miss their friends and taken them back to the beach. A motherless only child with an unsociable father who literally filled all his time with the demands of his practice, she'd been partly cared for by a succession of elderly ladies – grateful patients of her father, she later discovered. Secretly, and for many years, she'd expected her mother to return one day. Her father never spoke of his dead wife and had kept nothing of hers as a remembrance, not even a photograph. Conversely, that had helped Alice believe she was living elsewhere. But after a while she'd found it hard to picture her face.

One of the benefits of a seaside childhood was the ability to change, modestly and rapidly, into a swimsuit. Alice had left wallet and keys in the nursing home and now ran towards the water. That was another benefit: fakir's feet. She remembered how Richard had tried to make her laugh by tickling her feet, refusing to believe they had turned to unfeeling leather.

Then she forgot everything. The water felt freezing: she swam in an energetic crawl straight out to the horizon. Late husband, father, her children, the ever-present worry about her next interview disappeared in the flow of water over her skin, the splash of her arms and the bubble and spray as she lifted them out of the water. The colours, the no-holds-barred brightness of the sun, the blue of the sky and the blue-green of the sea, touched by gold at the edges. She didn't close her eyes – they were as immune to the salt as her feet were to the pebbles. She was a red-haired mermaid.

Alice swam back slowly, sometimes on her back, sometimes doing a leisurely breaststroke. She looked around now, noting who was on the beach, who was swimming, who had taken a boat out. Occasionally she raised her eyes to check the shoreline profile of pale Regency hotels and houses, to her right the long swoop of the pier. She had left it all when she married Richard, but the sea, shore and buildings contained her childhood.

'He's still asleep,' said Mary Rose. 'But your mobile's hardly stopped, the nurses say.'

She must have forgotten to turn it off. It rang again as she entered her father's bedroom. She hardly looked at him. 'Yes?'

It was Guy. If she could get back to London in time, he had the deep-sea diver lined up for interview. They could meet in the Kensington Hilton near Shepherds Bush.

'But, Guy, I've not done the research.' Briefly she pictured the blue-green sea bubbling past her eyes.

'Why ever not?'

He was right. 'I should say I haven't done as much as I'd like.'

'Don't worry, Blue's a great talker. Room 405.'

London felt stuffy after Brighton. The trees along Holland Park Avenue, with their blotched trunks and curled leaves, seemed saturated with the fumes and pollution of the city. The hotel was stuffy, too, but cold under sharply directed air-conditioning.

Alice stood in front of the reception desk, thinking that she would hardly need to stretch her arms to touch the ceiling and wondering why the famous deep-sea diver had chosen such a claustrophobic resting place.

'Mr Carroway says to go right on up.'

Alice stood in the lift with her fingers clasped round her pad, which was still inside her bag. She reminded herself that she had been here before – the interview for which she was ill-prepared, the place that made her shiver, the mood of unwilling lack of concentration. It was early to be doing another interview: the Brendan Costa piece wouldn't be printed till Saturday. It was only Guy's insistence that Blue Carroway mustn't be missed that had got her here at all.

Chivvying herself along the corridors, lit in a Hades-like orange glow, she came to Room 405. The door was open, allowing music and stripes of low sun to cross the threshold.

'Welcome and enter.'

He stood, possibly consciously posed, in the beam of the golden spotlight. He wore close-fitting, electric blue shorts to just above his knees – like a runner's shorts, Alice thought – and absolutely nothing else. Which was not entirely accurate because his chest was decorated with a gold necklace and the hand he held out to her with a heavy gold ring inset with a large green stone. The spoils of diving, she supposed.

'I'm glad you had time for me.' His body was a warm golden, too, not of the oiled-sunbathing variety but of the open-sea and salt-air kind. She couldn't suppress the ridiculous thought that it was as if a Greek god had landed in the middle of this anonymous hotel.

'Iced tea, coffee, champagne or Blue Carroway's special?'

Alice turned her attention to his face. Amazingly that, too, was spectacularly good-looking, although perfection was marred by a flattened, once-broken nose and a deep scar puckering the skin above his left eye. His bleached hair was cut short but still tried to form into curls.

'Iced tea.' It struck her that she had never seen a truly beautiful man before or even a half-way handsome one, unless she had just failed to notice them during her early and long-married state, and it was only now, in this heat-wave of new susceptibility, that they sprang into her vision. Although it would have been hard to miss Blue, whatever your state of mind. Perhaps she had moved in the wrong circles – where women were supposed to be beautiful and men clever.

'Shall we sit by the window?' He had produced two bottles of tea, then turned away to pull on a white sweatshirt. 'I've been in high temperatures around the world but city heat's something different.'

'Where've you come from?' Alice sat down at a table by the window and took out her pad. Once again she didn't have a tape-recorder, this time because she had come from her father. She dismissed an image of his bony limbs collapsing under the bed.

'I'm about to set up an office on the south coast.'

'I was brought up in Brighton.' What was this? Already giving information about herself? Despite her cool dress, her skin felt prickly with heat.

'Cornwall's more my sort of place.'

'Guy Vernon's a friend of yours?'

'We've sailed together. He said he'd try to get me a bit of publicity, but that I might not be famous enough for you.'

Alice laughed. 'I guess I wouldn't mind a glass of champagne.'

Blue went back to the fridge and pulled out a half-bottle of Moët. 'Will this make me more famous?'

Alice didn't answer. His eyes were as blue as his shorts. She watched as he opened the bottle, filled two glasses and handed her one. 'Cheers.'

'So, how did you get all this money you want to give away?'

'Not give away, use. I like diving but not for ever. I've had the bends on a couple of dives recently. Do you know what happens to the body if you go too deep?'

As Blue described in precise medical detail the punishment for staying too deep too long or coming up too quickly, Alice scribbled assiduously. A single gulp of champagne had sharpened her wits and the evening air was lowering the temperature.

'But all this is hardly important,' Blue concluded. 'The technicalities of diving only interest those who do it. Do you dive?'

'Nothing serious.'

'You should.'

'But how about the deep dives, the treasure-seeking dives? Can you tell me a bit about that?'

'If UNESCO had its way, there'd be no more treasure-seeking.'

Alice identified a slight Australian twang to Blue's voice as he rehearsed for her new measures limiting diving to historical sites and the removal of material from them. 'The US and the UK haven't signed up to them yet,' he said, 'but if they make sites only available to archaeologists you'll have wrecks all over the world passing their sell-by date and nobody doing a thing about them. Do you know the amount of research that goes into finding a suitable site for reclamation?'

'No. I can't say I've ever thought about it.'

'I was involved in the investigation of a Second World War wreck, the HMS *Hood*, a battleship sunk by the *Bismarck*. Well, we didn't find that by peering into charming coral reefs but by slogging it through the fucking Public Records Office, the libraries, the wartime archives.'

He looked up now, as if for approbation or even, judging by a new aggression, disagreement. 'So, you're researchers,' ventured Alice.

'Right.' He stood, retrieved the champagne bottle from the fridge. 'Divers are hired hands, mostly. I've had enough of it. I've been lucky. I've made money. I've still got my health. So now's the time to quit.'

'Quit?' Alice looked at her pencil.

'Unsexy word?'

'What?' He was standing close to her, champagne bottle poised over her glass. What was happening to her? Why this urge to reach forward to the bulging blue shorts now a few inches from her face? 'Oh, no. No, thanks. So how do you get the money for this course you're planning? And how are you going to pick the lucky youth offenders?'

He sat down opposite her again but Alice knew that he had clocked her response to his closeness. Probably he'd embark on another lecture and she'd be able to compose herself. In years of odd interviews, this was one of the oddest.

'Over the last fifteen years I've been involved one way and another in salvaging many millions of dollars' worth of tin, nickel and copper sunk in the Second World War. Then there are the merchant ships – some of them lost quite recently. I've worked hard. I'm good at my job so I have seed money of my own. I'll need much more to run it.'

'Just like a banker,' said Alice, who'd never met anyone less like a banker in her life. 'So how about the tan? Don't tell me you lie on a sunbed?'

He seemed surprised, turned the gold ring on his finger. 'Sailing. Surfing. I've been in Cornwall. I guess you Londoners don't notice the sun.'

'Actually, I was swimming in the sea at Brighton today.'

'Filthy water, isn't it?'

'I feel as if I've been rolling in a mixture of lard and cat's pee.'

'My power-shower's vacant.'

'I—'

'Then we could have supper together. Unless your husband's waiting?' He looked at her with eyes now green and the colour of the stone in his ring.

'No husband.' Could it be that, after all those years happily married to a kind, clever lawyer, she had turned into a pushover for a pretty face, a muscular body? My light was on red, she thought, remembering a comment made by Mitzi (which at the time she'd considered ridiculous and vulgar) and now it's, at very least, on amber.

Alice went to have a shower and enjoyed every minute of the coolish water sluicing off her body. She dressed again in the bathroom and brushed back her hair, darkened to a mahogany colour by the water.

'Wow!' He had put on white trousers and sandals. 'I didn't realise you were this beautiful.'

Alice smiled and thought she must have been looking frightful before. 'I know a Greek place two streets away.' She would keep control a little. She took her mobile from her bag and turned it on. It rang immediately.

Punishing herself or him, Alice listened to seven messages as they walked through the hotel and on to the street: Florrie, Sister Mary Rose, Mitzi, Guy, Sir Brendan's secretary and two about work. It was a roll-call of her week. Only Peter to go. The phone played the final message.

'Hi, Mum. Nothing special to say. Just calling.' There was Peter.

They were on Holland Park Avenue now, filled with warm darkness and the sweeping lights of cars. The trees above their heads blocked out the sky and stars. They reached an area filled with cafés and shops, most of them still open.

'I only like night-time in the deep countryside or at sea,' announced Blue, irritably.

Alice put away her mobile. 'Our restaurant's round the next corner.'

It had a small courtyard at the back into which all of its customers were crammed.

'I think it's cooler inside.' Blue took Alice's arm. She broke away sharply and felt rather than saw him smile.

Mountains of food arrived as soon as they sat down: green peppers, hummus scattered with fresh parsley, radishes, black olives with garlic, yoghurt with cucumber and dill.

'This is what you get for free.' Alice decided to drink sharp retsina and wake up her wits. Guy's message had asked about Blue and repeated his qualification as a great talker. He was talking now, telling her about a ship that had been carrying gold from the USSR to England during the Second World War. It had sunk in such deep water that divers couldn't get down to it except in special tiny submarines. He had been part of the group who'd finally located it and brought up the gold. He half shut his eyes. 'That's some experience, to hold in your hands a gold bar worth a cool thirty thou.'

They had the retsina now and Alice wasn't inclined to find her notepad. She couldn't think why Guy had pushed him. Really, he wasn't famous enough. Beautiful enough, certainly. Sister Mary Rose had phoned to report her anxiety that Dr Featherstone was staying awake to be ready for the return of his imaginary visitor.

'You're not eating.' Blue had ordered red snapper with rice and herbs, which he was enjoying.

'I'm sorry. It's been a long day.'

'We can leave any time.' He took out a roll of banknotes, which prompted the immediate arrival of a waiter.

'Perhaps I can interview you tomorrow?'

Blue looked surprised, as if he found her suggestion incomprehensible.

Alice picked up her bag. She pictured her large apartment, with its many rooms and its view of the street. She had somehow lost track of the time but she imagined that the revellers at the pub across the road would still be quaffing and laughing. 'I live in such an ugly flat.' She sighed. Florrie had phoned to inform her that she had just had the most wonderful day of her life. Now, why should that be depressing?

'But you're coming back with me. For one last glass of champagne.' He tucked her arm into his and led her out on to the pavement where the stars were sparkling through the canopy of leaves as they whirled about her head. Oh, God, I'm drunk, thought Alice.

Sir Brendan's secretary had rung with dates for the weekend at his country house. She had talked of train times and road maps.

Alice glanced sideways at Blue. 'Of course I'm coming back with you.'

Alice rode Blue as if she were a charioteer, with her red hair streaming behind her.

'I'd never have guessed.' Blue put out his hand to catch her as she fell down beside him. 'You are . . .' Their bodies heaved like the swell of the sea after the wind has dropped.

'You mean we make love well,' Alice murmured. Four years ago or more? She couldn't even remember when she'd last made love. And never like that. Never with a stranger. It was just luck, she thought dizzily, absolutely nothing to do with love. But his hand was on her body again, stroking and holding.

'No, I'm too tired.' Probably she was whispering too softly for him to hear.

'Tired? You're not tired.' His fingers were so warm, delicate and knowing. How could he *know* so much about her? She should be shocked he knew so much.

'You don't understand. I'm a grandmother...' Perhaps she wasn't saying it out loud. Her body had begun to shudder, rising to his touch like a fish rises out of water. 'Blue...' But her protests were tiny streamers of bubbles soon dispersed in the great roaring of the sea.

Chapter Seven

Friday

Alice pictured the scene in *Gone With the Wind* when Scarlett O'Hara wakes up after a night of love with Rhett Butler, and stretches in the luxury of love-making remembered. She was absurd. It was all absurd.

'Hi.' Blue lay beside her.

Alice turned to look at him. By daylight, his appearance was even more startling.

'How did you break your nose?' She put her finger on it to avoid touching his lips. They were far too red and curved for a man.

'It was born this way. Breakfast?'

'And the scar?'

'That, too. My mother had one just the same.'

Why haven't I a headache? wondered Alice, before admitting to herself the reason.

'Are you going to interview me over breakfast?'

This was a downer. But, then, Rhett Butler had come in angry. This was not serious thinking. Could he have made love to her in order to secure his place in her paper? And if he had, did it matter? She had made love to him at least as much as he had made love to her. 'Breakfast in bed,' she said lazily. She watched him move round the room. The curtains were undrawn and he was naked. He brought her orange juice and a packet of biscuits. She ate them hungrily.

'Where's your notebook?'

'In my bag.' He brought it over and watched while she took out pad, pen and mobile, which she turned on. It rang immediately.

'Why the fuck did you do that?'

'I have children, a granddaughter and an elderly father.'

He went into the bathroom while she listened to her messages, all from the same people as the evening before, all asking why she wasn't at the flat. Alice reached under the bed and found her watch. It was after nine.

Blue came back in his white trousers and a blue T-shirt. He stood over her. 'You used my body.'

Alice, still listening to the mobile, decided to assume he was joking. 'I'm sorry,' she said. 'I can't interview you this morning. I have to get home. Besides, I feel befuddled. I couldn't take in what you have to say. I feel unprofessional.' As she heard herself say the word, she laughed, and at least he smiled.

'I can't stay long either. What will I tell Guy tomorrow?'

Alice stopped laughing. 'Not too much. Actually, nothing. I will interview you. Trust me.' She smiled again. It all seemed unreal. 'Shall I visit you in Cornwall? Whereabouts are you?'

Instead of answering he began to gather things from the room, emptying it of his presence. She should be doing the same. He came back to her. 'Be my guest.' He took her pad and wrote down a telephone number. 'If you lose it, Guy will help.' He kissed her rather formally on the cheek, then relented a little and ran his hand over her shoulder and breast.

'It's another warm day,' she whispered, shivering. But he had turned away. Reluctantly, she got out of bed.

Alice lay on the couch in her living room. Someone had untied the white curtains, which hung straight and still. It hadn't been her, she was sure, but she couldn't remember who else had been in the flat.

'It's sometimes the way, Guy. You know that.' She was on her fourth telephone call. Everyone needed placating. In the time it had taken her to get home she had decided she couldn't chase after Blue to Cornwall but Guy was refusing to accept her decision.

'He told you about this young offenders' project, surely? That's newsworthy. He'd make a great photo.'

Alice thought it best not to admit that Blue's project had only been briefly mentioned. 'He's great-looking, of course—' She stopped abruptly as various images presented themselves.

'You can come west with me tomorrow. I'm leaving around five or six in the morning.'

'No, Guy. I've got to see Florrie tomorrow.' She must be firm.

Blue wasn't a suitable interview subject. He'd done nothing except have a few dreams. At best he was a photo-opportunity, as Guy had suggested. Then she decided to be a bit more honest with herself and admit that the last thing she wanted was to meet him again with Guy, although she wasn't clear as to why that should be so. 'I just can't make it tomorrow.'

'So who are you going to interview? The Master's keen on Blue too, you know.'

What was all this? Since her earliest days on the paper she'd learnt to take direction but she felt there was something more here. 'I'm thinking about it. There's Robin Nutford, the Nobel Prize winner who's never given an interview. I got an email that he'd let me talk to him.'

'You know the Master's view of Nobel Prize winners. They'd have to be female, under twenty-five and bust size thirty-six treble D for him to show any interest.'

'Then there's that Arsenal footballer, Liam Dailey, who's published a novel.'

'It's being serialised in the *Telegraph*, Alice.'

'Look, I'll think about it. It's only Friday, after all.'

'OK. You think. But I'll keep tabs on Blue Carroway in case your thoughts fall his way.'

After she had finished this uneasy conversation with Guy, Alice returned to her computer and dealt with as many messages as possible by email, then checked over the various alternative interview subjects. It was always like this, she reminded herself. People outside newspapers envied her what they saw as an easy job: just one piece a week and a reliable contract. Mitzi liked to say that anyone who could work at home should pay a toll to those like her who had to take on the London transport non-system twice or more a day. They didn't understand the pressure of producing a suitable interview each week, pinpointing someone high profile enough to grab the interest of several million readers who would also agree to speak to her. Worse still, it couldn't just be a trawl through *International Who's Who* because she was writing for a daily paper, and daily papers want today's news. Her candidate had to be hot news that week, which meant she couldn't plan ahead more than a few days and, if she did, the piece was more than likely to be scrapped as another more up-to-the-minute candidate presented themselves.

Alice got up and walked through the flat to stand on the balcony and stare rather blindly at the street. It was her critical thinking post. The truth was that she had become lazy recently. To do her job properly she had to be in touch with the life of the city, every day invitations for lunches, openings, drinks parties, charity functions, publishing launches, lectures and riverboat trips arrived. At these sometimes entertaining and sometimes not, events, she met people in the news or, better still, about to be in the news. She made contacts who gave her access to those she wanted to interview or, more importantly, her editor wanted her to interview. A few years ago she would cover two or three such events a week. Her address book filled rapidly, which was probably the main reason her position at the paper was fairly unassailable. She knew how to get hold of people and, quite often now, they got hold of her.

When Richard was alive, she had occasionally felt guilty at allowing this busy social life to cut into their evenings together. But he encouraged her, if she hung back, almost pushed her out; if she stayed in, he spent most of the evening working, piling papers round himself like fortress walls.

But when she looked back on the first six months of this year – and the whole of last year, if it came to that – she could count the drinks parties she'd attended on the fingers of one hand. She'd become picky, going where she already knew people, supporting authors she liked, shrugging at the idea of a lecture by some bright new hopeful, a young don with a radical theme and a handsome face, a novelist from Eastern Europe who was taking a fresh look at Communism. She was jaded, she supposed. Or lazy, lacking Richard's goading.

Alice turned abruptly off the balcony and walked through to the study where she searched for the bag she'd been carrying on Tuesday when she went into the office, the day she'd come home on the boat with Guy. She found it stuffed into a corner and took out of it a dozen invitations. On rifling through them, she found some already out of date (one made her jump by playing a tune – possibly 'The Bluebells of Scotland') several for the current week and just one for Friday. Friday was an unusual day for a party of any sort. The card was thick, white, traditionally printed in black and gold with a coat-of-arms embossed on the top. It had the pleasure of inviting her to a reception at one of the city livery halls to celebrate the foundation of the London City School. It was in the bottom five per cent of alluring prospects.

Alice took the card to the telephone and rang the RSVP number. 'I'm so sorry to be replying so late to your very kind invitation . . .'

'Not at all,' replied a courteous lady. 'It's those who never reply at all who make our life harder. I'll add your name to the guest list.'

Alice went the whole hog, and dressed herself in chic black, accompanied by purple slingback high-heeled shoes with long, pointy toes. They were very expensive shoes that were not appropriate for the Underground but she wore them anyway. There was no other sensible way to get to the City but the Underground, although the continuing heat of the early evening choked her with the fetid smells of the subterranean and unaired. When, with some relief, she spotted a seat and sat down, an old man opposite her stared fixedly at her legs. She decided to take this as a compliment, although his partly shaven rubicund face and crumpled copy of the the *Farmer's Weekly* didn't suggest he was a worthy admirer. Perhaps they were linked by a shared sense of being out of place among the regular daily travellers. Alice noted this as a further sign of how she had allowed herself to become out of touch.

She got off at St Paul's station and walked along the pavements, hard and hot to her thin soles. It was a pleasure to turn off between the tall glass buildings, that reflected evening light in sudden, disconcerting angles, and go through a cool courtyard to an even cooler entrance to one of the medieval stone halls.

Having made such an effort, her arrival was something of a let-down. She took a glass of champagne and looked round the hall. It was after seven and already the high-ceilinged room, with its arched stained-glass windows and heavy stone carving, was three-quarters full. With a practised eye, she picked out six or seven people she knew – a publicity agent whose job was to go to every party, a publisher who specialised in educational books, the chairman of a chain of bookshops, the glamorous author of a bestselling novel for children, the presenter of a television history series who had just left his wife for his PA. At least, thought Alice, I know that bit of gossip. Maybe the rather plain girl, definitely young though, who was standing as close to him as a bodyguard, was the PA in question.

Alice knew she must speak to one of these people – that was why she had made the effort to come and they were all interesting by any standard – but found herself curiously reluctant. Just out of practice, she told herself bracingly, and had taken a step forward when her elbow was grasped by someone she couldn't see.

'Whatever are you doing in this gloomy place?'

Alice turned round quickly. 'Same as you, I suppose.' She had forgotten the impressive size of Sir Brendan Costa. Tall as well as broad, it was hard to believe he was the son of an Italian father. He wore a double-breasted suit, which expensively emphasised the width of his chest. She noticed that he held a glass of water – unless it was vodka.

'Luckily for you that's impossible. In a manner of speaking I'm one of your hosts. Or, rather, I helped pay for this shindig. Your name wasn't on the guest list.'

'I rang late.'

'You know what I'd like to do?'

'Sorry?'

'What I'd like to do is talk to you for a little while longer and then take you to dinner at Sheekey's. But unfortunately I can't. I have the official dinner to attend and, worse still, I have to make a speech – more of a few words than a speech – for which reason I must leave you now.'

'Cheers,' said Alice.

'However, when I've finished my few boring words and we've listened to a few more boring words, very probably at sadly greater length, I shall come back to you for five minutes more of the pleasure of your company. So don't leave too soon, please.'

'I've only just arrived,' said Alice.

'Excellent. À bientôt.'

Alice watched him make his way through the crowd and reappear by a dais where a microphone waited. She moved into the centre of the throng. Whether it had been the champagne or the unexpected presence of Sir Brendan – one of her interview subjects, after all – that had energised her, she found it easy now to congratulate the novelist on her latest success and listen appreciatively to the charitable ways she planned to spend some of her money, and move from her to the bookshop-chain chairman, who invited her to a seminar on bookselling, and from there to the publicist, who had two potential interview subjects. She was even irritated to be just starting on the television presenter when they were interrupted by the speeches.

Usually, and unlike most people, Alice enjoyed speeches. She supposed her interest was an extension of her interviewer's role. A man or woman on a dais revealed all sorts of things about themselves. She had already seen Brendan the man of power, and Brendan the little-boy-lost, but now she saw Brendan the showman. The school they were celebrating was, he informed his listeners (politely attentive but not enthralled), the nearest thing to 'heaven on earth'. If he had enjoyed such advantages as a child, such insightful teachers, such dedication and imagination, he would not be a mere businessman scrabbling to make money for England but a figure of Gandhian insight and usefulness. This school, he assured his more interested listeners – and his echo of a northern accent had become just a touch stronger – had the potential to turn out children superior in every discipline, from maths to morals, from gymnastics to geography, from PE to politics . . . The only trouble was, there was not enough financial support forthcoming from the local education authority.

This was a high-class pitch for money. Alice admired it, particularly the peroration. Then, looking in her direction, Brendan produced a chequebook and wrote out, as he informed his now spellbound audience, a cheque for fifty thousand pounds. 'Buy yourself a few test tubes,' he said, handing it over to the bashful and rather bewildered-looking headmaster.

The rest of the speeches were, as Brendan had predicted, long and dull. In normal circumstances, Alice would have slipped away – to another party, another set of contacts – but this evening she hung around.

'Stylish or what?' Brendan came to her with an unashamedly smug smile.

'Did others follow suit?'

'Promises, promises. They don't want to look vulgar or ridiculous. Luckily I don't mind. But they will give eventually. Now, how are you?'

With his enthusiastic face glinting at her and his arm drawing her out of the crowd, Alice tried to think how she was. There was Blue, she remembered, with Guy's pressing invitation to accompany him westwards, and the unsolved question of whom she should interview for the following week if not Blue. 'Your interview will be in the paper tomorrow,' she said. 'It's a pity I couldn't have described this scene.' She was half joking.

'That wouldn't have done at all. It would have looked like boasting.'

How perceptive of you, thought Alice.

Brendan grabbed a passing waiter to refill both their glasses. 'I assumed my interview would be in.'

'You should never assume.'

'So who is it next week?'

'I'm not certain. It's often like this. I did talk to a deep-sea diver.'

Brendan, who was in the process of downing his champagne, jerked the glass sharply. His eyes fixed briefly on her, then looked over her shoulder. 'What's this diver called?'

'Blue Carroway.' Alice willed herself not to blush as she pronounced the name. But Brendan suddenly seemed inattentive. He was still looking past her round the room. 'I have talked to him briefly but now he's gone down to Cornwall. I'm tossing up whether to follow him there.'

'What part of Cornwall?' Brendan asked casually. 'I have a house in that direction. Maybe I can give you a lift.'

Alice felt confused. Behind Brendan, she could see the headmaster and a man who had talked about the mercers heading in his direction. Clearly he was about to be removed for dinner. The room was emptying rapidly. 'I haven't decided whether to go.'

Brendan also seemed to sense an interruption. He took out his wallet, selected a card from among many and handed it to her. 'If you do want a lift, call this number. I'll be leaving about lunchtime.'

'Oh, I'd probably go earlier.'

His minders or hosts had come. Brendan took a step towards

them. 'We'd be there in time for tea on the lawn,' he said. 'That's the kind of difference flying makes.'

He was gone then – not, Alice noticed, stopping to introduce her. She left and walked back to the Underground, picking up, as she'd paused to stare up at the great dome of St Paul's Cathedral, the publicist she had talked to before the speeches.

'I hear you've interviewed the famous Sir Brendan Costa,' she said.

She was younger than Alice, dark and pretty, but her face was obscured by an excessive amount of make-up. In her job you need protection, thought Alice. 'It'll be in tomorrow.'

'He's quite a charmer. At least, until you disagree with him. I once went to try to sell a good cause to him. He more or less threw me out.'

'Why ever?'

'He said I wasn't prepared. I *was* prepared, but I told him he needed to improve his image. Maybe that's why he did your interview.'

'How long ago did you see him?'

'Last year.'

'He's taken a long time to take your advice, then.'

The girl, called Bea, laughed. 'Bread on the waters. Not very helpful for me, though. He cut me dead this evening.'

They were at the Underground now and went down the escalator one behind the other. Alice wondered whether Bea's information, assuming it was true, should put her on her guard against Brendan. But then, she reminded herself, she was on her guard. That was one of the things she was good at: she didn't need blusher and eyeshadow to protect herself. She had learnt as a child, when her mother was no longer around and her father had made her feel tiresome. She knew about keeping her guard up and herself to herself. Richard had once said it was what he most valued about her.

'You'll probably think I've been too kind to him,' she said, as they parted, Alice for one platform and Bea for the other.

'Sir Brendan, you mean. I guess that's your style and why they keep saying yes. Which reminds me, I'll email you on the latest in fashion-designer chic tomorrow. I'm talking about a man, you understand.' The two women waved and Alice took up position on the almost empty platform to wait for a train.

The flat was deliciously cool and silent. Alice made up a plate of salad and cheese and sat with it on her lap in the living room. She was hungry, and thought, with sudden acute pleasure, of the last proper meal she'd eaten – in the Greek restaurant with Blue. She didn't think of the food, which she had hardly noticed, but of her thudding heart and shaking hands, prelude to the night she'd spent with him. Why shouldn't she go and see him again? Why shouldn't she interview him, if that was what the Master wanted (rather inexplicably) and Guy advised? Blue himself had been keen enough, almost throwing her out when she put away her pad in the morning. Neither was there any reason why she shouldn't accept Brendan's offer and fly – by private jet presumably – to Cornwall. Unless she wanted to end up a dried-up old maid, if such persons existed in a post-feminist age, she must be prepared to take some risks with the people in her life. Correction: the men in her life. And although this diagnosis offended her sense of dignity she allowed it to remain.

Alice took off her shoes and jacket and went into the study. Guy had sent her a lot of material on Blue, on deep-sea diving in general, on treasure-seeking, on great wrecks and expeditions. This time she would be properly prepared.

It was after midnight and Alice was already in bed when she remembered she should ring Guy and let him know of her changed plan. It was odd to hear his voice as she lay in the darkness. It was heavier and richer than she remembered.

'Oh, God, I'm so sorry. I forgot you were leaving early. Did I wake you?' Had she also woken a partner, a body beside him, a head on a second pillow?

'Alice?' He sounded a little dazed, although warm – his voice was very warm.

'Yes. It was just to say I am coming tomorrow. I'll ring you when I arrive. Tea-time probably. Maybe you can line up Blue?'

'I thought you weren't coming?' He had woken up. His voice was more clipped, less warm.

'I changed my mind. Go back to sleep.'

'Thanks.'

'I'll ring you.'

'So you said. Alice?'

'What?'

'Why did you change your mind?'

'You persuaded me.'

'Did I really?'

He seemed about to say more, perhaps ask more questions, but Alice cut him off. 'Between four and five. Goodnight now.' She put down the phone. And then remembered she hadn't asked him where they'd be. What town, village or beach? It seemed impossible to ring him back so she lay for a while, reminding herself she was a journalist with a journalist's powers of detection. Eventually she recalled that she'd written down the name of the place Blue was planning to set up his school during her interview with him on Thursday evening. It would still be safely there in her notepad.

Chapter Eight

A Second Saturday

Sitting in bed with a bowl of cereal, Alice turned off the *Today* programme and turned on her mobile. Ten messages had been recorded on the previous day. She got as far as two from the nursing home.

'May I speak to Sister Mary Rose? . . . It's Alice here, Sister. I expect you were trying to reach me yesterday.'

'Indeed I was. Yesterday morning. Several times.' Mary Rose's voice was severe, yet there was no edge of tragic news to be imparted. Unless, working where she did, tragedy, in the form of death, was an everyday occurrence.

'What's the matter? Is my father ill?' Alice put down her spoon and remembered that, when she was a child, her father had railed against the sugar content of cereal and banned it from their house.

'The doctor disappeared. Remarkable for a man of his age. He was gone on Friday morning but we think he went in the night. His bed was quite cold.' Her voice was unemotional.

'Disappeared!' She imagined her father, who could take no more than a few steps, even with his zimmer, dashing along Brighton pier. Jumping off the end. 'With his zimmer?'

'That was the strange part. The zimmer was parked, as usual, neatly in the corner. We keep it out of range, you know.'

'But he *disappeared*!' The word was extraordinary.

There was a pause. 'You did get my message?'

'No. No.'

'I see. Well, of course, we found him,' Sister Mary Rose laughed, 'just as I picked up the phone to the police. He was in the next-door room, temporarily empty. No one had thought of looking so close to home. Very hungry, poor old dear, but quite unharmed. Used the furniture to get to the bathroom, then found an empty flower vase. Hasn't altogether lost his wits, you see.'

Alice noticed she had been holding her breath and took a long gasp. 'Why did he run away?'

'"Disappear" was the way he described it. Of course, there has to be a deterioration after an adventure like this.'

'But why?'

'I did tell you all this in my message.' Her tone was patiently unreproachful 'It's this woman he's dreamt up. This "harpy", as he calls her. He's scared she'll come and get him. Harm him, that is. We try to reassure him but I'm afraid he's not quite reasonable. But you needn't worry now. We've put cot sides on his bed and a couple of straps – non-invasive, you understand, just enough for his own safety. You can trust us to look after dear Dr Featherstone as if he were our own father.'

This remark, essentially true, as Alice knew, ended the conversation. She put down her mobile and finished her cereal. Her father's productive life was in the past. Every Thursday she visited him. She was a dutiful daughter. The nursing home was expensive and she was paying for part of it with her own money – well, Richard's money. Above all, she must forget the matter of non-invasive straps.

She rang Florrie. 'I've got to work today. I'll try to get down later tonight or tomorrow. How are you all?'

'It's too early, Mum, to know how we are, although I doubt I could ever answer the question in the way you pose it.'

'Heavens, Florrie. Did Lily have a bad night?'

'I was with the mushrooms.' Florrie had a dignified tone, which made Alice suspicious.

'So your Baz friend looked after her?'

'My Baz friend, as you so whimsically put it, had a lovely night. I've often told you how well Lily sleeps. She's not a chore, you know.'

'I love Lily!' exclaimed Alice, surprised at her vehemence. Was Florrie cross that she couldn't babysit today, thus releasing her and her friend to jaunt off somewhere?

'Of course you love Lily. What a strange thing to say. Dear old Mum. Always keen to be in the right.'

After this comment Alice decided it was time to move on and

finalise arrangements with Brendan. She had been Florrie's champion against Richard for so many years that it still felt strange to harbour her own critical thoughts. 'I'll let you know my movements as soon as I know them, darling. Hug Lily for me.'

They were flying to Plymouth, his secretary informed her. 'Sir Brendan apologises but the car won't be able to pick you up as it's already being driven down to Cornwall. He suggests I arrange a cab . . .'

Everything was being organised for her. Alice had a curious sense and, she had to admit, an agreeable one, of handing over control. Her next step was to buy the newspaper and see how her piece looked in print. If she was in London, she liked to go down to the local newsagent so that she could check out how it looked on the shelf among other papers.

Today was a good day. 'Your picture's on the front page,' said her friend the newsagent who, over the years, had learnt to care as much as Alice about such things. It still gave her a shock to see her smiling face, in colour now, red hair a little wild, over a byline not written by her: *Costa Goes Personal with Alice Lightfoot*. Not too bad. Perhaps Bea had been right and this was all part of Brendan's plan for a more human image. She read the piece walking slowly back to the flat. Nothing to worry her there either, although someone had added a few more figures about his surprisingly large donations to the Labour Party, and a sub had put a heading that hardly tallied with her story: *Costa Cools on the Market*. Where had she written that or even implied it? But, all in all, it was a job done well and he should be happy. She had made him seem both powerful and vulnerable. He should be very happy.

Alice felt her body relaxing in the warm sunshine. In a moment she would start to think about Blue and how she was going to deal with him. And Guy. She felt herself tensing a little and stopped to shrug her shoulders up and down, up and down, before she went into the apartment block.

Alice was struck by how incredibly *rich* Brendan looked. Perhaps it was his off-duty clothes that did it: his blue polo shirt, the obviously cashmere sweater draped round his neck, his exceptionally leather leather belt, his well-oiled loafers with funny-looking tassels. 'It's very kind of you to offer me a lift. I've never been given an airlift before.'

'For Sir Brendan read Sir Galahad.'

They were at a small airport on the outskirts of London to which Alice had been efficiently whisked by a black cab on account. An early-afternoon haze seemed to reach out from the city as if to drag them back into its grasp.

'Sometimes I hate London,' said Alice, impulsively.

'You seem distressed. A woman of your intelligence and beauty cannot deserve it.'

'You must have liked the interview.' Alice smiled at him.

'It was charming. You painted me as a little-boy-lost. My wives will be furious, but I'm delighted. We are, perhaps, kindred souls.' He turned and, crouching to accommodate his considerable height, entered the aeroplane. Alice followed warily, with a feeling that she was going into the lion's den.

As at their lunch meeting, Brendan was the perfect host – if given his own way. On the aeroplane, as they sat by side and the ground dropped at a rather hair-raising angle, he explained that Goose-fields, his house in Cornwall, was his dream palace, as far as possible from the hard north of his youth. 'I'm training myself to be a sybarite, which comes so easily to you southerners.'

Alice objected, not very seriously, that as his father was Italian and his mother Irish he had much more sybaritic blood in his veins than most southerners. 'I can hardly think of you as a northerner at all,' she added.

'It's impossible to talk with someone who knows so much about me!' He had decided to take offence and punished her by going up front to talk to the pilot.

His absence allowed Alice a moment of vertiginous doubt. What was she doing flying to Plymouth in such unlikely company? But he was back too soon for her to have found an answer. 'We're about to land,' he advised and, petulance banished, checked her seat-belt solicitously.

This being looked-after was seductive, Alice acknowledged. She was even more aware of enjoying it as they landed on a Tarmac strip among green fields and stepped out into an afternoon of softly glowing sky.

'You'll come to the house first?' He knew she would.

'I have to call my colleague.'

'And after tea on the lawn Harry will take you wherever you want.' Harry and the Bentley Azure had met them and now drove them through cavernous trees.

'Are you all right?'

Moody himself, Alice couldn't help enjoying the way he noted her moods. It had not been one of Richard's strong points, although she suspected that, if a problem had been brought to his attention, he was more likely to act on it than her present host. He was now listening attentively to his mobile. This reminded Alice unpleasantly of her many unattended messages. She decided that this was not the moment, leant back and closed her eyes. She, too, could be a sybarite. Not that she believed Brendan could ever be that. She opened her eyes for a flash and saw his short, square fingers opening and closing on his knee. He was far too energetic.

'How near is the sea?' asked Alice. As promised, they were sitting on the lawn. Tea had been set on a table with a white tablecloth that shone rather too stridently in the gentle green all around them. The silver teapot also glinted fiercely. Alice still had not called Guy.

Brendan pointed beyond her. 'Ten miles away, but there're two hills in between. I used to keep a yacht but only my son had time for it. Isn't that right, Harry?' This was addressed to the chauffeur, who nodded in agreement while putting down a fresh pot of hot water. He muttered a few more words as he departed. 'What was that, Harry?'

The dictator's command, thought Alice, wryly.

'Jago was the problem. That's all I said.'

'Quite.' Brendan let him go and turned back to Alice. 'My first wife took my son to California during his formative period. Need I say more?'

'I'm sorry.'

'Your children are still too young to do wrong.'

Alice remembered the scene with Lily. If he believed she was the mother of a baby, he should be surprised to see her free and independent to fly about England, although it was amazing how men could overlook obvious truths in their own interest. Something had been nagging at her since they had arrived in this little paradise and now at last she remembered what. 'Surely the house to which you invited me for the weekend is in another part of the country? Was it Gloucestershire?'

Brendan allowed a pause. He folded his napkin and Alice listened to the wood pigeons calling softly from a row of tall red beeches. She looked again at the house behind him, a perfect small manor built of soft yellow stone, encompassed by a close network of gardens, two of them walled. This was not the swanky mansion of the northern self-made millionaire. There could hardly be more than four or five bedrooms. 'This is my secret house.'

'I'm honoured.' But a little trapped too. 'If you'll excuse me, I'll make my call.'

'Be my guest.' He waved his hand at the garden and watched Alice as, rising hastily and rather clumsily, she set off for a protective wall, a shadowing tree.

'It's me. Alice.'

'I know it's you. Where are you?'

'Not far away if you're near St Mawes.' Why was she avoiding his question?

'South, north or east?'

What difference did it make where she was? 'North.'

'OK. Come to the Blueberry Arms at Little Hanbury.'

It was only after Alice had switched off the mobile that she realised Guy hadn't mentioned Blue, her only reason for coming to Cornwall. Presumably Guy had arranged for him to be there too.

Outside the pub, Guy sat in a garden where the grass was yellow from pressing feet and a large weeping willow draped delicately over three or four tables and a small stream beside them. Alice got out of the air-conditioned car and felt the heat surging through the dampish air. She waved at Guy, while looking anxiously to see if Blue was going to appear from a doorway. But there was only one pint of beer in front of him.

'Where's Blue?' she asked, before she'd even reached him. It was easier at a distance.

Guy stood up to greet her – how tall he was, much taller than he'd seemed in London – but he didn't answer, except to say, 'That was Sir Brendan Costa's car, wasn't it?'

'Yes. Yes.' She tried to brush it aside. 'He gave me a lift. Heavens, it's so hot. I thought the country was supposed to be cooler than London but this is stifling.'

'Would you like a drink?'

'Just water. No, perhaps a spritzer.' While Guy went inside the pub, Alice tried to understand what was going on. Where was Blue? Beyond the willow she could see a corner of the Bentley. Harry had his orders to wait for her and was determined to do so, despite her protests.

Guy came back and sat down opposite her. For once he wasn't wearing glasses and she could see his rather large hazel eyes. 'I know you've come to see Blue.'

At the name, Alice felt a delightful warmth spread through her body, followed almost immediately by something much more complicated. She certainly didn't want Guy to pick up any vibes. 'Where is he? Weren't you sailing together today?'

'Blue's disappeared. That sounds too dramatic, but he took my sailing boat out on Friday afternoon and hasn't been seen since.'

'Disappeared.' The word brought with it an image of an old man crawling from his bed and clawing his way into another, safer to him.

'Yes. Maybe he suddenly decided on a trip to France.'

'Why would he do that?'

'He's done it before without telling me. He likes feeling free.'

Alice considered this in silence. It was the sort of thing Florrie would say.

'You were the last person to talk to him. Did he give you any idea of what he was up to?'

Alice felt her heart give a distinct thud, almost painful, and loud enough, she felt, for Guy to hear. She took a long gulp of her drink. 'But, Guy, I met Blue for the first time ever on Thursday. Just for an interview, set up by you.' Her heart gave another thud. 'Why ever would he tell me his plans?'

'He wanted to be interviewed. He asked you to come down today, didn't he? Or perhaps he didn't.'

'I suppose so. Sort of.' Alice heard herself mumbling. She was unable to meet Guy's unprotected eyes. What would she see there? Knowledge? Understanding? Disapproval? Blue had wanted to be interviewed the morning they parted and she had wanted to make love again, and neither had happened. That was the truth of it. Or, at least, all she could remember.

'Never mind.'

Guy rubbed his face and she noticed he hadn't shaved that morning. He looked tired, too, and after a second or two she remembered why. 'It must be annoying for you, getting up so early and not having your boat to sail.'

'The sea's so calm it wouldn't have been much fun. That's partly why I don't understand what Blue was up to. He'd have had to tack for miles before he caught a wind. Also, there's a storm forecast for tomorrow.'

'No wonder it's so hot.'

'Shall I get you another drink?'

'No, thanks. So, what shall I do? Hang around hoping or look for another subject?' Suddenly Alice felt as tired as Guy looked, and found herself thinking, with a kind of yearning, of Brendan's peaceful house and garden and perfectly run establishment. Before she had left Brendan had invited her to stay the night. She had said no, but he'd only shaken his head and smiled.

'I'm going back to St Mawes to see if he's turned up. I'll ring your mobile with any news,' Guy told her.

He wasn't advising her, Alice guessed, because he was assuming she would get into Brendan's chauffeur-driven car and be whisked away. She stood up with an uneasy sense of being pulled in various contradictory directions – not that Guy was suggesting she came with him. 'I should go to Florrie and Lily,' she said.

They were both standing now and Guy walked ahead of her out of the garden. 'Do you need a lift to the station,' he offered. But he looked ironically at Harry, who had already opened the door of the Bentley.

'Thanks.' She was too confused to explain.

'I'll be in touch.' He walked away then, in the direction of an unlikely turquoise Volkswagen, not the modern streamlined variety but an older, battered version, with some peeling paint showing a lighter colour underneath. It seemed unlike the Guy she had thought she knew in London.

Half-way back to Goosefields, her mobile rang. It was not Guy as she'd expected. 'I'm so glad you're accepting my invitation,' said Brendan. 'I've finally found a woman in the village who can manage a perfect steak *au poivre*.' Alice didn't like steak. Nevertheless she decided Florrie would have to do without her. 'She's also prepared your room.'

'You're very kind,' said Alice. For some reason, she found it difficult to take Blue's 'disappearance' seriously, which was odd since Guy had seemed distinctly anxious. Perhaps at the moment she had too much to take on board. Or perhaps it was due to the sense of unreality that had been growing steadily since her night with Blue.

The wood pigeons called dreamily to each other. It was dusk, although still very warm. Soon it would be completely dark and they would go quietly to their roosts.

'So, did you interview your diver?' Brendan sat across from Alice. They had just finished dinner at the same table where they had had tea earlier, gently lit this evening by two candles in high glass bowls. His voice was alert, unconversational, to the point. Until now they had spoken about general matters. Brendan had held forth about the present government's inability to understand that the City had 'its own rules and requirements'. Alice told him about the pressures of pleasing her editor on a weekly basis. She hoped she sounded hardened professional rather than weakling woman. His question about Blue had come out of this conversation.

Alice sat more upright and tried to collect her thoughts. It struck her that Harry would have already told him that she'd met only one man so he had no reason to ask. 'Unfortunately not. That's why I have to stick around another day. He went out sailing and hasn't got back yet.' What was wrong with the truth, after all?

'What a nuisance! And how irresponsible.'

'Oh, he didn't know for certain I was coming.'

As quickly as Brendan had switched on his attention, he switched it off, saying dismissively, 'I've always heard that these people who prefer life under water never quite get the hang of behaviour above the surface. Now, my dear, I've had coffee arranged in the orangery.'

He came round to Alice and took her arm with a kind of old-fashioned formality. As if they were moving from one room to another, he led her over the smooth green grass to one of the walled gardens where, among vegetables neatly segmented with box hedges, a shapely conservatory clung to one of the walls.

'What a magic place!' Feeling like a child in fairyland, Alice entered. Orange trees, hung with fruit ranging in ripeness from rich orange, through yellow to acid green, grew from huge, decorated urns. Sometimes the trees were flowering, scenting the whole room. Candles flickering in the corners were reflected two or three times in the glass walls and a candelabrum stood on a table set with two chairs.

Brendan looked gratified. 'I'm glad you like it.'

It was impossible not to accompany the coffee with a glass of golden Tokay and a chocolate topped with a wild strawberry, impossible not to feel pampered and desired, impossible not to reward Brendan for all his wizardry. It was a little confidence, after all. 'Lily, the baby you saw with me, belongs to my daughter.'

Brendan put out his hand and covered hers, as if for consolation. 'Your granddaughter.'

'I should be with them now.' He must know that she was a responsible woman with a family, not some picked-up journalist with no background beyond newsprint.

Alice looked down at his hand. She had at first characterised its square lack of elegance as a sign of his coarseness, even brutality, but now it felt and looked utterly comforting. Her own father's hand, even in middle age, had always had a claw-like, unpadded quality, which was odd in a doctor. How much soft flesh had his horny digits prodded and poked? Not hers, she'd made sure of that. As a child, she'd often imagined the soft hands of her mother until that image had faded, like her face. So why was it in her mind now? To her horror, she felt tears pricking at her eyes, wanting to increase and fall.

'What is it?'

'Nothing. Nothing. A busy week.'

'You looked as if you were about to water my oranges with tears.'

'I never cry.' It was true. Even at Richard's funeral, so absolutely shocking, she hadn't cried.

'You're fortunate.'

'What?' She tried to resist rubbing her eyes.

'Don't you remember? When you interviewed me? Who cried then?'

Oh, heavens. It was true. Tears had spouted out of his little blue eyes. And she had even put it into her piece. Had he hated that? She hadn't asked him.

'But, as I told you then, I cry easily. Unlike you.'

She had recovered, shaken off the shades of the past. 'I'm fine,' she said.

'Time for bed, all the same,' said Brendan, in oddly nannying tones. He stood up and picked an orange blossom, which he presented to her before kissing her cheek. His lips were hot on her skin. 'When I was younger I grabbed what I wanted as soon as I spotted it, but now I've learnt the art of patience.' Was this an apology for not jumping on her? Alice didn't know. But she was glad when he took her hand and led her back across the lawn to the house. The soft grass was wet with dew and their feet made a shushing sound. Otherwise there was complete silence.

The house had a slightly musty but not unpleasant smell, as if the scent of centuries of wood fires lingered in the old panelling. Brendan led her along dim corridors to a room through whose open door she could see a large four-poster bed.

'Sleeping Beauty.' Once more he kissed her cheek tenderly, then passed his pudgy fingers lightly over her eyes. 'I'll see you in the morning.'

Chapter Nine

A Second Sunday

When Alice awoke, the curtains were too heavy for her to tell whether it was still night or morning so she climbed down from the high bed and went over to the window. It overlooked the lawn they'd walked across the night before and she saw it was early morning: a thick white mist curled from under the beech trees and rolled over the grass, like dry ice across a stage. Something had woken her. There was another window to the right of the bed. She drew back the curtains.

Her room was at the side of the house, overlooking a courtyard bordered by stables and garages. A car had just driven up, a turquoise car.

'Guy!' She spoke aloud and the name resonated in the high-ceilinged room. He looked up just as she jerked shut the curtains.

On becoming more sensibly awake, she told herself that he was simply coming to tell her the latest news of Blue. Probably he rang last night but she hadn't checked her mobile. She looked out of the first window again, and saw that four sprinklers were jetting water over the lawn. It seemed hardly necessary as the mist had cleared and the sun was already heavily barred by blue-black clouds, gathering swiftly in intensity. There had been a whole week of hot, dry days. Was this the predicted storm? She must dress, 'be prepared' for anything, in the Boy Scout motto.

Alice became aware of a knocking sound. She took a moment to connect it with the door. 'Come in.'

'Madam's breakfast.' It was the steak *au poivre* woman from the village with a charmingly arranged tray, which she put down beside Alice.

'Good morning.'

'You like storms, then, do you? Sir Brendan sends you up this breakfast. He's got a visitor. But Harry's around, Sir Brendan said, if you need to leave in a hurry.'

The visitor could only be Guy.

By the time she was dressed, the sun had gone and the sky was dark, but the sprinklers were still turning. Leaving her bag half packed, Alice left the room. She could do with a bit of fresh air before the journey.

In fact, the air was not at all fresh but hot and heavy and filled with approaching change. The garden was bigger than she had thought the night before, each walled garden an acre or two, one planted with an orchard of various fruit trees – quite recently, to judge by the pristine labels and clean stakes; in another there was a comma-shaped swimming-pool, sculpted into a grassy slope, topped by a changing-hut built like a temple and protected by flowering hibiscus. Such evidence of extreme wealth, particularly at a second, lesser country-house, was startling just when she had begun to think of Brendan as a normal human being. No one as rich as this, with all the power it implied, was normal.

Alice stared into the azure waters. What was the meaning of Blue's so-called disappearance? Guy had talked of a calm sea, not the setting for a shipwreck. Then why had she picked up from him such a strong sense of anxiety? Why had he come to find her? Could he have been hinting at something like, for example, suicide? This was transparently ridiculous. Alice managed a smile. As far as she knew she hadn't spent the night with a man who had suicide in mind. She walked a little further round the pool, coming within a few yards of the changing-hut. She glanced briefly at the black, reflecting glass. Disappearance as in death?

Alice returned her attention to the smooth blue of the water. She saw her face, magnified and distorted, still smiling at the idea of Blue killing himself. It made no sense. Suddenly the surface broke up, swirling in mighty circles as if something or someone was going to break it apart and emerge. In a flash of the imagination, Alice saw Blue's golden, tanned body, shimmering trunks, beautiful, slightly battered face, stand up in front of her, drops of crystal water flying out from him.

Then she saw it was raining. Huge drops were splashing into the pool, causing the ever-widening circles. One fell on to her bare arm.

73

In a moment, she would be soaked. Such a long week of sun must be followed by a great storm, thought Alice, as the increasing gloom was split by a wide swathe of lightning, followed by a slow rumbling of thunder. The storm was still some distance away. Should she try to run back to the house? The gleaming white temple was much closer.

As the rain splashed in single giant drops, Alice hurried to the end of the pool and was starting up the steps when the black glass door opened.

'We were wondering when you'd do the obvious. Welcome! I hope you slept well. You received the message that I was otherwise engaged?'

'Yes, thank you,' panted Alice, confused by Brendan's large, comforting but unexpected presence. He took her arm and led her into the small, dim room. The shrubs growing round gave it an eerie greenish light.

'And here's an old friend come to find you,' continued Brendan, in his jocular manner.

'Hello, Alice.' And there was Guy, standing up from a canvas chair, looking extraordinarily as usual. 'I tracked you down. But Sir Brendan persuaded me you were absolutely whacked so I didn't bother you.' His words were punctuated by lightning sweeping across the room followed by a colossal explosion, which was even more frightening because the thunder was still not overhead.

'It looks like we're marooned here.'

'It's scarcely raining.'

Guy was right: the expected deluge, which had driven Alice inside, still hadn't arrived. Even the drops had stopped falling. 'Isn't it dangerous to be near water when there's lightning?' Alice was sure she had read that somewhere but both men looked at her with the same benign lack of concern. Perhaps she was being over-sensitive but they seemed bonded in some male way, possibly against her.

'I was once caught at sea in an electric storm,' said Guy, looking pleased at the memory. Alice remembered their boat trip down the Thames and how he had explained that he liked tuna sandwiches because it made him feel like a storm-tossed mariner wearing a sou'wester. It felt an age ago, but it was only five days.

'I've never been a good sailor,' said Brendan. 'I don't think the

Irish or the Italians like the sea. For starters, they don't believe in swimming.'

'No self-respecting sailor believes in swimming. I'd almost call it a sporting tautology.'

Alice thought this frolicsome conversation sounded strangely unconvincing. Now they were both looking to her but she felt unwilling to ask about Blue. 'It's going to be a huge storm,' she said.

Brendan walked to the door. 'You're right. I'd better get up to the house while I can.' He smiled. 'You two can stay here and get on with it.'

Get on with what? thought Alice. But the moment the door was closed, Guy began to speak with urgent intensity. 'I'm afraid it's more serious than I thought. About Blue, I mean.' Alice saw he was sweating. It was oppressive in the hut. 'My boat's been spotted empty. No Blue. A fishing-boat's trying to bring it in if the storm doesn't get there first.'

'What do you mean, Guy? You mean . . .' she hesitated over words that sounded absurd in real life '. . . you mean there might have been foul play?'

Alice didn't get an answer to this question. Just as she finished speaking, the room was filled with a jagged glitter, followed by a raucous rending of wood, as one of the giant beeches, struck by lightning, tore itself apart and a vast branch heavy with leaves was flung across a wall and into the pool. Guy and Alice leapt to their feet and stared out in amazement. As if automatically protecting her, Guy put his arm round Alice's shoulders and pulled her close to him. The smashed branch, bigger than a normal tree, filled the pool and ejected a blue tidal wave of water on either side, rather as if a liner had been launched fast down a ramp. Dark red leaves whirled above, accompanied by a background chorus of outraged wood pigeons.

'Phew,' exclaimed Guy, when things had settled a bit. 'That was a close call. It's astonishing how long a vertical becomes when it lies horizontal.'

Alice found she was speechless and her legs were shaking. She felt for a chair and sat on it. Another flash of lightning illuminated the scene further. A wind must have got up because leaves and twigs were flying wildly round the sky. She noted it wasn't raining yet and reminded herself that despite the murky light this – incredibly – was a summer's morning. 'What about Brendan?' she remembered.

'Do you mean did the tree get him?'

'He only went out a moment before.' Alice still felt shocked. She wished Guy was holding her but he was standing by the door.

'Oh, I wouldn't worry about our Sir Brendan Costa. He's a survivor.'

Alice didn't feel like worrying about anyone. She felt like going home. 'Perhaps we should check. He might not have hurried away.'

'You mean he might have been eavesdropping on our conversation? Don't worry, he knows all about Blue's disappearance.'

'You told him.'

'That as well.' Alice stood up and found her legs had stopped shaking and now felt like jelly. 'Let's go, then.' Guy opened the door. 'I'll look in the pool and you look under the branches.'

Alice didn't try to understand his ironic tones but, not wanting to be separated from him, followed him out of the hut. It was a miracle, she thought, that the little building, with its glass windows from roof to floor, hadn't been stoved in and pierced them both with flying shards.

Outside, as they picked their way round tangled branches, which occasionally harboured intact nests, she began to revive. Besides, it soon became clear that there was no drowned or flattened millionaire. The lightning still lit the sky every few seconds and thunder rumbled more or less continuously, but the wind had dropped again and the air raised her spirits.

'There's still the rain to come,' commented Guy. 'What will you do now? Go home?'

Now Alice wanted to ask him more about Blue but he was walking away from her. Harry was coming towards them, a large black umbrella clasped under his arm, and just behind him, Brendan in a long mackintosh almost to the ground. He waved and shouted, 'Thank God you're all right. What a noise! What a falling! All over in less than a minute. I got out my stopwatch. Just forty-five degrees to the left and you'd both be in an early grave.' He had reached them and took Alice's arm in what she now recognised as his habitual way.

'Alice was worried about you,' said Guy. 'We've been sifting through the leaves for your remains.' He gave an odd chuckling laugh.

Brendan laughed more heartily. 'It would take more than a bit of one of my own trees to knock me off my perch.'

'That's just what I told Alice.'

Alice thought that what she'd earlier perceived as male complicity was a mutual hostility that produced louder voices and false laughs.

Brendan sighed and stepped back a little so he could look at her. 'I believe you're a witch with your red hair and green eyes. A catalyst for us all.'

'My eyes aren't green, they're hazel,' objected Alice. 'Gold, if you want to flatter.'

But Brendan wasn't interested in that sort of reality. 'You probably drew the storm towards you. A beautiful lightning conductor.'

'Absolutely not.'

'Alice wants to go home,' said Guy.

'Not worried about the storm, then?'

'Not really—' began Alice, but Brendan interrupted her at once.

'Quite right and proper. Harry will take you. Harry's never had an accident in his life. What would you say is the opposite to accident prone, Guy?'

'Accident proof.' He sounded brusque. 'Like you, Sir Brendan. I must go too.'

A few more minutes of uncomfortable dialogue later, Alice found herself in the back of the Bentley leaving the courtyard. Her bag sat beside her, efficiently delivered by Brendan's housekeeper. When she turned round, she saw Guy having what she assumed was a last word with Brendan. She waved, but neither man saw her.

'It should take two hours,' said Harry.

'Thank you,' said Alice and, lying back on the spongy seats with her eyes shut, determined not to speak another word. For half an hour or more she felt herself speeding along the road with no more accompaniment than a soothing spatter of rain.

'Now we're for it!' Harry's exclamation, which caused Alice to open her eyes, was immediately followed by a bolt of lightning and a roll of thunder. 'It's coming in another way,' he muttered. 'And look what it's bringing on its coat-tails.'

Rain hit the car in a slashing grey wave. The windscreen wipers swung frenziedly but without effect as cascades sluiced down the glass. At least it makes it possible to see through, thought Alice. But after a few minutes the pattern changed and the rain became individual needles, that hurled themselves at the car, bouncing in puffs of spray against the glass.

'Can't see a thing,' mumbled Harry.

'Better pull over.'

They sat in a lay-by while the heavy car was rocked by the fury of storm. In this remote part of the country on a Sunday morning, no other cars passed them in either direction.

'I wonder how long it'll last,' shouted Alice, above the sound of the rain. She reached for her mobile, switched it on. She certainly didn't want Harry to take it into his head to return to Goosefields.

'No saying.' He drummed on the dashboard. 'Just look at that blasted lightning and the thunder going round and round like it's playing with us.'

'I can't get any reception on my mobile.'

'You won't hereabouts. Can't hardly get radio reception.'

'Thank you.' Alice lay back again in her seat. There seemed nothing else to do. She didn't even know what had happened to Blue. Perhaps Brendan was right: she'd become a catalyst for the dramatic and the unexpected. Over her twenty years of marriage to Richard nothing like the events of the past week had ever happened to her. Or in the years since his death. It had all begun, she thought, on that afternoon when she had imagined a woman at the window of her flat.

'Might as well get going.' The rain had hardly lessened as the big car pulled again on to the road. Harry drove quite fast, water flying where the road was flooded, as high, sometimes, as the windows. Alice imagined them planing off the surface, turning upside down and landing in one of the many deep rivers that cut across the countryside.

'These tyres have got good grip.'

'I'm relieved to hear it.'

They proceeded for another half-hour or so, the rain following them all the way, as if the band of dark cloud raced in time with their own motion. West to east, thought Alice, and wondered if anyone at her cottage had remembered to bring in the deck-chairs.

'You might get a signal now,' Harry shouted, then leaned forward to find earphones, which he clamped over his head.

Alice pressed her own number but heard the engaged tone. Almost immediately, the mobile rang. 'Mum!' She could only just hear Florrie's voice above the rain and the swish of the tyres on the road.

'Florrie, you're breaking up. I'll be with you in about an hour.'

'Mum ... Lily ... Sleeping.' Alice could only pick out a few words and, knowing Florrie's garrulous mobile technique, repeated louder,' I'll see you soon, darling,' and cut the call.

At last the rain was subsiding. Alice seldom drove in a westerly direction from her cottage so the countryside round her was still unknown. The land had flattened again and green water-meadows stretched on either side. Much to her surprise they were not flooded in the way she'd expected, and she concluded that the storm had not yet arrived.

'How much longer?' She saw Harry's eyes rise to the rear-view mirror. She thought he was looking at her until she noticed he was staring behind her head. She turned. A massing blackness had gathered with hardly a lighter streak.

They had gone no more than a few miles before she felt rather than saw the first sharp finger of lightning and heard thunder that cracked and split rather than roared or rumbled. Ten seconds later darkness descended on the car and they were once more in a world of aggressive rain.

'We'll take a pit-stop!' shouted Harry.

Through the veiling weather Alice spotted the lights of a large petrol station ahead. The big car swerved left and they were in the relative peace of the covered area. They stopped by a pump.

Alice watched Harry dash to the side of the building ahead. If the gents' was on the left, the ladies' was probably on the right. But was it worth getting soaking wet? She got out of the car, stretched and watched another sliver of lightning trickle from the sky. Only one other car stood in the garage, beside a pump, black and unidentifiable. For a moment, she wondered what had happened to Guy in his unexpected turquoise car. Had he gone back to London or continued to wait for Blue in St Mawes? Probably London. The

Master wouldn't let him out of the office tomorrow. Monday was a big meeting day. In an attempt to divert herself from the continual nagging anxiety about her interview subject, Alice reached for the umbrella that was propped in the front seat and got out of the car.

As soon as she came out from under the cover, the wind tried to tug the umbrella out of her grasp while the heavy rain came at her from all directions. She pulled it down lower so that she had better control but, as a result, could only see the ground ahead of her. She had rounded the corner of the building when she saw a woman's legs coming swiftly towards her. They were inappropriately clad in pink trousers, already spattered with mud. Above the rain and wind, she heard what sounded like the protesting cry of a baby, followed by a volley of comforting but incomprehensible words from the mother.

Alice arrived at the open door of the ladies' with relief.

The room was small and not very clean. A nappy protruded from a bin. Not the easiest place to do nappy changing, thought Alice, then noticed something shining on the floor. It was a ring, silver or platinum with sparkling stones, possibly diamonds.

Alice abandoned the umbrella and dashed out of the ladies'. She reached the forecourt in time to see the black car moving out. She ran forward, shouting, 'You've lost a ring!' But the woman didn't hear or even see her and, rather than slowing down, drove faster, so that Alice, still waving the ring, was forced to jump out of her way.

'Is anything wrong, madam?'

'Yes. No.' Alice was thoroughly discomposed. And wet. 'That woman with the baby dropped a ring in the ladies'. I tried to give it back to her, that's all.'

'And then she nearly ran you over.' Alice looked at Harry suspiciously, but he wore a solicitous, servile look.

'Now I suppose I'll have to take it into a police station – if one's open on Sunday. And I left the umbrella in the ladies'.'

'Allow me.'

Alice allowed him, and went to sit in the car. She'd cross her legs till the cottage. She turned the ring in her palm and, fearful of losing it, put it on the third finger of her right hand. It fitted snugly.

'Down this lane,' commanded Alice, 'entrance on the left and we're there.' The sight of the ash tree that formed a marker to the house, the slate roof and the creeper-covered stone walls cheered her.

The car had barely stopped before Alice had leapt out, taking her bag with her. She ignored the front door, which was never used, and opened the side door.

'It's me! Home at last.'

The door sprang open. 'Oh, Mama!' Florrie flung herself into her mother's arms, a bundle of childish misery.

'Darling, what is it?' Alice eased her daughter inside where she found Baz hovering uncertainly.

Since Florrie seemed unable to speak, it was he who answered Alice's question. 'You see, we were sleeping. It is Sunday, isn't it? Time for a lie-in. And Lily's a good sleeper. But not that good.' At these words Florrie, who must have been listening despite being overwhelmed by sobs, shuddered alarmingly.

'Sit down, darling.' Alice pushed Florrie into a large armchair, then asked Baz to continue.

'It was the silence that woke me. I looked at my watch and it was, like, midday. Well, you know, Lily never sleeps till—'

'Oh, Mama!' Florrie interrupted. She jumped up and stood in front of Alice, tears streaming down her face. 'Lily's gone! Lily's gone! Oh, I'm such a bad, bad mother!'

'I think a cup of tea's what's needed here.' They all looked at the owner of this sane voice.

'Oh, Harry,' said Alice, gratefully. 'That's such a good idea.'

They made tea, and toast with Marmite, and although only Baz and Harry managed to eat anything, Florrie became calmer.

'The police haven't come yet?' asked Harry, suddenly. It turned out that neither Florrie nor Baz had thought of contacting them: Florrie had been too upset and it seemed likely to Alice that Baz's life experience had taught him to avoid officers of the law.

Alice looked at her watch. It was already two thirty. Lily could have been missing for hours. With a hideous sense of disbelief, she dialled 999. Somewhere on the edge of her brain, a memory was striving to surface. 'Police, please ... Yes ... I'd like to report a missing baby.'

Florrie began to cry again the moment the two police officers stepped through the door, as if the sight of their uniforms triggered a deeper understanding of what had happened. 'Lily!' Lily!' she wailed, weeping inconsolably, and left the room. Alice was torn between comforting her and welcoming the officers. Guiltily, she thought that her own absence had allowed the kidnapping.

One of the policemen – they were both young, tall, clean-cut – looked meaningfully at the teapot.

'I'll do it,' said Harry, handing a white handkerchief to Florrie. 'Tea for six.'

The small kitchen was crowded.

'I'm Detective Constable Smith and this is Detective Constable Hendricks.' They were rock-like – Alice was grateful for this. 'So, let's get down what happened. Hang on while I pull out my pad.'

The rain had finally stopped and the light in the room gradually lifted until streaks of sun came and went through the garlanding of creepers at the window. As if the storm had washed the sky, the sun was piercing and brilliant. As Alice raised her hand to push back a falling lock of hair, her eye caught the ring, glinting. She'd forgotten all about it. She twisted it off her finger and held it out to DC Smith. 'I was going to hand this in at a police station tomorrow, but perhaps you wouldn't mind taking it now.'

The policeman looked surprised, as if babies and rings didn't mix.

Alice explained the circumstances: the rain, the lavatory, the mother changing her baby's nappy, how she had failed to catch her before she drove off.

'What did she look like?' asked Hendricks.

'I don't know. I had the umbrella pulled down low.'

'With a baby, you say?'

'Yes. I . . .' She stopped. The memory that had so distracted her came back. The woman in the car had had white hair.

Into the silence, as DC Smith took the ring and held it up to the light, Florrie came back. She had washed her face and looked more composed. Her eyes turned slowly to the ring, glittering between the policeman's fingers.

'Where on earth did you get that?'

Alice explained.

'It's hers,' said Florrie flatly. 'Dora's.' Alice gasped. Baz – who had been more or less excluded from the proceedings – since it had been established that he was not Lily's father – gently led Florrie to a chair. 'She kept trying to give it to me,' said Florrie. 'She said her

82

fingers had shrunk and it was too big for her. She said an old woman like her didn't need a ring like that.'

'But you told me she was a cleaning woman!' Alice found she was almost shouting and lowered her voice. 'Cleaners don't wear diamond rings like that.' Had she failed to recognise her grand-daughter from those protesting baby cries at the garage? Was it possible that she could have raised her umbrella and seen her own granddaughter being abducted by a lunatic? 'She must be mad!'

'Mum! No!' Florrie began to sob again. 'Dora wouldn't hurt her, I know that. She loves her.'

Alice caught the two policemen exchanging a look.

'This is all very distressing,' said Smith, 'but good news if it does turn out to be the same woman.'

'It has to be!' shouted Florrie.

Harry took a step forward into the group.

'Officer?' The policemen turned to him. 'I took the precaution of memorising the registration number of the vehicle.'

'Now, that *is* news.' Hendricks smiled, as one sensible man to another. 'As a matter of interest, why did you decide to do that?'

'Because she nearly ran over Madam here.'

'Probably just a bad driver,' said Alice weakly. 'She could have had no idea who I was.'

'No,' agreed DC Smith. 'But now we've got the registration, we'll easily trace her.'

Alice felt extremely tired as well as a bit more hopeful. The policemen made phone calls and took down as much detail as they could. Florrie hadn't seen her so-called cleaner that morning and didn't know what she had been wearing, but Baz volunteered that she favoured bright colours. This reminded Alice of the pink trousers. DC Smith allowed a cheerful tone into his voice and Harry took up his hat to leave.

Florrie, Baz and Alice sat on wet deck-chairs in the garden. They'd covered them with rugs but the damp still came through.

'She'll be back any minute,' said Alice. Baz said nothing and Florrie, following her protest that Dora wouldn't hurt Lily, was also silent but alert, as if waiting. At one point Baz had produced a joint, which he returned to his pocket. Alice saw that his hands were shaking and repeated, 'She'll be back any minute, I'm sure.'

After the storm the whole garden was soaking. Any breeze strong enough to rustle the leaves of the apple trees produced a waterfall of crystal drops. A song-thrush that Alice had known for years began to flute and whistle. Perhaps it was a good omen.

Tentatively, she tried closing her eyes. But almost at once the blackness was torn apart by a dizzying kaleidoscope of recent events: Brendan at their first meeting, his square face and bright eyes doused in tears; Jonathan's ridiculous declaration; Peter departing guiltily with his father's shirts; Guy and Brendan in the changing-hut before the tree crashed down and Blue – of course, Blue. All of this before Lily, darling, innocent Lily . . . Alice, who hadn't cried at all, stood up hastily and turned her back on Florrie and Baz.

To calm herself, she walked round her small garden. She saw how the rain and wind had tugged a wineberry bush off the wall and brought down a branch of a young apple tree. Six or seven small green apples clung to it still, like babies attached to their mother. She picked it up, planning to put it in water. Fingering the tear in the wood of the trunk, she pictured the great branch that had landed in the swimming-pool. Its strength and weight compared with the little tasselled wand she held made her feel tearful again.

Restless now, she decided to go inside and make another pot of tea. As she turned off the tap after filling the kettle, she heard a car in the lane. A few moments later Florrie was shouting from the garden, 'Ma! Come here now!'

Alice looked out of the window.

Florrie stood on the lawn with Lily clasped to her so tightly that their pink cheeks were pressed together.

'She's back, then,' Alice whispered to herself.

In the end Baz made the tea. He brought it to the living room where mother, grandmother and granddaughter sat in a tight row on the sofa.

'You see?' said Florrie, as Lily guzzled contentedly from a bottle. 'I was quite right. It was Dora who took her, just for an outing. And now she's brought her back.'

Alice was outraged. 'She kidnapped her! We called the police. Where is she now? Florrie, I know you're glad Lily's back – we all are – but the woman's dangerous. She might do it again. You should think of some other poor mother.'

'She knew you'd be upset. That's why she went so quickly.'

'Upset!'

'It was only a few hours, Mum. If you'd just listen, I could explain. She told me something really important . . . The thing is, Dora isn't exactly what she seemed—'

'She certainly isn't! A cleaner who turns into a kidnapper and wears diamond rings. So, who's going to ring the police?'

Florrie sighed. Alice, picking up the telephone, saw her exchange a glance with Baz. More unconsciously than consciously she clocked that there was something they knew that she didn't.

Alice spoke to DC Smith, who was extremely happy at the return of the baby but said they would, of course, check out the woman involved. 'You can't just take a baby at will without the parents' knowledge.' Parent's, in the singular, thought Alice to herself.

'I was planning to be in touch anyway.' The policeman explained in a rather embarrassed voice, that he had received a request to contact a Mrs Alice Lightfoot for questioning in regard to the disappearance of a Lionel Brian, sometimes known as Blue Carroway.

Alice's heart began to thud. 'I only met him once.'

'I quite understand. I'm sure it's just a formality.'

'Would tomorrow morning be all right? I haven't properly recovered from the disappearance of my granddaughter.'

'No problem.'

But it was a problem for her. She supposed she wanted to help but, by sleeping with Blue, she felt as if she had cut herself off from the honest approach. Alice put down the telephone and turned to face three curious faces. 'It's nothing,' she said. 'Just someone else who's disappeared, a man I interviewed on Thursday. I'll pop into the station on my way back to London tomorrow.'

How quickly they lost interest when it didn't concern them! 'I'm going back into the garden,' she said. 'The sun looks surprisingly warm again.'

Alice walked round and round the small garden, which was steaming with the combination of rain and sun. Why ever shouldn't she, a free, independent woman, sleep with whomever she liked? In a heat-wave. So, it had been an impulse, quite unlike her usual behaviour, but what was wrong with that? She'd been a celibate widow for quite long enough.

The police's questioning would force her to remember that evening in Blue's hotel bedroom. She imagined him as she'd seen him, in nothing but his scintillating shorts. Even the image made her feel flushed, and she moved on speedily to her attempt at an interview. What had he talked about? The police would certainly ask her. At least she could check her notebook. They had gone to eat Greek, her suggestion, and at his suggestion they had avoided the crowded garden and sat alone in the gloomy little room. But, of course, it hadn't seemed gloomy because both of them – well, she, certainly – were consumed by one thought: that later they would go to bed together.

Again, Alice felt a flush rising up her body. And that was exactly what had happened. And it had been wonderful, and she didn't want one person to know about it. Blue had been nothing but a pick-up, a one-night stand, a cheap stud.

Alice pulled out her mobile and rang Brendan.

'My dear. I was hoping you'd call me. Harry told me about your granddaughter. I trust she's returned by now.'

Alice was surprised by his voice. The northern inflection was quite strong and she picked up an artificiality in his concern. She had cast him as comforting teddy bear on the basis of one evening at his little paradise. Now she remembered his reputation as a bullying man of business.

'Yes, she's back and I want to thank you for Harry,' she said. 'Without him we'd never have traced the woman who took her.'

'Good. I'm sure there's no cause for further worry.'

'Thank you.' There was a pause. Alice took a breath. 'And now the police want to question me about this Blue Carroway's disappearance.'

'Oh, yes. That. Guy told me. Most unfortunate you have to be dragged into it. The man was a crook.'

'A crook!' Alice heard the shock in her voice.

'So I understand. Hiding money, that sort of thing. He had every reason to disappear.'

'But he's a friend of Guy's.'

'Sailing companion.'

'Guy wanted me to write a piece about him.'

'I'm sure Guy had no idea what was going on.'

'I didn't mean—'

'You've certainly got a good story now. Just say as little as you can to the police. Always the best way. Let me know how it goes.'

After he had hung up, Alice turned off her mobile. Blue a crook? Why was she upset to hear this? She hadn't admired him for his good moral sense. And yet it did shock her because, quite definitely, she didn't believe it. So why would Brendan say it?

'You know, there's absolutely nothing to eat in the house.' Florrie had come out silently. Lily, half asleep, lay in her arms.

'There's always spaghetti.' Alice held out her arms. 'Give me Lily to hold and put some water on.'

As Florrie handed over the baby, Alice became aware that an alien perfume rose from her hair and cardigan. It was sweet, strong, and somewhere, long ago, she'd smelt it before.

Chapter Ten

A Second Monday

Alice stood in the police station. The walls were painted lime green, the colour of grass hidden under a stone. Neither of the two policeman she had met was behind the desk, instead a woman talking on the telephone whose hair was drawn back into a tight band. To look at it made Alice's headache even worse: it had been pounding ever since she had woken early that morning. With Lily's safe return, she must strive to return life to normal. The Master had rung her mobile before eight to ask her how much material she had on Blue Carroway. Obviously he had been told about his disappearance by Guy because there'd been no mention of it in the media. She'd checked. She'd admitted she had only a few notes, certainly not enough for the sort of in-depth profile she usually wrote. 'I was thinking of a news piece. Keep me in touch with your plans.' By plans, she'd presumed he meant her substitute subject.

The trouble was, she had no plans and found herself curiously lacking in good ideas, also curiously unwilling to tap into her usual sources. Once again she recognised that she had let herself get out of the swing. She should race to London, put her finger back on the pulse. Yet here she was, trapped in a country police station, waiting to be interviewed about the mysterious Blue Carroway. She hadn't told the Master about that.

'Excuse me.' Alice took a step forward.

At that moment another female officer appeared from the green wall to her right and she found herself ushered warmly down corridors into a small grey room. This woman was to interview her, 'ask a few questions to help us with our inquiries about Mr Carroway', as she put it.

'Of course.' Alice nodded eagerly. A woman made all the

difference. She might tell things to a woman that she'd never tell to a man.

The officer was talking about Lily's return, how relieved everyone had been at the station. 'So, down to business. It won't take long. I understand you saw Blue Carroway on Thursday evening?'

Alice felt happy that Lionel Brian had left the scene. 'My newspaper thought he'd make a good subject for an interview.'

It had been Guy, not 'the newspaper', who had suggested meeting Blue. And Guy hadn't even been in touch since he had watched her driven off in Brendan's Bentley.

As the officer looked down at her pad, Alice decided to ask a question herself. 'Is there any suggestion that Blue . . .' she paused '. . . Mr Carroway could be more than missing?'

Detective Constable Susan Paradise – she had introduced herself by this extraordinary name as they sat down – frowned and tapped her pencil. Unlike the other female officer's, her blonde hair was free to swing in an unrestrained bob. 'This is a missing-person inquiry, Mrs Lightfoot. In fact, if I were to be formal, I'd have to say it isn't even that yet. He was last seen on Friday and today is only Monday. He has been reported missing by Mr Vernon but that doesn't mean he's missing.'

'Naturally I'm glad to help, although Thursday evening was the first time I met . . .' this Mr *Carroway* business was beginning to depress Alice '. . . I met Blue,' she finished.

'And did he seem agitated in any way?'

'I don't know him well enough to be able to answer that.'

'Quite. But he didn't seem obviously depressed?'

'No.' Alice looked at the policewoman's face with its well-applied makeup and felt uncooperative.

'He didn't disclose any worries that might have led him to disappear?'

'Commit suicide, you mean?'

'Not necessarily. At this stage we're open-minded.'

'He was worried about the possibility of a new UNESCO ruling that would make it illegal for individuals to salvage wrecks.' Well, she'd remembered that, at least. She watched Susan Paradise write this down laboriously.

'Did Mr Carroway say anything else that might be of interest?'

'He was hoping to set up a diving school for young offenders. That's why I interviewed him.'

'Quite.' Detective Constable Paradise scribbled assiduously. She looked over her notes. 'When did you part from Mr Carroway?'

The question Alice had dreaded, coming in so quickly and unobtrusively, threw her. 'We went to supper at a Greek restaurant I knew. Then we parted. Not very late.' Alice was horrified: she had told a direct lie – a lie, moreover, that could be easily discovered from the hotel staff or, indeed, any of the people who had found her not at home that night.

'What time was this? Ten? Eleven?'

'Between the two,' said Alice, amazed at her idiocy but unable to stop herself. 'Can I ask you a question?'

'Certainly.'

'When was he last seen?'

DC Paradise stared at her pad. 'He was *seen* on Friday afternoon, taking out Mr Vernon's boat, but it seems no one spoke with him. You have the honour, as it stands at present, of being the last person he talked to. That's why we're interested in your conversation.' She closed her pad. Apparently the interview was over. 'You've been very helpful. I don't expect we'll need to call on you again.'

This news made Alice feel both relieved and slightly ashamed. But, then, how would the knowledge that Blue and she had spent the night together help the inquiry? Alice realised she had just missed a remark made by the policewoman as she led her back to the reception area. 'I'm sorry?'

'I was just saying how much we all enjoyed your interview with Sir Brendan Costa.'

'You did?' Alice tried not to look as surprised as she felt.

'Well, of course – he's an important local benefactor. In fact, you might say there's hardly a project without his backing in it somewhere.'

'I see.' They had reached Reception and Alice had the curious sense that there was more to this information than was immediately apparent.

'Yes. Sir Brendan has quite a fan club in south Cornwall. That's why we were so pleased you brought out his human side. To think of losing both parents and three siblings in the way he did. Not many of us would go on to make such a success of our lives.'

'No,' agreed Alice, taking a step towards the door.

But the policewoman's loquaciousness on the subject of Sir Brendan seemed unstoppable. 'We believe that he was talking to Mr Carroway about backing his young divers' school.'

'Really?' Alice heard her voice too loud and too emotional.

It was after five when Alice arrived back at her flat. The sun was still high enough to blaze on the red bricks and remind Alice that, in the summer, the countryside was more desirable than town. She passed by the empty porter's desk, then turned when Joe spoke behind her. 'There's a woman up there for you.'

'A woman?'

'That tall Egyptian-looking one, with the son.'

Alice recognised this as a description of Mitzi and hurried up. She had thought she wanted to be alone but now she was pleased that she'd be able to unload some of her experiences on to her friend.

'Where have you been? I've been calling and calling. Finally I decided the best idea was to come over and squat. I've been here for hours!' Mitzi was in hyper-mode. Dressed in shorts and halter-neck top, she marched round the room.

'If only you knew.'

'You haven't even asked why I'm not at work.'

'Why—'

'I've been too upset.' Without drawing breath, Mitzi flopped beside Alice on her sofa and fixed her with large brown eyes. 'Yesterday afternoon *he* came over. To see Greg, he said. Well, Greg wasn't there. And then that huge storm came. Christ, it frightened me – booming and crashing, and lightning like the hand of Jupiter. Anyway, you know what Hughie's like, always the one for the main chance, so before I knew what was happening, we were in each other's arms, next step bed, well, the floor to be exact, and talk about a wild sexual experience. We were at it like—'

'Mitzi!' Alice was shocked. 'Are you telling me you slept—'

'We didn't do any sleeping.'

'– with your ex-husband who nearly ruined your life? Whom you loathe and despise? Mitzi, how could you?'

'I know. I know.' She tried to look shamefaced, but Alice knew her too well. The pleasure principle had always been one of her strongest weaknesses.

'I've listened to you for hours – actually, it would probably add up to weeks or even months – about your need for independence. And at the first temptation, just when things are going so well for you and for Greg – don't let's forget Greg—'

'Sssh. He's next door.'

'Greg's next door!' Alice was shaken. 'He might easily have overheard.'

'He's on the computer.' Mitzi was casual. 'I haven't even started on what I meant to say to you and here you are lecturing me out of existence. The trouble with you, Alice, is you're too controlling. You don't understand us more ordinary mortals.' Mitzi managed to sound reproachful, self-righteous and penitent at the same time. 'It just happened. I can't explain it. I was storm-tossed. What I wanted to ask you was what I should do next.'

Alice sighed. She reached out and stroked Mitzi's bare arm. It was perfectly clear that she would get no chance to talk about herself. 'So you're now thinking of resuming your life with this "male chauvinist, sexually deviant, financially amoral chancer", I quote. Who made you cry every night for a year. Am I right?'

'Only thinking,' replied Mitzi, unable to suppress a grin.

It was nearly eight before Mitzi and Greg gathered themselves to leave. It had been necessary to order takeaway pizzas and open some wine. Until Greg joined them, the two friends talked of nothing but Mitzi's situation. Sex, they agreed, was a force that broke the rules of good sense and good behaviour. Even then, Alice had not mentioned Blue: she removed him and the dazzlement she had felt to a dark and secret place. She was glad she had lied to Detective Constable Susan Paradise.

As mother and son went out through the door Greg, who had not spoken during the meal in order to concentrate on stuffing down the maximum amount of pizza, suddenly announced, with a kind of exultation, 'Wow! You should have seen that boat.'

'Come on, precious child. Can't you see our hostess has had enough of us?' Mitzi pushed him down the hallway.

'What were you watching?' asked Alice.

'Greg never knows what he gets on the Internet. Child porn—'

'I was watching the news!' interrupted Greg, indignantly. 'It was this ship, been washed up in Cornwall with the man who took it out gone missing. He's a famous diver called Blue ... ' As Greg reeled off the known facts, the boat presumably smashed by the storm, the man disappeared and now likely drowned, Alice had to suppress a longing to slam the door and run to the computer to check out the facts for herself. Eventually she was on her own.

As she hurried towards the study, the telephone rang.

'Guy!' She had been waiting for him to ring all day.

He spoke in a rather formal quiet voice: 'I wanted to warn you that Blue's made it on to the news – or, rather, my boat has.'

'I know. My friend's son picked it up on the Internet.'

'They don't know what it's about yet. It could be just storm damage. A boat without a crew can go very wild.'

'So, no Blue?'

'No. The Master wants you to write up a piece about him.'

'But I've got hardly anything!'

'You've got more than anyone else.' Guy was obviously surprised by her fierceness. 'It doesn't have to be long. Eight hundred words max.'

'I've been upset. Yesterday my granddaughter got kidnapped.'

'What? What do you mean?'

'She's back now. Actually, she was only away a few hours, but it was pretty upsetting.'

'Of course. Who took her? Kidnapped! My God.'

Alice regretted telling him. After all, if she was honest she'd have to admit she was using the incident to avoid confronting her lack of professionalism. She had always despised women who used their personal life to excuse failures at work. 'I suppose kidnapping is a bit strong. It was someone my daughter knows.'

'I see.'

But Alice could hear that he didn't see, and knew she was sending out mixed, not very honest messages. She tried to give things a lift with an ironic little laugh. 'I just don't seem very in control at the moment, what with one thing and another.'

'That doesn't sound like you.'

'Of course I'll do something about Blue,' she said.

'Fine. Email it to me. As late as you like. I'm stuck here for hours.'

'And then I'll get going on my interview. I'm sorry I was a bit feeble earlier.'

'I suppose you could always skip this week. I happen to know there's a two-page spread on bedsits coming back into fashion so you might easily get squeezed. Advertising's currently healthy too.'

'Bedsits coming back into fashion!' Alice was insulted at the idea of being supplanted by something so mundane.

Guy laughed. 'You make it sound as if I were describing a paedophile ring.'

After Guy had rung off, Alice stiffened her sinews and replayed on the Internet the short news item featuring the smashed sailing boat. It showed a fairly distant view of a vessel being towed to shore, and the accompanying story was so sparse that she was surprised anyone had thought it worth running. The item didn't even show a flattering photograph of Blue – he was in a tracksuit with a peaked cap hiding his face.

Alice put aside fantasy sexual encounters, read what little she had written about Blue in her notepad, and settled down to write eight hundred exceptionally dull words. For starters, UNESCO was a notorious turn-off. No one could possibly suspect that the author had spent an orgiastic night with her subject. Only when she'd emailed it to Guy did she allow herself to replay a few glorious moments.

There was a ping as an email popped on to her screen. 'Thanks.' Guy hadn't bothered to sign his name.

Chapter Eleven

A Second Tuesday

Alice stood on her balcony drinking her second cup of tea. She had already checked the health and welfare of all the members of her family and discovered them in reasonable shape. Even her father was calmer. Five minutes ago she had lined up a visiting American professor to interview: he believed that the Aids virus was linked to a new strain of flu that had been recently identified in China. She had run him past the Master, who had not used his veto, which was good news since he disapproved of downbeat stories unless they involved horrible injuries or the famous. Not for the first time Alice wondered if she was writing for the appropriate paper. She thought, with some satisfaction, that she had arranged it all without any advice from Guy. He was becoming too bossy. Or something. When the telephone rang, she went inside to answer it with a fairly light heart.

'This is Detective Constable Paradise.'

It was too fanciful a name for a policewoman. She had, Alice noted, quite a strong Cornish accent. 'I'm afraid I'm very busy.'

'I won't keep you a moment, but I felt it my duty to inform you that the case of Lionel Brian, otherwise known as Blue Carroway, may become a murder inquiry. Perhaps you saw the news last night. The boat was found. It contains evidence.'

Alice kept her voice calm. 'What kind of evidence?'

'I'm afraid I'm not at liberty to discuss any details. At this point, we are still very much in the dark. For example, we're not certain where he spent Thursday night.'

'Surely at the hotel?' said Alice, before she could stop herself.

'That seems most likely. But as his room was prepaid, perhaps he thought he'd no need to check out and no one has yet told us they saw him in the morning.'

It seemed odd to Alice that no one in the hotel should have noticed a man of Blue's striking appearance. Although it was true that they hadn't called room service for breakfast. Perhaps he had slipped away immediately after her departure. He'd hated the London heat, she remembered, and had been longing to leave. 'I'm so sorry,' she said, noticing a throb of pain in her voice. 'Is there no hope he'll turn up?'

'Until there's a body, there's always hope. I'll keep in touch.'

Such news could hardly fail to dent Alice's view of a benign world. She was sitting in the reception of the Hempel Hotel, all white marble and orchids, when the second blow fell.

'Alice Lightfoot?

'Yes.'

'I'm afraid Professor Stein will have to cancel his meeting.'

Alice looked uncomprehendingly at this pretty messenger of ill-omen. 'I only spoke to him this morning.'

'Unfortunately he's been taken to hospital.' The professor had suffered a heart-attack, not serious but bad enough to put him in hospital.

Alice walked home. It took half an hour and when she got there her feet, in high strappy sandals, were red and sore.

She lay on the sofa and rang the Master. He listened to her story impatiently, then even more impatiently to the list of unused pieces that could be slotted in. At her protestations that she hadn't given up hope of finding someone, although she'd deliver a little late, he broke in swiftly, 'No, no. The paper's very full this week. I've got a two-page spread I want to run. Save your energy and surprise me next week.'

So, she had been elbowed by the fashionable bed-sits after all. On the whole, she'd rather it had been a paedophile ring. And he hadn't even mentioned her piece on Blue. Well, that figured.

Barefooted, Alice walked on to the balcony. Abstractedly, she brushed her fingertips over the top of the bay trees. Her eyes focused abruptly as a large car pulled up under the block of flats. A man jumped out. Harry! What was he doing here? She stopped herself waving in an undignified manner. He and his boss had been kind to her at a difficult time – nothing more. At that moment Harry looked up, smiled and held up a letter.

'Coming down!' cried Alice.

The letter wasn't long. 'Due to overseas commitments, I have found it necessary to bring forward my weekend invitation . . .' Alice saw that the proposed new date was in three days' time. He must be very sure of his pulling power to expect that the high-profile guests he had reeled off to her would be able to change their schedules at such short notice.

Reluctantly, but with renewed energy, Alice put her phones on voicemail and pulled over the large pile of papers dating from Sunday. After she'd been through them, she'd start on the Internet and after that she'd ring round some of her friends. She could fail one week but, as the Master had somehow made clear without saying anything, she had some catching-up to do.

Five hours later, Alice returned to the living room and stretched out on the sofa. It was nearly nine. She should close the windows: a light breeze was blowing the curtains inward and a spattering of rain sounded against the glass. Instead she closed her eyes and drifted. The downstairs doorbell buzzed loudly. 'Yes?'

It was too odd. Guy and Jonathan were standing downstairs. She let them in wearily. This was not a dream.

'We were individually worried about you.' Indeed, Jonathan looked worried: his clever, concerned face was pale against his expensively cut pinstripe suit. Heavens, how tightly he knots his tie, thought Alice.

'When you didn't come to the office as usual,' Guy came close to Alice as if he was about to touch her, 'and all your phones were on answering-machine—'

'For hours,' interrupted Jonathan.

'We came here and met each other.'

'I'm sorry I worried you. I was only working.' How peculiar it was to see these two men from different parts of her life in the room together, Alice noted. 'I've had a disaster,' she said. 'My brilliant professor had a heart-attack so I'm getting ahead of the game for next week.'

'What professor?' asked Guy. He was still standing close to her with an expression on his face she'd never seen before. It struck her that he'd been drinking.

'Would you like a drink?'

'We certainly would.' Both men followed her to the old-fashioned cocktail cabinet, where Richard had always insisted bottles should be hidden. 'Go on. Take what you want.' She watched as they both poured themselves large measures of whisky. Neither looked for water to add to it.

They all sat down and, as nobody seemed inclined to speak, Alice found herself saying to Guy, 'Detective Constable Paradise rang me this morning to tell me the news about Blue. I'm so sorry.'

'Yes,' agreed Guy. 'That was partly why I came to see you, Alice. To apologise for involving you in all this. Your piece is fine, incidentally. With a bit added, it'll probably run tomorrow.'

'Blue? Isn't that the nickname of that diver who disappeared off Cornwall?'

Alice turned to Jonathan. 'I interviewed him at Guy's suggestion.'

'He's a man I sailed with occasionally.' Guy's voice remained flat. 'Unfortunately he took my boat when he disappeared.'

'Hard luck.' Jonathan was sympathetic. 'I saw the boat on the news. It took a bit of a pasting.'

'It was quite a storm.'

'Expensive things, boats.'

'Of course I was insured.'

'How long ago did you first meet Blue?' Somewhere there had to be another story. Why had Guy come uninvited to her flat? It wasn't enough that he'd been worried.

'In Cornwall. On the beach. Men like Blue congregate in places like that. He was different, of course. He had this plan to set up a diving course for young offenders. He wanted to be a philanthropist.' He was addressing Jonathan again.

'I'll heat some soup,' said Alice.

As Alice opened two cartons of 'home-made' soup, it occurred to her that Guy hadn't answered her question and that he had talked of Blue in the past tense. She heated the soup in the microwave, found a bottle of wine and called the men.

They sat on either side of her. Guy was already in his shirtsleeves, and Jonathan took off his jacket but left on his waistcoat, which made him look like a snooker player. They questioned each other about their working life. They wore relentless expressions and Alice wished they'd shut up.

'I had a case in Knightsbridge Crown Court recently when first a juror and then the accused vomited. Hangovers, that was all it was. Of course, it's not like that where I am this week. In the Privy Council. It's all heavy files and sober judgments.'

'What's the subject?'

'Mandatory execution in Belize.'

'It's extraordinary we still have jurisdiction over countries with capital punishment.' Guy's words were just a little slurred and he'd poured himself another glass of wine.

Alice looked from Guy to Jonathan. It appeared that they were talking to each other but she knew it was for her benefit. She predicted each would try to outstay the other. She had become the princess they wished to win, perhaps for no very good reason, and she couldn't believe Guy had come because he feared for her. It was more likely he wanted to talk about Blue. Perhaps she should chase him out first. And yet to be left with a besotted Jonathan – she had seen his eyes flash her way once or twice – was hardly a more desirable fate. Once they had stopped eating and talking – they were still on capital punishment – she would show them the door at the same time. There was safety in numbers.

Guy was once more addressing Jonathan, holding forth about the chain of command at the newspaper. 'It starts with the editor and ends with him. It's the same on any good paper, a strong man at the helm and success follows. Luckily I've always been close to our particular dictator and he trusts me, possibly more than anyone, but I'd still go crazy if I couldn't escape to the high seas now and again.' He was really quite manic, his skin flushed, his glasses sliding down his nose so that, now and again, his hazel eyes gleamed free of the frames. It was unlike him to talk about the Master like this in public. Or had she misjudged his nature, noticing only what she wanted, the supportive editor in the office with whom she lunched once a week?

At last they were standing, almost hanging on to each other, although it was only Guy who had drunk too much. Jonathan was as sober as ever.

'So you'll both drop into the Privy Council tomorrow?' He stopped her at the door, barring out Guy, who had seemed about to kiss her cheek. They sorted this one out, and made off together down the corridor, Jonathan waving a hand behind him. Had she really promised him the treat of her presence in some dreary legal battle?

'I'll try.' Alice watched their receding backs. What an unlikely interlude it had been.

Chapter Twelve

A Second Wednesday

Once again dressed up in strappy sandals, feet already hurting, Alice made her way through the glassy over-populated regions of her newspaper. She so seldom visited her desk that when she saw it was occupied she assumed she had mistaken the floor or the direction. Even her neighbours were hardly known beyond their byline and a word of congratulation – 'I liked your piece on Victoria Wood's passion for badgers.' But they were her neighbours. Moreover, beyond them, there were the even glassier regions where senior editors sat behind unsolid walls. She thought she recognised Guy's back.

Alice hesitated. A young woman sat at her desk, studying her computer – no, typing on it. Alice could see her bare, sunburnt arms as smooth as conkers, although not quite so dark. She must wax them. 'Excuse me.'

'Oh, hi.' The girl turned. She was very pretty and barely out of her twenties. 'You're Alice Lightfoot.' She smiled winningly, but without getting to her feet. 'I was put at your desk. I'm sorry. They said you never come in.'

Alice saw her letters had been pushed into an untidy pile behind the computer. She bent over to collect them and, in the process, was able to read a few of the lines on screen: 'Helga Smith was a refugee to England at the age of three. At the age of six she went completely blind.' Nearly up the Master's street, thought Alice, although, if she wanted to be kind, she could warn the girl that refugees were never his thing. 'I'm not staying,' she said. She needn't be cross but she needn't be helpful either. 'Be my guest. What are you writing about?'

The girl looked secretive. 'Nothing much. I won a prize. That's why I'm here.'

'I see.' Alice had never won a prize. 'Don't let me interrupt you. Good luck anyway.'

'Thank you. My name's Polly Omar, incidentally.'

Alice walked on between desks, exchanging the odd word. One or two people complimented her on her piece about Brendan. It seemed so long ago now. Someone said, 'So who's this diver?' But she didn't stay to answer that one. She was heading for Guy, still hunched over his computer while also, she saw as she got closer, on his phone.

'Hi.' Why had she said 'Hi'? She never said 'Hi'. Trying to imitate the youthful Polly Omar, was she?

'Alice.' He turned quickly but he was still on the phone. She found a chair and sat down. He, too, had words on his screen but she was too far away to read them. She looked down at the pile of mail on her lap, mostly invitations, flyers and a few fan letters, maybe, but she felt reluctant to open them. She stood up again restlessly. Guy hardly said a word apart from 'yes' and 'no'. Clearly he was busy and didn't have time to see her. She caught his attention and pointed to the door. He held up two fingers. Alice sat down again. As she would have expected, his office was orderly, although there were stacks of newspapers and books on the floor. A huge coloured photograph of a sailing boat was pinned on his noticeboard. Alice had been in this office often enough but never before noticed the boat.

'I'm sorry. It's a bit hectic.' He stood up, brushing his hair back from his face. 'I wasn't expecting you.'

'Clearly not.' He must have forgotten the plan to visit Jonathan. He had never made her feel unwanted before. She tried to laugh. 'One of the three bears is sitting in my chair.'

'Oh, yes. Polly, is it? Bags of talent.' He seemed distracted. 'I'd like to take you to lunch but sadly I've got a date.' He looked at his watch. 'In fact, I should be going any minute. I've got my car. Can I give you a lift?'

Alice wished she had a rival date herself. 'That would be great.'

The car, parked at the bottom of the glass building, was not turquoise and battered, the one he'd driven in Cornwall, but black and sleek. Alice sat beside Guy, who was still distinctly untalkative, and noted that it was the first time she'd been driven by him. He drove faster than she would have expected and with boyish concentration.

'So, what went on between you and Blue?'

Alice looked away. Was that a question asked with knowledge? If so, it meant he had seen Blue after she had, because only Blue could have told him what happened that night. He'd put the question as if it was an accusation, although that might have been her guilty conscience. She blinked against the sunlight, hard and sharp through the windscreen and repudiated the word *guilty*.

'What do you mean?'

Guy had taken off his coat and tie when he got into the car and was in his shirtsleeves with an open neck where she could see sun-reddened skin. His glasses were the sort that turned darker in the light so she couldn't see his eyes. 'I mean, did you get on? What did you think of him?'

Alice remembered that she had reported back to Guy after her meeting with Blue. She had explained he wasn't a suitable subject for an interview. That might have suggested she hadn't found him interesting. 'To be honest, Guy, diving isn't my thing. I would have thought my piece made that clear.'

'You didn't find him charming?'

She hadn't found him charming: she'd found him bedazzling, overwhelming, glorious. She had reacted to him like a schoolgirl. 'It seems wrong to discuss him like this when he's disappeared. Possibly worse than disappeared.'

'What are you saying?'

How could he ask? 'You know much more than me. DC Paradise said the case might be changed from a missing-person to a murder inquiry.'

'It's not certain. Not at all certain.' Now he was speaking unusually loudly. Alice opened her bag and took out dark glasses. 'Where are you going to lunch?'

'A prize-giving at the Grosvenor House.' He glanced at her. 'I won't talk about Blue any more, then.'

Alice decided to ignore this but she guessed that the evening before she had been right: he had come round to talk about Blue. Thank God for Jonathan's presence. 'You forgot about Jonathan's plan for us, then?'

'Last night . . . I had forgotten. I'm sorry I barged in like that. I'd had a glass too many.'

'That's OK.' Somehow the atmosphere had become lighter.

'I'm interested in your friend.' So Blue really had gone off the agenda. 'Lawyers are supposed to be the most hated professionals but I admire their brains. As far as I'm concerned, they deserve whatever they're paid.'

'But what about principles?' This was an old argument into which she could put little energy. Throughout her marriage she had conducted it, usually silently, because Richard took any discussion of the subject as a personal affront.

'Jonathan is trying to abolish executions in Belize.' Guy's tone implied he already knew Jonathan better than Alice did.

'It does sound a good cause,' agreed Alice, dutifully.

'Have you known him long?'

'He was my husband's oldest friend. They were at school together.'

'I see.'

'He's decided he's crazy about me now.' Alice laughed.

'A joke?'

'Are you going anywhere near Whitehall – or the Houses of Parliament, even?'

Guy caught her looking at her watch. 'Do you think we'd get into the court before they break for lunch?'

'We?'

'I can't bear those prize-giving lunches. They go on for far too long and everyone eats and drinks a ludicrous amount.'

Alice had never been through the gates of Downing Street. They were large, black, well guarded by police, and under the serious scrutiny of scattered groups of tourists. 'We can't just go in, can we?'

'We're going to the Privy Council.' Guy spoke through the bars to a policeman, who waved them on without asking for identification. 'Now, is that democracy or the law?'

Alice thought about this as they passed through a security check in the road and crossed to enter the Privy Council building. Outside Ten Downing Street an interview was taking place with all the paraphernalia of cameras and microphones. Inside the building it was quiet, although not grand, until they climbed some stairs and entered what looked a boardroom with an immense shiny table, panelled walls and a coat-stand. The court, they guessed, lay beyond it. As they went in, a woman and a man, both in lawyers' gowns and wigs, came out and began an intense, whispered conversation.

They found themselves in a large room with a domed ceiling, filled with people, benches, desks, files, books and boxes of papers. They sat on what seemed to be a public bench and tried to understand the proceedings or, at least, to pick out Jonathan. Despite the number of people present, the room was remarkably quiet, the only sound the monotonous voice of a man with his back to them. It was only when he stopped talking and turned profile that Alice recognised Jonathan.

She nudged Guy, who gave her a thumbs-up.

Alice watched the scene in front of her but the microphones were bad and the subject remained, to her, incomprehensible. She did grasp that the row of men sitting opposite Jonathan, although unwigged, were the superior legal figures, probably judges. A question from them would send backbench figures scurrying to look up some necessary legal procedure in a huge, uncontrollable book of loose pages. Jonathan, meanwhile, continued to present his case.

Suddenly the pattern shifted and the thirty or so people in front of them were no longer on benches or behind desks but standing in preparation for departure. At this moment, Jonathan turned and saw them. Alice stared: with his wig covering his thinning hair, the black gown showing off his height and broad shoulders, and his clever face alight with the battle to put across his case, he was an impressive sight. A man to be admired. Now he waved, mouthed, 'See you outside,' and turned back to talk to a younger man.

Guy took Alice's arm to lead her out, as if she might not have understood Jonathan's directions. She felt his fingers, broad and strong. She pictured them on the rudder of a yacht, then found herself substituting Blue's fingers. She shivered suddenly, and Guy looked at her questioningly. 'A ghost.' Alice pulled away from his hand. By now they were in the outer room. 'Richard always said Jonathan was a tiger in court.' She had forgotten this until now. It struck her, with ridiculous good sense, that Jonathan was worth a hundred of a diving stud called Blue. The absurdity of comparing them made her smile and restored her equilibrium. This Jonathan was not the same desperate suitor who had poured out his love to her. Successful men should always make sure they are seen in their workplace, she thought. But that introduced an absurd image of Blue diving into azure water.

'Why are you smiling?' asked Jonathan. He had appeared suddenly, gown flapping. He still wore his wig and was still touched with intellectual glory, and knew it. 'Could you pick up what was going on?'

Guy responded immediately: 'It seemed to me things are going your way. How many more days?'

'Three.'

'They still have the death sentence in America,' Alice pointed out. She noticed Jonathan was taking little aborted strides to right and left as if he was too wound up to remain still.

'A solicitor friend of mine specialises in Death Row cases.' He fixed them both with his sharp brown eyes. 'A remarkable man. He goes over to the US at his own expense and gives counsel for free.'

Guy took a step back. 'So you believe no one deserves to die?'

'What do you think?' exclaimed the new, intense Jonathan. 'How about continuing the discussion over lunch? There's a little Italian café up towards Trafalgar Square where we can get a simple—'

'No. No, I don't think so. Thanks.' To Alice's surprise, Guy had made a precipitous lunge towards the stairs. She followed him with Jonathan and they watched him stride determinedly along Downing Street, past the police and out of the gates.

'Did I say something?'

'He had a lunch date but I thought he'd jettisoned it.' She had no idea why Guy should run away.

'Let's eat anyway. Hang on while I get rid of the fancy dress.'

Alice and Jonathan walked up Whitehall. With the removal of his wig Jonathan looked less charismatic but more approachable.

'We'll go in here.' Jonathan guided her into a well-lit modern café with gleaming steel tables. 'I usually have the chicken salad. Would that suit?' He ordered, including two glasses of red wine, as they went through.

Alice looked at her anxious face reflected in a mirror on the wall. She needed an explanation for Guy's strange behaviour. It had struck some wriggling snake of uncertainty in her mind that she was unable to identify. 'Guy's usually so calm.'

'He's jumpy all right. But, then, I would be in his position, boyfriend down the tubes, in line for arrest quite possibly.'

Alice watched her mirrored face try to take in what she was hearing. 'I don't . . .' She cleared her throat and began again: 'I don't understand.'

'Guy's gay, isn't he? And this fellow who's disappeared is his boyfriend. I just assumed . . .' He tailed off, then began again. 'He *is* gay, isn't he?'

Alice saw the mirror turn a rosy hue. 'I don't know anything about Guy's personal life.'

'But haven't you known him for years?'

'He did kiss me once,' said Alice.

'What? When?' Jonathan's relaxed attitude changed so suddenly that Alice half smiled.

'Last week, actually, on Tuesday.' She paused. 'But, then, last week was strange.' She looked at him meaningfully. He said nothing. 'Of course, it was very hot. Heat lasting for so long in England is unusual and unnerving. People behave out of character.'

'I wasn't behaving out of character when I tried to kiss you. I love you, Alice. I always will.'

Why had she led him into this? Did this noble barrister, whom she had just admired weaving knots round five law lords, believe she was fishing for a renewed declaration? She wouldn't admit to herself that the turn of the conversation had arisen only because she dared not confront his remark about Guy and Blue. She pushed it even further to the back of her mind and replied seriously, 'I like you as a friend, Jonathan. Please don't spoil things. I admire you.' This was true, as of two hours ago.

'Thank you.' He seemed satisfied with this declaration and reassumed his conquering-hero glow. 'We'll leave it at that for the moment.' He smiled, and Alice tried not to think that his long, not very white teeth were wolfish. 'I've tickets for the Wigmore Hall next Wednesday . . .'

The moment Alice arrived back in her flat, she picked up the telephone: 'Mitzi. I've got two good parties tonight, one including a short talk on "The Writer as Hypnotist". Do you want to come?'

The truth was, she wanted to talk to Mitzi. Strange things were piling up inside her head.

'I can't, darling. No way. I've a meeting starting at six that will take me through dinner.'

Alice was just about to hang up when she heard Mitzi's voice again: 'Alice? Are you going to Brighton tomorrow?'

'I always go to Brighton on Thursdays.' Just how dull an answer is that? she thought. 'Why? Do you want to come?'

'You might just be lucky. The truth is, if I don't get a day out of the office soon I'll go crazy, and then what use will I be?'

'None. Bring your swimming-gear.'

That evening as Alice was going to bed Florrie rang.

'Your mobile's on constant message service, Ma. After what happened to Lily, I thought you'd be keen to know we're all right.'

Alice listened guiltily to her daughter's reproaches. She was right: her lack of concern was unnatural. She thought almost nostalgically of her granddaughter's delicious skin and cheerful chuckles. 'Oh, darling, I'm so very sorry. I just had to get back in the swing of things. I won't have an interview in this week.' Hiding behind her work was pretty low but better than hinting at the exploding feeling of her life at the moment.

Florrie's tone changed from accusatory to dignified: 'Perhaps you're not interested in developments?'

So ungrandmotherly were Alice's present concerns that her mind whirled meaninglessly for a second or two, then came up with the right response: 'Don't tell me! Have they caught the kidnapper? What's the news?'

'The police are still trying to catch her, which is a waste of time as she brought Lily back. They haven't found her, but they have got the car. It was hired on Saturday and delivered back yesterday.'

'And her name?'

'Mrs Dora Hurtado. I told you already, Mum. You know that.'

Alice was now properly involved. 'Spanish? Is she Spanish, then? You never told me her surname. You never said she had an accent.'

'She didn't. Well, I don't think she did.'

Having remembered that Florrie had always been too self-centred to notice minor details about someone else, Alice remarked, 'Well, I suppose she could be South American or Mexican. But they don't know where she is now? Poor Florrie.' Maternal solicitude raised itself a notch. 'You must be worried. It's so inexplicable.'

'I'm not worried at all. I liked her. Actually, I miss her. She was so lovely with Lily.'

'But she *kidnapped* Lily!' Alice heard her voice become shrill and tried to calm herself with the thought that this mode – Florrie relaxed and herself anxious – was a reassuring return to the north.

'Mum, I thought we were moving on from this kidnapping obsession you've got. Sometimes I wonder whether you couldn't use the space of meditation.'

'Meditation?' queried Alice. 'And I hate the way you call her Dora,' she added, with more spirit, 'as if she were a friend.'

'It is her name.'

'Maybe.' There was a pause, during which Alice had a strong sense that her daughter had put herself on this Dora Hurtado's side and she, Alice, on the other. 'Dora sounds a most unlikely name to me,' she said, and felt a little shift in the atmosphere as if her words meant something more.

'Do you want to hear what I have to tell you? What Dora told me when she brought Lily back?'

'Certainly not. I've got enough to worry about already without your absurd imaginings.'

'Oh, Ma.' Florrie laughed. 'You'd really fall for her, I promise you.'

'How's the mushroom-picking?'

Chapter Thirteen

A Second Thursday

There was a pleasure in routine, however uninspiring the project in hand. Alice sat on the same train she always caught for visits to her father and felt reassured enough to consider the question of Guy and Blue, Blue and Guy. Were they really a pair? Had she completely misunderstood her night with Blue? Had she used him, unwilling victim, in a rapacious, sex-starved way? Alice allowed herself to think again of riding Blue in the dark room and the images of light and water that streamed over them.

'Found you!'

She looked up to see Mitzi standing over her, holding a carton of coffee in either hand.

'Good morning!' How happy she was to see this dear and self-centred friend, with her snaky-thin legs in extra-tight jeans and her favourite red hoop earrings. 'You look great, Mitzi.'

'Thanks. I feel as if I've done a full day's work just by catching this train.' She sat opposite her. 'So, do you have lunch with your father?'

'He has lunch. I watch. Then he sleeps and I entertain myself till four when he wakes.'

'I've been recommended an excellent pub called the Mermaid's Hiccup. It serves Guinness and jellied eels, oysters and mussels. The thought of which makes me sick.'

Alice laughed, and then found she wanted quite badly to cry. She turned her head to the window, where the backs of office buildings, the backs of streets and churches and terraces of houses were soothing.

'Why are you looking like that?' asked Mitzi, over her carton of coffee.

'I'll tell you in the Maiden's Hiccup.'

'Mermaid's, if you don't mind.'

When they arrived at the station, Mitzi announced she was going walkabout and disappeared down an alleyway under a tunnel. Alice, who usually walked the mile or so to her father's nursing home, decided to take a bus. But the long straight road to the front was so congested with traffic that she got off and walked after all.

The sea was pearl grey under a colourless sky. The tide was so far out that she could hardly hear the swish of water over pebble and sand. On an impulse she climbed down and continued her walk along the beach. The sea smelt stronger than usual, as if the heat of the week before had brought out the fishy saltiness of it, the sweet undertone of sewer. Above her head a shrieking bunch of seagulls whirled about restlessly. As always, she marvelled at the wildness of the scene, in such contrast to the ordinary city life proceeding only a few yards away.

She noticed that the seagulls' gyrations, their sudden descents and abrupt reascendings were centring on a spot ahead of her, nearer the line of the sea. They were feasting, certainly, on something dead, a large fish judging by the number of eager marauders. As her rational mind produced this explanation, Alice's ill-disciplined inner eye produced an image of such disgusting vividness that she let out a cry, lost at once in the noise of the gulls.

She turned immediately towards the road, but not before her stomach had churned too far and she found herself bent double, vomiting her coffee and breakfast. She grappled in her bag for a tissue, then wiped her mouth and eyes. She must sit down and compose herself, not allow herself to be scared by her own ridiculous imagination. On the other hand, she must get away from those seagulls. She crossed the road and turned inland.

Now the traffic was welcome and the elegant symmetrical architecture of Regency Brighton soothed her. After five minutes' walking, she could tell herself, If Blue did drown, there's no way his body would end up on a beach in Brighton. He set out from south-west Cornwall. There are thousands of coves and bays and jagged gullies along the coastline between there and Brighton. I must pull myself together before Sister Mary Rose wonders what's happened to me. Rather bitterly, she thought her father would hardly know or care if she came or not.

The nursing-home door was closed, which, in the warm weather, was unusual. Alice pressed in the code and went into the hallway. She had just reached the bottom of the stairs when Mary Rose, who seemed to have been lying in wait, shot out of her office. 'Oh, Alice, dear, may I have a word?' This was not unusual but her flustered look contradicted the omnipotent competence that Alice had grown to rely on.

'Of course. I'm afraid I'm a little later than usual.'

Inside her office, Mary Rose shut the door – another first. 'There's no cause for concern,' she said, an opening that filled Alice with dire foreboding. 'Your father is safe and sound. But there has been an incident. In brief, he disappeared.'

'He disappeared again!' exclaimed Alice.

'I'm afraid this was more serious. An outside agent was involved.'

'But you didn't contact me!'

'Perhaps I was wrong. So much happened and then we had him safely back. And I knew you would be here today . . .' Her voice appealed for understanding. There might even have been a hint of a tear behind her large spectacles. Her pretty, plump, woman's complexion had coagulated into pink splotches.

Alice hardened her heart. Sister Mary Rose was in charge of a nursing home that was paid five hundred pounds a week for total care of her fairly demented father. They could lose him once, but not twice. 'So, what happened?'

'It was Wednesday and I had the morning off – so the first part is hearsay. At eleven o'clock, or thereabouts, a woman came to visit your father, a perfectly respectable woman, it seemed. Unfortunately, Sister Obu is new here and when this woman announced she was taking her father for a walk—'

'*Her* father for a walk?' interrupted Alice.

'I know. I know. Sister Obu has only been in this country for two months, although very experienced in her home country and a most loving soul. She assumed she was hearing the truth—'

'But for a walk!'

'In the wheelchair, of course. It was all done most correctly. The only trouble was that when I came on at two o'clock they still hadn't returned.'

'My father *hates* going out! He hasn't let me take him out for ages.'

'As you say. But I'm told he went quite calmly with his visitor. Of course, I was very concerned. We searched the home and the garden and the immediate neighbourhood, and then I felt it my duty to contact the police.'

'The police!'

'I would bring Obu to talk to you but the whole experience unnerved her, poor dear. The police were not very kind, with English not being her first language, and she hasn't been in today.'

'So what happened?'

'The woman, who was much older than you wheeled him to the front, up the ramp that leads to the West Pier, all broken and derelict as it is, and left him there.' Mary Rose sat back and joined her hands across her comfortable stomach.

'Abandoned him, you mean? An incapable old man in a wheel-chair?'

'Abandoned him.' Mary Rose nodded, pleased Alice had got the point. As the story unfolded, her air of guilt had dissipated, as if Alice's knowledge gave her dispensation.

'But what if he'd tried to get out?' Alice imagined the situation with horrible clarity. As a child, she'd loved that second pier, now so rusted, black and threatening.

'Luckily he fell asleep, and a concerned passer-by phoned the police from her mobile.'

Alice took a deep breath. 'And how was he? How *is* he?'

Mary Rose allowed herself a small smile. 'Proud is the best description of his state of mind.'

'Proud?'

'For getting rid of the woman. He didn't see himself as abandoned. He believes he drove away his kidnapper.'

'Kidnapper?'

Now Mary Rose looked embarrassed. 'Over-enthusiastic visitor, as we told the police. Perhaps someone from your dear father's past who wanted to do good but lost her nerve. Your father's reputation still lives in this town, you know.'

'He was an excellent doctor.' This was an understatement. During Alice's childhood, Dr Bingo Featherstone's surgery, which was held in their house, spread through all hours of the day and night. By the time she was seven or eight she could cook supper for herself and her father, then, more often than not, ate it on her own.

'And of course he never remarried after your mother's death.'

'He was married to his patients.'

'A saintly man, perhaps.' Alice was about to contradict this estimate of her father's irritable, impatient character but she saw that Sister Mary Rose had now assumed a bustling, busy look. Clearly the interview was over, information shared. They both stood but Mary Rose had one more thing to say. She placed her hand on Alice's arm. 'If the police should contact you, I'd be grateful if you played down the affair ... The reputation of the home is at stake. And your father is not an easy patient, if you see what I mean.'

Alice did see. Good Sister Mary Rose need not fear any complaints from her. In any case, by putting her father in the home, she had relinquished such rights. She left the office, commending Mary Rose for her care and attention.

Dr Featherstone was asleep. As Alice appeared a nurse removed his untouched lunch. He lay on his back, mouth open, fine nose pointing, prow-like, to the ceiling. How contained he seemed. So much life locked into that bony skull, a life he'd never shared with her. Apart from his skill and attention to his patients, which were obvious to everyone, she knew nothing about him. Had he mourned her mother deeply? She assumed so because he'd never married again, but he'd never spoken of his feelings, not even when she herself had been widowed – although, of course, by then he was already losing control of his mind.

With a start, Alice realised that her father's eyes were open and he was staring at her with a gleaming, sly look. To quell her nervousness, she went to him and gave him a hug, then a kiss on either cheek. He pulled himself up with surprising strength, knocking her aside.

'Well, she came back. But I wasn't going to run this time. I told her, "You do what you like with me. At least it'll make a change from sitting in this bed all day." So we got past Cerberus, a gentle, dark-skinned Cerberus, and we were out, below the sky, next thing the sea. We argued all the way, of course. She's always been a liar and a cheat and I got her to admit it.' Here Dr Featherstone lifted his arms above his head in a triumphant gesture.

Alice was amazed at his energy. It seemed that his strange trip to the sea had galvanised him into new life. 'So, will this woman come back a third time, do you think?' She had sat down to ask what seemed to her an important question, but her father closed his eyes.

'She cannot be predicted,' he muttered eventually, adding further words Alice could hardly understand except 'charm'.

'You knew her before, then? She was a patient?'

'Hah!' His eyes were open again as he gave a hearty snort. 'Patient. Patient. She was the least patient person I've ever met. She was impatience on a monument.' He seemed pleased with this allusion and gave a self-congratulatory smile, which amazed Alice because he hadn't smiled for at least two years. The sight made her feel as if he'd taken several steps nearer humanity.

'Oh, Daddy!' She clasped his hand.

'Yes. Yes. But now I must rest.' She understood from his expression that he needed to gain strength in case his mysterious visitor should return. It was not a descent into the meaningless abyss of exhausted old age, but a rest with a purpose, a preparation for the future. Alice mocked herself for thinking all this but thought it all the same, and left her father with a lighter heart than she had for years.

'I'm meeting a friend!' she cried gaily, although her father gave no sign of hearing. 'I'll be back at four.'

Alice skidded along to the Mermaid's Hiccup, but after a while her pace slowed. The sun was out again, hardening the edges of the white-painted buildings. In her day, Brighton had been shabby, no new paint or well-restored colonnades. Their house in Palmeira Avenue, red-brick and gloomy, had been over the invisible line into Hove but her school was in Brighton, a private school filled with the professional classes and aspiring others. For one terrible term she'd been sent to Roedean, a forbidding prison set on a windy cliff above the sea where large girls with purple thighs whacked small balls into the sky. She couldn't remember how she'd expressed her misery to her father and suspected that he'd removed her for reasons of his own. Perhaps the fees had been too high, or he'd missed having her around the house to cook the supper.

Alice found she was standing outside a shop with a long window filled with strange objects and unusual points of information. She saw bags of crystals, dangling crystal balls, packets of incense, piles of beads, painted dolls and a card announcing that within she would find a Tarot Reader, Iridology, Channelling, Palmistry, Clairvoyance, Hypnotherapy, Hopi Candles, NLP, Bonne Technique, Kinesiology and Naturopathy. Perhaps she'd find a present to put her back in Florrie's good books.

The shop was quite large, but so divided by bookcases, display cabinets and circular stands that, like a maze, there was no direct route to the counter or anywhere else. Indeed, the counter was not directly visible, and although Alice could see no one else in the shop, she could hear the low murmur of voices and feel the presence of others – palmists, clairvoyants or tarot readers.

She started down a row of shelves mainly devoted to erudite tombs of the magic arts, attracted by a vase of feathers hung about with silver and turquoise jewellery – probably American Indian, she thought. She was putting out her hand to touch a pair of pendant earrings in plaited silver when a voice came from her right. 'I thought we were meeting in the Mermaid's Hiccup?'

Alice smiled at Mitzi. 'I'm on my way. You look as if you've had a good morning.'

'Now you're *here*, let me introduce you to my new friend, the clairvoyant.'

Behind Mitzi appeared a Viking of a man with a blond beard and thick wavy hair to his shoulders. His eyes were piercingly blue. 'I'm Luke Nestor.' His voice was deep.

'Are you busy?' asked Alice, feeling foolish.

'I'm only in Brighton once a week.'

Alice wanted to disclaim the need for his services, but found it unnecessary as they were heading for the pavement. She rummaged in her handbag for her dark glasses and when she looked up saw Luke Nestor was staring at her.

'See anything interesting?' She tried to sound light-hearted rather than suspicious.

'No. No. I'm glad to have met you.' He turned abruptly and walked away in the direction of the sea-front.

Mitzi put her arm confidingly in Alice's. 'Now there's just us and we can talk.' At last Alice had located her dark glasses and felt more protected. She kept them on even as they sat in the Mermaid's Hiccup. It was an old building that must have been renamed since her childhood or she would have certainly noticed it before. The clientele were all foreign tourists, drinking dark beer with a look of resigned distaste on their faces. She and Mitzi decided on a glass of sauvignon to accompany their fish hors d'oeuvres.

'It's someone I interviewed,' began Alice tentatively. She got no further for Luke Nestor burst back upon the scene, backlit with rays of afternoon sunshine from the open door. Before he spoke Alice had time to think that he looked like an Old Testament prophet.

'I think it right to share with you what I saw on the street and now see with you here. A woman is both close and far away. In some sense she's inseparable and it's best for you that you make your terms with her. She's not exactly threatening but she is, and will continue to be, unless you act, a disturbance to you and your family.' He seemed to bow, or maybe he was merely ducking since the dark beams were low and he was exceptionally tall. Alice stifled a wild desire to laugh and stretched out her hand. 'Thank you, Luke,' she said solemnly. 'I shall take note.'

He bowed or ducked again. 'I'm at your service.'

She saw that he was holding out a flyer. 'Thank you so much.' Did he mean that the same woman who had kidnapped Lily had taken her father to the sea? And she, Alice, was the link. Was that what he was telling her? 'Wait!' she called, but Luke had already removed his bulk and closed the door on the sunshine.

'"From ghoulies and ghosties and long-legged beasties and things that go bump in the night, Good Lord, deliver us."' Mitzi recited. 'What was all that about?'

'A woman.' Alice felt helpless to explain. 'I should go back to my father in a minute.'

'I'll come with you and we can carry on the conversation we'd only just begun . . .'

They walked by the sea-front, passing the grisly black skeleton of the West Pier, which rose out of the glittering sea in its chains of black barbed wire and rusting, partly burnt-out ironwork.

'Yesterday, some madwoman brought my father here,' Alice said, pointing to the ramp that led up to the padlocked gates. 'The police had to rescue him.'

'There's a story!' Mitzi put one hand on Alice's arm. In the other she swung her bikini, as if she was about to jump into the sea. 'But it's not your story. Who is this man you interviewed?'

Alice took a long breath. 'I met Blue last Thursday, exactly a week ago. I'd been swimming. It was a really hot evening and I was all sticky from the salty water. We met in his hotel room and drank champagne and he let me have a shower. Then we went out to supper.'

'Phew,' said Mitzi. 'I thought we were heading somewhere else. Did anyone ever suggest you took up writing porn movies?'

Alice tried to smile but couldn't. They were still walking, which made it easier to talk. 'After supper in a Greek restaurant we went back to his room and I spent the night with him.' She paused or stopped – she didn't know which.

'Is that all?' Mitzi's face was expectant.

'He's disappeared.'

'Who is this Blue? He's not that deep-sea diver?'

'I don't understand what I felt for him, Mitzi,' Alice continued. 'I felt exhilarated, proud, powerful—'

'He's not married, is he?'

'And now I feel humiliated, pathetic, ashamed.' But that wasn't what she felt at all. She just felt muddled, out of control. 'And this weekend I'm going to stay with Sir Brendan Costa—'

'Well, I knew *he* attracted you.'

Alice hadn't been listening to Mitzi's comments. She stopped to face her. 'And then there's the question of this woman. She's called Dora and she kidnapped first Lily and then my father.'

Mitzi laughed. Above her head a few seagulls cackled sympathetically. 'You certainly go from one end of the spectrum to the other.'

'And then there's Guy. Jonathan says he's gay and was having an affair with Blue. But that simply can't be true. Or if it is the world is an even odder place than I thought it was.'

'Can we sit down, please?' Mitzi dragged on Alice's arm, which made her realise she had been walking very fast. They had crossed the border into Hove and any minute would turn inland towards the nursing home. 'Who is Guy, for heaven's sake?'

'Surely you know Guy. I've worked with him for years. Guy's a friend.' For the second time that day she felt like crying, she who never cried.

'And you say that your disappeared lover of one night was having an affair with him?'

'That's what Jonathan says – he, incidentally, now attempts to jump on me every time I meet him.' Alice turned appealingly to Mitzi, then took a long look at the sea. 'I don't know what's happening to me, Mitzi. I haven't even been able to write an interview this week.'

'Now, that *is* serious – but as for the rest of it, I wouldn't worry too much. It's just life, really, a bit heightened, perhaps, as if you're making up for lost time, but nothing that won't work out one way or the other.'

The act of speaking had made Alice feel better and an echo of Mitzi's words remained with her: 'making up for lost time'. It was true that time had never seemed to be on her side, not even when she was a small girl. Sometimes whole days would pass without anything worth remembering.

'We'll be at the nursing home in two seconds. Come up and meet my father, if you can face it.'

Mitzi shuddered. 'No, thanks. I can't bear old men. I'll wait outside in the sun.'

Dr Featherstone was sitting up in bed with the *Daily Telegraph* folded open at the letters page. He wore glasses and held a magnifying glass.

'Daddy, you've been reading!'

Her astonishment seemed to embarrass him. 'I may have lost my marbles but I'm not entirely illiterate. It's a case of keeping in touch. Lose touch and your brain knows it. Eyes aren't so good, though. Care to read this letter from some fool doctor in Minehead? Thinks he knows about the effect of diet on autism. Ignoramus.'

So Alice read the ignoramus's letter to shouts of derision from her father and a request to read it a second time, which she did, pausing for his commentary. At the end she put away the paper. 'Daddy, do you feel safe here in this home?'

'Noone's safe until they're underground.' His voice had returned to the more usual mutter. His eyes drooped as if he was going to sleep but then, surprising Alice, he was alert again. 'Sorry.'

'Sorry?' She didn't understand.

'Richard.'

Richard, her husband. Alice was even more surprised. In

Richard's lifetime, her father had taken little account of him, and after he'd died so suddenly he'd hardly mentioned him again. 'You mean because Richard's underground?'

'Something like. Sorry for it. A good man.'

Alice stared at her father. His unexpected words brought home to her just how far she'd moved from the grieving widow. Richard had been a good man, but he was no longer dictating to her heart. She used to think of him nearly all the time; now she seldom did at all. 'I'm so busy,' she murmured.

'Good. Good.' He lifted his ancient hand and stretched it out towards her. Alice saw by his flapping motion what he wanted: she laid her hand, lightly tanned, under his. He patted it. 'That's it. You enjoy your life. Can't count on second chances.' He took back his hand and Alice saw that humanising smile transform his face. 'Now, you should go. Don't worry about me.'

Alice left, bewildered, and not altogether sure why. Had her father been as different as she felt or was it as much a change in herself? Why did she feel as if he had given her permission for something, although she was not sure what? Certainly he had been a hard taskmaster when she was a child but she trusted she'd never held that against him. To the contrary, he might have been the reason she'd married so young, swapping one older man for another.

Meditatively Alice passed the window, where the seagulls swooped and screamed, and thought for a moment of the carcass, animal, vegetable or mineral, that had so upset her. She had actually vomited, she reminded herself, only that morning, but now she felt quite calm. Maybe her rambling confessional to Mitzi had straightened her head a little.

At the bottom of the stairs, Alice found Mitzi leaning against the door, waiting for her. 'She's a wonderful woman, your Sister Mary Rose. Can you credit it? She believes the old are just like the rest of us.'

It was rush-hour in Brighton as Alice and Mitzi walked back slowly to the station. Neither mentioned their earlier conversation, although as they reached the sea-front, Mitzi commented that she wished she'd swum because she might have got all hot and sticky and who knows what might have happened then?

'Fuck you,' retaliated Alice, although her heart wasn't in it.

'Thank you for coming,' she said, when they parted in the noisy bustle of Victoria station. 'You cheered me up enormously.'

'I never knew you were such a one for secrets.'

'It was the way I was brought up.' And what, thought Alice, as she waved Mitzi goodbye, had she meant by that?

Chapter Fourteen

A Second Friday

Alice opened her eyes and sat up in one movement. She was trembling all over and not from cold. Gradually her ears reported a hammering on the front door. It was that which had wakened her and dissolved what was only a dream: a woman with white hair looming over her bed, ready either to kiss or to kill. Her arms clasped round her chest, Alice hurried to the door and opened it a crack. She was faced by the curious eyes of Joe, the annoying porter. 'Yes?'

'There's a lady police officer downstairs. Wants to come up.'

'Fine!' Alice tried to sound airily confident, but the moment she'd closed the door she felt moved to reopen it and shout down the corridor, 'Tell her I need five minutes!'

She pulled on cotton trousers and a T-shirt, picked up the telephone and dialled. 'Jonathan, it's Alice. The police are here to question me about Blue Carroway. It may be a murder investigation. Do I have to speak to them? It seems I'm the last person he spoke to. I feel so nervous. I—'

'Alice. Calm down. Unless you murdered him, you've absolutely nothing to fear from the police.'

'Oh.' Alice was startled. Why was she so nervous? She remembered. 'But I lied to her last time.'

'Were you under oath?'

'Of course I wasn't under oath.'

'Then you were merely helping her with her inquiries. I can't say I recommend lying to the police but a great many people do. Was it an important lie? In which case you have an opportunity to put the record straight.'

'But then they'd know I'd been lying before and wonder why.'

'True enough. Why did you lie?'

Alice had a quick image of Jonathan's fierce despair as he declared his love. 'No reason. Just a muddle.'

'Fine. Put it right. But, remember, they're drawing on your goodwill. If it goes further I'll get you a solicitor, but at this stage it would make them think you had something to hide.'

'Absurd,' said Alice.

'Please come in.' Alice showed the policewoman into the living room with a certain amount of formality. 'Detective Constable Paradise, isn't it?'

'Please call me Susan.'

Alice placed herself with her back to the windows where the white curtains rippled gently. The sun had not yet come round the building but it would be another bright day, already warm despite the early hour.

'What a lovely flat,' said Susan.

'It was my husband's. He died nearly three years ago.'

'I'm so sorry. And sorry to bother you again. The truth is, we're not getting very far with our investigations on Mr Carroway.'

'I suppose you hoped a body would turn up,' commented Alice, trying to feel bold. 'Perhaps you'd like a coffee?'

'No, thank you. Yes. The sea usually gives up its secrets.'

'But not always.'

'Not always, and sometimes only after a long time. I wonder if I can go over some ground with you?'

'I think I'll have some coffee.'

When Alice came back from the kitchen Susan was bent over her pad. Her face was rounder and more complacent than Alice had remembered, perhaps because her blonde hair was looped back. 'I see you interviewed him in the early evening and then you had supper together before parting. Would it be possible to see your notes?'

'Nothing easier, but they're mostly in shorthand.'

'One of the older officers at the station will decode.'

Alice handed over the pad.

'Something new has come up,' said the youthful Susan, stowing away the pad in her shoulder-bag. 'Did Mr Carroway mention a plan to sail to Cherbourg? There has been a possible sighting. Unconfirmed, but we like to follow every lead.'

'No,' said Alice, glad to be truthful. 'When was he seen?' As she spoke, La Rochelle came into her mind and then she remembered it had been Guy who had mentioned sailing there.

'Very early Saturday morning.'

Alice calculated furiously, while trying to keep a casual expression on her face. It didn't take long to work out that there was no way Blue could have got to Plymouth from London and then to Cherbourg by early Saturday morning unless he had started around midnight when, in fact, he had been making love with her. They hadn't parted till well after nine on Friday morning.

'I see,' said Alice. 'Well, I hope he's alive. Is he married?'

'A loner,' pronounced Susan, in sober tones. 'So you parted between ten thirty and eleven p.m.?'

Alice wondered if they had known the truth all along and were trying to break her down. Maybe she was already broken down. Maybe honesty *was* the best policy.

'I think someone's knocking on your door.'

Alice felt irritated. Why were the porters incapable of using the intercom? She went to open it and there was Joe, hidden behind a huge bouquet of pink and red and orange and purple flowers. 'I thought I'd better bring them straight up,' he said virtuously.

The flowers were incredibly beautiful, the colours of a Persian carpet, the scent of an English country garden, the texture of velvet and silk and organza. Alice took the bouquet and put her face close to the pink skirts of a rose shaped like a peony and felt her heart melt towards whoever had sent them.

'That chauffeur brought them in.'

Brendan! Alice forgot Detective Constable Paradise and walked back to the living room with the flowers hugged to her.

'What a splendid bunch!' said Susan.

'Yes,' agreed Alice. 'Do you mind if I put them in water?'

'Go ahead.'

Alice thought Brendan's plan was to seduce her with beauty – although it wasn't clear whether he wanted to seduce her at all.

'Mind if I have a coffee after all?' The policewoman had followed her into the kitchen.

'Be my guest.' Without untying the flowers, which were

perfectly arranged, Alice filled a glass vase with water and plunged them in.

Coffee made, they returned to the living room. 'How else can I help you?' Alice took an upright chair, which announced (she hoped), 'I am a busy and successful woman.'

'So, he made no mention of visiting France?'

'Not that I remember. Perhaps it's in my notes.'

'Quite. And you parted between ten thirty and eleven on Thursday evening?'

'Yes. Yes.'

'I'll just finish my coffee, if you don't mind, and then I must be off.'

The moment Alice had seen the detective constable out of the door, she dashed to the telephone.

'Guy. I'm so glad you're there!'

'I'm always here. Remember.'

She now recalled his out-of-character flight from Downing Street. 'You left so abruptly on Wednesday.'

'Yes. Sorry. That empty chair at the feast got to me.'

But she knew it was more than that. 'I rang to run a few ideas past you for next week's interview.' For what other reason could she ring him?

'There are at least three politicians desperate for a bit of limelight.'

'I want a real heavyweight. Serious.'

'You could do that new junior minister who was quoted yesterday as saying the Prime Minister suffers from a personality disorder . . .'

'But he'll say no if he's any sense.'

'Or there's the new prisons minister. He's clever and ambitious.'

'And won't be in the job very long. He's famously horrible, too.'

'Whenever did that disqualify a subject for your column?'

Alice laughed. It had felt like a compliment.

'So,' said Guy, as she was about to put down the phone, 'I'll be seeing you this weekend.'

Guy was coming to Brendan's? Why was the idea so disturbing? Luckily, for the rest of the day, there was no time to do anything but check the availability of her names, convince the Master of the suitability of the chosen one, then start background research, including calls to 'friends' and colleagues. She had ended up with the new prison's Minister, who had radical solutions to the young-offender problem. Or so he said. She would see him in his office at nine on Monday, then accompany him on a visit to Wandsworth Prison. It would be another rushed deadline. His name was Ivo Swayne. She couldn't help noting, with surprise, that at thirty-eight he was still a bachelor. The main point was that next week she'd be in print again.

It wasn't until Alice had got into bed and fallen into a kind of drifting superficial sleep that she remembered her dream of the early morning. Perhaps it had been with her all day but only surfaced as her eyes closed once more. The woman was threatening to come again so she must stay awake and on guard.

Alice found she was sitting up. She switched on the bedside light. Instead of thinking about her ghostly visitor, though, she began to worry about her wardrobe for the weekend. How would she be expected to appear in the morning? What was the current wear for a helicopter trip, alighting at a grand country house? Did she dress like an intrepid reporter of the fifties in pressed khaki? (She had none of that in her wardrobe.) Or was it the modern equivalent of twinset and pearls – tight jeans and an Armani T-shirt? But she didn't much like that look. Her hair was too flashy, her body too feminine. If it was hot yet again, which seemed likely, perhaps she could wear a sleeveless dress with bare legs and sandals. Or would she look as if she were going, rather underdressed, to a cocktail party? Or, worse still, to the beach?

At midnight, Alice got out of bed and went to her wardrobe and drawers. Richard had almost cured her of sartorial panic by his amazement and lack of understanding at her wild rifling through her clothes. But now there was no one to help and she pulled down dresses, trousers, skirts, shirts and jackets, and flung them on to the bed. Soon the pile was so high that some toppled or slid to the floor.

Alice knew this progression from the past: the greater the chaos, the more the encouragement to sort it out. She had not reached that point yet. She went to her drawers and shuffled through pants, bras and petticoats, selecting some to add to the mountain on the bed. The phone rang. In Florrie's days as a wild teenager, the midnight call had always been her, sounding drunk or drugged or both, and pleading for an extension to the time she was allowed out. She seldom took any notice of the firm demand for her return, usually given by Richard.

Heart beating fast, Alice picked up the phone. 'Ma. I just thought I should let you know she's come back.'

'Who?' For a ridiculous moment Alice mistook 'she' for 'he' and thought of Blue.

'The woman. Dora. My friend. Who took Lily. She came back and was so lovely. Awfully sorry and all that, of course. She had to go and visit an elderly relative—'

'Florrie, have you gone quite mad? This woman kidnapped your baby. You were distraught. I was distraught.'

'Yes, I know. But she didn't mean to upset us. She was just giving Lily a bit of an outing and then that dreadful storm came and she got lost. She *loves* Lily. I've told you all this already.'

'Florrie.' Alice sat on her bed, squashing linen and silk. 'The police are looking for this woman you like so much. She's dangerous. She might even have kidnapped your grandfather too.'

'I don't know what you're talking about, but if you're going to be like that I'm sorry I told you. I didn't have to, you know.'

Alice felt weary. Her head drooped. 'She's not staying with you, by any chance?'

'No, but I've invited her round tomorrow. I can't tell you what a help she is.'

'What are you going to tell the police?'

'The truth.'

'The truth.' Alice heard herself stupidly repeat the word. Somewhere in her head an echo, which in itself was hardly more than an echo, was stopping her thinking straight.

'Don't you worry about a thing. I assure you Baz and I have everything under control. I was just calling to keep you informed. Tomorrow we're taking Dora to the police station and then she's coming to live here for a bit. You'll meet her next weekend.'

Blearily Alice surveyed the jumble on her bed. Hardly hesitating, she tugged out the duvet, causing a further cascade of clothes, and went next door to the room she'd shared with Richard. It was time she moved back. Or, to put it another way, time she moved forward.

Just as she was falling asleep, she got up again and went in darkness to the living room, which was faintly lit by the street-light outside. She picked up the heavy vase of flowers Brendan had sent, carried them carefully to the bedroom and set them on the chest of drawers. She hadn't drawn the curtains across the window behind them and could easily make out their intricate outline and even the stained-glass colours.

Chapter Fifteen

A Third Saturday

Harry carried Alice's bag to the car with an air of formality.

'Welcome, my dear.' Brendan sat forward on the edge of the seat, but he hadn't got out to greet her. Then she saw that he'd been putting away his mobile phone.

'This is so exciting!' she exclaimed. 'You give me all my firsts. First a private plane and then a helicopter.' She'd forgotten both the smallness of his eyes and their brightness.

He kissed her cheek and took her hand. His hair was greyish-brown and cut close to his scalp in fine layers. 'We'll be buffeted about the sky with this wind. I hope you're not nervous of flying.' He gave her hand a squeeze. The journey to the heliport in Battersea would take less than half an hour, he told her, and the flight thirty-five minutes. He began to fill her in about the other guests. As far as she could remember, there was no one who had been on the previous weekend list. With a queasy sense that, once again, fate was shaping up with more surprises, she heard him pronounce the final name: 'Ivo Swayne.'

'But I'm interviewing him on Monday.'

'That's no reason why he shouldn't spend the weekend with me.' Still holding her hand, he was teasing her in an avuncular yet flirtatious way. 'You do get around, don't you?'

How could she find such a man attractive? And yet she did. She felt her heart flutter a little at his warm, rather massive closeness. 'Now that we know each other a little better,' she said, in her interviewer's voice – sympathetic with an edge of school-mistress determination, 'may I ask you why none of your marriages succeeded?'

'They didn't fail,' he answered quickly, then conceded, 'Well, I suppose divorce is generally considered failure. You ask me because I seem to you such a warm, even sentimental old fellow. Is that it? Tears before bedtime.'

'No. I—'

'It's boringly simple. None of my three wives and six mistresses ever interested me as much as my work. I wasn't a *bad* husband, merely inattentive.'

'You mean there were no rows, no throwing of glasses, no furious silences?'

Brendan sighed, smiled and let go of her hand. 'You're such a romantic. And so young.'

'Wrong on both courts. I'm not at all young and I'm very unromantic.'

'I must remember you know everything about me.'

'Well, let me tell you something about me. When I was sixteen I read *Madame Bovary* with a total lack of sympathy for the heroine. I felt the same about Anna Karenina and Elizabeth Bennet.' This was a lie but he deserved it.

'How sad. So beautiful and never to have known love!'

'I was married for twenty years!'

'Quite.' He touched her hot cheek gently. Why did she let him do such things? 'You're a very passionate woman.'

Alice laughed at the absurd, corny, old-fashioned seducer's line. Brendan stared at her for a moment, then rolled down his window and gazed out in a meditative way. 'You must have married very young.' He made it a statement.

'Yes. I had my first baby before I was twenty.'

'That explains it.'

'Being a grandmother, you mean? And Florrie was only nineteen when she had her baby. Too young. It's the most extraordinary thing but she's forgiven Lily's kidnapper and invited her to stay – as a kind of housekeeper, I think.'

'How very odd. Although a good housekeeper is worth her weight in gold.'

'I've washed my hands of it,' said Alice, wondering at having such a conversation with such a man. Yet it was only another example of the immediate intimacy she felt with him, even when he was irritating her.

'Very wise. I said the same after my third marriage. People are unpredictable and uncontrollable. The property market is a poodle by comparison.'

'So you won't marry again?'

'I'm as unpredictable and uncontrollable as anyone else.' Brendan looked at Alice closely, perhaps meaningfully. 'Let's say I've no plans to marry again. I'm on fine terms with my ex-wives – two of whom have remarried. My eldest son hates me, but he's a fool.'

They were crossing Albert Bridge now and Alice remembered how she had come up to London in a school party when she was eight and the teacher had told them that if they walked in step over the bridge it would begin to swing. How gingerly they had tiptoed from their coach parked south of the river! They'd hardly dared to talk as they crossed, watching each other with sharp, childish vigilance for any tendency to synchronisation.

That visit to London had made her give up the idea of her mothers' ever returning. She'd decided, while still in Brighton, that London was just the sort of place a missing mother would be, and even on the swinging bridge she'd kept a careful look-out for her. Once she'd spotted a redheaded woman, slim and smart, hastening along the pavement, but when she turned her face was all wrong, and then she saw that there was a little boy on her other side. She had one other false alarm, in the grounds of the Tower of London, but this redhead had been no more than fourteen or fifteen years old. When no mother had appeared by the end of the long day she'd finally given up hope.

Other children had been met off the coach by their mothers. She made her own way home. Later, when her father had asked her if she'd enjoyed her day out, she'd answered, 'Fine,' and refused to say another word.

'Can this bridge swing?' Alice asked Brendan, watching the brisk wind whip up ripples on the water beneath.

'Officers command their men to fall out of step, of course.' He patted her knee indulgently. She wondered if this frequent touching was his usual style or reserved for her and, if so, whether she felt flattered. 'We're nearly at the heliport. Ivo Swayne will be meeting us there. I'll give you one piece of advice for free. You should never be afraid of mixing work with pleasure.'

Ivo Swayne was an unprepossessing man, not very tall, with frizzy mouse-coloured hair, a bulbous nose set too high in his face and gappy teeth in a full, lopsided mouth. In both face and figure, he tended to corpulence. If I can find *this* man attractive, thought Alice, I need to go back to my shrink. She rethought: Unless he's a genius.

'What are you smiling at?' She could only lip-read Ivo's words because they were sitting inside the helicopter and, although they hadn't yet taken off, the propellers were rotating with an appalling din.

Alice smiled more and shook her head. Suddenly the ground was disappearing below them and London, at a crazy angle, spread ever wider. The angle straightened, but every now and again there came a new slant, as if a giant hand was pushing them in a swing. Even so they continued to rise, high enough to see sky and a floating range of clouds ahead. Brendan was sitting by the pilot and they seemed to be shouting at each other in an argumentative way, or maybe their voices raised to be heard above the aircraft noise. Alice watched the sky with amazement. The clouds were racing towards them, although above. One had a grey cushion – like a wad at the bottom – which opened to pour forth slanting strokes of rain, just as a child would draw it. 'Look.' Alice nudged Ivo, then noticed that his already pallid complexion had become an even more unhealthy colour. 'Are you all right?'

He put his head between his knees – or as far as he could get it over his stomach. It seemed he was about to vomit. Certainly the helicopter was now sliding and slithering on the air-waves in a disconcerting manner. Out of the window she saw more clouds above but less city below, with a wide belt of fields emerging ahead. The helicopter, she noticed, was not only swinging but juddering as if gamely fighting an unseen force. Brendan had finished shouting at the pilot and now twisted round to face Alice. He shook his head and pointed downwards. His mouth was thin and cross.

Almost at once, the helicopter started circling downwards, which cut out the juddering if not the slipping and sliding. They touched the ground rather hard in the wide grassy verge of a field planted with turnips.

As soon as they were out of the helicopter, Ivo wearing a look of supreme thankfulness, Alice saw that Brendan was in a rage.

'Ridiculous wimps,' was all he said in passing. Soon he was on his mobile.

'He hates things going wrong,' whispered Ivo, quickly recovering his spirits. 'He takes it as a personal defeat. We should never have set off at all in that wind. When I was an under-secretary in the Foreign Office, we took a helicopter to Srebrenica. I vowed never again. But today I thought, At least we won't be under fire this time. Do you know Brendan well?'

Alice was about to remark that it might have been wiser to ask that question before criticising their host, then recalled that she must treat him carefully as he was Monday's interview subject.

'You don't seem his usual type,' added Ivo, as she didn't answer.

'Obviously you know him better than I do.' This came out more tartly than she'd planned.

Ivo looked at her with surprise. 'He's a big party donor. Surely you journalists know things like that.'

Mortified on two counts, Alice remembered that that piece of information had been given prominence in her interview with Brendan and understood that Ivo was not one of her readers. 'I interviewed him,' she said briefly.

It was three-quarters of an hour before Harry found them. During this time, Brendan remained a solitary figure at the edge of the turnips, either talking on his mobile or staring sulkily at the ground. His image, in Alice's eyes, took a dive. She was left to talk to Ivo who, after a while, preferred his mobile too.

Alice noticed that the tufty tops of the turnips were no longer waving furiously but now stood almost unwaveringly upright. She looked towards the helicopter but the pilot, who had also been on his mobile, suddenly leapt inside it and turned on the engine. He was not taking them anywhere.

Ahead, a wooden gate was shut but not padlocked. Alice let herself through it into a wide, sloping field, the grass short-cropped and pale. Behind her there was a huge noise as the helicopter rose upwards, casting a black shadow like a vast witch. Almost at once from the far side of the field, a stampede of black and white cows came towards her; behind them, at a steady pace, with his hand on the horn, drove Harry in the Bentley.

Alice felt dismayed. All this disturbance in a peaceful pastoral scene caused by one ill-tempered man. The cows came closer, their udders swinging in an undignified manner. With the helicopter directly overhead, they wheeled round and set off at right angles. The car came to stop beside Alice. Harry leant through the window. 'Lucky the helicopter took off or I'd never have found you.'

'You've probably curdled those poor cows' milk,' said Alice severely.

'Do them good to stretch their legs, madam. I was glad about the baby returning unharmed, if I may say so. Do you need a ride?'

Brendan didn't recover his good humour until his house was in sight.

'Shall we walk the last stretch?' The house was at the end of a long driveway, which twisted and turned through parkland to a highish, probably man-made rise. The building, even at this distance, was clearly modern and, judging by the young chestnuts planted on either side of the driveway, recently constructed. Brendan's suggestion that they should walk the last stretch was filled with schoolboy enthusiasm.

Alice was immediately charmed, which made her realise how much she wanted to like him and the weekend to be a success. Since Ivo declined to leave the car, Alice and Brendan were able to stroll along together, the latter explaining in great detail the architect's concept of the house. 'Everything is turned outwards,' he said. 'You'll see when we're in it. You feel as if you're sitting in the middle of a field filled with buttercups. The very few walls that aren't made of glass are painted in white tinged with yellow and the white ceilings washed with blue. Even people who never stir from the house feel as if they've been picnicking in the country.'

By the time they reached a cattle grid and the final climb to the house, Alice was hot, and glad she'd rejected all her smarter clothes in favour of a pale cotton skirt and sleeveless shirt. Every cloud had been blown from the sky and the sun was at its highest. Brendan, despite his bulk, seemed unfazed by the sweat shining on his face and blotching the back of his shirt. But as they neared the glass and plaster front of his mansion, where the car was already parked, he grabbed Alice's arm. 'Don't let's go in yet.'

He guided her to the left where trees, densely planted and underlaid with a tangle of low-growing flowers and shrubs that

Alice couldn't identify, disguised a narrow brick path. It was deliciously cool and shady, a place to linger, but Brendan, strode on, letting Alice follow single-file behind. Since he obscured her view ahead, she was taken aback when the trees ended abruptly and she was faced by a flight of stone steps leading down to a wide blue lagoon.

Even more unexpected was Brendan's behaviour. By the time they'd reached the bottom of the steps, he'd thrown off all his clothes and, just giving Alice time to appreciate a grizzled bear chest, executed a resounding belly-flop into the water. Bobbing up at once, he shouted, 'Icy, absolutely icy! Like a mountain lake. You can't resist!'

Alice found she couldn't. But she did hesitate as she reached her underwear. Breasts were no problem but red pubic hair looked so very naked. In the water, Brendan ploughed resolutely up and down, making whale-like spouts of water and indeterminate animal grunts. Alice stripped off her pants, ran to the edge of the pool and dived gracefully in.

Brendan hadn't been joking. The water was so cold she felt like shrieking. In fact, she did shriek as she surfaced, a child's shriek of adventure. The pool must have only just been filled or, even without heating, the sun would have made it warmer. She swam as fast as she could, puffing and panting. After a while, she noticed the even noisier form of Brendan had left her. Treading water, she saw him wrapped in a large white towelling robe, holding another over his arm. 'You're a star!' he called. 'But don't turn into an iceberg.' He held open the second bathrobe.

Alice came out of the water. He didn't move towards her so she had to cross several airy yards but her body felt so filled with well-being that any self-consciousness was banished.

'You're pink all over,' commented Brendan, wrapping her up tenderly.

It was impossible not to kiss him then or to enjoy his already warm hands feeling through the wrap. Her breasts tingled, her skin glowed.

'That was very nice.' Brendan removed himself.

Alice was surprised at his tone and, turning away, caught sight of Guy hovering at the end of the pool. 'Your guests feel they can't start lunch without you,' he called, without approaching further.

Alice wondered how much of the last few minutes he'd seen. 'Hi!' She waved.

Guy moved towards her. He wore an open-necked orange shirt and pale blue trousers, more flamboyant than his usual style.

'I'll go on.' Brendan squeezed Alice's arm and moved away.

Alice was pleased to see Guy. 'Who are these guests?' she asked, trying not to sound anxious.

'Well, you've met Ivo.' Guy crouched and dipped his finger in the pool. 'Ouch! I hope you were wearing a wetsuit.'

Was this an ironic way of informing her he'd seen her naked? 'We'd got hot walking. So, who are the other guests?'

'Aren't you going to dress? It's quite a formal lunch party.'

'Then I'll go to my room and smarten myself up. Guy?'

'Yes.'

'When did you first meet Brendan?' Did he look evasive or was it just the angle as she crouched to pick up her clothes?

'Not long ago. Last year. He's got fingers in a lot of pies.'

They were now walking upwards, through a pleached lime-tree avenue, elaborately planted but still young enough to see through. A rose garden lay ahead bordered by low box hedges, and beyond that the shimmering glass of the house.

'What sort of pies?'

'Business ventures. Mainly property development. Look, you should know all this. You interviewed him.'

How could she explain what more she was looking for when she hardly knew herself? 'Yes. Of course I know he's a big party donor.'

Guy laughed. '*Ergo* Ivo. To check him out. Brendan doesn't just make *you* nervous.'

Alice thought she hadn't said he made her nervous, and considering their closeness on Guy's arrival by the pool, he might have deduced the opposite. The garden was planted with old-fashioned shrub roses whose pink and red and purplish-coloured blooms gave off a rich scent. Many had fallen, the petals lying in wave-like patterns on the dark earth. The sun was very hot. Alice glanced at her watch: it was already one thirty.

'I've never seen you look so beautiful,' said Guy. His voice was husky.

Alice smiled at him questioningly but he was already moving

away. With a little spurt of feminine triumph, she knew what he'd said was true. The wild trip in the helicopter, the hot walk, the ice-cold swim and the moment of shared lust with Brendan had all given her a sense of physical exhilaration. She put her hand up to her hair which, unsurprisingly, felt tightly curled, verging on frizzy, but even that failed to depress.

The lunch was formal with serious waiter service and many glasses to choose from. But the room in which it was held – or, rather, the atrium – was literally filled with birch trees dappling the table with delicate shade. Alice, who had found her clothes unpacked in her bedroom and a freshly ironed white linen dress laid out on the bed, took her place without losing her sense of a benign world. She shook her head slightly so that the earrings she'd chosen, turquoise and silver, jangled. Even finding that Ivo was her neighbour couldn't dampen her spirits.

'This is all in my honour, you know,' was his opening gambit.

'Oh? Why?' Alice, scanning the table, didn't take much notice. There were twelve places, and Brendan was sitting between a very old woman and a very young one.

'How much champagne have you drunk?'

'I haven't had time for anything like that.'

'Sensible girl. I've been at it since we arrived. Surviving the helicopter seemed something to celebrate. I haven't forgotten you're a vile hack but, off the record, our well-heeled host's on a sticky wicket. The only problem is, he may drag us into the treacle too.'

Ivo was drunk. His bulbous eyes swivelled and his nose flared. Nevertheless, she was surprised he should be quite so indiscreet.

'What do you mean by "us"?'

'My dear girl, if I need to tell you that, then I wouldn't dream of telling you more.' At this point, Alice caught Brendan's eye – he was staring at her intensely. 'Try reading *Private Eye* more often and leaving *Woman and Home* to the other pretty ladies.'

With Brendan's eyes still on her, Alice felt it imperative to give an insouciant laugh, although she felt much more like slapping Ivo's loutish face. 'How ridiculous you are!' she said. 'If I want to know the latest gossip I consult my friends.'

Ivo, having given her a secretive leer, spooned some vichyssoise into his wide mouth, which cut out the possibility of an answer. Alice had forgotten that she was supposed to be eating and spooned some herself. It was very good. What had Ivo been on about? Or, rather, not on about? It was true she seldom bothered with *Private Eye*.

'The thing is,' said Ivo, dribbling a little, 'we don't need crooks as our supporters.'

'Crooks!' Perhaps he really did think she knew something about all this. That could be the only explanation for his behaviour. As she came to this conclusion, she was claimed by the man on her left: Guy.

'I thought the special adviser would hold you in his beam for ever.'

Alice allowed her nearly full bowl to be taken away. 'He was implying all sorts of scurrilous things about our host.'

Guy was unperturbed. 'He's absolutely plastered, I'd say.'

Alice thought about this and decided that, if she didn't want her day to be spoiled, it was the best approach. 'I won't believe a word he said. What happens in the afternoon, do you think?' she added.

'A tennis tournament, I'm informed, followed by a short period at leisure before we go out for a charity evening at the local castle. Brendan likes to keep his guests entertained.'

'Well, I'm delighted to be entertained.' Alice turned to welcome an exquisite plateful of fresh salmon, surrounded by equally exquisite tiny vegetables. 'I'm here to enjoy myself.'

She must have raised her voice because Ivo clutched her arm. She turned towards his greedy eyes. 'And yet you look so cool.' He lowered his voice. 'The tennis also is to flatter my ego. Once upon a time I was Wimbledon's hope for a British champ.'

This was further proof of just how drunk he was, but Alice didn't argue. She herself was being plied regularly with a sumptuously golden chablis. From then on she hardly took any notice of what either of her neighbours said to her. By the end of the lunch, they were talking to each other across her and she was able to sit back. Let them get on with it, thought Alice, contentedly.

The tennis court and its environs were not very attractive. Like everything else in and around the house they were new and the spectators' hut smelt of glue. Alice found herself sitting next to the old woman, Lady Waterford, who was thin and elegant and had clever blue eyes surrounded by aristocratic wrinkles.

'Don't you play tennis?' Lady Waterford asked. 'You look pretty fit.'

'Badly. I play it badly. And I don't like being seen to be bad at things.' Alice leant back in her colonial cane chair.

'In my childhood, girls had to do everything, however badly, tennis, piano, poetry, even Greek in my case.'

'Do you live nearby?'

'Most of us here do. Turning out to check over the new money. We're all involved in some deserving charity or other. Mine's my house.'

Alice gathered that Lady Waterford, although Irish by name, lived in an English stately home – or perhaps she had two. Two courts were in use and several of the players hadn't been at lunch. There were only two women and the men included Ivo, extremely active despite his alcoholic intake, Guy and Brendan himself.

'I read your interview,' commented Lady Waterford, as Brendan went through an elaborate warm-up routine. His whites were very white and he wore a towelling headband and wristlets. 'You were kind to him, considering.'

Considering what? Alice wondered. One of an interviewer's worst dreads was getting a subject entirely wrong. Were there things to expose that she'd failed to bring out? For ten years her track record had been one hundred per cent, giving her excellent credibility. She was kinder than most, perhaps, but never foolishly, which enabled her to interview people who turned down her sharper colleagues. She remembered, with a sense of shock, that today was Saturday and she hadn't looked at the paper because she didn't have an interview in it. Suddenly she had a desire to see the loathsome two-page spread that had replaced her.

Perhaps she should concentrate on the game nearest her: Brendan and the young girl against Guy and an unknown male. Brendan was left-handed and steamed about the court with more energy than elegance. Guy had a strong service and a deceptively undercut backhand. His partner leapt and parried at the net, which made them an effective team. 'Brendan and Juliet will win,' said Lady Waterford, confidently. Juliet, it appeared, was her granddaughter and at the moment devoted her life to tennis. 'It's the only thing she's good at,' explained her grandmother, sanguinely.

'I'll think I'll go for a walk,' said Alice, after a while, then noticed her ladyship was asleep. As she crossed the lawns and terrace she thought how much less attractive this brash estate was than Brendan's house in Devon. Or was it Cornwall? Arriving by plane had rather dimmed her sense of geography. She was glad she'd seen Goosefields first; even though it had ended in such a ferocious storm, she remembered her stay there with pleasure.

It was nearly five o'clock when she entered the house, which was delightfully cool and empty. Through an open door, she spotted a pile of newspapers on a table. Her own was on top.

'May I be of assistance?'

It was Harry, approaching from behind. Perhaps he hadn't recognised her because his gruffness was that of a mastiff guarding his master's goods.

'Did you think I was a burglar, Harry?' She smiled.

'I keep an eye on things when the house is empty.' He remained stiff, if not belligerent.

'Does Sir Brendan have so much to hide, then?' She was opening the paper and spoke casually. There was the piece, six interviews with transvestites, not about bed-sits at all, and the byline was a certain Polly Omar, looking as pretty in her photograph as she had in the flesh. Shit and shit.

'That's not for me to say, ma'am.'

'Oh, Harry. I wasn't being serious.' But he had turned to go, apparently offended.

Clutching the despised newspaper, Alice wandered back to the tennis courts. Happily, the wine was operating as an excellent pain-killer. Holidays aside, she'd missed very few weeks, a couple of times when she'd been ill, and when Richard had died. It wasn't a bad record.

She could hear shouting, clapping and cheering from quite a distance. In the pavilion, the atmosphere was no longer somnolent. On court, the partnerships had shifted. Now Brendan was playing with Guy against Ivo and Juliet. Brendan was serving, an ungainly almost underarm action, which nevertheless sped and swerved dangerously over the net.

Alice settled down to watch. Guy and Brendan are like Beauty and the Beast, she thought, noting the former's long, tanned legs and hard-hitting style. His hair seemed thicker and blonder and his face, behind narrow dark glasses, more defined. Most important of all, he was calm and in control of himself. Brendan, on the other hand, was raging all over the court, his face scarlet, sweat pouring down him, making it clear that the wristlets and headband were for practical not fashion reasons. Despite his height, his legs, Alice thought critically, were hardly longer than his torso. Nevertheless, Brendan was winning far more points than he lost and not only because Ivo was making stupid mistakes.

'Even Juliet can't save him,' commented Lady Waterford, wide awake again.

Despite the gladiatorial drama, Alice took up her newspaper. After all, no one had bothered to explain the rules of the tournament to her. She therefore missed the moment when Ivo, reduced to impotent failure, hurled his racquet to the ground in disgust. She looked up in time to see Juliet picking up the two halves. Meanwhile Brendan, sweat flying, was bounding up to the net to shake hands. The match, or perhaps even the tournament, was over.

'And now we can go home,' commented Lady Waterford, rising to her feet.

Alice wondered if she wanted to go home too but acknowledged she was enjoying herself far too much. She left the paper under her chair and went to congratulate Brendan.

'Quite a win. Quite a win,' he agreed, failing to look modest.

Alice remembered Ivo had said that the tournament had been designed to flatter him, but the opposite seemed to be true.

'What's the next event?' she asked Guy, after congratulating him on his win.

'Culture.' He surprised Alice by kissing her cheek, his face hot and a little damp but somehow attractive too. 'The Jane Austen Society's annual beano. A black-tie do, Juliet tells me.'

Chapter Sixteen

A Third Sunday

At one o'clock in the morning, with an owl hooting dolefully outside the window, Alice finally reached her bedroom. The evening's events whirled in her head, making her inclined to laugh hysterically – but that might have been too much late-night champagne. The Austen dinner had been held in a large, beautiful house that the celebrated author had once admired in a painting. The host, overwhelmed by the importance of the evening and his distinguished guests, drank himself into incoherence, which was unfortunate since he was the principal speaker. Brendan, on ebullient form, proposed an unscheduled toast to 'scribblers everywhere – in particular the one presently seated on my left', which was Alice. While Ivo, tennis defeat and ugliness notwithstanding, flirted outrageously with the host's wife and was successful enough to be seen escorting her into the garden. Alice lost track of Guy, who seemed mostly engaged with his tennis partner, Juliet.

I never thought country-house life could be so diverting, she thought, as she removed her clothes and tipped herself into bed. In seconds, she was asleep.

She awoke, just as suddenly and not much later, to feel the warmth of another body beside her and a hand on her breast. Even if she had drawn the curtains so that the moon couldn't shine in, she would have known it was Brendan. 'You don't mind, do you?' he said, quite loudly in her ear. 'I just couldn't resist any longer.'

Alice found herself giggling weakly. Where were the protestations of undying love, of eternal loyalty? Where was the romance, the poetry? 'You're not very romantic, Brendan.'

' "My heart aches, and a drowsy numbness pains my sense, as though of hemlock I had drunk ..." '

'That's an ode to a *nightingale* not a *woman*.'

'You *are* my nightingale.'

What happened next was inevitable. Or, anyway, it seemed so to Alice at the time. It was impossible to deny the bear-like form stroking her so seductively. He was tame enough now, but what if he became fierce and turned his wrath on her? The idea was exciting rather than alarming and as his mouth searched greedily for her nipples, Alice found herself already uttering little moans of pleasure. Soon he was guzzling her all over, his big form weighing heavily on her so that she was incapable of movement even if she had wanted to make any.

She seemed to have come a hundred times before his head reappeared beside hers and his voice, rather snuffily, requested permission to enter her. This made Alice laugh. After what he had been doing to her over the last minutes or hours it surely wasn't necessary to ask permission for anything.

'Darling voracious beast,' she whispered, holding him close, 'I would love you to come inside me!'

This acted as a green flag to the bull he now became and Alice joined in his bellows of joy. It didn't take long, for which he apologised, tenderly touching her face, then rolled away and fell at once into a noisy sleep.

Not long after, Alice also fell asleep, for the second time that night.

The morning light woke Alice to an immediate and sick-making sense of dread. At least there was no one beside her; her searching hand met nothing but clammy sheets. Her brains boomed and boiled inside her skull as if they planned to crack it open. She staggered out of bed and made it to the bathroom where she gulped down two glasses of cold water. From the mirror above the basin a grey and wrinkled hag stared despairingly at her. She fled back to her bed.

How could she have let Brendan make love to her? And, worse still, enjoy it so much? Nostalgically, she recalled her night of love with Blue. His beauty and the democratic nature of their love-making gave it elegance and even innocence.

Alice stumbled out of bed again. She flung up the bottom of one of the windows and stuck her head out into the air. Where was her independent spirit? Her self-respect? Her instinct for survival? She wouldn't trust Brendan as far as she could throw him.

Alice went back to bed again. The garden had been grey and quiet. It must still be early. At least her faithful watch was on the bedside. Five to five. She had been asleep for hardly more than a couple of hours. She must force herself to calm down and at least rest a little.

But the sheets smelt of Brendan – and herself, too, she supposed. It was impossible to lie calmly between them.

Alice sat in the large armchair by the window, shivering from the cold and enjoying the sense of penance. Now she was strong enough to face the consequences of her action. Brendan, she felt sure, wouldn't resist bragging about his conquest, if only by the arm of ownership on her shoulder or those bright blue eyes resting too long on her face, or legs – Alice tucked them under her and shivered more violently. And yet, in this analysis, she was forgetting her instinctive sense, right from their first meeting, that he would look after her. Where did that sit now? Just why was she filled with such shame and dread?

Alice allowed herself to think about Richard and felt fractionally soothed by memories of low-key loving and safe order. When he had been alive the most dramatic part of her week was her interview, the careful preparation, the meeting with her subject, the slow and intense writing of the piece. Now her work had to be fitted into the hurly-burly of her personal life, which, ever more threatening and disorderly, entwined and overlapped one with the other.

At least Blue had had the good taste to disappear after their liaison. This bad-taste thought produced a lightening of her mood. She discounted it at once, of course. But it contained the truth that she'd made no plans to see Blue again. On the other hand, his sudden, quite possibly tragic, disappearance had made everything more complicated.

Alice walked slowly back to bed. She was so cold and exhausted now that she hugged the tumbled bedclothes round her so that she was warmly cocooned. At last she fell asleep.

The light was brighter when Alice woke again, but still grey.

According to her watch it was only seven o'clock, but the hour or so of sleep had given her a little more confidence. It struck her that what would really sort out her head was an ice-cold swim.

The pool was in use. Without coming too close, Alice stood watching in dismay. It was a male body, moreover, and she was rather off male bodies at the moment. At least it was definitely not Brendan's: his huffing and puffing style would be quite distinctive. This was a smooth male, swimming away from her now in a regular fast crawl. He turned and came back towards her, his face lifting neatly sideways at every second stroke.

Guy! An empty pool would have been best but Guy was not bad at all. Guy was her friend without entanglements. 'Good morning, Guy.' She had pronounced the words too loudly and her head protested with a throb.

Guy trod water and waved. 'Hi! I can't stop for long or you'll have to chip me out.'

Alice, who was already wearing her costume, lowered herself gingerly into the water, trying to avoid the waves of Guy's wake. She swam vigorously up and down.

When she got out, Guy was waiting for her. Wrapped in their towels, they sat down together. Guy tore in half a large bread roll he was holding.

Alice gnawed gratefully. 'However did you get it?' The icy swim had anaesthetised her body and soul as she'd hoped but roused a sharp hunger.

'Last night's supper. Smuggled up. I find breakfast is never early enough in other people's houses. Particularly on Sundays.'

Vaguely, Alice wondered what other people's houses he stayed in. 'I didn't sleep very well.' She had no intention, of course, of telling him about how she'd spent part of the night, but needed some kind of sympathy.

Guy picked up his glasses from the ground and put them on. 'You do look rather green round the edges.'

Contradictorily, this comment irritated Alice. Surely one of the positives of raging sex was a radiant glow? 'I'm frozen.'

'Quite.'

'The thing is, I've got to interview Ivo tomorrow, as you know. I'm not properly prepared and it feels very odd being with him here in social surroundings.'

'Like a surgeon dining with his patient before putting in the scalpel.'

Alice found she was irritated again. 'I've never used a scalpel but I do like to feel professional.'

'And he behaved so absurdly badly yesterday. Is that off your record?'

Alice warmed to her theme – it had an impersonality, which was soothing. 'That's what I mean. I can hardly put it in when I'm talking about his high ambitions to solve youth crime but it has to be in my mind.' All at once this regular dilemma of most journalists' lives seemed an insurmountable barrier. 'What do *you* think, Guy?'

'I think you didn't have enough sleep.' He took her hand and, amazingly, his was warm and strong, while hers felt cold and crumbly, like a half-frozen fishcake.

'You know what I just might do.' She looked at him imploringly.

'Cut and run.'

'However did you guess?' Alice put her case for this cowardly behaviour with all earnestness. She should never have come in the first place. She absolutely must read the mountains of material sent by Ivo's office and from the Prison Reform Trust and Nacro, besides making some essential calls to two or three personal contacts she'd dredged up.

'Open and shut case.' Guy still held her hand in his comforting grasp. 'How are you going to make your escape? Helicopter? Foot? Harry's car? Pumpkin turned to coach? Brendan won't let you go easily.'

Alice felt a horribly revealing flush turning her face and neck from green to crimson. 'He is quite keen on getting his way,' she muttered weakly.

'I'd invent an illness in the family. What about your aged father? You could pretend you're going to Brighton, then scuttle off to London.' He was smiling.

Alice thought he liked the idea of doing down Brendan but was far too taken up with her own situation to consider this. 'I mean, I'm not his prisoner.'

'Certainly not. I'll back you up. Just remind me of your father's name?'

'Bingo Featherstone. He was a doctor.'

'Dr Bingo Featherstone, you're due to have a minor stroke at breakfast.'

Unfortunately there was no sign of Brendan at breakfast. Ivo was hugely present, stuffing himself with fried eggs on toast and bacon. Judging by the pile of disordered papers beside him – including the *News of the World* – he had devoured the morning's news as well.

'Where's our host?' asked Guy, helping himself to kippers.

'Church, nine thirty. Town. He's a Papist born and bred. Back at eleven.' The politician returned to the matter in hand. 'The opposition's half-baked proposal for secure hostel accommodation for young offenders, whatever that might be, hasn't caused much of a stir, I'm glad to see.'

Alice saw he was looking for a response from her but she lowered her head quickly and poured a meagre amount of cornflakes into a bowl. When she raised her eyes again Guy, who was sitting opposite her, gave her a huge wink.

Two more guests came into the room, two women whom Alice had hardly spoken to. Seeing more responsive prey, Ivo began to lecture them about the causes of violent crime.

Like conspirators, Alice and Guy whispered over the silver coffee pot on the sideboard. 'That's screwed it,' said Alice.

'On the contrary. It smooths the way. I'll drive you to the station and deliver your explanatory note on my return.'

'Do you really think I could?'

'Just remember your poor old father.'

The sky was still grey as they sped along the country lanes. Alice's escape from Brendan was making her feel as carefree as a truant schoolgirl. She admired the tall grasses at the side of the road, bleached yellow by the weeks of hot sun. They passed through a small village and she admired the unusually pointed church spire with a weathercock on top. She admired Guy's profile. It looked *wholesome*, she decided, enjoying the word.

'I've never asked you before, but how did a sporty chap like you get into the snake-pit of journalism – moreover, into the grip of the Master? And, even worse, condemn yourself to that dreadful office for five days a week? Or is it six or seven?'

'I love journalism. If I wasn't a journalist, I'd be a beachcomber.'

It was while Alice was considering this unlikely reply that a shiny and substantial car drove into view coming towards them. Guy muttered imprecations under his breath.

The two cars crossed and Alice could see Brendan peering out of the back window with a paper folded on his knee. Guy drove on rather faster. 'They'll follow us, of course.'

'Let's stop and wait for them and I can explain about poor old Bingo.'

'We've no choice.' Guy slowed down abruptly. 'They've turned round.'

'Phew,' said Alice. Her earlier panic had subsided and she was ready to face him. 'Let's pull over.'

Guy did so, and she sprang out of the car. 'I'm so sorry! My poor father!' She almost ran towards Brendan, exclamations and explanations pouring from her lips.

'My dear Alice, what has happened?' Brendan stood still. He was wearing a soft blue jacket that matched his eyes and he looked nothing like the bestial seducer who had dominated her night-time and early-morning imaginings. His expression was of concern and affection.

'It's my father,' stumbled Alice, 'he's had a minor stroke in Brighton. I got the news on my mobile and Guy's kindly taking me to the station. I left a note.'

'I'm so sorry.' Brendan came towards Alice and put his arm round her. At his touch, her traitorous body performed the sort of warm, relaxing exercises that follow a successful sexual encounter. The truth was, she wanted him to enfold her in his arms and carry her away to some safe and sexy place.

He held her away and looked into her face. She found she was glad Guy had stayed in the car. 'But of course you must go to your father. Why don't you let Harry drive you to Brighton?'

'No,' gasped Alice. 'I mean the train's so quick, and I can work on it.'

'Then you'll let him put you on the train. I'll hitch a ride with Guy.'

So Brendan let her go, as if by giving her Harry he'd taken over her journey.

Alice's flat seemed very empty. The grey day had entered the rooms and the white curtains hung limp even when she opened the balcony windows. She had surrounded herself with worthy literature on the problems of dealing with youth violence but her concentration was nil. Whole pages passed without her taking in a word.

'Mitzi! I'm so glad you're in.' Dialling Mitzi had seemed like an excellent idea. What a pleasure to pour out her new nymphomaniac tendencies, so obscure in a previously steady wife and grandmother! Even before she began, she felt the relief of words and laughter. Mitzi never took anything too seriously.

'Thank God, Alice. Don't you pick up any messages any more? My life's been in absolute *turmoil* and I've been *desperate* to talk to you. Greg has run away because Hughie spent the night here. At least, he did run away but he's come back on condition I absolutely promise never to see his father again. It's like I have to choose between my son or my . . . Well, I don't know what Hughie is any more. Except that he actually seems to be working to get me back. Which must mean something, mustn't it? I feel as if I'm living in one of those *horrible* episodes of *EastEnders*, all mixed up in a great bubbling cauldron of drama. You've got to help me, Alice. What I need is some of your wise-woman talk.'

Half an hour later, Alice was about to put down the telephone when Mitzi stopped her with a 'Hey, Alice. I've been meaning to tell you . . .'

'What?' said Alice wearily.

'You know you mentioned that friend, working colleague whatever, that guy called Guy, when you were listing the men in your life? Well, I met him the very next day. Wasn't that odd?'

'Where did you meet him?'

'We gave a bribery-type lunch for a few well-placed newspaper people. He was one of them. I would have remembered earlier except for everything that's going on with Hughie. He talked about you.'

'He talked about me!' Why was she so surprised? So pleased? 'How did you make the connection?'

'You forget, it's a small world. He thinks you're terrific.'

'Terrific in what way?' This was Guy, her colleague Guy, Mitzi was talking about.

'What do you mean, "*in what way*"? In what way does any man think a woman's terrific? *In that way.* Honestly, Alice.'

'I'm sorry. Thanks for telling me. I could do with being thought terrific. I was going to tell you what happened today. Guy was there too—'

But now Mitzi had delivered her message, she lost interest. 'Actually I thought he was terrific, too, but given my taste in men . . .'

Fearful that she was starting up on her husband again, Alice said goodbye and, even more distracted than before, turned back to her papers. '"The Chief Inspector's report on Holloway Prison includes information that seventy-five per cent of new inmates were found to be suffering from some form of identifiable mental disorder . . ."' she read aloud to see if it would help it sink in. But her voice echoed in the empty room. She stood and went over to the window. It was four o'clock. If she had been going to Brighton, she would be there now. It was not a very reputable act, using her father as an excuse to avoid her lover, but it had been Guy's suggestion, not hers. He had organised it.

Alice stared out at nothing very much and felt a mounting panic. What if her father really had had a minor stroke and Sister Mary Rose hadn't been able to find her? Alice dialled the nursing-home number with trembling fingers. It was all a punishment for allowing her life to get into such a muddle.

'Hello.'

She didn't recognise the voice. 'It's Dr Featherstone's daughter here. I'm just checking how he is.'

'I guess he's asleep just now.'

'He's fine, then?' It was such a relief to find her urgency sounding ridiculous.

'Oh, yes, perhaps a little disappointed his ladyfriend still hasn't come back.'

'His ladyfriend? Are you . . . ?' Alice racked her brains for the name of the sister who'd been on duty when the mysterious woman had taken Bingo for a walk.

'I'm Sister Obu. I know it turned out wrong but she was a lovely lady. Next time I'll send a nurse along with them.'

'Thank you,' said Alice, preparing to ring off.

'Just a minute, dear. I knew there was something. A man rang for you earlier. Didn't give his name when I said you weren't here. That must have been where you got your idea Dr Featherstone wasn't too well. This man seemed quite certain he'd had a stroke.'

'Thank you,' Alice repeated weakly, and put down the telephone. Of course Brendan would ring, whether he was concerned or suspicious. But he shouldn't have. Alice felt angry. He should have rung her mobile like any normal friend.

Alice threw aside the papers, found her handbag and left the flat. Her earlier tiredness had been replaced with a restless energy. She was seldom in London on Sunday but she liked the feeling that the weighty populace of workers had been swapped for lighter, more adventurous spirits. Although she had come out with no plan, except to pick up some milk and bread, she headed briskly for Kensington Gardens.

She sat on the bench facing the unrippled stretch of water and, beyond it, a statue of Queen Victoria in front of Kensington Palace. To get to the pond she had passed the elaborate Peter Pan playground built in memory of Diana, Princess of Wales, and now she was facing the battleground where that unhappy marriage had been fought.

Alice's earlier restlessness had gone, leaving her with a sense of loneliness and desolation. All the passers-by spoke in foreign languages, or so it seemed to her, increasing her feeling of alienation.

Alice reached for her mobile. As she did so, she sensed that someone was trying to attract her attention. She looked up. A man was waving at the other side of the pond, walking towards the trees on her right. But the sun was low and gave the water a metallic gleam, which confused her. Besides, he was not advancing towards her as a friend would do.

'Hello. Hello. Alice.'

Guy had answered her call and seen her name on his fascia. She felt unnerved.

'Guy. How are things?'

'Fine. Much tennis. Ivo broke another racquet, although this time by chance. Brendan retired victorious but hurt.'

'Hurt?'

'He pulled a muscle. Said he'd had a sleeplesss night. He went off in search of a physio. He's not back yet. How are you?'

'Fine.'

'And the dear old doctor?'

'Actually, I'm not sure that was such a brilliant idea. Brendan rang the home and discovered I wasn't there and my father isn't ill.'

'It doesn't matter, does it? It'll just convince Brendan that you're not very interested in him.'

Alice could hardly disagree. Besides, her attention was diverted towards the dark trees into which the strangely familiar figure had merged.

'Guy,' she said slowly, 'I think I just saw Blue.'

There was a long beat of silence before Guy spoke. 'That's most unlikely.'

'I know. I know.'

'Where are you?'

'In Kensington Gardens. By the pond. He was miles away, the other side of the water, and the sun was in my eyes.'

'There you are. Of course I wish it were true.'

'Yes.' There seemed nothing more to say but Alice was unwilling to ring off. 'I suppose his young offenders' project's been put on hold?'

'I assume so. I don't really know much about it.'

'No.' But surely he had been the first person to tell her about the project when he'd been persuading her to interview Blue? 'You never told me you met a friend of mine on Friday.'

'You're quite right. I didn't. I liked her.'

'She liked you too.' How foolish that sounded.

'Must go. Packing and journey to London.'

'Of course.' But Alice made one last remark, a bid for sympathy, she supposed. 'Things were never like this when Richard was alive.' So far she had only thought it. Out in the air, it sounded pathetic.

Guy's voice had an unmistakable smiling tone. 'From what you told me at the time, your late husband did veer towards over-protectiveness.'

Alice walked through the dark trunks of trees into which the probably-not-Blue apparition had disappeared. Close to, they were quite pale and speckled with scaling bark. As if they had a disease, thought Alice.

She was surprised by her mobile ringing. She must have forgotten to turn it off as had become her habit.

'Alice.'

'Jonathan.' Why did he always make her feel guilty now? It wasn't her fault that he'd fallen in love with her.

'Just checking you've remembered our date on Wednesday.'

'Of course,' she lied.

'How was your weekend?'

Neither did she remember informing him about that. 'Fine. On Saturday night we went to a dinner organised by the Jane Austen Society.'

'That doesn't sound like Sir Brendan's style.'

'I wouldn't know him well enough to tell.'

'And you're safely back in your flat?'

There was a definite question mark. 'Yes,' she lied, again.

'I'm in court all day so I'll meet you there, if you don't mind.'

There was a pause, which Alice gradually recognized as meaningful. 'See you—'

'Sometimes I imagine,' interrupted Jonathan, in a heavy voice, 'that when Richard died he left me to look after you.'

He had said such things before but never so forcefully and Alice found herself acutely irritated. 'Oh, I don't think so,' she said, and turned off her mobile.

But in a way he was right. Richard and he had been so close, such old friends, that sometimes they seemed to speak with one voice. She remembered an evening, perhaps ten years ago, when she and Richard had gone to Covent Garden to see a new production of *Don Giovanni* and had unexpectedly met Jonathan as they went upstairs to the bar. It was still the old Covent Garden then, and the two men had stood close together, each with a hand on the golden banisters, making fun of the Don whose voice was not matched by his figure. She had thought they were like brothers and, for a couple of minutes, had felt completely cut out, until both, as if realising at the same moment, had turned to her and asked her opinion. They had listened politely when she gave it, as if to a stranger.

Chapter Seventeen

A Third Monday

Every ugly inch a minister, Ivo Swayne sat at the end of a long table, flanked by his private secretary and a press officer. Alice tried not to smile as she pictured him standing, furious, over his broken tennis racquet. Already he had submitted to being photographed, showing a surprising amount of personal vanity as he folded his arms and set his lips, and was now looking expectantly at his press officer – a woman so fat that the arms of her chair were lost in her folds.

Alice, too, looked expectantly at the woman. She was feeling delightfully strong this morning and too old a hand to rush in with her questions.

'The minister apologises, but the hour he promised you must be reduced to forty minutes.'

This was obviously a punishment for witnessing his humiliation on the tennis court and then running away. 'I was hoping to accompany him to Wandsworth prison later.'

'I see.' The personal secretary came round to the press officer and they had a private little chat. Meanwhile Ivo looked as if he were somewhere else. 'I'm afraid I hadn't been informed of that,' admitted the press officer. 'I understood you were talking about youth crime.'

'Mainly,' agreed Alice, hedging. She looked at her watch ostentatiously. Soon her forty minutes would be reduced to thirty.

'I think we'd better begin and settle this later,' said the minister. Now everybody looked at Alice.

She always enjoyed this moment, poised on the edge of her dig, an archaeologist about to excavate the truth. 'I understand you had no experience of prisons before you took on this job?' It was an aggressive question but, then, Ivo was an aggressive man. Besides, she knew that being prisons minister was considered an insalubrious job, best avoided if at all possible.

'I've put it on record that I intend to visit a prison every day I'm in office.'

'And have you managed it?'

Ivo turned to his private secretary. 'Have I managed it?'

'There have been very few cancellations, Minister.'

'Thank you.'

This exchange set the pattern for the rest of the interview. Ivo either quoted himself, as if Alice should have already known the answer, or if put on the spot turned to his private secretary and, occasionally, his press secretary to supply the answers. As forty minutes approached, Alice found herself relieved to end the charade. He had uttered nothing but platitudes. Although she was recording him, she had also taken some notes, the shorthand filling the space beside her questions. 'Education as the foundation for rehabilitation', 'Removal from families and peer group', 'Care in the community developed into a seamless joined-up policy'. Words, all words. She waited, hopefully, to be shown out, but now Ivo was enjoying the sound of his voice. Where was his urgent appointment? thought Alice dismally.

At last she was being hurried out. 'So,' the private secretary faced her in the corridor, 'you want to come to Wandsworth with us?'

'Yes,' agreed Alice, without enthusiasm.

'There may be a security problem.'

'Can't the prisons minister vouch for his guests?'

'Prisons have their own rules. I'll let you know by lunchtime.'

Alice went back to her flat, but she didn't bother sketching out her interview. Without a prison visit, it was nothing. Unless, of course, she used her experience of him over the weekend. Alice sat in front of her computer. 'Ivo Swayne is a very ambitious man. It's easy to know that because he's such a bad loser. And a coward. Our first meeting was in a helicopter when his usually rubicund face quickly turned green. Our second was on the tennis court when the minister raised the art of racquet abuse to a new level . . .' Alice amused herself in this vein for some time. It was just a pity her paper was not scurrilous – at least, did not wish to be thought scurrilous. Now she would write up Ivo's seduction of the drunken Jane Austen Society chairman's wife. 'Although not blessed by good looks or charm, the minister's approach to women is characterised by absolute confidence, which leads to some unlikely successes . . .' Time passed merrily in this way until the telephone rang.

'You're on. Wandsworth entrance at two. Bring identification and no camera or mobile.'

Alice had never been into a prison before and never thought it odd that she hadn't. But the moment she had passed between the outer world and the inner, delivered via a process of sealed chambers that might have sent her equally to the deepest ocean, she found herself amazed that she had never been curious.

'Here we are.' The cheery prison officer had brought her to a large room, murkily lit, which held twenty or so men, plus the press officer: several prison officers, Ivo Swayne plus his entourage, and a large group dressed identically in blue and white striped shirts and blue trousers – presumably the prisoners. Ivo, with a bored expression on his face, was being introduced to a couple at a time.

Suddenly he spotted Alice. In contrast to his cold, formal manner in his office, he sprang towards her, arms spread, almost as if he wanted to give her a hug. The prisoner, interrupted in mid-flow, looked crestfallen and took a step back.

'Alice! You came!' He did kiss her, although not with a hug.

Alice thought he must dislike prison-visiting a great deal to be so welcoming. 'Of course. I had to see you on the job, didn't I?'

'Ah, you're a cruel woman,' replied the minister, leaving Alice to wonder what he meant.

Meanwhile, his escort, probably a prison governor, had caught up with him and, after introductions, led him back to the prisoners, with Alice following.

His visit was to be brief, it seemed, and he had already completed a walkabout. Tea appeared, brought in by further inmates who were also introduced to the minister and allowed a moment to say their piece.

Alice, to give herself a role, took a few notes: '. . . word-processor access has made studying much easier . . . pre-release courses definitely a good idea . . . being able to be involved in organised

drama most rewarding'. They certainly seemed a satisfied represen-
tation of HMP's customers, but she wondered how any of it would
help her interview. At one point she tried edging an inmate out of
the group so she could talk to him privately, but Ivo instantly called
her back: 'Alice, I know you'll want to hear what Doug has to
say . . .' Not long afterwards, the visit was over.

'The minister says can we give you a lift anywhere?' The press
officer, the overflowing large lady, approached Alice.

'Thank you.'

Alice left the prison feeling no wiser about its affairs than when
she had entered. Nor, she believed, could Ivo have been much
better informed.

'You know what I truly believe?' Ivo's eyes bulged towards her.
They were settled in the back of his car, with the press officer
having joined the female chauffeur in the front. 'All music is
orgasmic.' He assessed the effect of this pronouncement on Alice,
who overcame her surprise and laughed caustically. 'Whatever
made you think of that?' she asked.

'I think about it night and day.' He was very serious.

'Music?'

'Sex.' His voice was triumphant, like a schoolboy learning to
pronounce the word. 'Take Beethoven's Grosse Fugue in B. It
winds up and up and up. A kind of exquisite torture looking for
happy relief.'

If this assertion was true, it might explain Jonathan's passionate
declaration after an evening of music.

'Have you no comment?'

'I'd like to ask you a few more questions about your vision for a
better-functioning prison service.' Primly, Alice produced her tape-
recorder.

'Restorative justice. Those are the two words I want you to note.
It's the way of the future. Taking into account the victim. The
young offender must meet and take into account the offended-
against.'

Alice listened as, fluently, he detailed this new initiative, and
supposed that now she had a bit of meat to her interview. She was
still in professional listening mode when he abruptly turned off the
tape-recorder and leant very close. 'I need to talk to you about
Brendan. Off the record. You understand?'

'No.'

Ivo frowned and nodded towards the driver and the press officer. Alice was about to raise her voice even louder when he whispered in her ear, 'You can't pretend you don't know him, unless you make a habit of sleeping with strangers.'

Alice was outraged. 'I never discuss my private life and I know nothing about Brendan's work or personal life that could possibly be of any use to you. That is to say, I know nothing. Full stop.'

'I see.' Ivo leant forward and tapped the press officer on the shoulder. 'Barbara, dear, do you remember I told you about this coffee bar that serves fab Viennese coffee topped with real cream and dark chocolate flakes? Well, it just happens we're about to pass it. Helga, love, would you mind?'

The car stopped and, before Alice could take in what was happening, Barbara had been ejected into a noisy South London street. Alice turned on Ivo furiously: 'If you think I was holding back because of that poor girl, you're quite wrong. Anyway, we're still not alone.'

'Helga, I have the feeling you'd like to listen to some loud music.' He added, in a whisper, 'Helga's terribly butch but she won't admit it.'

'Correct, Minister,' said the driver, switching on the radio.

'You're so childish.' Alice glowered out of the window. Had Brendan told Ivo about their night together or was it merely speculation? 'I think I'll get out myself.'

'The car will take you wherever you want after dropping me off. Seriously, I'll tell you something, Brendan's got himself into big trouble and my job is to see it doesn't harm the government.'

'I thought your job was to be prisons' minister?'

'That, too.' Ivo suddenly became patient and understanding. 'You see, the whole thing is too much of a coincidence. You have to be involved or at least know something. It's not just Brendan but Guy Vernon – *and* you interviewed this Blue Carroway, who seems to be at the heart of the whole business.'

Alice wanted to ask, 'What business?' but thought he might construe this as encouragement. The truth was, she agreed with him: it did seem too much of a coincidence that these three men, linked in some way she didn't understand, had recently become, in one way or another, important in her life. 'I've known Guy for ages. I work with him.'

'On your newspaper.' Ivo sighed. 'If you lot would leave us alone, we could do our job a sight better.'

'You asked to be interviewed.'

'If you can't beat them, join them.' Ivo sighed again, more deeply. In fact, he seemed to be sliding fast into melancholy, his jowly face falling further towards his paunchy stomach.

'Is this on the record?'

'Everything about Brendan's off the record. I suppose he was a real between-the-sheets charmer?'

Alice turned away her face. They were going at quite a pace over Westminster Bridge so there was no escape.

'Jump. Break a leg. I've known women do it before.'

This turned out to be Ivo's final barb. He ordered Helga to turn off the music, which had been raging cheerfully throughout their conversation and produced a mobile on which he proceeded to make a date with a woman he called 'Sugar'.

Unfortunately Alice could only escape the minister's physical presence. She had to write up the interview with him as soon as she returned to her apartment. But she found herself incapable of starting. Remembered images were much stronger than puny computer-screen words: Brendan and Ivo competing on the tennis court, Brendan and her in bed – she had to get up for this one and wander round the flat until she found herself facing Brendan's huge bouquet of flowers, whose vibrant colours now seemed overpowering, even vulgar. In order to lower the emotional tone, she forced herself to consider the group of prisoners, shadowy in the neon lights of the prison. It was telling that twenty years of marriage to a barrister had not inspired one conscious thought about the potential prisoners that were his bread and butter, with a fair dollop of jam too.

Alice walked into the living room and sank down on the sofa. The landline telephone at her elbow rang.

'Alice. I'm so glad I've found you. How's your father?' It was Brendan.

Alice couldn't remember whether her father had suffered a heart-attack or a stroke. 'Fine,' she said. 'We're all fine.' She found a bit more energy. 'You were kind to ring the nursing home. As you gathered, it was all a bit of a storm in a teacup.'

'A storm in a teacup?' repeated Brendan, as if the words were in a foreign language.

A diversionary tack seemed needed. 'I spent most of today interviewing Ivo.'

'Ivo. Dear boy. I hope you two took the opportunity for a bit of bonding over the weekend. In the sadly short time you were with us. I've known him since he was nineteen. We were at Oxford together.'

Alice recalled her research on Brendan and was quite sure his education hadn't included three years at Oxford – or any university, if it came to that. Ivo was also considerably younger than him. 'What did he read?'

'Geography. Then he tried to be a businessman. Most unsuccessfully.' Brendan laughed. 'I think he wanted to be me.'

Alice, the interviewer, thought how little she had learnt about Ivo. She might as well face the fact that she didn't *want* to know. Curiosity was an interviewer's most important weapon. Without it, there was nothing but questions and answers. When she was married, she had gone out from her quiet home, like a warrior, bristling with nosy determination.

'I called to ask you out to dinner. I've a table booked at the Ivy.'

'I've absolutely got to write up this interview with your old mate.' Alice heard the whine in her voice and remembered how Brendan made her feel cared-for, which resulted, it seemed, in childish weakness. 'I don't like the Ivy,' she added. 'I'm afraid I'm in a bad mood.'

'You work too hard. No one should work in the evenings. It's bad for the metabolism. Dearest Alice.'

Alice felt her body respond to his voice. 'Dearest Alice,' he had said. He would never even pretend to love her. She knew that instinctively. He only wanted to *fuck* her. She pronounced the word to herself almost triumphantly. The trouble was, she wanted to fuck him.

'Shall I bring you round a glass of champagne to cheer you up?'

'No. No.' She cut him off. 'Not today. My interview . . .' Her voice sounded unconvincing even to her ears but he didn't try to persuade her further and rang off.

Alice felt even more gloomy than before he'd rung. She looked at her watch. Seven o'clock. Guy would still be at his desk. She would beg him to come round.

Guy walked into the flat as if he'd been there more than twice. Alice discovered she liked this attitude. Probably it was a measure of her loss of nerve over her piece. Not only over that.

'You look strange.'

'How strange?'

'Distraught. I never thought you were a distraught sort of person.'

'Let's have a drink.'

They sat on the sofa with their glasses and Alice felt disinclined to answer his unspoken query. 'It was very nice of you to help me escape yesterday.' Had it really only been yesterday?

'Come to think of it, you were on the road to being distraught yesterday. How can I help? Write your article? Pull out one of your back-drawer items? Or go the whole hog and tell the Master you've had a stroke? These things run in families, you know.'

Alice looked at Guy consideringly. Every time she saw him now she was struck by his regular up-and-down good looks and the peculiarity of her not having noticed them before. 'Have you changed your glasses recently?'

'What? No. So, what's it to be? Substitution, evasion or sudden death?'

'I thought you were an editor, not a writer?'

Guy smiled. 'Leader writers don't get a signature.'

'So that's why you're so close to the Master.'

'We went to school together.'

Alice was amazed. 'You never told me that before either! I always imagined he was born at the desk as a ready-made twenty-four-hours-a-day editor. You know what Brendan told me today? He and Ivo were friends at Oxford.'

'That's the only part of the story I know isn't true.'

'What story?'

Guy looked into his glass, which was empty. 'I thought you might know quite a bit.'

Alice's mood of pent-up dissatisfaction exploded. 'I don't know anything. I don't know what the link is between Brendan and Ivo. I don't know what the link is between you and them. I don't know who Blue was or why he disappeared. I don't know the first thing about anything or anyone.' Her voice rose alarmingly, then fell suddenly flat. 'I don't even know who my mother was.'

Guy stared, amazed.

'I've no idea what that was about,' Alice muttered. Silently, he took her hand.

'I'm sorry.' Alice tried to compose herself. 'It comes down to my inability to write this piece. I simply can't miss a second week.' Alice stood up, reluctantly detaching herself from the warm and tender hand. She went over to the telephone. 'Guess what I'm going to do?'

'Have another glass of wine.'

'That's a good idea too.' She picked up the receiver. She knew the Master never left his desk before ten when the paper was put to bed. 'Is the editor there? It's Alice with something urgent.' '*Urgent for whom?*' she could imagine him saying.

'Yup.' That was how he talked. Without even a question-mark, forcing you to provide question, answer and proposition.

'I'm not delivering this week either. I've blown out. My granddaughter was kidnapped. My father had a stroke. Ivo is a pig.' Alice gathered momentum. 'I'm fed up with talking to conceited men who are all liars anyway. I'm not giving notice, Ted, but I need a break. I *deserve* a break.' She had never dared speak like this to him before. She should be proud of herself. Ted was his real name. In person he was unassuming, grey to the point of disappearing.

'For how long?'

Alice almost laughed. She could imagine him making a note. 'Alice out of order. Replacement?'

'Three weeks.'

'We'll call it "away on holiday", then. Have a good time.'

He had put down the telephone. Alice wondered what it felt like to be quite so single-minded. She might have been about to commit suicide, after all.

A mobile rang in Guy's pocket. He took it out, seemed about to cut it and then changed his mind. 'Guy here.' He listened. Alice felt only slightly curious. The conversation was brief. 'Certainly,' said Guy, and put away his phone. He smiled at Alice. 'Don't you want to know who that was?'

'I've lost all curiosity, particularly about men. I need a holiday.' Alice sat down close to him.

'It was the Master. He wants me to get your notes on Ivo so someone else can write it up.'

'That takes the biscuit! Are you telling me that I'm so utterly unimportant, just a recording-machine in fact—'

'You know how papers work, Alice.'

'Oh, do I? Do I?' But of course the Master would want the interview. It was the measure of her collapse that even with this she couldn't face writing up her notes herself. 'I'll hand them over but only if you write up the story. I don't want that Polly Omar messing about with my stuff.'

'Fine,' said Guy, who had remained annoyingly calm. 'I'm going to take you out to dinner now. Italian, Indian, French or Greek?'

'Not Greek. Blue and I went Greek.'

It wasn't until they were settled into Mario's, an Italian restaurant which, with its Chianti bottles strung overhead in fishing nets, seemed to have been left over from the sixties, that Guy followed up Alice's comment.

'I'd forgotten you had dinner with Blue. Or perhaps you never told me.'

Alice regretted this indiscretion. 'Oh, please don't talk about Blue. It's just too dreadful. I couldn't have seen him in the park, could I?'

'No. It is dreadful.' Guy was meditative. 'Did you know Brendan was supposedly backing him?'

'People say all sorts of things.' Alice was wary. It provided some protection from the memories of her night of love with Blue. She could not and would not deny the joy but she'd rather not dwell on it, just at the moment. Perhaps, she thought, trying to be wry, Guy felt the same emotions.

'As a matter of fact, in my view Brendan is quite a dangerous man,' he said. 'Do you remember when the tree was struck by lightning and fell into the swimming-pool?'

'You can't blame him for where lightning strikes.' Surely Guy's role was to convince her of a benign world, not play out his own anxieties.

Guy ignored her comment. 'Just before the lightning struck, we'd been talking about Blue. I was very fond of Blue, you know.'

'Yes?'

'Of course, you didn't know him at all well.'

A strong desire to tell the truth tempted Alice, but at least one part of her journalistic training held firm: never stop a man half-way through his story. But as she leant forward a little to show interest, Guy picked up the menu, which took all his attention. Alice, who had been keen to avoid the subject of Blue a few minutes earlier, felt let down but still couldn't bring herself to probe. When she saw he definitely wasn't going to say any more, she sat back in her chair. 'I think I'll go to the seaside.'

Guy, still engrossed in the menu, spoke meditatively. 'Have you ever been to the Scilly Isles?'

'No.' Alice was surprised by the seriousness of his tone. The lighting was low and the candle on the table only reflected itself in his glasses. 'Do you recommend them?'

'Yes.' His voice was almost dreamy. 'If I wanted to get away from it all, I would choose the Scillies.'

'Good!' said Alice, energetically. If she could have set out at that moment, she would have. Somewhere in the back of her mind, she considered with satisfaction Brendan's discovery of her further flight. A new idea struck her. 'I promised Florrie to visit this weekend. Instead I shall whisk her off for a seaside holiday.'

'You may have trouble booking.'

'I'm not short of money.'

'No. Money isn't your problem.'

If the waiter hadn't arrived at this point, Alice might have thought more of the unpleasant word 'problem'.

Chapter Eighteen

A Third Tuesday

Alice drove out of London in a confident way. That was a relief. She could still do something confidently. When Guy had left her the night before she had scuttled about the flat, throwing clothes and books into a suitcase, making calls to Florrie and Peter – one excited at the prospect of an all-paid-for holiday by the sea, the other sensibly anxious at her announcement that she'd lost it. Mothers shouldn't say such things to their sons, she regretted briefly, then decided that Peter needed a bit of shaking up. 'I'm inviting you to come,' she'd told him, but he'd talked of work and Jennie until she'd stopped listening.

So here she was at Chiswick already and it was only seven o'clock. Since she was heading west the sun had risen behind her, a promising glow in her rear-view mirror, which was fast dispelling an equally promising hazy mist. She would like heat now she was on holiday. There were niggles, of course, a slight backache reminding her that her period was due – not many years left for that sort of nonsense, she thought, with satisfaction. Her father, to whom she had managed to speak, had reacted selfishly to her announcement that Peter would be coming to see him on Saturday as a replacement for her usual Thursday visit. 'I am old but not senile,' he had said, 'and know the difference between you and my grandson, and Thursday and Saturday. And I suppose you've made sure *she* isn't coming either?' Alice had refused to consider this 'she' with the seriousness her frightened heart suggested so merely added, probably falsely, 'And Peter's bringing Jennie too.'

Then there was the question of Jonathan and the concert they were supposedly attending the next day. But tomorrow was another day. In fact, for three whole days Alice was entirely free since there was no room on Tresco, the Scilly island picked by Guy, until Friday when Florrie and the rest would join her. She had half-heartedly rung Mitzi, who'd been amazed at the invitation to a few days' holiday by the sea. 'I'm a working woman, you know that, and I'm tiptoeing towards a seriously important account.' At least she hadn't brought up her odious, hopefully still-ex-husband.

As she reached the M4, an unbroken river of traffic coming the other way – workers heading for London – raised her spirits an extra notch. Why had it taken her so long to see that although work and weekly scheduling were important, regular release was essential to avoid a regime becoming a stranglehold? Alice smiled again as she heard herself repeat this as a mantra to Richard, who had hardly understood life outside work.

Alice began to sing, snatches from *Oklahoma!*. She'd found the record in a cupboard as a child and played it quietly in her room to avoid her father's disapproval. The sun rose higher, warming the car till she wound down her window and pressed open the roof, allowing noisy air to come rushing through. In such natural exuberance of light and wind, Alice drove for several hours until she realised suddenly that she must stop for a break. Her hands were shaking on the wheel.

The Little Chef served a healthy mix of sausages, bacon, egg, tomatoes and mushrooms. Alice felt as if she hadn't eaten for days, which made her recall last night's outing with Guy. It had ended strangely. After acting like a true friend by suggesting the holiday in the Scillies and even helping her book via the Internet on their return to the flat, he had become withdrawn and almost cold, muttering bitterly, 'The sea is nothing but a delusion. It corrupts everyone in the end. How about changing plans and heading for the Spanish plains?' Alice had laughed, upon which he'd looked at her with what she interpreted as dislike. This was a *Blue* moment in every way, she decided, but before she could summon sympathy he had left, hardly bothering to say goodbye. It had reminded her of his dash from the Privy Council, after which Jonathan had laconically declared that Guy and Blue had clearly been in a gay relationship. She couldn't bring herself to take the idea seriously, yet Guy had worn the same haunted look of despair.

The sun was stretching itself into gold streamers over the sea. Alice parked the car near the St Mawes harbour wall and got out stiffly. So this was where she had ended up, on the bit of the coast where Guy kept his boat, from where Blue had sailed and not returned. It must have been in her mind all along, but she hadn't admitted it to herself until the last couple of hours when she'd had to study the map and find her way. 'Excuse us.' Two large, sunburnt boys, with tousled sea-going hair and faded shorts, knocked into her with some bit of a ship they were carrying.

Alice felt small and fragile. She told herself it was the effect of the long drive, but actually it was the reality of St Mawes. She had pictured a romantic fishing village, more or less cut off from the world, but on this hot afternoon in August it was as crowded as Oxford Street. Even the sea, illuminated by the sun's rays, was a writhing mass – here she knew she exaggerated – of sailing boats, motorboats and water-skiers.

'Sorry.' Another procession of over-healthy young men, plus a couple of indistinguishable girls, passed by. They were all going the same way. Alice glanced behind her and saw a plain building with wide glass windows facing towards the sea; it proclaimed itself the Yacht Club.

Looking for a way down to the beach, Alice moved further towards the harbour. She was trying to picture Blue in this environment. His seductive blue shorts and gold chain were quite different from anything she was likely to meet here. Guy would fit in easily enough, but never Blue.

At last Alice found her way past the harbour to the shingly beach. She could see now that the speedboats and water-skiers had almost gone and the sailing boats, too, were turning in or finding moorings on the other side of the bay. If she sat down long enough, the scene of frenzied activity would clear and she'd find a little peace. So she sat and soon the sea had almost emptied and a dusky cloud was creeping over the sky.

'Hi. Haven't seen you here before?'

Alice had always been pleased, if not exactly flattered, that she'd never been the sort of woman men tried to pick up. Stares yes, pick-ups no. She'd decided that her hair, so very richly red and thick, acted as a warning beacon. But this man – young, with tousled black hair, one earring, dark sunburn – was sitting down beside her with the air of a chap who intended to stay.

'Where are you staying? Polvarth, I expect. They get all the pretty ones up there.'

Alice found she was pleased with this compliment. After all, she'd driven the whole day and wasn't wearing a scrap of make-up.

'You're local, are you?'

'Born and bred.' He waved his arm vaguely behind and to their right. He brought out two cans of beer from a plastic bag. 'Want one?'

'No, thanks.'

'I prefer to eat my dinner on the beach, rain or shine. My name's Squid. What's yours?'

'Alice. I wouldn't mind a swig of beer if the offer's still open.' Her heart was thudding madly as she took the can. She knew her next line but she needed a bit of extra courage. 'You haven't come across a diver called Blue Carroway?'

'Blue Carroway!' He was looking at her with amazement. 'Everybody round here knows the name and a good many of them the man himself.'

'Oh, I see. I was just interested.'

'It was in the news.' He seemed delighted to find someone he could instruct in the history of Blue Carroway. 'He's a famous deep-sea diver who sailed out from St Mawes and never came back. Murdered. Could be.' Abruptly, Squid lay back on the pebbles and shut his eyes.

Alice stared at him. He was drunk or high, she guessed. The bag was filled with cans. She mustn't believe anything he told her. Blue had been on the news, as he'd said. Anyone could make up stories about him. On the other hand St Mawes was a small place. 'Was he a friend of yours?'

'I know things about Blue Carroway.' He spoke without changing his position, eyes still closed. 'I even know where the boat – or what's left of it – has been impounded by the police. I can take you to it, if you like.'

Why should he make this offer to a stranger? It sounded like a child's boasting. A chill wind blowing off the sea made Alice shiver.

It was when they got out of her car and climbed a padlocked gate before crossing a field towards a ramshackle shed that Alice thought of Detective Constable Susan Paradise. How could she, Alice, ever explain away her decision to see Blue's boat? A journalist's curiosity to follow an unexpected lead? Ahead of her, Squid was bounding cheerfully along, the remaining beer cans rattling against each other in their bag. With a guilty urge to hide, she wished the sky would darken just a little – but there was still brightness all around, even in the pools of water on the sand at the edge of the sea, far away now at low tide, even in the yellow grasses growing round the shed. *That* was black enough, and far more substantial than it had appeared at a distance.

'This side!' called Squid.

The doors were at the front, heavily barred, but he was calling from the far side. 'See? There's a slice of rotted panel. You can look right inside. How much closer to tragedy can you get?'

Quite a bit closer actually. Alice had assumed they would get inside the shed so she could touch the shattered wood, imagine the fierce scene, if there had been one, that had taken place there. Peering through a crack in the wall made her feel like a peeping Tom.

Alice peered. As her eyes got used to the gloom, she heard Squid open a can of beer behind her. 'I can't make out much,' she said. But then she could: the boat was far bigger than she'd expected, barely squeezing into the shed. Its outlines were smoothly intact, the damage, as far as she could tell, confined to the dark middle of the interior.

'Most of the mast went, of course, smashed, lost in the water, and a lot of the cabin.' He was talking over her shoulder. She smelt his beery breath.

'But why do they suspect foul play?' The words sounded absurd. 'There was a dreadful storm when he was at sea. I was in it myself.' Again, Alice recalled the terrifying moment when the tree had crashed into Brendan's swimming-pool.

'He was too good a sailor to let a storm dish him. Then there's no body. And there's the gossip.'

Alice jumped, not because Squid had delivered these words with meaningful weight but because he had put his hand on her neck. 'Don't do that!'

He stepped back several paces, tripping over his bag of beer, which he'd put on the ground. 'Sorry. Sorry.'

'That's not why I came here,' said Alice, severely. 'I'm sorry if I misled you.'

'Yeah. Yeah. Next thing you'll accuse me of rape and I'll be thrown in prison. Look, you can walk on me, if you like.'

Alice stared as he collapsed among the grasses. 'You're drunk,' she said.

'I had a bad day.'

'I've had a bad two weeks.' Alice wondered if this was true. 'Bad' was definitely not the right word.

'It's a cruel world.' He turned on his elbow to stare up at her. 'You know why Blue Carroway died?'

'But that's not certain!'

'If he did die,' amended Squid. 'It's because of a big fish round here called Sir Brendan Costa.'

After this, Alice felt certain about her next course of action. 'That hotel you mentioned, I've forgotten its name. I think we should go there and find something to eat. I'm starving and getting cold.'

Alice longed to leave the shed now. It loomed darkly over the evening with its cargo, which she could hardly make out and didn't wish to try further, of smashed bones. Didn't they talk of the bones, or perhaps the skeleton, of a boat?

Polvarth stood above the town, looking seawards with a long terrace planted with palms and filled with happy residents, some still eating delectable fish dishes.

At last the light was dropping. The sea had a purplish glow and there were no white sails to lighten it. Alice, at a table for two, looked about for Squid, who had vanished on their arrival at the hotel. Perhaps he had lost his nerve, thinking his battered jeans and T-shirt inappropriate for pink tablecloths and palm trees in terracotta pots. She felt too tired and relaxed, with a Campari-soda in her hand, to ask herself how much she cared.

'I'm back.'

Alice hardly recognised him: his T-shirt had been swapped for a well-ironed white shirt, his black hair was wet and slicked back.

'I sometimes work here,' he said, 'when things are slow.'

'So, what will you eat?'

'Do you know anything about diving?' Squid's question, delivered with some intensity, arrived at the same time as their lobster salad.

'I can scuba dive.'

'You asked if I was a friend of Blue's. A few years ago – well, six now – I went on a deep-sea diving expedition with him. I mean I met him there. He was at the top of his profession, I was just back-up, in case anyone had a serious case of the bends. No one did so I never went down. Just hung out.'

'What was the expedition?'

'It was treasure-seeking, although they didn't like to call it that. "Salvage" is a nicer-sounding word. The divers were going very deep. Nearly a thousand feet. They went down in what are called submersibles. To be honest, I wasn't sorry not to be called, although I wouldn't admit that to anyone but a sympathetic lady like you.' He gave Alice a roguish grin. 'Divers are a macho lot, British, Australian, American, German, they all know each other. They have to rely on each other underwater. There aren't many of the really good ones.'

'Why were *you* there?'

Squid sucked a lobster claw as if the question embarrassed him. Eventually he muttered, 'Someone must have dropped out at the last minute.'

Alice had her doubts about the whole story. 'What were they salvaging?'

'Gold.' Back on track, he let the word resonate. 'Not pieces of eight on some ransacked-through-the-ages Spanish galleon. Real solid-gold bullion. Thousands of shiny gold bars, sent by Stalin on a British ship during the second World War to pay the Russians' way. The ship was torpedoed and the gold went to the bottom of the Barents Sea, along with a good part of the crew. It made the news at one point. There was a bit of a row because the wreck had been declared a war grave. Maybe you remember.'

Alice reflected that Blue had referred to something similar. Now she could believe Squid again. 'The gold was raised?'

'Nearly fifty million's worth. I saw it stacked in a cabin. I even held a bar. At the beginning everyone was so excited.'

'I should think so!'

'It was a tough dive. The divers had to spend a week in the decompression chamber after they came up.'

'A week!' exclaimed Alice.

'Do you know what happens if you come out too quickly after a dive that deep?'

'Sort of.' Alice made an effort to recall Blue's description of the bends. 'Something to do with breathing a mixture of oxygen and something else and the something else taking time to disperse from the body.'

'Helium,' said Squid. 'It forms in bubbles in the tissues. A hundred years ago in Greece, coral sponge divers used to explode when they came up. The medics advise joint pains, paralysis and heart failure as risk factors. Our divers were careful about that but one of them caught a seabed ear infection and had to give up and another broke his hip in the diving bell. I tell you, watching all that scared the shit out of me.'

'Was Blue scared?' Alice only asked such an idiotic question to bring Squid back from the general.

'Nope.' He was suddenly silenced. Meanwhile the waiter arrived and asked for Alice's room number. She signed the bill.

'Can we just sit?'

'Of course we can sit,' answered Squid.

The waiter smiled, cleared their table, the last one, and left with a pile of tablecloths over his arm. 'They shut up shop so early,' said Squid, restlessly. 'Do you know who owns this hotel?'

Even before he told her, Alice remembered she knew. She had not done much homework on Blue before she saw him but she had been thorough with Brendan. Polvarth had been one of the properties whose complete renovation and redesign he had financed. He still owned it. 'I interviewed Brendan Costa,' she said. 'It's his, isn't it?'

'So *you* wrote that interview. He financed that expedition I was telling you about too. We were all on his payroll, although I suppose he raised the money from some poor suckers.'

Alice tried to keep a grasp on the facts. 'But they got their money. You told me. Millions of pounds' worth of gold.'

Squid looked out to sea. There was some light from the road below them but the water was an oily black. 'Shall I tell you something really strange? I can hardly believe it myself. Sir Brendan Costa is my father.'

Alice, leaning back in her chair, hand over her face despite the darkness, thought that the way her life was going she should have guessed it. Squid must be Jago – she could even remember his name

– Brendan's son by his first wife. She had got the impression that he was a playboy with fast boats and an irresponsible lifestyle.

'I can't think why I've told you. I hardly ever see him.'

'I'm sorry,' said Alice, from behind her hand.

'Just sometimes I get fed up,' Squid continued bitterly, 'at his becoming so successful when you consider the things he's done. At least I'm not a thief.' Suddenly he stood up. 'Oh, let's cut it. What's the point of whingeing? Nothing will change him and nothing will stop him and, to be honest, I don't give a fuck.'

He was going away, the story was not going to end. 'But Blue?' tried Alice.

Squid turned back. 'That's where I started all this, wasn't it? With Blue. You see, Blue knew what went on the ship, the ship stacked with gold bullion. All those years ago. And then he got fed up with hawking himself round the world and got this idea for a diving school.'

'For young offenders,' nudged Alice, as Squid became silent and took another step away.

'He was properly obsessed.' By now Squid had receded into the deeper darkness of a palm tree.

Alice could hardly see him. Was he trying to link Blue's disappearance with his father? With this expedition he'd financed?

'Squid! Don't go!' But she was too late. The palm tree waved its flat leaves in a negative gesture.

Chapter Nineteen

A Third Wednesday

Alice woke up slowly. It was nine o'clock. She'd slept for an age. The room was extraordinarily quiet, facing not to the sea but the garden. She could now see that the hill behind was an unusual oval shape, the burial ground, perhaps, of a Viking ship. The sky above it was lightly veiled with white clouds. Her long sleep had cleared her mood, bringing something near happiness or, at least, calm.

Alice went along to the almost empty dining room. Only an elderly couple, like twins with short white hair and trousers, ate toast and marmalade. She placed herself with a view outwards and her back to the room, and admired all over again the layers of stone terrace, palms, walls, sea and sky. Small boats chased across the smooth water each with the silhouetted figure of a water-skier behind. Further out several sailing boats zigzagged lazily from left to right. She couldn't see the shoreline but she could picture the swimmers and splashers and surfers.

Alice looked at the newspaper lying folded beside her plate. There was no need to open it and search, as she normally would, for the persons or person newsworthy enough to be a subject for her next interview.

Alice walked along a coastal path, climbing steeply above the village, then following the curve of the cliffs. The sky was now a cloudless blue, and even though it was early August, wild flowers sprang exuberantly around her. Some of them, which she assumed were particular to the south-west coast, she couldn't name – a white convolvulus with silver leaves, for example – but there were also clumps of drying thrift and bushy green spikes topped with the ubiquitous orange flowers of montbretia. Alice slung her bag on her shoulder and set herself a good pace; she soon overtook the elderly couple from breakfast.

Walking is freedom, thought Alice. But not freedom from thoughts, she mused, after she had passed the couple. Is it better to be one of a couple? She had been so young when she'd married Richard. He had proposed three months after they met – at a dinner party in Brighton. After ten months Peter had been born, and not much more than a year later, Florrie. When most of her friends were still at university, she was married to a serious husband, with two children and a very grown-up flat in London where they gave quite elegant dinner parties, food cooked by her with slavish attention to the just published *River Café Cook Book*.

Occasionally her father had come to London and his face, for the first few years at least, always wore the same expression of surprise. Once she'd dared to tax him with it. 'Do you *really* want to know?' he'd asked, which made her anxious that it was something to burst her world apart.

'Quite,' she'd answered. He'd looked a little scornful, or perhaps only relieved, and told her nothing. Florrie was the family member he rated most highly, for reasons Alice couldn't fathom.

The sun had become extremely hot in the last half-hour and she had an uncomfortable feeling that her face and arms were bright red. Perhaps she could make a parasol from some large, flat-leaved plants out to her left. Here the path wasn't following the contour of the cliff, which jutted outwards like the prow of a ship, but took the shortest route directly across. The plants grew at nearly the furthest point of the prow. Alice skipped towards them.

She found herself staring directly at a huge depth of dark green water. With a vertiginous sense of toppling forward, although in reality she stood straight enough, she imagined Blue, not as a corpse bloated and nibbled by fish as had spooked her so at Brighton, but as a diver, cylinders of oxygen strapped to his broad shoulders. The vertical drop suggested the water continued under the cliff. As she felt sweat gathering at her back and waistline, she pictured him splicing the cold water and making his way to the cave under her feet. Watching the dark swell made her feel a little cooler. She leant further forward. If she'd been a poor Mexican boy, she thought, she'd have called for spectators now and dived, or perhaps jumped in, to collect pesos from the bottom of the sea. Caught in a sharper whirl of vertigo – a breeze had caused it, rippling up from the sea – Alice sat down abruptly.

The greenery beneath her, so close to the cliff edge, was springy like a mattress with little coils of grey-green, topped with a few tiny flowers. Now that she had crushed them, they smelt of the kind of herb good cooks dropped into their casseroles. Maybe she was lying on a bed of thyme, although the flowers didn't seem quite the right colour. Alice closed her eyes against the sun and saw blackness, spotted like a tropical fish with red and green and blue. She reached for her bag, which lay beside her, and felt for her dark glasses, but her fingers found instead the torpedo shape of her mobile. Almost automatically, she switched it on. A mistake. Immediately its cheery tune sang out. But you don't have to be bossed about by your mobile. Eyes still closed she was about to switch it off again when an image of Jonathan's handsome, troubled face replaced the whirling tropical fish. He was still expecting her to accompany him to a concert this evening. It was just possible, after all, that he was the lynchpin to her life, the secure centre, old friend of her husband's.

Eyes open now, but screwed up against the sun, Alice dialled his home number and then, when there was no answer, his chambers. All this was easy because when Richard had died Jonathan had put both numbers into her mobile, saying he would always be there for her.

This morning his clerk answered and offered to track him down.

'Alice! I was about to ring you with tonight's schedule.'

'Oh, Jonathan. I'm afraid I'm lying on a Cornish cliff looking at the sea.'

'Why are you lying down?'

That was class, thought Alice, an immediate acceptance of the situation. 'Because I felt queasy. Vertiginous. I'm so sorry to let you down.'

'Yes. I'm sorry too. Are you interviewing someone?'

'I'm on holiday.'

'How bold of you. Tell me, have you spoken to Brendan Costa recently? Since the weekend?'

Alice felt herself blushing to the blue sky. Why was he asking that? And, even if he turned out to be her lynchpin, did he have the right? 'Hold on, I've got to find my dark glasses.' Alice sat up and, with her glasses on, felt more able to prevaricate. 'I told you about the house party. Guy was there.'

'It's Guy who's been in touch. Sir Brendan wants my professional advice about something or other.'

'And will you give it?'

'Money has no smell, according to the Emperor Vespasian.'

'What do you mean?'

'Just rumours.'

'Men like him attract rumours.'

'In fact, I may pass on Sir Brendan.'

'I'm going on to the Scillies on Friday,' said Alice. 'Florrie's bringing Lily. We'll make sandcastles for her.' There was a short pause. Somehow Alice knew what he was going to ask. She even had time to prepare her reply.

'Would you let me join you for the weekend?'

'Oh, Jonathan, that would be nice. But I've promised Florrie it's just us. Three generations. All female.'

After this call it took Alice a few minutes to return to her previous blitheness. But as she stood up and returned to the path, she noticed a wave of sea pinks, a few still flowering or flowering again. A breeze became continuous as she turned the corner of the headland and some seabirds, gulls probably, kittiwakes possibly, flew out calling from the cliff edge. She found she could rise above the plots and intricacies of life. Let Jonathan turn his astute mind on Brendan, if that was what he decided. He might discover something useful. But just now she wasn't going to think of either of them.

Alice walked for more than an hour. The sky clouded a little, taking the edge off the heavy midday heat, and the sea was sometimes turquoise, sometimes the blue of lapis-lazuli and sometimes a deep, rich emerald. There were a few other walkers, all properly equipped with hats and backpacks and binoculars strung round their necks. It was not particularly odd, therefore, to see a tall, stocky man standing with binoculars raised towards a further headland. It was odd, though, to recognise him as Brendan.

He came to her swiftly. Short of jumping off the cliff, there was no way she could avoid him. 'Whatever are you doing here?' It sounded like an accusation. 'You know Goosefields isn't far away,' he reminded her. 'And, of course, I have to check out Polvarth now and again.'

'I'm on holiday.' She hoped he didn't think she'd chosen the hotel because he owned it. Maybe he had the guest list sent to him.

'I spotted you earlier.' Brendan tapped his binoculars. 'You were on your mobile. I thought, Who is that stunning person with wonderful hair? And then I saw it was you.'

'Isn't that behaving like a voyeur?'

'Nothing wrong with voyeurs. In point of fact, I was trying to check on a patch of samphire.'

To Alice's surprise he began to recite in a sing-song voice.

> *The crows and choughs that wing the midway air*
> *Show scarce so gross as beetles; half way down*
> *Hangs one that gathers samphire, dreadful trade!*
> *Methinks he seems no bigger than his head.*

'Remember your Shakespeare? Poor lads were lowered on ropes to pick samphire off the cliffs. The precious stuff was sold to cure the gallstones of the rich. A dreadful trade indeed.'

'It's from *King Lear*, isn't it? Gloucester jumps off the cliff, which isn't really a cliff at all. Just Edgar's description.'

'So much deceit in life.' Brendan sighed unconvincingly.

'How does it go on?'

'Oh. About fishermen walking on the beach who look like mice and a tall ship that looks the size of its cock, which is not what you might think but a coracle or dinghy. That kind of thing. It ends,

> *I'll look no more*
> *Lest my brain turn and the deficient sight*
> *Topple down headlong.*

' "Topple down headlong," ' repeated Alice. 'That's what I felt like earlier on the edge of the cliff. Was it samphire when you checked?'

'No. Sandspurry. Not the same thing at all.'

Brendan came and sat down beside her. She tried to hide her sense of threat. Also the attraction she felt for him.

'So, why did you run away from me?'

'I felt ill. I'd drunk too much. I needed to learn more about Ivo. I needed a holiday.'

'At least you've given your dear father a clean bill of health.' He put his hand, hot and heavy, on to her bare arm, which was also hot, not just from the sun. 'I must assume that if I asked your permission to take off your clothes and make love to you here and now I would get a negative?'

Alice concentrated on the image of her two elderly walkers coming across such a scene. She managed a rueful and, she hoped, light-hearted, 'Not just now, thanks.'

'Think of the joys of sea air and sun on naked flesh. Never mind. Another time.' He waved his hand at the cliffs where Alice had walked from. 'How much money would you need to be let down on a rope and pick that samphire?'

'You said it was sandspurry.'

'I can't be certain.'

Alice twisted round. 'Lend me your binoculars.' They were heavy and Alice had trouble holding them to her eyes and focusing on anything other than sky and sea, but suddenly she found herself at close quarters to a beady-eyed gull, poking his head out of a hole in the cliff face. 'I'm on a sheer cliff and I'm terrified!'

'Imagine swinging from the end of a rope gathering samphire. Have you found the clump yet? Sweep the binoculars down the cliff.'

Despite the horrible sense of vertigo, Alice obediently lowered her gaze but too fast: in a second she was at the base of the cliff, from this angle and at low tide footed by shingle. She was about to move upwards again when a figure walked into view. It was a man, instantly familiar. 'It's Guy!' she cried, and regretted it at once. She put down the binoculars. 'I thought it was Guy but it was only someone like him.'

She wished the people in her life would stay in separate boxes and present themselves one at a time and never in each other's company. She thought it perfectly possible that the drive she and Squid (Brendan's son, oh my God!) had taken last night to find Guy's boat had been in this direction. Perhaps he was making his way to it along the beach. 'I think I'll walk back to the hotel now.'

'I must push off too. Harry's waiting in the road.'

The sight of Guy, so substantial through the binoculars, as if she could touch the checked cloth of his shirt, had unnerved her to the extent that she longed to be enclosed by the four walls of her bedroom. Once Brendan had scrambled to his feet and set off inland across a field, she went back along the path the way she came, almost at a run. So much for holiday relaxation. She might as well have stayed in London.

Polvarth's late-lunching guests were still lingering over their coffee on the terrace. 'It's beginning to rain,' said a woman, smoothing a drop off her naked arm. Alice was glad. She'd order a sandwich and lie on her bed. Perhaps she'd even turn on the television and be lucky enough to catch a fifties black-and-white film where the women wore tiny clasping hats over their perms and the men were shaped like tree-trunks.

'Room twenty-seven.' Alice leant on the reception desk.

'There's a person waiting for you.'

'I'm not expecting anyone.' Alice felt confused. This person waiting must be Guy and yet he had been walking in the opposite direction away from the hotel. 'I'm going to my room now. Would you send up a ham sandwich?'

The phone rang as soon as Alice had finished her sandwich, as if the caller had known how to time it. Sighing, Alice picked up the receiver.

'I am sorry to bother you on holiday but when I heard you were in the area I couldn't pass up the opportunity for a word. It won't take long.'

Although expressing apologies, Detective Constable Susan Paradise's voice had a commanding edge that disconcerted Alice.

'It might be easiest if I came up to your room or maybe I can arrange to use an office.'

The so-called office was very small with only one window looking to the back garden and half obscured by the boughs of a tall, dark plant. More like a cell than a room, thought Alice.

'It has come to our notice,' Susan Paradise began immediately, 'that Mr Carroway spent the night at the Hilton Hotel with a woman. We wondered if you could throw any light on this? When you parted,' she looked at her notebook, 'at about ten thirty or eleven p.m., did he mention any plans for a further visitor?'

'No,' said Alice quickly, pleased that she could kick off without a lie. So it had come, the moment she had been waiting for.

'I see. So you have no idea who this woman could have been?'

Alice thought. 'How do you know there was a woman?'

The policewoman paused, consideringly. 'She was seen leaving by hotel staff.'

'So you have a description?'

'We do.'

Alice wondered how many red-haired women could have been wandering about the Hilton Hotel in the vicinity of room 405. Still playing for time, she asked, 'In the morning, was it?'

'Late morning.'

Late morning! She replayed the scene. Blue had almost hurried her out. He had wanted to leave stifling London and get to the sea – or that was the impression she'd received. What was the explanation? Had the hotel staff misremembered the time? Alice found she was staring fixedly at the green bars as if the answer lay in the garden beyond. She shifted her gaze to the policewoman, who was waiting patiently. 'Was she distinctive in any way?'

'She was dressed in tight black trousers and top. Peroxide blonde hair. Pale skinned, heavily made-up. Medium height, slim build.'

'Peroxide blonde,' gulped Alice. She didn't know whether to laugh or cry. Blue had entertained a lover after she left. Her visit, therefore, was of no importance to anyone but herself. This other woman would set the time of his departure.

'Are you all right, Mrs Lightfoot?'

'I walked too far in the sun this morning. Without a hat.' Blue had thought so little of their encounter that he'd immediately enjoyed another. A blow for her self-esteem. Presumably she was just one in a line of women besotted by his beauty who threw themselves at him.

'As you will appreciate, it means there's no way Mr Carroway could have reached France at the time or place he was spotted.'

A new question occurred to Alice. If Blue was a two-women-a-night man, where did that leave Jonathan's always unlikely view that he and Guy were lovers?

Chapter Twenty

A Third Thursday

Alice woke on Thursday with a sense of catastrophe. The day before had become confusing, both the interlude with Brendan on the cliff-top and the interview with Detective Constable Paradise. In the evening she'd left her room and walked by the harbour, watching the sun fight its way through the clouds for a last orange flare. She had felt truly widowed with no one to confide in, a feeling accentuated by the constantly expected appearance of Guy, who never materialised.

At seven she'd rung Mitzi and tried to explain the continuing oddities in her life but Mitzi wanted to update her on her own saga with her ex-husband and only became properly interested when she grasped that Alice had slept with Brendan. 'I knew you fancied him!' she exclaimed. 'Right from the beginning.'

'But I don't like him at all. He's an utter shit,' Alice had protested.

'All men are utter shits,' Mitzi advised cheerfully. 'Treat it as a first-base negotiating position.'

Despite or because of this advice, she had eventually become calmer and had even enjoyed her supper alone on the terrace – no sign of Squid or Guy. She propped a book against a bottle of wine and told herself that in a couple of days she would be called on to be a mother and grandmother. This was irresponsible time, precious despite its disturbances.

Which made this waking with a sense of catastrophe so unnerving. Shakily, she went to the bathroom and there, sitting on the lavatory, she worked out that her period was ten days late. She got up hastily and went to the basin. As she washed her hands she stared fixedly, unseeing, at her anxious face while she frantically rehearsed all the reasons why this lack of bleeding was insignificant: she was over forty, she was a grandmother, she might even be entering menopause, she had seldom bothered with birth control during the latter years with Richard and nothing had resulted. She had been upset over the last week or two with changes in her pattern of life. Surely that made it quite likely that her cycle would become irregular too. But none of this good sense could avert the awful sense of doom: she had slept with not one but two men, and with neither had she taken any precautions. And nor had they.

Alice leapt out of bed and pulled on random clothes. It was perfectly simple. She would find a chemist and buy one of those testing kits. Just for reassurance.

Alice left the hotel. She hadn't looked out of the window before her departure and was shocked to find it was raining heavily. She stood undecided, letting the warm water drum on to her head, then returned to Reception.

'Can I help you?'

'I was looking for a chemist.'

'I'm afraid there isn't exactly a chemist in St Mawes. What is it you wanted?'

No answer to that one. 'Where's the nearest chemist, then?'

'Percuil.'

'My surname. I took it by deed poll.'

'Squid!' A hot flush made Alice put her hand to her face. Could she be going to present him with a sibling, a rival for his father's millions? She must stop herself imagining such ridiculous possibilities.

'I'll show you the way, if you like. You'll never find it otherwise.'

Alice was certain she rejected this offer, understandably not wanting him to witness her purchase. But he was in the car with her all the same, peering through the still deluging rain and explaining that there was not much work for him in wet weather. 'Although it does flatten the sea,' he added, 'good for water-skiing.'

'You're an only child, are you?' Alice knew she was obsessing.

'My mother lives not far from here. She creates innovative pottery but she's never mastered the art of making it dishwasher-proof.'

'That must be hard.' Alice remembered how Brendan had commented bitterly that of his three wives only the first refused to be reconciled to the situation. Certainly 'innovative pottery' had an ominous ring. 'What I meant was, how many other children does your father have?'

Squid gave her an '*et tu, Brute*' look, then answered, with more spirit, 'I thought the whole world knew. And particularly you, who interviewed him. A few years after I was born when, according to my mother, he'd already decided I was a loser, he decided children were a waste of time. He dressed it up as something else, of course – the pain of losing so many of his family in that famous bombing raid, children as hostages to fortune, et cetera, et cetera. But the truth was he didn't like the thought of rivals, someone taking over when he wasn't there any more. Did you ever hear about that unscalable mountain in Ethiopia where the emperors dumped their princes to keep them out of the way? Well, that was our Sir Brendan's attitude. Except there was only me to dump.'

'Didn't his later wives object? And what about mistakes? Mistakes often occur.' Alice heard her voice a little breathless.

Squid gave a bitter laugh and announced, in a rather theatrical manner, 'My father caters for mistakes.'

'What do you mean? I don't understand.'

'He had an irreversible vasectomy.'

'You're not kidding!' Her expression of joy startled them both, and Alice giggled, not least at Squid's astonished expression. She could not be pregnant by Brendan – the worst dread of all. To have conceived from their casual unloving meeting in the night would have been loathsome. If Blue's seed had impregnated her, it would be the work of magic, the fruitful seed of an underwater being. Well, perhaps that was pushing it a bit, particularly considering his later assignation.

There was no escape from Squid's solicitude as they entered the brightly lit chemist, no way she could smuggle out a Pregnokit. By the time they came out again, Alice was laden with unwanted purchases of homeopathic remedies, *Kali-b.* and *merc-v.*30. The rain had stopped, and there was even a wet gleam in the sky.

'I must get back to my clients,' announced Squid, so Alice drove him back to the hotel. When she arrived, Reception informed her that a person was waiting to see her and this time, instead of Detective Constable Paradise with her bob of yellow hair and upsetting news, the person was Guy.

'Oh, Guy!' He had risen from a comfortable-looking sofa in the sitting room, a newspaper in one hand. They stood for a second, smiling warmly at each other.

'How's your holiday?' he asked.

They sat on the sofa and Alice tried to decide how to answer him. 'I thought I saw you yesterday. I was on the cliff-top with binoculars.'

'Two glinting eyes. Yes. There's stuff to do with the boat and Susan Paradise wanted to talk to me again. I had to come down. I didn't want to bother you. How about a pot of coffee?'

'That's an excellent idea.'

'Why are you looking at me like that?'

'Nothing.' But Alice continued to watch him as he went out in search of coffee. He returned and settled beside her again. 'So what are your plans for today?'

'I've already been to Percuil. And now it's stopped raining, I'll go for a walk. I might even take a picnic.'

'I wish I could take you out for a sail. Maybe I can borrow a boat.'

This was the cue to tell him that she had seen, or rather spied on, his poor smashed sailing boat. But a waitress had arrived, pouring them cups of coffee.

'Susan also wanted me to take her round my boat again,' Guy began again. 'Give my view on how the damage was caused. That sort of thing. She's a bright lady – not easy to pull the wool over her eyes.'

'I found her quite stupid.'

'Really?'

They drank reflectively.

'Would you be interested in seeing my poor old boat or do you think it too...' he paused '... too macabre? I've been given permission to take an insurance assessor round there.'

'I'd like to come.'

'Put some decent shoes on, then, and we'll go in about half an hour. I just need to check on the tides.'

'Tell me,' Alice said, as they left the hotel and headed for a pathway to the sea. They would walk along the beach and meet the assessor at the boathouse, 'do you have two distinct personalities? One for the office and London, and one for here, time out?'

Guy didn't answer before he had indicated a rough pathway scrambling down an incline between hedges of crimson-flowering fuchsia and eventually depositing them on the beach. 'Whatever do you mean?' he said. He looked at the sky.

Alice saw shifting white clouds clearing to reveal geometric patterns of blue. It was like a Matisse cut-out, she thought. 'You were so very City,' she said, 'even if sympathetic, a cog in the newspaper machine . . .'

'Thanks.'

'I don't mean to be rude.' She heard her voice childlike in its earnestness. 'I guess it's what city living does. I expect I seemed just the same to you.'

'No.'

They had begun to walk along the beach. A few boats were pulled up above the high-water mark; the shingle moved under their feet and they had collected an airy escort of seagulls. 'I just would never have imagined you as quite such a sporty, outdoor sort of person. To be honest, I put you more in the category of the Master, inseparable from your desk and computer.'

'Except when we had lunch at one of our pubs?' suggested Guy, with only a touch of irony.

'Quite.' But there was something here she couldn't understand, which gave their relationship a sense of unreality. 'If I hadn't interviewed Blue, I'd have gone on with my blinkered view of you.'

'I don't expect so.'

'But why should anything have changed? I'd already known you ages.'

'Or not known me.'

'That's precisely what I'm trying to say.'

'Things do tend to move forward.' He stopped walking and turned to look at her. 'However long it takes.' He took her left hand, which was clenched into a fist at her side and gently loosed the fingers. 'Is that your wedding ring?'

'Yes.' Alice looked at her fingers in his. His were very sunburnt, even the hairs on his fingers bleached blond.

'Platinum. And that's your engagement ring?'

'No. I lost that years ago. This was my mother's engagement ring. An opal. My father gave it to me after she died. She never liked it much, he told me. Her tastes were flashier, so he said. That was just about the only thing he ever said about her. She just vanished out of my life and after a while I gave up expecting her back. Then I hated her for leaving me.'

'But you still wear her ring?'

If this was a question, she had no answer. They began to walk again but now Guy led her towards the edge of the sea. The tide was low, perhaps as low as it could be, so that she felt a long way from land, isolated in the expanse of wet sand, patched with shingle, shells, seaweed and the odd bottle or can. The sea on their left trickled towards them lazily, occasionally lapping at their feet with a longer tongue of water.

'I had planned to go along the top for most of the way.'

Alice didn't ask him why he'd changed his mind. It suited her here. Already there was less activity out to sea and that, too, seemed far away, the voice of a skier or sailor coming disconnected across the water and therefore making no impact. 'It's more peaceful here.'

He nodded, and watched as Alice took off her shoes. The water was hardly cold at all and her toes nestled tenderly in the sand. She bent down and rinsed her fingers. The opal of her mother's ring swam mistily in the ripples. She had worn it for so long – ever since her father had given it to her when she was about sixteen – that she hadn't thought about it for years. Initially it had been on her right hand, but after she had lost her engagement ring, she had switched it to the left. It was a sad teardrop of a ring, she thought now and, almost inevitably, pictured those glittering diamonds she had picked up from the garage's lavatory floor. Dora's ring. But she didn't want to think about that. Not yet. Not now.

'We'd better get a move on or we'll miss the assessor.'

Alice replaced her shoes and they walked more quickly. The trouble was, she thought, that the spider's web woven round her in the last three weeks was too thick for any easy unravelling. But, at least, on this peaceful strand, with Guy at her side, she felt a lessening of anxiety.

To arrive at the boat, they had to climb round a headland where the sea came up close and there were piles of shingle and rocky outcrops. Alice recognised it as the spot where she had seen Guy with her binoculars. She also realised, with a postdated shock of surprise, that there had been someone with him, moving out of the focus of her glasses, perhaps a man. But then she remembered when she'd lowered the glasses and looked with her eyes, that there'd only been one figure: Guy.

'In rough seas, this is a dangerous bit of coastland.' Guy scrambled just ahead of her over the rocks. 'There's a marker buoy but in darkness or heavy seas it's not much use.'

'Do you think Blue smashed up here?'

Guy turned to her. 'No. No. Blue's not such a fool. It was out at sea.' They walked on faster. The tide was no longer standing still but coming in fast, rippling over the sand and sometimes breaking in lines of thin white foam.

'The boathouse is round the next headland. You can only get to it at low tide.' Alice imagined the fast trickle becoming surging waves, strong enough to hurl them against the cliff face. Although she had grown up in Brighton, she had no real experience of that sort of sea. Sometimes she had swum at Camber or Cooden, but Camber was edged by billowing waves of sand, where she always imagined Lawrence of Arabia had been filmed, and little clutches of nudists hidden behind the dunes, while Cooden had the sort of flat acres of beach that attracted families with small children. That was another place she'd thought her mother might come back: among the crowds at Cooden where she was watched over by someone else's mother.

'I want to talk to you about Blue.'

Alice, a few paces behind Guy, stopped, hoping she'd misheard. But he was waiting for her to catch up.

'He's a quite exceptional person.' Only just consciously, Alice heard the present tense and was surprised. 'I don't think I told you much before. He got into trouble as a boy. His father left his mother, and then his mother found another partner and they emigrated to Australia. But after a year or two Blue decided he preferred England and somehow got himself back here. He was still only eleven or twelve so he got put in care. In theory, at least. That was when he had years in and out of various young offenders' institutions. For drug-dealing mostly, with a touch of burglary thrown in. Soon he scaled up, with violence adding to his sentences, and upgraded to adult prisons. Not many men get out of a situation like that and make a half-way decent life for themselves, but Blue decided to turn himself into a success. He got a bit of backing from some philanthropic businessman and began his new life, as far away from the old as possible. First he reinvented himself as a sailing instructor and then as a deep-sea diver. He even went back to Australia for a bit. He was – is, I trust – among the top half-dozen divers in the world.'

'Yes.' Alice thought of the man she'd found in the hotel room. His golden glamour was almost mythical by now, but Guy was telling her a true story.

'I thought you'd see the point of him. That's why I sent him to you.'

How was she supposed to react? 'I did see the point of him, if not in quite the way you'd expected'? 'I thought he was almost unbelievably glamorous,' she said. 'But that doesn't fill an interview – at least, not my sort of interview.'

'Perhaps I hadn't given enough background. Perhaps you didn't give him enough time.'

They'd reached the second headland now and, as she negotiated the rocks, submerged now in an inch or two of cold water, Alice was glad to have an excuse for no comment.

'He's brave too' – again the present tense – 'not only physically. He wasn't afraid of anyone.'

Was this a clue she should note? Alice peered into a rock pool and saw her frowning face reflected. The stone was encrusted with limpets, which gave her the outline of a weathered gargoyle.

'There it is!' Guy pointed towards the outline of the boathouse in the pale grass at the edge of the sea.

'But why did Blue need to be brave?' Alice couldn't let the moment pass. 'What happened to him? Why did he disappear?'

'It'll all become clear enough.' Guy slowed down and waited for Alice. 'There is one thing I want to tell you.' As the light had got brighter in the course of the afternoon, Guy's glasses had got darker so that Alice found herself staring at black goggle eyes. 'Don't believe everything you're told. You shouldn't worry about Blue, that's what I wanted to tell you.'

Alice felt confused. Why did Guy think she'd worry about a man whom, as far as he knew, she'd only met once and had not appreciated enough to interview? Only she knew he might be the father of her unborn child. Alice failed to suppress a mad smile.

'Why are you grinning?'

'I'm not grinning. It's the wind.' She made an effort to appear normal. 'I'm glad about your friend Blue but I can see a Range Rover driving towards your boathouse.' It was all his affair, she wanted to imply; she was a mere spectator.

By the time they arrived two figures had emerged from the car. Guy frowned. 'Whatever's he doing here?'

'Phil asked me to show him the way,' shouted Squid, apparently spotting the frown, 'so I couldn't say no.'

While Phil, the tall, stiff-looking assessor, shook hands with Guy, Alice found herself warmly embraced by Squid. As he kissed her other cheek, he whispered, 'I promise I won't say a word.' Sharing a secret with Squid was hardly the act of a sensible adult, thought Alice, as Guy disappeared to open the shed with the assessor.

'We won't be too long,' he called back at her.

Alice decided to return to the seashore, to paddle, perhaps even to swim – it was quite hot enough now – but, of course, Squid followed her. He seemed in egregiously cheerful mood, beaming and bobbing round her like a large puppy.

'I thought you went to find your clients?'

'I'm a jack-of-all-trades. Phil offered me a ten spot to escort him here. He's come all the way from Plymouth and didn't want to lose his way for the last few miles.' He gambolled a bit more, kicking a loose pebble as if it were a football, then came back. 'You never said you knew Guy.'

'He's a working colleague.'

'He's got quite a reputation here, in demand, but you must know that.'

'I've no idea what you're talking about.'

'Nothing bad.' Squid laughed, irritating Alice further. 'You know what they say, "A single man in command of a good fortune..."'

'"In possession of a good fortune..."' So now this drop-out airhead was misquoting Jane Austen at her. Was he implying that Guy had a lively Cornish love life? It seemed so. Alice had only just got used to the idea that he wasn't gay, and this information was flummoxing. Must she look on him now as a Cornish Casanova, or was Squid merely amusing himself?

'Take yourself off somewhere,' she told Squid, 'while I go for a swim.'

'I am used to the unclothed female form, you know. I won't ravish you or something.'

Alice suddenly took in that Squid was high. No expert on drugs, it had taken her a while to identify his air of manic energy and the jerky wildness of his movements. 'Just shut up,' she said firmly, 'and go away.'

He went at once, attacking at a run the headland Guy and she had come round, then hopping from rock to rock, the surfaces only just visible above the sea, until he had disappeared.

Alice removed her clothes, glad that she'd worn a bikini underneath and slipped into the advancing water. It was much colder than she'd expected, reminding her unwillingly of that liquid glacier she'd endured before being warmed in Brendan's bearlike hug. She swam a fast crawl straight out to the horizon, only stopping when her arms were tired and her body beaten into enjoyment. She turned round to face the shore while treading water energetically. Above the swell of the sea she saw the boathouse, almost as if it were riding the crests. The doors were wide open and the afternoon light, cleared by the morning's rain, lit the interior to show the two men standing inside the boat. One raised an arm and then the other with an abruptness that had the air of violence.

What if this was a replay of the scenario at the time of Blue's disappearance? Maybe one man had raised his arm and then the other. Blue and Guy. They had fought and Blue had disappeared over the side. But why should this happen? Could Guy be in Brendan's pay, employed to knock off Blue, and all the wonderful things Guy had insisted on telling her about him – they had seemed over-fulsome at the time – merely cover for a dastardly deed? This was crazy. Forgetting to tread water, Alice sank down among the waves and found herself taking a briny gulp. She began to swim for shore, this time performing a leisurely breaststroke.

Guy and the assessor were out of the boathouse now and looking her way. Since the sea was moving inwards at a frantic pace, this drew them quite considerably closer together. Suddenly Guy was running at great speed towards her. He shouted something and waved his arms. Instinctively, Alice looked behind her. She remembered the scene in *Jaws* where the swimmer fails to notice the threat flashing her way. Snap! A leg gone. Snap! Snap! And both arms.

'Your clothes,' shouted Guy.

Indeed, there they were, floating on the surface of the water. He would reach them before she did. She couldn't spot her shoes at all. How utterly stupid! Born and bred by the sea yet caught out by the oldest trick in the book. There was no point in swimming any faster: everything would be soaked by now.

She stood up in waist-high water, peered down and saw the quavery outline of first one shoe, then the other. 'Drowned, utterly drowned.' Mocking herself, she waded in, holding them, dripping, away from her.

Guy was looking up at the boathouse. 'I don't want him to drive away without us. You'll freeze if we have to walk. Here.' He took off his shirt and handed it to her. Underneath he wore a tight, dark blue T-shirt. 'I'll tell him to wait a moment.'

The shirt was made of a very soft cotton, thick enough to feel immediately warm. Alice undid her wet bikini top and slid it out. She felt like a respectable woman. She followed Guy up the beach and decided that, on the whole, she didn't regret missing a sight of the doomed sailing boat close-up.

Phil the assessor's four-wheel drive car had an efficient heater that blew air up Alice's legs. By the time they arrived at the hotel, she was quite dry and snug.

'You can give me back my shirt later,' said Guy. 'I've planned an outing for us, if you like the idea. What about six o'clock at reception?'

Automatically, Alice looked at her watch before remembering she'd put it into one of her shoes before swimming. 'Great idea.' She was not going to reveal another ridiculous bit of incompetence. As she went upstairs to her room, she imagined the supposedly waterproof watch, given her years ago by Richard, floating out to sea, then gradually sinking to a sandy resting-place at the bottom of the ocean where it would tell the time for the fishes till the batteries ran out.

She took off Guy's shirt in the bathroom and, as she removed a fragment of shell that was clinging to her left breast, an echo of the catastrophic feeling of the morning came to her. Did her nipples look darker and more pronounced than before? Was the swell of her breasts more luxuriant? She smoothed her stomach tenderly. That certainly seemed no bigger. She went over to her sponge-bag and took out shampoo and conditioner, bath oil and body lotion.

*

'It's where I keep my boat in winter.' Guy and Alice were standing on the edge of a graveyard that sloped steeply into a wide estuary of the sea. Alice couldn't imagine how the graves clung to their corpses, preventing them sliding out, down the vertical bank and on to the rainy beach. From there, she imagined, a high tide would take them, bones or bodies, and swirl them out to sea.

'It's an amazing place,' she said. The graveyard was covered with still brilliant green turf, shaded, now and again, by groups of cedars. The length of the estuary was thickly edged with trees and, in the evening light, the water changed from deep emerald to amber and imperial purple.

'This was where I first met Blue. He was reading inscriptions on the tombstones. He took me to read one he'd just found:

> *He came to bring us joy*
> *But his maker took him back.*
> *Now his joy is our sadness.*
> Samuel Swinnerton Thomas, 1837 to 1840.

It was then he told me about his childhood. It was the first thing I knew about him. I told him about my crazy parents and he told me about a world of madness. It was a very wintry day, still windy after three days of storms. I'd come to check the boat and he came with me.'

'He seems an unlikely friend for you.' Alice shivered a little. She had put on her lilac sleeveless dress and, even with a pashmina wound round her shoulders, it felt cool under the pines. 'Which gravestone was it?'

It was right at the edge of the cemetery, leaning backwards, weathered and mossy, so that the letters were difficult to read.

'You got it wrong. It's not a "he" it's a "she" who died, called Sarah, not Samuel.'

Guy came closer. 'I never looked at it for myself. He just waved in this direction.'

'I would have thought the death of a three-year-old girl was just as affecting as the death of a boy.' Alice was still crouched over the stone. 'I told you my mother died when I was three,' she said, following Guy away, 'but there wasn't a gravestone. My father was

– is – an atheist, or humanist, as he prefers to call it. It's a kind of reverse, isn't it? A three-year-old mourning her mother.'

They were walking away from the estuary now, taking a path edged by stone tablets on which lines of poetry were written. But the trees were clustered darkly overhead and Alice could only make out the odd line.

Ever near us though unseen,
The dear immortal spirits tread.

'This morning you said you grew to hate your mother because she'd left you.'

'I don't know. I expect I was exaggerating. I was so young. I didn't believe my father for years. Not fully, anyway. I expected her back any day. I was so muddled and confused. Mourning a death would have been a relief.' Alice read again: 'Stranger in peace, pursue thine onward road, But ne'er forget thy last and long abode.' She thought about the words. 'If I were honest, I'd admit my mother's death was never likely to be very convincing. There was no evidence for it, you see. Just my father's word.'

'What a burden for you to carry. But she's never turned up, has she?'

'Do you mind if we don't talk about it any more?'

'Of course not.'

Alice was glad when they reached the turquoise car. They were going to the Smugglers' Cave, Guy told her, with a fabulous view across the harbour. They served real ale and paella made with fresh fish. It was, he informed her, his favourite eating-place in the world and she should be honoured he was taking her there.

'I am honoured.' Guy drove at his usual fast pace, through dim, narrow lanes enclosed by high, overgrown banks into which rabbits and other larger animals scuttled nervously. Alice was sure she saw the heavy flanks of a nocturnal badger heaving itself into the safety of tangled stems. The car was climbing all the time and when they emerged on to a headland she was surprised by the brightness of the sky. But, then, they were winding downwards, not far, just enough to tuck themselves into woods where a cottage, white-painted and thatched, appeared.

It was only when they had parked and walked towards its low

door, that Alice turned and saw the view: village and harbour, shimmering beyond the indigo blue bay.

Guy took her arm. 'Don't bang your head.'

'I feel as if I'm at the centre of a secret.'

'It's certainly an improvement on the Monkey's Tail or the Admiral's Telescope.' Guy smiled.

They were shown to a table by a window. All five other tables were filled. Guy must have reserved this one. The large owner, bending under the low beams, was introduced as Arthur. He brought them a jug of ale, hunks of homemade bread, taramasalata and olives.

'Arthur used to be an actor,' Guy said. He paused a moment, then added, 'He was the one who spotted Blue going out to sea.'

'On the day he disappeared.' Alice's tone was sympathetic but she didn't want to think about Blue. Not tonight. She was filled with sea, sun, beauty, and happy in the reassuring presence of Guy. The ale, which she would normally have rejected, tasted cool and smoky and light and dark. How infinitely more subtle than the ice-cold vulgarity of sharp-bubbled champagne or narrow-shouldered wine. Across the table, she saw, Guy was looking at her curiously.

'I always wondered if you really were quite such a contained, competent, assured woman,' he said.

'I was,' agreed Alice, emphasising the past tense. 'I thought that's what I was. On Monday I wrote up my interview, on Tuesday I delivered it and had lunch with you. On Wednesday, I tried out some new subjects and went out with Jonathan or Mitzi, my girlfriend. On Thursday I visited my father in Brighton. On Friday, with any luck, I was interviewing and over the weekend I went to the country and saw Florrie and Lily. Oh dear,' she added, after a small pause, 'I've forgotten Peter and Jennie.'

Guy laughed. 'It's incredible.'

'Well, I am exaggerating. There were days when the mould got twisted. Once I had to spend six very hot days in South Beach, Miami, because the fashion designer I was supposed to be interviewing got himself shot and the editor decided I could write a news story. I never was any good at news stories.' She hesitated. 'I suppose I'm not very good at interviews any more.'

'That's why you're on holiday. Remember?'

Alice looked out of the window. She wasn't going to ask him if he'd written up her Ivo interview. Instead she found herself thinking of Richard. 'It's odd carrying on life after your husband dies. I had a counsellor from Cruse, a kind man called Lennie. He told me to think of the future one day at a time. So I guess that's what I did. I thought it was what Richard would have wanted. Even when Florrie had her baby I thought of it like that. One day at a time. It seemed to work very well. I never broke down, you know.'

'I know,' said Guy.

Of course. She'd been having her almost weekly lunches with him when Richard had died. In fact, she had a feeling that if she tried very hard she would dig up the memory that she'd been lunching with Guy on the day Richard had his stroke. 'Lennie said I was his best client. But I've always liked order. I wouldn't have married Richard otherwise.'

'What did he look like?'

'Looks weren't the point of Richard. Did you never meet him?' It was a stupid question. Her office had been separate from Richard, just as his office had been separate from hers.

'He did pick you up once. I can't remember why. Perhaps you were ill. I heard his voice. He had a booming voice.'

'Booming?' Alice was surprised. He had been too tall and thin to boom. His chest was not broad enough to boom. But he had had a loud voice.

'Barristers tend to boom.'

'Isn't that a cliché?'

'So, what did he look like?'

Alice waited while Guy poured from a fresh jug of ale. Why was he so interested in Richard all of a sudden? 'I never notice looks. Don't you remember those memos from the Master? "Where's the description?" Do you care about looks?' But she had noticed Blue's beauty.

'I can see you're very beautiful. But I have to take into account that I've got a thing about redheads. Not the carrotty sort with pale skin and white-mice eyes. I like the auburn Italian variety with golden skin, amber eyes and plum-coloured hair. Your sort.'

Alice was so taken aback she drank some more ale too quickly and half choked. Then she laughed. 'Do you know, for a period of several days, until the day before yesterday in fact, I thought you were gay?' She laughed even more at Guy's expression. 'To be precise, I was told you were gay.'

'Whoever could have told you a thing like that?' He was relaxed, mocking.

'Jonathan. He was quite certain of it. He said you and Blue were lovers.'

'Paella.' Arthur appeared over her shoulder with a huge dish and so many fat prawns that the middle of the table seemed filled with waving pink whiskers.

'This is a spectacular place.' Alice served them both with greedy portions.

'What did you mean just now?' he asked, after they'd both eaten two or three mouthfuls and Alice had pulled out from its shell a particularly juicy prawn.

'Jonathan's fantasy, you mean? I thought it was pretty unreal at the time.' She didn't add that everything had seemed pretty unreal lately. 'I don't suppose you made a pass at him?'

Guy looked at his plate. 'You've known him for ages, haven't you?'

'Beyond ages. He was at school with Richard. They were best friends or whatever boys are. Poor Jonathan.'

'Why do you say that?'

Alice had a sudden strong image of Jonathan's imploring eyes as he declared his love and was just about to betray an old friendship with a jokey description when Guy spoke meditatively: 'Of course, he *is* gay.'

Alice's mocking complacency about the distinguished barrister who loved her wasn't up to taking in this latest shift. She looked across at Guy for a clue but, as usual, she was met by the barrier of his glasses. 'But he was married for years! His wife was called Joyce.'

'I know. He told me. We had lunch. He wanted to quiz me about London night-life, among other things – he assumed I knew a thing or two as a bachelor and a newspaperman.'

'And do you? You'll probably tell me Richard and Jonathan were lovers next!'

Guy didn't answer, then offered Alice some more paella.

'He jumped on me only the other evening, you know, the week everything began. I had to fight him off. He was ridiculous. Like a teenager.' Alice laughed, but still Guy said nothing. An unwanted memory surfaced. Something she had not thought of for years, for two decades at least, when Richard – casually, in some sort of schooldays conversation – had referred to the amount of homosexuality at his school. Jonathan had been there too and she had gathered from what he didn't say, more than anything else, that they had had a childish fling. But only at school. Like everyone did then. Even so, she wouldn't tell this to Guy. He wouldn't understand that Richard and Jonathan were from another generation, eighteen years older than they were, when 'the gay' hadn't been invented and homosexuality in public schools was merely a temporary substitution for girls, currently unavailable.

'I don't meant to upset you,' said Guy, 'on such a beautiful evening.'

'I'm not upset. Frankly, Jonathan's sexual proclivities have no relevance to my life one way or the other. I would say, however, if you're only half-way right, he's quite an actor.'

'I suppose he must be. What was his wife like?'

'Joyce? Clever. Serious. She never wanted children.' Alice decided that talking about Jonathan and Joyce was worse than talking about Blue. But what did she want to talk about? What were the customary subjects over their Tuesday lunches? Of course, it had been work, who was in the news, whom she could get to and write a sparkling piece about. But now she was on holiday. Suddenly the whole idea of communication in words was enormously complicated and she imagined solitude with affection, as if silence was itself a companion. Perhaps this verbal loss of nerve – because, she thought now, she'd been suffering from it for some time – had been at the root of her swift sexual capitulation to both Blue and Brendan. Her heart gave a hideous somersault. How could she be quaffing real ale with Guy when she still hadn't laid to rest the spectre of pregnancy? Pregnancy! A baby. A baby like Lily . . .

'What's the matter? You look as if you've seen a ghost.' Guy said this sympathetically with not too serious an expression, but Alice was still gripped with panic.

'I'm just going to the ladies'.' She rose so quickly her chair tumbled behind her.

'It's over there.' Guy pointed and retrieved the chair.

The ladies' was dimly lit by an orange bulb and Alice knocked against the basin in her rush to see if she'd begun to bleed. But of course she hadn't. So she sat on the lavatory for several minutes hoping for a philosophical point of view. And although that was putting it a bit high, she did consider that the paella and real ale would have been out of the question in either of her last two pregnancies: she'd lived off a diet of dry toast and Lucozade with an occasional splurge on a Marmite sandwich. One look at the prawns' triumphantly waving whiskers would have sent her running for a sink. Gradually, her earlier cheer returned, so on her return she was able to reassure Guy that she was very well indeed.

He'd been talking to Arthur in the relaxed mumble of old mates. 'I sometimes stay here,' he said, in answer to Alice's curious look.

'And tonight?'

'Tonight I want to walk by the sea with you. Do you see? The moon's come up.'

Alice looked out of the window and saw that while they'd been eating a large moon had taken the place of the sun. 'Is it full?'

'Oh, yes. A harvest moon. Wait a little longer and we'll see the aureole.'

'Do you know about the sky?'

He did. In fact, he had once done the research for a commissioned book called *The Layman's Guide to the Heavens*, but by the time he got to write it he wasn't a layman any more and found it impossible to bring himself down to the proper level. 'I'm an editor, really,' he said, 'not a writer, even if I can knock out the odd bit of polemic for an editorial.'

As he talked on, this time about the book on sailing he'd never write either, Alice's mood swung back to holiday complacency. She didn't even have to speak.

'Chocolate cake to round things off? It's another speciality.'

Chocolate cake would really settle the fate worse than the fat-worse-than-death issue. 'I'll share a slice with you.'

It was still warm when they came out of the Smugglers' Cave. Alice shut her eyes, and when she opened them, the moon was set in a jewelled belt of stars. Guy took her elbow. 'There're two steps a little further down.'

He was right, she thought, about the beach. It was too beautiful an evening to end abruptly. In Brighton, on nights like this, before she'd married, she'd slept on the beach, unrolling a sleeping-bag over the pebbles as if they were cushions. Once she had told Richard about it, half hoping he'd like the idea, but he hadn't been able to believe she went on her own and referred mockingly to her hippy past. She'd never been sociable enough to be a hippy: she'd just liked the sea at night. Richard had been her first lover.

Guy stopped the car short of the village – nowhere near the black boathouse with its sinister contents, Alice was relieved to note.

'We might need a torch to get down there.'

But they didn't. The stars and the moon, with its glowing harvest haze, lit their way down a path that ran beside a derelict stone barn, occasionally cutting down more steeply with two or three stone steps.

'They used to keep nets and fishing tackle in there but a storm took the breakwater out to sea and it's never been replaced.'

'It seems so sheltered.' They had arrived. It was a small beach between two headlands.

'In the summer. And I guess there're fewer fishermen. We're lucky we've escaped the late-night revellers.'

Alice could see signs of past barbecues above the shoreline but it was hard to imagine the beach anything but deserted. 'It's perfect.'

'Cornwall is full of perfection.' Again he took her elbow. Alice felt his warm fingers gripping her cool flesh and remembered that last ordinary Tuesday when they had taken a boat down the Thames and he'd taken her hand. It had been so hot. Stifling hot. Later he had come back to the flat and kissed her. Without passion, she had thought afterwards. Was that what she'd thought? The tranquil kiss of a storybook prince with a storybook Sleeping Beauty.

Alice broke apart from Guy, chose a well-angled spot and lay down on the smoothly rounded pebbles. 'I'm on holiday,' she said, when Guy came to join her. He lay down near, but not too near, and began, slowly and quietly, to tell her the names of the stars.

I'll never remember any of them, thought Alice, lazily. When she was ten, her father had told her she had a woman's brain, just like her mother – about the only time he'd mentioned her. She knew it wasn't a compliment. Perhaps that was why she'd never tried for university and married so young. And yet she had made a success of her job. She had used to protest that to Mitzi she had had no strong feminist longings before she started working and it had annoyed Mitzi dreadfully when she became successful. But the journalistic bug had caught her quickly enough. Of course she'd worked terribly hard and of course she was terribly proud of herself. Proud of her pay packet too. Why, she wondered vaguely, had Richard wanted her to work quite so much? His earnings had been ridiculously high after he became a QC. Maybe he thought she'd become boring otherwise. Maybe she would have. But she'd never been bored. Once, when Florrie was about fifteen and impossible, she'd terrified them by disappearing for three nights. Alice had gone to Richard and suggested stopping work so she could keep a closer eye on their daughter but he'd refused to discuss it. That was when he'd said Florrie was the most selfish, self-centred, self-regarding person in the universe. It had been 'the universe', she felt certain now. 'The world' wouldn't have been big enough.

Guy had stopped talking. 'Thank you,' she said. 'I'm afraid I listened to it like poetry. You know, every other word.'

'Good. I like that. Nature, music, poetry: the three gateways to the soul.'

Alice said nothing. But she thought that he had left out love. Perhaps he didn't believe in it. He was a bachelor, after all, in his late thirties or even forties.

'What are you thinking about?' He put out his hand and found hers.

'I was thinking that shingle has grown harder since I was a girl.'

'Here.' He pulled her to him as if he'd guessed what she wanted. Now they were lying with their faces upturned and only a few inches apart. She noticed that he wasn't wearing his glasses.

Alice remembered the last time she'd stared at the sky for any length of time. 'Where were you during that eclipse three years ago?'

'I had a telescope and I drove to Land's End. But it was all a waste of time. The cloud was far too thick. I told you about it at the time.'

'Oh.' She had forgotten. 'I went up the tower of the little village church near our cottage. I got the key. No one else was at all interested. The children had gone off west somewhere and Richard said he'd rather watch it on television. So I was all on my own. Because of the clouds I decided not to bother about buckets or special protective glasses. I just lay down on the lead roof – it had a nice little bit of a slant – and watched the sky. At first the sun seemed completely muffled but every now and again the density thinned till it was almost clear and then, for a second or two, I could see the sun and the darkness spreading over it. I was transfixed. If someone had shouted, "Fire! Volcano! Earthquake!" I wouldn't have moved. When the shadow blacked out the sun to nothing, I was startled by a flock of birds. They reeled round my head in the dimness, then dashed off again. I'll never forget it. Even though I had a headache for three days afterwards, I felt special, somehow chosen.' Alice relived the experience she hadn't thought about for so long. 'It's strange,' she said, 'that something can feel momentous that has no obvious relevance at all. Do you think it's the being on one's own?'

'No,' said Guy. 'I don't.'

When he kissed her, she could taste the chocolate, a sweetness in both their mouths. For a moment, she remembered that fairytale kiss in her flat, but this was immediately different. No one had ever kissed her so carefully or for so long, and very soon she stopped thinking. Only a sensation of the sky, the stars and the moon rolling over their heads stayed with her.

Guy moved slightly apart. Alice lay where he had left her, eyes open or closed, she hardly knew which. Some lines from a poem learnt in childhood made half an echo in her head:

> And whilst our souls negotiate there, We like sepulchral statues lay . . .

'Guy.' She put out her hand and found his. He held hers tight. 'I've got to catch the night sleeper,' he said.

Alice felt bewildered. He was leaving *now*? She stared at the sky and saw that the moon was less hazy and had changed its position. 'Why?'

'I only had today off to see the police. The Master calls.' He squeezed her hand. 'I'm sorry.'

He was sorry. Alice sat up. The movement made her feel dizzy.

'If you like, I'll leave my car at the station, then you can use it to meet your family at Penzance.'

They both stood up. Alice suspected bitterly that he had been planning this while they were kissing. 'Fine,' she said. 'Thanks.'

They walked back to the car quietly, and Guy drove to the hotel, hardly saying a word. Alice thought she hadn't been on a date since Richard's death and this was what it was like: the dinner, the telling of an important story (she had never told anyone about the eclipse), the kiss and the farewell.

'I'll be in touch,' said Guy, and this, too, was part of the date. 'The key will be *in* the glovebox.'

Alice went up to her room and looked at her bed. But she was too restless to sleep. Why had the eclipse been so important to her? Of course, because Richard had died a few days later – it was a Tuesday when she had, indeed, had lunch with Guy. All through that dreadful afternoon and evening the guilty memory of her happiness; alone on the top of the church tower – even though she had had that headache – had been at the back of her mind. The headache had stopped when she heard of Richard's death or perhaps she had no longer noticed it.

Alice went to her bag, which was still only half unpacked, and searched for her reporter's pad. It was a habit: she took it everywhere. She wanted to make a few notes, *try* to make a few notes, about what was happening to her.

She was surprised by how thin the pad was until she remembered she'd given her notes on Blue to Detective Constable Susan Paradise and those on Ivo to Guy. Brendan was still there: 'Childhood tragedy, even if unremembered, is a sound launching pad for worldly success . . .' She was about to flip forward with a derisive snort when her eye saw one word and a number that made her clasp the pad to her breast and sit on the bed.

Blue had given it to her as she left in the morning and she had scribbled it down on a random page of her pad. She'd forgotten till this moment. Unable to resist, Alice grabbed her mobile and was about to press in the number when she remembered there was no signal unless she climbed up the hill. It would have to be the hotel's telephone.

The number rang for a long time. As she listened to the tone, Alice's impatient excitement changed. Why had she assumed this was a direct line to Blue? Much more likely his mobile was lying at the bottom of the ocean ringing among scuttling crabs and starfish.

Just as she had given up hope of an answer, a recorded voice came on. 'This is Blue's number,' and then another man's voice cut across the message: 'Hello.'

Alice had heard the voice too recently to be in any doubt. 'Guy! Why are you answering Blue's telephone?'

There was a pause. 'Why are you ringing it?'

'But you're on a train,' retaliated Alice, definitely not answering the question, 'on your way to London.'

'I missed it. I had to come back to the Smugglers' Cave. The next train's at five in the morning. I'll still leave the car for you.'

But he wasn't answering the question. She had to ask again. 'It is Blue's number, isn't it?'

'Yes. He stays here often.'

'But it's a mobile!' How could he think she wouldn't know that?

'Quite. He left it here.'

Alice thought that nobody left their mobile behind when they went sailing. Surely not. 'Didn't the police find it? They must have searched.'

'No. I found it.'

'And you didn't give it to the police?'

'No. How *did* you get the number?'

She would answer him now. 'Blue gave it to me after the interview. I scribbled it down on my pad. I only just found it. By chance. So I rang. Out of curiosity.'

'Like a journalist.'

'I suppose so.'

'Well, you'd better get some sleep.'

'Yes.'

'I'll be in touch.'

Alice felt even less like sleep now. Why should Guy miss his train? He hadn't seemed in a rush on the beach. A long kiss. A kiss that had gone nowhere. Perhaps he *had* been in a rush. Surprising herself, Alice prepared for bed – checking for bleeding as had now become habitual (with the usual negative result) – and got in. Convinced she couldn't sleep, she nevertheless felt exhausted: the day of sunshine, sea, walks and strange events weighed her down to the mattress. Briefly, she recalled the hard roundness of the pebbles as Guy and she lay kissing, then hurtled down into a deep sleep.

Chapter Twenty-One

A Third Friday

Florrie's train was due in Penzance at midday. Alice woke late, then hurried to pack and check out of the hotel before the next step of picking up Guy's car from the station. She'd already ordered a taxi to take her there when she remembered that her own car was sitting in the hotel car park. She must get a grip.

It was another golden day, as if the great storm and yesterday morning's heavy rain had been aberrations in the endlessly hot weeks. As always, Alice felt soothed by driving, enjoying the lanes dipping through overhanging banks with the occasional wide view of sky and even more occasionally of sea.

At last she stood on the station. The train was delayed by half an hour but she didn't mind. It gave her time to admire St Michael's Mount, rising romantically out of a brilliant sea, and to look forward to Lily's luscious baby charm.

The train arrived in a rush and stopped with a series of rapid jerks, like a horse that doesn't want to be reined in. She searched the windows eagerly for a first sight of Florrie and Lily. Near the back of the train, a group was climbing down with the maximum noise and confusion. It was Florrie's kind of muddle so Alice watched, but the first to descend to the platform was a middle-aged or even elderly woman with white hair, followed by a young man whose face she couldn't see. Now the train was emptying and she still hadn't spotted Florrie.

'Mum! Mum! We're here!'

Alice dashed to answer the cry and hugged Florrie with all the joy of motherhood. Her body felt so young, so slim, so perfect. 'Darling. How wonderful you've arrived!' They separated. 'Where's Lily?'

Florrie whirled round, frowned, then flourished her arm. 'Mummy, meet...' she hesitated '... meet Dora.'

'Dora!'

The white-haired woman, whose face was not as old as her hair, held Lily in her arms. Her eyes, bright and amber brown, gleamed above the baby's smooth head. 'I am so happy to be included,' she said, looking in Alice's face, 'in such a family party.'

'And there's Baz, too.' Florrie, dazzling in full white skirt and cropped top, whirled about even more.

'Baz, too,' echoed Alice stupidly. I'm not up to this, she thought, this kidnapper joining my peaceful holiday, plus this flaccid, nearly convicted drug addict. She turned to the latter as the lesser of two evils. 'Hello, Baz.' Showing surprising strength in his lank wrists, he was organising and lifting several large suitcases onto a trolley.

'Cheers, Alice.' He smiled. This, in itself, was out of character. But now they were gathering themselves together and she still hadn't said hello to the woman called Dora. She couldn't or wouldn't yet. That was all there was to it.

'I'll take Lily.' Alice lifted the baby as she spoke, with eyes only for her.

'Mama! Mama!' shouted Lily, waving her fat arms at Dora.

'Her speech hasn't moved on much,' commented Alice to Florrie, attempting a light-hearted laugh. Soon they would all have to bundle into her car for the ride to the heliport and then she could hardly overlook the existence of this alien woman in their midst. She could feel the concentration of her gaze, those bright eyes and her unconvincing silence. She sensed Dora was an unquiet person. The big leather case with the faded gold initials and a multitude of straps must be hers. It was a very unquiet case, and extremely unlike anything that could belong to anyone remotely resembling a cleaning woman or even a housekeeper.

'Dora and Baz were brilliant at entertaining Lily on the train.' Florrie tickled her daughter under the chin. 'Dora sang Mexican folk songs. She's been living in Mexico, you know.'

Alice gritted her teeth. 'I only booked two of us on the helicopter. They're very full at this time of year.'

'Dora got cancellations, Mum. You mustn't worry about a thing. This is your holiday.'

Alice gave up temporarily. Florrie had taken in that she was on holiday, which was amazing in itself. She didn't even try to organise the seating in the car so, naturally, the alien came in beside her. On her fingers, as she did up her safety belt, Alice spotted a glittering diamond ring. The same sweet scent that she had recognised on Lily after her kidnapping, filled her nostrils. In the back Lily chortled while Florrie and Baz made funny noises. At least that excluded the possibility of conversation.

At the heliport, also, there was far too much travel activity for any sentences beyond 'Surely you were carrying four bags not three,' usually directed at Baz who had turned out to be a dedicated beast of burden, and once they were on the helicopter, the noise was overwhelming. Alice was amazed to realise that her last, ill-omened trip on a helicopter had been a mere six days ago, last Saturday to be precise. This commercial helicopter was far bigger and her mood, she tried to calm herself with the thought, was altogether different: no pressure from a predatory millionaire, or from his guest and her interviewee, the horrible Ivo Swayne, whose profile she should have delivered on Tuesday. All swept away into the great blue yonder.

The great blue yonder seemed even wider after they had landed at St Mary's and embarked on a boat for Tresco. The trouble was that such a paradise of beneficent sun and frolicsome waves was sure to have a snake.

'This is not my usual lifestyle,' pronounced the alien, as they stepped off the boat and watched their bags manhandled on to a three-wheeler truck – there were no cars on the island. But that was all right, Alice thought. It was not her usual lifestyle either. That was the whole point. 'Take your time.' Dora turned to Alice, came closer, although she didn't try to touch her. 'However this happened, it was always going to be a shock.'

Alice looked away. She felt a frown torturing her forehead, a lump in her throat, tears behind her eyes. She felt like a child who wants to be invisible. Perhaps later she'd be stronger. Now she couldn't even speak.

It was still only five thirty when they arrived at their rented cottage, a square, three-bedroomed house in a row of others. There was only a strip of grass and a track that seemed to run round the island between the houses and the sea. This should have been charming. Soon she was standing in a little hallway.

'Who sleeps where?' Alice asked Florrie, out of earshot of the others.

'Oh, Ma. You're in the best room that faces the sea. Lily's in the little room at the back and Baz and me in the yellow one.'

'But I thought you and Baz didn't . . . ,' she hesitated '. . . share a bed.' She hesitated again. 'And what about . . . ?' She couldn't complete the sentence.

'There're twin beds and Dora's going to stay in a hotel. In fact she's off already.'

Alice looked where Florrie was pointing through the still open door and saw that, indeed, the woman had hitched a ride on the little truck, legs swinging on the back, leaning comfortably against her distinctive luggage. Confusingly, she felt the grit of disappoint-ment. 'How can a cleaner afford to pay for a hotel?'

Florrie gave her a disbelieving frown, then went upstairs and began to empty clothes onto the twin beds.

Alice watched her for a few moments but the atmosphere of waiting for something to be said became oppressive so she went to her own room and lay on the bed. She could see the sea. It was darkening now, the sun barely skimming the surface. At last she made up her mind. 'I'm going for a walk!' she called, and went quickly down the narrow stairs. As she passed the living room, she saw that Baz was changing Lily's nappy while she chewed contentedly at a stuffed rabbit.

The island, Alice knew, was only three miles square, although more round than square. The sense of the great blue yonder might easily be swapped for prison claustrophobia. Napoleon, for example, had never seen much to praise in Elba.

Alice walked for ten minutes or so, uphill with dry feathery grasses tickling the sides of her legs, until she saw ahead of her, tucked in on the bow of a small inlet, a large building that could only be a hotel. It was one floor high, with a grey-slated roof, but at the back there was a walled area that might contain a swimming-pool, and in the front a series of three terraces, the lowest almost level with the sea.

'It's good of you to check I've settled in comfortably.'

Alice found Dora sipping a glass of champagne on the terrace furthest from the sea. She'd changed into a pale blue silk blouse and a pair of purple trousers. The effect, with her white hair and a string of amethyst beads, was impressive.

'I'm afraid I'm not smart enough for you.' She heard her voice, distant and polite, as if she was talking to a stranger.

'It's a habit I have, changing for dinner. My husband insisted. But, then, he was Mexican.'

Alice thought, It's not too late to run – but where could she run to? She must remember she was captive on the island. The island she had chosen. 'My late husband would have liked that too. But he was English.'

'Men enjoy a woman who dresses up. It feels like a compliment, I suppose. Even Baz notices if Florrie puts a flower in her hair.'

Alice didn't want to discuss Baz and Florrie. She needed a little more time. She sipped the champagne that Dora had ordered for her. 'It's a great view,' she said eventually.

'Very dull, I'd say, all that sea. I've never been fond of the sea since I was married to my first husband.'

It was her heart that was popping and fizzing, Alice thought, not the bubbles in the champagne. 'Have you been married often?' After all, they both knew that she knew the answer to the big question: who was your first husband?

'A modest amount, given the circumstances. My first husband wanted to cage me, the second was a crook, and the third died three months ago.'

'My husband died.'

'Have some more champagne.' Without waiting for an answer, Dora called over the waiter. 'I prefer Bellinis but I can imagine the sourness of the peaches here. Sourness is a curse of the northern isles. It affects everything. People become addicted to disgusting sweets called Popsicles or Love Hearts but it doesn't help. My second husband, with whom I ran away from the first, was very sweet, like sherbet that dissolves on the tongue. He was Hungarian, but he might have been anything. He was a type, totally charming, totally unreliable.' Dora smiled and drank from her second glass.

'How long were you married to him?'

'Impossible to answer. Even before we were married, I tried to return to your father . . .'

Alice lifted her refilled glass of champagne. The bubbles exploded aggressively against her nose. Beyond them the sea, Prussian blue and flat, provided no escape. Screaming was an option, she supposed. She was vaguely aware of other guests on the terrace but they didn't matter. Continued denial was perhaps more sensible. On the other hand she could try protestations, accusations and rage. Words like 'impostor' might be useful in this scenario. She rolled it inside her head – *'impostor'* but it dribbled around pathetically and went away. Perhaps facts were the answer. 'Facts put order into the chaos of emotion.' Who had said that to her? Richard, probably. He had taught her so much. Did she really have to change the whole basis of her life?

'The curtains moved in my flat and I thought it was a burglar. A woman burglar. But when I took the porter up there was nobody. He thought I was ridiculous.'

'Your porters *are* ridiculous. They'll do anything for a crisp ten-pound note. Or a soggy old one, I expect.'

'When I looked down from the balcony, I thought I saw a woman in a fluttering dress as the curtains had fluttered but she was a friend of the Hunters, who'd just arrived back from the country.'

'If you smile, compliment the children, you can talk to anyone. It doesn't make them your friend.'

Alice wanted to accuse her of cruelty but she'd come to her willingly and posed questions. 'You've been following me,' she stated.

'Stalking, actually.' Dora retained her cheerful air.

'And you're not called Dora.'

'Very nearly.'

Alice knew her dead mother had been called Pandora. The past tense was momentarily soothing.

'It's true I've been stalking you and Bingo, Florrie and Lily, and Peter, of course. But you were the hardest. How should I have behaved?'

Alice stood up. 'I don't believe you!' she tried saying. At last there was anxiety, even guilt on the face of the woman in front of her.

'But you won't go, please! You'll eat with me? We can telephone Florrie on her mobile. She'll understand.'

Alice sat down again. 'Does Florrie know?'

'I could hardly kidnap her daughter and not tell her, could I?'

'You told her, then? All those weeks ago?'

'She was supposed to break the news to you but she said you wouldn't listen so we opted for secrecy instead. I knew she could keep a secret. She advised against telling your son. Even from a distance I could tell he was far too like his father.'

'You didn't know his father!'

'His grandfather, then. As you get older, generations become muddling.'

'But his grandfather kept a huge secret. If it's all true. I don't believe you. You understand that, I hope. I'm just keeping you company.' Alice knew she was talking wildly but at that moment it seemed a better option than any other. 'I think you're an impostor!' There, the word was out, the *p* ringing imperatively.

'An impostor?' Pandora frowned enquiringly.

'Trusting Florrie is mad.'

'But she kept her word. She didn't tell you.'

'That's because – because...' Alice tried to think why Florrie hadn't told her own mother about this impostor (she could run this line a little longer), '... because she's perverse.'

'Daughters always favour their grandmothers over their mothers.'

Her complacent tone was too much for Alice. 'You don't know anything! Nothing! You haven't existed for forty years! You don't exist now. You're not real!' But she gave up with 'impostor' this time round. She thought of all those years when she'd searched for her mother and the day she had given up, in London, when she was eight.

Pandora looked round the terrace. 'We're driving the punters away,' she noted, in an unconcerned manner. 'The management won't be pleased.' She tried to catch Alice's eye but she stared determinedly out to sea. 'Of course, Bingo was thrilled to see me. I knew he would be, silly old bugger, despite his truly appalling behaviour. Can you imagine any human being separating a mother from her baby?'

'But *you* left! And I wasn't a baby. I was three!'

'You were quite backward, as a matter of fact. I was delighted when I saw how well you'd turned out.' She interrupted herself. 'Waiter! Two more glasses of champagne, if you please. Your father was in the wrong, even if I left. He drove me to it. He was domineering, selfish and insensitive. It was mental cruelty. He didn't physically abuse me because he wasn't man enough. Even so, for your sake, I returned.'

'No, you didn't!'

'You were at school.'

'I didn't go to school till I was five.'

'You were at play-school. He sent me packing in an hour. He said I was sullied goods.'

'Well, you were, if you went off with another man.'

'Nonsense. I was enhanced goods. Perry taught me all sorts of things. But Bingo didn't want to know. Sheer obstinacy. He *longed* to have me back.' Pandora paused to give a languorous look at the waiter, who was refilling her glass.

'You're ridiculous. You couldn't be anyone's mother!' Vacantly, Alice watched the waiter scuttle away.

'It's true I never had any more children. After Perry left me and Bingo read me such a lecture I had to leave him again, I rather lost heart for that sort of thing. Children need security, unwavering affection, total commitment.'

'No!' said Alice. 'They just need you to be *there*!'

Pandora took a larger gulp of champagne than usual as if this shaft had shot home. Alice thought they were both becoming drunk – a necessary anaesthetic.

'When I saw Bingo in the nursing home—'

'How could you? As if I didn't exist.'

'What was I supposed to do?'

Alice put her head in her hands.

'I couldn't believe you hadn't guessed it was me. Lily and Bingo—'

'He told me you were dead. Dead. As in *gone for ever*. He told me you would never come back.'

'He was wrong to do that. I told him so. Death is an act of God, irrevocable. Divorce is an act of man, easily reversed.'

'There were no photographs. Nothing. I didn't even have a dead mother!' Alice could feel herself becoming a wild thing.

Pandora sighed as if with resignation. 'Bingo was a cruel man. I don't overlook how he made you suffer. And now, of course, having taken it out on you, he's absolutely thrilled I've come back. He said his life was so boring he was contemplating suicide. He showed me his secret cache of pills. When I turned up, he was a man without hope.'

'He says all sorts of things. He's got Alzheimer's. Very nearly anyway. Didn't you notice? I visit him every Thursday.'

'As an act of duty. He told me.' Pandora gave Alice a stern look. 'He felt he was a burden to you. He felt humiliated by his age, his mercifully occasional incontinence, his life in a prison cell. But don't think I'm unsympathetic.'

'It's a very expensive nursing home!'

'When my dearest Homero was dying – he was twenty-seven years older than me – I looked after him night and day. With the help of a nurse, of course. The Mexican Indians make wonderfully patient nurses. He died in my arms.'

'My father is not dying.'

'No. But he isn't living either.' This was delivered with the certainty of incontrovertible truth.

For a few moments they were both silent. Darkness was unrolling itself across the sea. Alice wanted to say, 'Everything's happened because of you,' but she wasn't ready yet.

'We should eat,' said Pandora, eventually.

'If they'll let us into the dining room.' Alice hadn't meant to set up a spark of complicity between them but she could hardly take it back.

'Yes. Now, you call dear little Florrie and I'll go and freshen up a little.'

As Pandora walked away, Alice took her mobile from her bag and obediently rang this *dear little Florrie* whom she'd never known.

'I'm having dinner with *Pan*dora,' she said, with what she hoped was a vicious edge to her voice. It's hard to be made a fool of by your own daughter.

'OK, Mum,' said Florrie, calmly. 'We'd already guessed as much and Baz is cooking us lentils.'

Alice put away her mobile, avoiding imprecations from her message service, and walked through to the dining room.

Pandora hadn't yet arrived but a waiter showed her to a reserved table at the window. She resolved to be as calm as her daughter, listen and judge.

Pandora returned, swanning across the room with a silvery throw coiled round her shoulders. 'I guess I'm a flamboyant dresser,' she responded, to Alice's look, 'my own taste, not my husbands'.'

Alice remembered the bright pink trousers in the service station when the rain poured down and a baby cried. She struggled to remain calm. 'Why have you come back?'

'I told you, poor old Homero died.'

'So you had nowhere else to go?'

'Certainly not. I had plenty of places to go. Or to remain. Look, if you're hoping I'll play the humble penitent, you're going to be disappointed. My life has been no easier than yours. Shall we order?'

While they ordered, Alice examined closely the appearance of the woman opposite her. The white hair, she noted impartially, still held a trace of something brighter ... possibly – it was impossible to avoid the thought – red. The face had the leathery look of skin that had seen too much of the sun, yet the outlines of the features were still clear and made Pandora look, sometimes, surprisingly young. Despite her last comment, it was not a face that had let responsibility or anxiety weigh too heavily. 'How old are you?' she asked abruptly.

'Eighteen years younger than your father. That was part of the problem.'

With a start Alice recalled that eighteen years had been the age gap between herself and Richard.

'I came to England,' continued Pandora, 'because I felt sorry for you when your husband died. I knew you would need a mother.'

'He died nearly three years ago! And how did you know that anyway?' She could hear her voice rising. She sliced a piece of fish pâté and stopped her mouth with it.

'I could not leave Homero till now. Surely I told you that? And Bingo is either craftier or not quite such a monster. He wouldn't tell you about me, but he told me about you: marriage, births, your husband's death. Enough for him to know he hadn't lost me for ever. I see he gave you my engagement ring too.'

Alice looked down at her finger without seeing it. 'How could he keep up such a pretence, such a lie?'

'He was busy saving the world – the world of Hove. Busy men don't find personal affairs important. They're odd like that. I once knew a busy businessman who hadn't noticed his wife had gone deaf.'

'Why didn't she tell him?'

'Oh, she couldn't worry him with a thing like that.'

They both ate more of the pâté, although Alice was feeling a little sick. The cocktail-party tone of their last remarks seemed hardly appropriate, although she couldn't imagine what would be better. Must she accept that this extraordinary woman, folded in silver, was her mother? She couldn't deny the fact, if it were a fact, but she could refuse to admit her into her life. Bitterly, she considered Florrie's disloyal behaviour in secretly siding with her grandmother, if it were her grandmother.

'Shall we have some wine?' asked Pandora.

'Not for me,' Alice answered stiffly, and regretted it at once.

'I'll order a bottle just in case. One should always drink too much in times of crisis. I have been there. I know.'

Then there was her father, Alice thought, just as disloyal and even more secretive than Florrie. Really, Peter was the only one in the clear and that was because Pandora hadn't thought him worth telling.

'What are your plans for my father? Are you planning merely to disrupt his life or have you something more positive in mind?' She could have been asking the same question about herself but she didn't want to think about that.

Pandora smiled leniently. 'Silly old fool. He's lucky I haven't given up on him. I took him out for a stroll by the sea, you know, and he was so rude I left him by the pier. I nearly pushed him into the water. In fact, I probably would have pushed him in but the chair wouldn't go over the pebbles. He's a barbarian! I told him so, and when he started to spew forth insults again I reminded him that, whereas he'd been able to treat me that way when he was in the prime of his life and I hardly more than a schoolgirl, things were different now. I'm a strong woman, hardly past her prime, and he's a weak, doddering thing who needs a bottle to pee in and a zimmer for even one independent step. That shut him up. He called me a bully but I could see it was meant affectionately.'

They both watched silently as a waiter removed their first-course plates and presented them with large fishes.

'So why did you abandon him by the pier?' Alice began again.

'A whim. No, I lie. I left him there to reinforce my point. You don't want to know what went on between your father and me. It's all too long ago for recriminations or even accusations. Let's just say I was glad to see him look so pathetic.'

'Sister Mary Rose called the police. If it wasn't for her concern about the reputation of the nursing home, you could have been charged.'

'Is that what she told you?' Pandora eyed her large fish speculatively. For a slim woman she seemed to eat and drink an awful lot. 'Of course, I put dear Mary Rose in the picture.'

'You put Mary Rose in the picture ... You mean Mary Rose knew who you were?'

'Don't be so upset. She's the one closest to poor old Bingo, after all – she had to know my plans.'

'I'm his daughter!'

'Yes. Yes.' Pandora smiled kindly. 'So you'll be more pleased than anyone to hear that I'm taking him out of that dreary place and we're setting up home together. I've got my eye on a very nice flat in a mansion block in Kensington.' She looked at Alice's horrified face. 'Don't worry. That was a joke. But I will find a flat somewhere in London, or maybe Brighton. Not Hove. I have bad memories of Hove.'

'It's no joking matter,' said Alice, with a mixture of severity and resignation. The waiter had poured her a glass of wine, which she gulped thirstily. Thinking about the practicalities of looking after her father was a comparative relief; she drank some more. 'He needs round-the-clock nursing.'

'So did Homero.'

'There're no Indian slaves in England.'

'Filippinos, Ghanaian or Nigerian, I'm advised.'

'Aren't you ashamed of yourself?'

Pandora rearranged her stole on her shoulder. 'I know what you mean. Although primarily a businessman, thank God, Homero was also a poet. His brother was a priest. Is a priest. A remarkable man.'

Alice wondered how much she wanted to know about this woman's life outside England. Not very much, she decided. Please. She tucked into her own fish fiercely.

'You asked me why I came back. You'll be wondering why I'm eating fish.' She waited expectantly.

'Everybody eats fish on an island.'

'My reason is that today is Friday. On Friday Catholics don't eat meat.'

'Yes, they do,' said Alice. 'All that bogus stuff was swept away in the sixties.'

'Not in Mexico.' Pandora looked nettled. 'Or among the old believers.'

'But you can't be that!' Was the woman mad or merely eccentric?

'You're right. I wasn't telling the truth when I said I'm no penitent. But I'm a very new believer, new to shame and penitence and guilt. It doesn't always come easily but I'm here to try. Looking after your father is part of the penitence. You, of course, if you will allow it, are the reward.'

Just for a second, Alice felt herself seduced by the warmly glowing eyes but then she hardened her heart. She pushed away her plate. 'You've had the reward already. Florrie and Lily have fallen into your lap.'

'What a curious expression! But they do understand how much I love them. They're free spirits, as is that charming boy Baz.'

Silence seemed the only response to this, broken by the waiter's reappearance.

'My daughter and I would both like some zabaglione,' announced Pandora, grandly.

Alice felt bemused. She was not up to anything further, not tonight anyway. She had heard the words 'my daughter and I' pronounced as if they had real meaning.

'I think I'll skip the zabaglione, if you don't mind. I should be heading back while there's a glimmer of light in the sky.'

'I understand.'

Alice was aware of Pandora watching her closely as she stood up. 'I have to go because . . .' Did she even want to try to sum up the evening?

'I understand. We'll meet tomorrow.'

A spurt of anger fuelled Alice with the thought, 'We'll see about that', but she didn't say it out loud. Perhaps she was too tired. 'Goodnight, then.'

'Goodnight. You may not believe it, but I can appreciate how difficult this is for you and I thank you for coming.'

It was true that she had come of her own free will. Thanks were in order. And very much more.

Alice walked slowly down the path. After the lights of the hotel faded, it was almost completely dark: the great moon of last night and its starry mantle were swathed in soft cloud. But the air was windless and warm. If it hadn't been for the need to peer down for rabbit holes and brambles, she'd have shut her eyes and allowed herself to drift along with the night. She thought of Guy's warm shoulder, his mouth joining hers. But he had left her alone, answering the call of the Master – or of someone else.

'Hi, Alice!'

Who was calling out of the darkness? Possibilities presented themselves like Macbeth's parade of ghosts.

'It's Baz,' said the voice. 'I brought a torch.'

Baz had come to look after her, the sort of caring a loving son-in-law might perform. His torch came flashing up to her. She must remind herself that he was part of the plot to bend her to Pandora's will.

'Thank you,' she said reluctantly, as he lit the path ahead of her.

In the cottage there was an air of festivity. Lily was still up or had got up again. She wore a white Baby-gro, decorated with what looked like strawberry juice.

'Did you have a nice time?' called Florrie, almost as soon as Alice was through the door. Florrie never asked her if she'd had a 'nice' time.

'Interesting.' She'd drunk too much to confront her daughter with her deceitful behaviour. 'I'd love a cup of camomile tea.'

'How wise! She does drink an awful lot.'

She, of course, meant Pandora.

'Who?' asked Alice, going over to Lily, who wore a solemn, sleepy look like an owl. 'You are up late, my darling.'

'Her teeth woke her,' said Florrie. 'They're gnawing away at her gums.' Even Florrie wouldn't answer the 'Who?' with 'Granny' or 'your mother'. Florrie had always had a mother.

Baz put on the kettle, which began to hum like a spinning-top. The atmosphere should have been sweetly cosy, thought Alice bitterly. Really, something had to be said.

'Do you think she's a fantasist, Dora or Pandora, or whatever she calls herself?'

'Oh, Mum!' Florrie gave a long sigh.

'But you can't believe all the stories she spins!' Out of the corner of her eye, she saw Baz edge out of the room as if he were clearing the space for action. But she couldn't deal with action. Apart from anything else, her head was whirling in a rather sickening way.

Florrie poured water over the teabag before she answered. She put the cup carefully on the table. 'You know, Mum, life is all about accepting things and moving forward.'

Alice felt herself gaping. Florrie's tone had been compassionate and patronising, like an elder person advising a younger. Alice thought of what she'd faced up to and moved forward from: the death of a mother when she was three, the death of a husband when she was forty. Even Lennie, her Cruse counsellor, had not talked to her like this. The only response was rage, but she couldn't indulge in that with Lily at her side. The baby was now emitting sharp squawks, like a nightjar. Alice bent to stroke her cheek and found her finger grabbed and stuffed into Lily's mouth.

'I told you she's teething,' said Florrie. 'Babies have a very hard time, you know.'

Alice felt the pain of being chomped on by Lily's silky gums with some pleasure. Did Florrie believe that recognising and accepting (to use her term) a mother who had been dead, as far as she knew, for forty years, was on a par with Lily's teething problems? Well, she wasn't going to play that game. 'I can't talk to you,' she said, liking the firmness in her voice. 'If you take the trouble to think a little more you may understand why. Perhaps I'll feel different in the morning but right now I'm going to bed.' Without looking at her daughter or granddaughter further, Alice left the room.

At least Florrie had the good sense not to make any comment.

The bedroom, now that Alice could no longer see the sea, seemed small and stuffy and she didn't feel energetic enough to unpack her bag.

Perhaps this was the moment to pick up her messages. The first three were from Brendan. Perversely, she was pleased by this. Perhaps she did mean more to him than a notch on his bedpost. She entertained, for a moment, the idea of being married to someone seriously rich. She pictured Goosefields, his first house that she had visited, his conservatory that smelt so seductively of orange blossom, the charming four-poster bed where she'd slept alone. That night was the innocent peak of their relationship, she decided, before the storm, the tree falling into the swimming-pool and everything that had followed. In his first and second messages he was trying to lure her back to Goosefields: 'I hope they looked after you especially well in my hotel. Unhappily I have to fly to New York for a couple of days but I'll be back for the weekend. Perhaps you could come over.' In the second message, he added the information that 'There'll be no house party.' As if no other guests was a positive, reflected Alice, indignantly. In the third message, Brendan sounded bad-tempered and as if he were on a plane. Perhaps his deal or his reason for going to America hadn't worked out, she speculated, with a sense of satisfaction. He was regretful, reproachful, even, that she hadn't answered his earlier calls. 'We're too old for games-playing,' he said, in a waspish tone.

'We certainly are!' Alice responded aloud, then cut him off and moved to the next three messages. The first was from Peter, reporting at length on his visit to his grandfather. 'He complained of loneliness,' he said, but it was not the night for hearing about that so Alice cut him off quickly too. The next was from Mary Rose, who received the same treatment, and the final one from Jonathan. Nothing from Guy. Jonathan's was as long as Peter's, telling her all about the concert she'd missed and detailing his plans for their next outing. After Guy's revelation about his sexuality (true or false?), she felt muddled about the proper reaction and saved the message for later. She was about to shut off the mobile when it rang.

'I caught you. What luck!' said Guy's voice. Alice felt it was luck too. 'Just checking to see you're making out OK. You didn't take the car.'

'No. I forgot I had one already. My own.' After the evening she had just passed, Alice was surprised to find herself laughing. 'I must have been moonstruck.'

'Me too. Harvest moonstruck.' Guy paused. 'So you like the island?'

'The island's great. The cottage is great. I've got a sea view.' Should she tell him about Pandora? What could she tell him about Pandora?

'No more news?'

'Some time I'll tell you. Another time. Not tonight.'

'You're making me curious. Nothing bad?'

'I shared a bottle of champagne with a bit of history. I'm glad you rang, Guy.'

'Sleep well.'

'You too.'

Just before Alice fell asleep, she wondered how Guy known that she hadn't removed the turquoise car from the station.

Chapter Twenty-Two

A Fourth Saturday

Alice turned over so that she faced away from the light shafting energetically through the thin curtains. When it came down to it, what was so wrong with being 'in denial'? She heard the words in quotes, mocking them to herself. Why shouldn't she deny this so-called mother, an old and eccentrically glamorous Mexican widow? Well, a widow any way. Certainly, by staying away for nearly forty years she had lost any rights due to her. Frankly, denial had a lot going for it. Denying Brendan, who had caught her at a time when she was sexually unstable, could hardly be bettered. Denying Blue was less attractive, since despite his later guest, she continued to believe in the romantic ideal of their lovemaking, but denying any resulting pregnancy was absolute top priority. She was forty-three. Most women's periods became irregular at her sort of age. When she returned to London, she would get her hormones checked or whatever was needed. What else could she positively deny? Jonathan was the prime candidate. Even Mitzi merited a dose, for her ridiculous obsession with her ex-husband. And her father and Mary Rose who had hidden the identity of their visitor deserved it doubly.

Of course, she saw that this kind of denial was not exactly Florrie's kind or, at least, a combination of various forms. But there seemed no reason why she shouldn't define her own terms. She would have a day off, in bed, in denial.

An hour or two later, when Alice had fallen asleep again, Florrie's voice called cheerily outside her door: 'Breakfast!'

'I'm in denial,' mumbled Alice, pulling up the duvet.

Later Florrie, who might or might not have heard her mother's words, tried again. She even opened the door. 'We're all going on a picnic. It's a lovely day. Baz has made delicious egg sandwiches with mayonnaise and fresh dill.'

'I told you, I'm in denial,' responded Alice, who had clocked the 'all'. After she heard them leave, she got out of bed and went down to the kitchen where she ate toast and Marmite for a while, then returned to her room. She hadn't even drawn back the curtains. Since she couldn't sleep, she began to think. It seemed worth considering the idea of throwing up her job altogether. She had obviously lost any gift or, indeed, appetite for interviewing, failing to spot Brendan as a crook (if he was one), failing to write up Ivo, who was the prisons minister even if he was personally revolting. And, anyway, wasn't it time she did some good in the world?

This thought was so exhausting that she fell asleep for another hour or so. When she woke she could hear noises downstairs. 'I'm dying for a swim!' called Florrie.

A little later there was a knock at the door. 'Would you mind babysitting for us while we go for a swim?' Florrie's voice – she hadn't opened the door this time – was polite but insistent.

'Get your Mexican fantasist to do the job.' Had they still not got the message?

'Pandora's having a rest. She brought a flask of tequila to the picnic and drank most of it herself. She was very disappointed you didn't come too.'

Alice ignored this last sentence and concentrated instead on listening to Lily chirruping on the landing. She imagined her sweet soft skin and chuckling laugh.

'OK,' she called. In a second the baby had tumbled out of Florrie's arms on to the bed and they were alone together.

'Mamamama . . .' drooled Lily, then rolled onto her stomach and tried to catch a strand of Alice's hair. Alice twisted it behind her, sat up and pulled the baby on to her knees. She began to bounce energetically, waving her hands as if to an admiring audience and ululating a song of happiness: *'Praise to thee, my Lord, for all thy creatures, Above all Brother Sun, Who brings us the day and lends us his light . . .'* When had she last thought of the song of St Francis? Not since she was six or seven when an unusual and beautiful book had appeared in the house with pictures of flowers and animals. Of course, she had guessed, or at least hoped, it was from her mother.

'Dearest Lily!' Alice felt reproved and hugged the baby, who immediately hurled herself forward in an effort to grab a necklace off the bedside table.

'No! No!' It took a good deal of strength to right her again and encourage the resumption of bouncing and joyous babbling. Only a few weeks ago, when Alice had stayed in the cottage, Lily had lain in her Moses basket or on a cushion and kicked and slept and fed, or cried and slept and fed. But now she had found language of a sort, action, independence.

'Well,' said Alice, pulling a witch's face, 'you are a surprise. When did this change happen? When Grandma wasn't looking, I suppose.'

'Moomoomoomoo,' responded Lily, delightedly, but Alice was hearing her own words again and considering an unwelcome idea. She gave Lily a serious look. The baby held it with wide-eyed attention.

'So it was *she* who changed you? Out in the rain and storm. Snatching you from your mother and grandmother, teaching you that life was yours and for the taking.'

'Gagagaga,' replied Lily, in full agreement.

'Yes, she's definitely that sort of person. Determined to do things her way. She abandoned me, you know, when I was hardly more than a baby, just because she thought my father was too domineering. No sense of responsibility at all. But that won't surprise you.' Alice half closed her eyes.

This was clearly the chance Lily had been waiting for: she launched herself once more at the bedside table, this time capturing the necklace, which she attempted to stuff into her mouth while sliding dangerously near to the edge of the bed.

'That's exactly what I mean,' cried Alice, as she caught Lily's leg and hauled her to safety. 'You and your great-grandmother both like living life on the edge.' She reinstalled Lily but allowed her to retain the necklace, which hung out of her mouth like a limb from a crocodile's jaw.

'I'm a very different sort of person.' She wagged her finger reprovingly at Lily, which made her giggle so that the necklace dropped out of her mouth, entailing another tussle before order was restored.

'I was brought up to believe in duty, particularly to those closest to you. It's no good hiding from someone as clever as you. With

Richard, who was the grandfather you never met, it wasn't always easy. He was a very private person and very exacting. But he chose me, carried me off from my home, which was extremely flattering, considering how young and stupid I was. To be perfectly honest, our sex life was predictable at best but you mustn't tell anyone else that. It's between you and me.'

Alice tickled Lily's tummy where the T-shirt had ridden up and decided that, even with a baby, she should change the subject.

'I admired him so much and it seemed amazing that he admired me. But he did. And we loved each other, of course.' Alice leant over Lily as if a tear might fall but nothing did. Instead she felt a rope of hair tugged painfully. 'Lily! That hurts!'

'Mamama,' shouted Lily triumphantly.

Perhaps she was not the best confidante. The extrication process took time and tact, and at the end Lily sat chewing her own knuckles, making sounds like a discontented seagull.

'I think you're hungry,' said Alice, 'but as your mother's still away, I might as well finish what I was going to say. The point is that Pandora, your grandmother, my mother – I just can't be bothered to deny it any more – is the sort of woman who makes me jealous. To be honest, if Florrie wasn't my daughter, I'd feel much the same about her. I think that ridiculous term "free spirit" would probably describe her, the very opposite of what the two men in my life, my father and my husband, believed was important. And yet here she is posing, because it is a posture even if it's a biological truth, as my mother.'

Lily's squawks were now rising so Alice took her in her arms and held her over her shoulder, then continued to speak: 'And the trouble is, I can't let all this wash merrily over me. I have to take a position. Not a posture, you note.'

'Muhmuhmuhmow.'

'Now, ssh, darling, and listen. As I was saying, I can't just run away. After all, she's planning to live with my father. I have to take a line, be involved. However much I might want to take the next boat to an even more remote island than this one, I can't.' Alice smiled a little. 'Well, I could, perhaps, just for a day or two, take off again. They wouldn't miss me. Of course I would miss you, my cherub. What do you think? I'll let you make the decision, yes or no?' Alice squeezed Lily tenderly and lifted her downy head from her shoulder so she could see her face.

But Lily was fast asleep, all emotion save placid contentment cleared from her face. Alice laid her in the bed beside her. This time, she didn't speak out loud but she thought, Yes, that is what I'll do. Take off in the morning and find a bit of peace.

Chapter Twenty-Three

A Fourth Sunday

The boisterous waves banged at the sides and bottom of the boat. Ahead, the sea was deep emerald, decorated with the diamond flash of breaking waves.

'Is this always a rough stretch of water?' Alice shouted, at the man at the helm. When they'd left Tresco harbour – waved off by Florrie, Baz and Pandora, with Lily in the latter's arms – the sea had been quite placid.

'Can be in winter.'

So this was not rough at all. Alice shrank back as heavy spray came drenchingly over the side. The man at the helm, she noticed now, wore oilskin trousers. He had a grim, weatherbeaten face under a flat cap, and could have been any age between thirty and sixty. Also in the boat was a box of three chickens, which were completely silent, perhaps from terror.

Perversely, since her aim in this trip was to cut herself off from mankind, Alice felt a strong urge to talk to this dour representative. 'Do you bring many people over?' she shouted.

'Enough.' He glanced over his shoulder to where she sat huddled in the stern. What did he see? Alice wondered. A cowardly middle-class, middle-aged woman, inappropriately dressed in a cotton skirt and light sweater. But actually she wasn't frightened, just astonished at the fierceness of the sea. She didn't even mind being wet, although she hoped her B and B had drying facilities. Perhaps that did make her old and dull.

This further island had seemed at first a black stripe on the horizon but now she could see to the right, the west, a slow ascent to a sharpish point. Gradually colours emerged from the black, bright yellow-green on the lower easterly side, rusty gold in the middle and a darker green rising to black on the tallest silhouette. All this blurred into a whirling kaleidoscope as a particularly large wave burst as high as her face.

She noticed that the helmsman was steering into the waves to avoid the boat being hit broadside and tipping right over. They were now at the furthest point from both islands, the wind gusting merrily. The sea was much darker, reflecting a layer of cloud that was gathering above them.

Alice considered what would happen if the captain misjudged their course and the boat suddenly flipped over, throwing its passengers, chickens included, into the churning water. The chickens would drown, presumably, but she and Terry (she remembered his name) would swim, although perhaps he was not able and would cling to the hull, while she struck out boldly for the island ahead, thrown up eventually, like the shipwreck in *The Tempest*, on an alien shore.

This dramatic fantasy so entertained Alice that she failed to notice their progress had become smoother and more direct. Suddenly a harbour was in view, a rugged stone wall on either side of a small beach. A few boats were moored and one or two figures were already visible on the right-hand pier. At their present speed they would arrive in five minutes or so. Momentarily panicked, Alice tried to prepare herself for a new landing, a new start.

The welcoming party, if that was what it was, was as dour as the helmsman, without being actively unfriendly. There were two women and a man. One of the women took the chickens while the other picked up Alice's bag. The men moved to the side and began a conversation using so few words that Alice wondered how they could get their meaning across.

Following the two women, neither of whom exclaimed at her wetness, Alice left the coastline and trekked across low-lying pasture where a large herd of bullocks grazed.

At a gate the women waited for her to catch up. The younger, with dark hair and rosy cheeks, pointed ahead. 'That's where we're going to.' Across another wide field, encircled by a group of trees, a couple of whitewashed houses stood at right angles from each other. Beyond, she glimpsed sea. They would have crossed the island, which at this end was hardly more than half a mile wide. Looking at the sun, in the south straight ahead, she understood why the buildings had been positioned in what must be the warmer, even if more exposed, side of the island. Perhaps the force of the prevailing westerly winds was broken on the rugged further end before they reached this little enclave.

'Shall I take a turn with the bag?'

'No. No.'

Beyond the pasture, to her right, were several more fields, filled with dark golden stubble, then rough grassland, broken with rocks and overgrown with patches of bracken, gorse and thistle, sloped upwards ever more steeply to a wilder part of the island. It must be about seven or eight miles long, she estimated.

A dog came to meet them as they neared the houses, a black-and-white sheepdog that crawled ingratiatingly at the older woman's feet.

'He chased the stock,' she explained to Alice, 'so he's in disgrace. Aren't you, Gyp?' As she bent to pat him, Alice saw he was attached to a long rope. 'I'm Pat,' continued the woman, 'and this here is Demi what you'll be staying with. Here, now,' she handed over the case, untied the dog and went into the nearest cottage. Demi led on.

'What a spectacular view!'

Demi put down the chickens and looked at Alice in surprise, then glanced quickly at the huge sweep of sea and sky before them. 'It's just the sea,' she said indifferently. 'We don't even get much shipping, not real ships anyways.' She opened the door to the house.

Alice was reminded of Pandora's similar condemnation and wondered at the idea that two such different women should come to the same conclusion. Her bedroom was similar in size and clean austerity to the room on the previous island, except it had a huge, low-set window, obviously put in fairly recently. This time Alice didn't voice her awe at the expanse of water and air displayed there.

'Terry put it in when we married.' Demi seemed worried that Alice was standing transfixed at the window. 'It's too cold in the winter so we prefer the back. It's all right in the summer, though.'

'I like it.' Alice could easily imagine that someone who didn't like a sea view wouldn't want to wake up in this room every morning. But she felt sorry for the husband – her helmsman – who had chosen to create for his wife such an unwanted wedding present.

I'll give you sandwiches for lunch and a hot dinner in the evening.'

'That's fine,' agreed Alice, although there was clearly no choice in the matter. If the weather held, she could take her sandwiches and explore. 'Is there anywhere I can swim?' she called, after Demi's retreating back.

'The bird-watchers go in further along the coast, Terry says.' She clattered down the uncarpeted wooden stairs, giving the impression that only bird-watchers would be mad enough to do such a thing.

Later, armed with her sandwiches, Alice set out, walking slowly westwards.

She stayed as close as possible to the coastline, and soon found herself in thick bracken, sometimes tangled with brambles or prickly gorse. This wasn't the flowery Cornish path with its sea pinks and sandspurry, but a much wilder world. She remembered what Guy had told her about the ships wrecked along this coast and inevitably thought of Blue. Once again she replayed the evening and night they had spent together, literally seeing it in images rather than hearing any accompanying words. Even the knowledge that he'd seen the 'peroxide blonde' afterwards didn't tarnish him. She pictured herself coming off the sticky London streets into the artificially cool hotel, finding her way via many low-ceilinged corridors to the room where Blue, spot-lit in slanting sunshine, appeared to her like a golden apparition, yet with so much physical and sexual energy sparking off his sunburnt body, shiny blue shorts, gold chains and Greek-god face that it was hardly surprising she had lost her head. Alice stopped walking and smiled and sighed, but she wasn't going to reprove herself. Neither would she shame herself with memories of a different kind of sex shared with Brendan. At least she was doing very well in not thinking about the person she'd come here not to think about.

Alice walked on, in delightful uninhabited silence. After a while, she looked at her wrist but, of course, there was no watch – therefore no time. No sun, either, although it was perfectly warm. Soon she'd find an unbrambly patch and sit down with her sandwiches. The land had been gradually sloping upwards so she was now well above the sea and had seen no path leading down or, indeed, any obvious beach. In fact, after her wetting on the boat, her question to Demi about swimming had been more for form's sake than out of any real desire. It felt fine to be dry and comfortable, with only the choice of picnic spot to concern her.

Alice sat down to eat her sandwiches. She had rounded another headland and below her, some distance away, she could see a group of three cottages, so small that each looked as if it contained hardly more than one room. They must be where the bird-watchers stayed, she assumed. It was a remote place on a remote island. At the back of the cottages there was an even smaller shed, which she guessed was an outside lavatory. As she watched, a male figure wearing a peaked cap came out of the shed and went into the furthest cottage.

When Alice got back Demi was preparing supper. On looking at the kitchen clock she saw she had been out for nearly five hours. She hadn't gone any closer to the bird-watching compound, giving up the idea of finding a beach, but dawdled her way back, turning inland for a change and crossing a long field of crackly stubble. There, tiny birds flittered up from her feet and a reappearing low sun made the second run of poppies glow like rubies. Alice had pulled one through a buttonhole in her jacket.

Now she sniffed the smell of frying onions with hungry anticipation. She'd flung away half of the sandwiches, which had been made of white bread and tasteless cheese.

'Cottage pie at six thirty,' said Demi.

'Can I have a bath before?'

'You didn't swim, then? I'll put on the immersion. It's extra, mind you.'

'That's fine,' said Alice, going upstairs.

It was absurd to have no watch and no mobile that worked, although she knew there was a landline in the next-door cottage.

The kitchen was very hot, the oven still on, heating not only the cottage pie but the whole small room. Terry was already sat at the table in his shirtsleeves, his reddened face matching his coppery hair, and bent over a newspaper. He lifted it when Alice came in. 'All right?'

'Fine, thank you.' Alice saw that he was about forty, a good-looking man, although with something indefinably hangdog about him. She realised Demi was watching them closely. She brought the pie to the table as Alice sat down and Terry folded away the paper. They helped themselves and began to eat.

'You enjoyed your walk, then?' said Demi, eventually.

'Very much.'

'It'll be better weather tomorrow.' Terry put down his fork and stared at her. 'Demi says you want to swim. You've got to be careful round here.'

'Where's the best place?'

'There's a safe enough beach near the bird-watchers' place. Don't go out too far, though, or you'll meet the current.'

'I won't.' Alice was touched by his concern, although she supposed a drowned guest wouldn't be too good an advertisement for their B and B business. 'What happens if you do have an accident?'

'Helicopter,' answered Demi. 'I've been in it twice.' She said this with her eyes on her husband in what looked like an old reproach. He frowned heavily but said nothing.

'Anyway, if I feel I'm drowning, I'll shout for that bird-watcher.' Alice heard her bright voice cut into what had become an uneasy atmosphere.

'He'll take no notice,' muttered Demi.

'You'll be all right on that beach if you stay close to shore.'

'Yes,' agreed Alice, who was fast losing any desire to swim. This exchange seemed to have exhausted her hosts' appetite for conversation and the rest of the meal was carried on in silence apart from the odd request for bread or butter.

Afterwards, as Demi cleared away, Terry invited her to join him in watching television at his mother's cottage. So Pat was his mother. But Alice definitely hadn't travelled so far to watch television. She looked out of the window and saw it was still light, even sunny. 'I think I'll stroll a little.'

'Please yourself.'

The water beyond the harbour was immediately dark and deep, unbroken by glittering ripples as it had been in the morning and only brightened by the sunset's reflection. She could still see a clear outline of the island she had left and, despite her vacuous mood, which had persisted, pleasurably, all day, she couldn't resist picturing the cheery family scene being enacted there. Very possibly they'd all had supper at the hotel, Lily passed from hand to hand. More picnicking in the day, no doubt, with sandy bathing in shallow water and plenty of screams and laughter. Certainly, they wouldn't miss her, even though, she thought, just a little bitterly, she was paying for the rental of their cottage. But that was the price of her freedom, she told herself bracingly.

Restless now and rather cold, she took the quickest route back to the cottage, made even faster by her nervousness as the herd of bullocks seemed intent on beating her to the gate.

She burst into the kitchen to find Demi standing by the stove. 'Are those bullocks dangerous?'

'Oh, they're all right. Just a bit playful – like children.' As if these words had removed her energy to stand, Demi slumped into a chair at the table.

Alice tried to decide whether to suggest a cup of something.

'I shouldn't have mentioned the helicopter!' Demi's voice was loud and anguished, the opposite to her usual lacklustre tones. Alice stared helplessly, then also sat down. It was clear there was more to come.

'Now Terry'll be upset for days. I promised myself I wouldn't bring it up again but I can't forget, can I? It's not that he doesn't want kids too, I don't say that. But it's not the same for a man, is it? They don't have them and lose them, do they?' She paused in her flow and looked up at Alice, although her eyes were blinded by the passion of her thoughts. 'I expect you have kids?'

'Two,' said Alice. 'I'm so sorry . . .'

'It's not just the miscarriages and the helicopter being late and everything. That's not Terry's fault and I'm not stupid, you know. It's the whole thing, the island, my life, our life.' She paused again, this time without looking up.

Alice understood that she was playing the role of stranger as listener and must not, could not escape.

'It's been ten years now and my sisters have got seven kids between them.'

Alice considered her options. Either she could make meaningless sympathetic noises or she could intervene in an attempt to shift the picture. Clearly, the first option was the sensible course – Demi was already talking again, filling in more details about what she obviously felt was an insoluble problem, without looking for any response. 'Why don't you leave him?'

'What!' Demi stopped in mid-sentence.

'Just walk off,' Alice amended this quickly. 'Leave the island. Tell him you're too unhappy. You can't bear it any more. Shake him up a bit.'

'For a holiday, you mean? I do that already. Twice a year.'

'For good. Your life together isn't working, so leave him. You can find someone else more sociable and he'll find someone who enjoys island life.'

'But I *love* him!'

Oh, yes, love. Alice wondered how she had managed to leave that yawning chasm (why did she call it that?) out of the equation. At least it had released Demi from her depressive Ancient Mariner cycle. She was now speaking excitedly about the wonders of Terry and how they had hit it off straight away. Suddenly, and much to her surprise – she had assumed herself more or less invisible – Alice found she was under attack.

'You're all the same, you single women who come here for a week or so, licking your wounds. Old and bitter, and thinking you know better. Let me tell you, divorce isn't the answer. I see it in your faces, wrinkled and cold and unloving, unloved . . .' More of this followed, delivered with flashing dark eyes and flaming cheeks. Alice debated whether to inform this wrathful goddess of love that she was, in fact, a widow. Presumably it would puncture the hot air of rage, based as it was on a wrong premise. But, then, did she want to puncture it? It seemed her suggestion had indeed shifted the picture – for the better, since Demi was now passionately advocating a loving marriage, whatever the problems. Besides, if she said nothing she could slink upstairs.

'I'm sorry,' said Alice. 'I shouldn't have spoken.' And now male steps were approaching the cottage. 'I'm off to bed.' She fled.

Alice lay in bed in the extraordinary silence of the island. For quite a while after Terry and Demi had come to bed, it hadn't been silent at all. Alice had been embarrassed by the enthusiasm of their love-making, which she considered a bit of showing-off by Demi to her 'wrinkled and cold' guest. But now there was silence, no birds, no barking foxes, sniffling animals in the hedgerows, scampering mice in the wainscoting. What was it she was avoiding thinking about?

Alice touched her shoulder, her arm, her thigh. You could hardly think about sex – you either did it or you didn't. In the early days of her marriage when Richard had brought home *The Joy of Sex* and several other manuals, they had experimented quite successfully but she had become pregnant with Peter so quickly and Richard had immediately become less interested, although he had enjoyed stroking her rounded belly. She had been keener than him.

Alice rolled over on to her stomach as she was pricked with the dagger of the unresolved pregnancy issue. The room was cool and she had put on a long T-shirt, which rucked up uncomfortably round her hips. She ran her fingers along her warm inner thigh. She supposed she could make love to herself, but whose face would she hold in front of her? Whose body would she imagine approaching hers? She'd always needed that stimulus, which was why, after Richard's death, she'd seldom touched herself at all. She would have felt like a necrophiliac to conjure him back and she'd no one to put in his place.

She supposed she had two new candidates now. She smiled ironically to herself: this had been her attempt to get away from humanity. Besides, the whole exercise might become rather squalid compared to the celebration of True Love so recently enacted next door. There was another reason why she hesitated. She could feel it hovering somewhere without being able to place it. Another reason, another person? Never mind. Enough was enough.

Alice pulled down her T-shirt brusquely, then turned on to her side.

Chapter Twenty-Four

A Fourth Monday

Alice was a long way across the island before the sun had come round from east to south. She had left the cottage early, not because the atmosphere was strained – despite their conversation, Demi was friendlier than she had been on Alice's arrival – but because she could tell it was going to be a stunning day and she felt mad keen now for a swim, imagining herself breasting the ocean rollers watched by an interested party of seals.

She had strode out boldly, well equipped with water, food, a book, a towel, a sweater, neatly stowed into a borrowed backpack. 'I'll see you for supper,' she'd told Demi, cheerfully. That would teach her to think her withered and cold.

All this was fine, but she'd forgotten what a long and tricky journey it was to the bird-watchers' commune. There were brambles to be avoided, springing at her like sharp-toothed elastic, there were rabbit holes subtly disguised at the side of the path. Once she thought she'd wrenched her ankle really badly, but she'd managed to shake out the strain. There was the path itself, which would veer unexpectedly near the cliff edge so that there was only a net of vegetation saving her from a hundred-foot drop to the sea. And now, after a couple of hours, the sun was back to its previous scorching habits and reminding her that the one thing missing from her backpack was sun-cream. At least she wore a hat.

At last the little group of houses was in view. Alice pulled off her hat, which was making her even hotter, and sank down thankfully on a useful sponge of heather. She took the water from her pack. After half a bottle or so she felt recovered enough to go forward and search for the beach. There it was, a bright patch of shingly sand, indeed a desirable destination. It was efficiently sheltered by a headland on either side. Now to climb down there. She took one last look before she started on a twisting path and stopped abruptly. A figure had just rounded the far headland and was striking out firmly for the shore.

Why shouldn't the bird-watcher, because it must be him, go for a swim on such a dazzling day? She felt unreasonably annoyed that her solitary idyll had another occupant. Surely a bird-watcher's habitat was a disguising bush where he would crouch for hours, large stomach and hips covered with a knobbly sweater, eating his way through a packet of toffees in special noise-free wrapping?

Alice started down the path. Swimming was what she had come to do and she'd not be put off. Since the path swung to the right, she soon lost sight of the swimmer, and when she could see the bay once more it was deserted. The cottages disappeared, too, hidden behind a rise in the ground, although she could just see the chimney of one.

Alice swam. The water was much colder than she'd expected, shocking her into quick energetic strokes that sent the blood racing round her body until she felt the longed-for glorious exhilaration. With a gasp at her bravery, she ducked her head under water so that her brains could feel the effect too.

She swam less fast now, at first watching the smooth horizon ahead but the sun, shining directly in her eyes, beamed off the water in blinding rays so instead she took up a diagonal course, first one way and then another. Now she could see all the little inlets, bays and gullies in the rocky cliffs.

Still zigzagging outwards, she was reluctant to turn but, in another few strokes, she'd be past the bay and into open sea, presumably with all the dangers of currents and undertows about which Terry had warned her. Although she was warm, the water had become colder and darker, so dark she could see nothing below her: it might have been a huge, empty chasm or a great vault alive with ocean-going creatures, catfish and sharks, eels and octopi. A little frightened by these images, fish faces swimming out of the void, some with rubbery, sneering mouths, others with rows of champing, pointed teeth, she had started to turn when she felt a mind-stunning whack on her left knee. That side of her body went limp and became useless. Tears filled her eyes as she flailed automatically with her right arm. Even so, she began to sink, salty water lapping into her mouth, which was open with the desire to scream.

This was a bolt from the blue, an unfair, unexplained, torturing pain. The scream, if it had come, would have expressed as much rage as suffering. But, spurred on by danger, her brain came to life again: she had swum too close to the cliffs and caught her knee on a rocky outcrop, submerged and invisible. At this point, as her head bobbed almost under the water, the imagined fishy teeth seemed child's play to what had attacked her. The situation only improved as her knee became numb.

Now she turned her anger on herself. It was not fate but her own idiocy that had led to this wounding. Everybody knew you kept an eye open for hidden rocks. At this point, she took another gulp of water, which sharpened her wits further: the rocks might provide a resting-place if they weren't too smooth-sided or jagged-topped. Slowly she felt her way forward until her fingertips touched the cold hardness, lightly encrusted with ancient limpets. Now to see whether there was a flat seat for her or just an anarchic tumble of sharp pinnacles. Although the sea was calm, it still washed and sucked against the rock, which made the exercise harder. She realised, also, by the pull of the water, that the tide had turned and was now going out, which would presumably bring the shore closer to where she was stranded.

The tears started again as she hauled herself painfully and carefully on to a ledge about a foot below the water. The trick was not to get washed off again but the tide was whisking away the inches and soon she could see her injured knee, blood fanning from it in red whorls. At least she was in the sunshine or the shock, which was making her shake in rigid spasms, would have been far worse.

As the water fell away from her she saw a new problem. If the rock became too high above the sea, she'd never get off it again, a human mermaid with the wrong sort of tail. Rather hopelessly, she gazed around her until her attention was caught by what looked like several balls floating a few metres into the open sea. Then one disappeared and reappeared closer to her. Her eye clarified by salt water, she recognised they were seals, come to cheer a maiden in distress.

Even from this distance, she could see that their wide faces were filled with curiosity and good humour. 'Oh, come and rescue me!' she cried, and they came nearer, performing a bobbing dance towards her until she could see the charming individuality of each whiskery, snub-nosed face. They were different colours, from pale to dark, although one was a surprising skewbald. He or she, Alice couldn't tell the difference, was the leader of the group, advancing closest, rising highest out of the water. 'I love you!' cried Alice, since there was no one to judge her a raving lunatic.

So intent was she on this new love affair that she didn't hear splashing from the shore. Not that there was much splashing as the swimmer executed a smooth, gliding crawl.

Suddenly the seals dipped into the sea and vanished. Almost at once, Alice heard a loud man's voice: 'You'll be cut off soon!'

She turned her head sharply. He was already about ten metres away, and his face, when it rose sideways from the water, was obscured by large goggles. There seemed no point in yelling so she waited till he was closer. She supposed she should be immensely relieved at a potential rescuer – presumably the bird-watcher she'd seen swimming earlier – but her first reaction was of annoyance that he'd scared away the seals. Experimentally, she stretched her knee a little and found it would move. Although it was painful, it was not the knockout agony it had been before.

'Are you hurt or just stupid?' He was right up to her now, goggle eyes glinting in the sunlight.

'Both,' said Alice. 'Stupid first, then hurt.'

This seemed to mollify him because he helped her gently off the rock and, as she winced and bit her lip, he suggested she turned on her back and he'd tow her in. Alice shut her eyes and let herself be drawn through the water. Although it felt cold now, she was curiously relaxed, like a child in the secure arms of an adult.

When the water was waist-deep, her rescuer stood, although still supporting her. 'Can you walk?'

'I'll try.' But the pressure of the water against her leg was too painful.

'Float in,' he commanded her. So, again like a child, she floated, arriving on the beach with the thankfulness of a shipwrecked mariner.

'Have you got a towel?'

'In my pack.' She was shivering much more violently than before, her teeth chattering in a quite unreal manner.

The rescuer went to where she had left her things. Soon he returned, minus his goggles, and began to rub her vigorously with the towel. It was only then that she knew.

'Blue!'

'Have you only just realised?' Kneeling on the sand, he made a funny little bow. 'I hoped I'd made more impression than that.'

'Of course I've only just realised!' Forgetting her knee, Alice tried to crouch and let out a cry of pain.

'I thought you'd come to find me, put a stop to the boredom of being incarcerated on a fucking desert island.'

'How could I know? I thought you were dead. I thought you were a bird-watcher.'

'A dead bird-watcher, that's a gas.'

'I saw you yesterday, I . . .' Alice stopped trying to explain and looked at him. He was sitting on his haunches. With one hand he was playing with the sand, letting it run through his fingers, like a filter, then inspecting the little shards of shell caught there. Despite his avowed boredom with his situation, he looked very at ease and not at all impatient. She remembered how he'd seemed to her in London, the incredible golden beauty that had knocked her sideways at the time and overlaid all her memories of him since.

'Are you staring at me or about to pass out?'

'I'm so grateful,' said Alice. 'In a minute I'll try standing.' He was deeply sunburnt, but in the brusque seaside light, she could see the blotches and wrinkles of imperfection. He was older than she had guessed, fortyish probably, and his face, even accounting for the scar and the flattened nose, was more battered, the dark stubble lightly mixed with grey. His curly sun-bleached hair had grown a bit longer, showing that it was receding and thinning a little. All the same, his eyes were that unforgettable dazzling turquoise-blue and he was still a remarkably handsome man . . . but, thought Alice, different. Then she thought, Maybe I'm the one who's different.

'This is like Robinson Crusoe meets Man Friday. Would you be even more grateful and stare less if I fried us some chicken?'

'I do have some sandwiches.'

'If they come from Terry's house, I'd take the chicken. I killed it myself this morning.'

Those silent chickens cowering in the boat.

'I won't be long.'

Alice watched Blue walk away from her. She'd asked him no questions – no serious questions. The present had left no time for investigating the meaning of her past. It seemed to her, as she lay quite comfortably in the sun, that the present had taken over her life for several weeks now. Blue seemed to believe she knew his whereabouts and had followed him. But how could she have known without anyone telling her? It was all chance. Alice shut her eyes with a strange mixture of bewilderment and content. When she opened them again, a dark shadow lay across her face.

'You fell asleep.'

'Did I?' Alice got to her feet. She walked slowly to the edge of the sea, intending to freshen herself with the water.

'Your leg's better, is it?'

Alice looked down, surprised. In her sleep she had forgotten about it, and now that she remembered, it only hurt a little. 'It throbs rather, but nothing worse.'

'Then you haven't sprained or broken anything. I'll give you a hand.'

Blue took Alice's elbow and, for the first time since their unlikely second meeting, Alice felt a quaver of desire. After all, their bodies which had known each other so intimately, were almost naked: she in a bikini, he in faded cotton shorts. But Blue showed no sign of feeling any attraction to her. He might as well have come across a Boy Scout in distress as a semi-clothed woman with whom he'd once made love.

They walked up the beach, through scrub, past a few stunted thorn trees, bent inland by the westerly wind, until they reached the first building and a barbecue made of bricks upon which chicken pieces were neatly laid. Blue brought her a wooden chair. 'It smells delicious.'

'Wild rosemary.' He handed her a nicely charred chicken leg, carefully transferring the three folded leaves that were stopping his fingers getting burnt. Alice was taken aback by his orderliness when in her imagination he was a free spirit. He went away again and returned with two bottles of beer. 'I keep them in a stream behind the houses.'

'The cottage must be horribly cramped.'

'Bird-watchers are out all day.'

'But you're not a bird-watcher.'

'I'm used to small places. Even the biggest ships have small cabins – especially for their divers. I've always lived in small places. When I was a kid, I had a cupboard under the stairs, then there were other rat-holes far worse.'

Prison. He was referring to prison. Alice had never managed to put together the god-like creature in the London hotel with the young victim/criminal whom Guy had described to her. It had been easier to forget it. Besides, Blue had been missing or dead at the time Guy had told her. He had said it was the reason Blue wanted to start his diving school, which was why Guy had wanted her to interview him in the first place. That had to be true. Alice shivered.

'You're cold.'

'I left my clothes with my backpack on the beach.'

He set out at once to get them. Alice recognised that this constant physical energy was very attractive. Probably its containment in the claustrophobia of a London heatwave had held her attention as much as his striking appearance. Richard's energy had been almost entirely intellectual. His expression of deepest intensity was reserved for whatever brief he was currently working on. Alice sighed and drank her beer.

Blue came striding up from the beach. Her towel hung round his neck. From a distance, at least, he looked like an advert for an aftershave lotion. Again, that quaver of lust rose.

'More chicken? More beer?'

'Yes. Please.' She took her clothes from him. He was real now, that was the thing. She put on her sweater and watched him delicately pick up a piece of chicken. On second thoughts, he was still surrounded by far too many mysteries to be real. He was just a little more like an ordinary mortal than he had been before. 'I don't think I'll try putting trousers over my knee.'

He studied it. 'The salt water's cleaned it fine. It's hardly more than a graze. The bruising's the problem.' He went inside and reappeared wearing a sweatshirt with his shorts, plus more beer and another chair. They sat together in an oddly companionable silence. Alice supposed she should ask him some questions now but was unwilling to break the mood.

'I like that you don't ask me anything.' Blue leant forward. As the light slipped westwards, his eyes were changing to a dark navy. They were watching Alice intently. 'I might have told you something in London. If you'd asked the right questions, I was prepared to then. But now the story's not mine to tell, even though it is my story.'

'How did you know I was planning questions?'

'It's only normal, isn't it? We meet, have sex, part, I disappear, perhaps drowned, perhaps murdered.'

'Murdered!' He must be playing games with her – and why should he want to do that? 'But you can't or won't tell me the story?'

'I told you. It's not my story any more.' He stood up. 'I'd like to show you something.'

She could have begged, she supposed, reassured him she was an off-duty journalist, in her case not a contradiction in terms, but he had taken her hand and was pulling her up gently.

'It's a walk. We can go as slowly as you like. Anyway, you don't want to let your knee stiffen.'

They set out westwards to the wilder part of the island, which Alice hadn't explored. Blue brought with him a shooting-stick, which he said one of the bird-watchers had left behind. In fact, the walking was not too hard as the soil became thinner, with grass or heather barely covering the rocky underlay. After a while, seagulls gathered high over their heads, escorting them noisily as they would a ship at sea.

Every ten minutes or so they stopped, Alice resting on the shooting-stick. Despite the birds, the atmosphere was tranquil and neither of them talked much. Alice wondered what there could be to look at in such a barren landscape. The ground sloped gradually but continually upwards so the westerly sea was still out of sight. Maybe that was what Blue wanted to show her, a great expanse of the Atlantic rippling away under the reddening sun. But that was nothing new. Or maybe it was a lighthouse rising dramatically from a rocky islet. There were plenty of lighthouses, one, she'd been told, with a heliport on the top. 'Are we on a lighthouse tour?' she asked.

Blue smiled. 'I've seen too many lighthouses to find them interesting. You know, they had to put one out of commission on the western end of St Agnes. It was drawing sailors to their deaths instead of warning them.'

Alice thought of how she had imagined Blue shipwrecked and at the bottom of the sea, but she wasn't allowed to ask him about that. 'This is a dangerous part of the world.'

'The ocean's always dangerous but you get to understand its ways. I feel more threatened on land.' He didn't allow time for Alice to comment before he added, 'We're on the last leg now.' He went ahead too fast for her to keep up. Without his guidance, the ground seemed more uneven and steeper and her knee was throbbing badly. There was more tangling vegetation, too. For the first time, she wondered how she would walk back to the bird-watchers' house, let alone to Demi and Terry's.

'Here we are!' He was standing just the other side of the crest of the hill, half silhouetted against the sea and sky. Alice limped up to him. 'Look.' She peered and discerned the top of a large, rounded stone, like a tombstone, jutting out of the ground. She went closer. It was so disguised by vegetation that if Blue hadn't pointed it out she would never have noticed it.

He pulled back some bracken and brambles. 'It's best kept covered. You never know when a visiting tourist might get out his penknife.' He ran his finger tenderly over the deeply carved lines. At its base there was a ditch big enough for a man to lie in. 'It's a man's face carved into the stone, do you see? He puts things into perspective, don't you think?'

Alice didn't know what to think. She opened the shooting-stick and sat down. The face looked back at her. It had wide eyes, broad lips and a flattened nose. 'He might almost be African.' She had to say something in response to Blue's enquiring expression.

'It's one of the earliest carvings of a human figure in the British Isles. Neolithic, if you like that sort of thing. But Terry calls him Billy.'

'He doesn't look very like a Billy to me. Did Terry show it to you?'

Blue turned away as if he might not answer, then relented. 'Guy told me about it.'

'Guy?' Here was another question she had to ask. 'He was our point of contact, wasn't he?'

'Guy's a great fellow.'

'I've known him for quite a while but there're lots of things I don't know about his life. Until a few weeks ago I'd never met him out of the office except at a nearby pub.'

'He wanted me to talk to you but we got a bit diverted, didn't we?' Blue smiled, irritating Alice who thought it had male-smirk undertones. It reminded her of something she'd rather forget: the woman who had been spotted coming out of Blue's hotel room.

'Is that what it was? A diversion?'

He took no notice of this. 'Guy and I only met last summer. We hit it off right away. Sailing, of course, but more than that. I told him about my plans. He was enthusiastic so I told him more of my story.'

'The story you can't tell me?' Alice was unmollified: that word 'diversion' still rankled. She had carried the memory ever since, three weeks now, and to him it was nothing.

'An earlier story.'

Alice found she was also annoyed by the word 'story'. As if he were important enough to be a hero in events, if such events could be strung together in some truthful and shapely order, which she sincerely doubted. In her view, everything that happened happened randomly and was so filled with lies that it was hardly worth recording. In a bitter little flash, she recalled the lie at the heart of her childhood: her father's lie about her mother's death. Perhaps, after all, 'story' was the right word, if it implied the untruth of fiction.

'What's the matter?'

So he was not entirely insensitive. Alice knew nothing about a man like Blue, with his background. He'd run back to England from Australia, she remembered, in search of his mother. Had it been in search of his mother? Now she couldn't remember exactly. She hadn't wanted any of this dark history to enter her golden memories.

When Alice didn't answer his question, Blue had come right up to the stone effigy and crouched down so that he could run his fingers over the lines of the face. 'He could tell us a thing or two about fucking survival.'

'So that's the issue, is it?' Alice was still cool.

'Yeah. You wouldn't know about that.' Suddenly he came right up to her, thrust his face into hers. 'I don't understand you. You live like you're in fairyland. Don't you see anything? What do you think it's all about if it's not survival? I might have been fucking dead, that's all. What a baby's life you must have led!' He gave Alice a look of disgust and turned away as if to walk homewards.

Speechless under this unprovoked attack, Alice watched. After a few paces, he turned round. 'And what were you doing sitting on that rock like the fucking heroine of a romantic novel waiting for Sir Galahad to rescue you? What if I hadn't come?'

Alice decided to defend herself on that particular issue. 'I'd have got off somehow,' she said. 'I'm not such a helpless idiot. The knee just hurt a lot to begin with—'

'Hurt? What do you know about hurt?' His anger, which had come out of nowhere, was escalating with her defence. But she wasn't as feeble as he thought her.

'And then the seals came to cheer me—'

' "The seals came to cheer me!" ' He was mimicking her voice, making her sound like an English middle-class twit. 'What have we got here? An inhabitant of La-la Land, the place where grapes grow on trees and the sunset's always red. Don't you ever try to imagine what's going on outside your own pretty world?'

'Yes!' screamed Alice. She had gone from calm to furious in one and it felt good. She hopped towards him because her knee was hurting – yes, hurting horribly. 'Of course I wonder what's going on. These last few weeks I've felt as if all the bits of my life had broken apart and were whirling round in a kaleidoscope, making no sense at all. And then all these new bits got thrown in—'

'Ta, oh, ta,' he interrupted, with a nasty satirical expression on his face. 'I've been called all sorts of things but I have to admit a "new bit" is a first. Any other revelations you'd like to share? Let me guess, your kaleidoscope is made up of darling psychedelic colours, which would explain why you reacted so positively to the little bit of something I popped into your champagne. Call me old-fashioned but I do know how to get a widow going.'

'You called me "a diversion"!' shouted Alice, hardly hearing his last words. 'If you think that makes me feel good—'

'But that's what it was, wasn't it? You came on to me like you hadn't seen a man for a decade. What did you want me to think? That it was romantic love with stars bursting overhead? You wanted me. You got me. With a bit of encouragement, we had a fucking good fuck. Didn't we? Isn't that what we had? Tell me different. Can you? Can you?' Now he was shouting. His sunburnt face was purple and distorted.

'You're ugly,' wailed Alice. 'You're ugly. What you say is ugly. What are you saying? You drugged me. You put something in the champagne. That's such an ugly thing to do—'

'So ugly is worst, is it?' He advanced on her and, for a moment, Alice thought he was going to take hold of her shoulders and shake her. But he passed by to stand once more in front of the Neolithic man. The sight seemed to calm him but she felt no better.

'Who are you to tell me what's worst or best? You've no idea who I am. I don't know about you, I admit it, but you don't know about me either! We're strangers!' She rethought, then yelled, 'We're strangers who shared a great experience. We're intimate strangers! And I don't care if you did put some pill into my drink, or if you fucked some tart the moment I left. It just shows what an insensitive whoring lout you are!'

Blue looked up at her, then back at the stone monolith. 'Billy here says if that's what you want to call me you must be right. Like a lady is always right about affairs of the heart. But Billy does have one question.' Blue's voice was quiet, almost meditative, so Alice was unprepared for what followed. 'Tell me this. If we're "intimate strangers"' – he imitated her voice again – 'what the fuck's your relationship with that murdering bastard Sir Brendan Costa?'

Alice thought of herself as non-violent. She had had no brothers or sisters to fight with, she had very seldom smacked her children, she had never thrown a plate or anything else at Richard. But Blue's accusation, combined with his mimicking, so enraged her that she found she had raised the shooting-stick as if it were a pike and rushed at him.

Blue parried it easily, catching the end, and laughed. 'I like it: "Late Lawyer's Wife Attacks Missing, presumed Dead, Deep-sea Diver". We could sell it for thousands.'

Alice sat down on the rocky ground. She had no heart to shout any more and neither it seemed, did he. The silence of the barren landscape and broad sea beyond was merciful, soothing the angry vibrations in her ears. The seagulls had gone. It must be getting late. However badly Blue had insulted her, she still needed him to help her back. He was staring moodily out to sea where the light of a lighthouse had just come on, not very bright yet.

How did he know about her night with Brendan? Probably that was a silly question. Probably everybody knew. She felt too weary to think about it now. At least Blue's continuing silence suggested he didn't plan to pursue the topic.

'I'm sorry,' Alice tried to catch Blue's attention but he gazed sturdily into the distance, 'I'm a fool. Call me what you want. I expect whatever you popped into the champagne was just the right prescription.'

Blue turned round. 'Yes. We'd better be getting back.'

'OK.' Alice got up obediently, but she wished he'd said sorry too.

It was a dismal walk to the bird-watchers' house. Blue didn't talk at all, striding ahead but waiting every so often for her to catch up. By the time the little cottage with its sloping roof and tall chimney was in sight, she knew she couldn't walk any further. Blue must have guessed the same because he opened the door for her to go through. As she'd guessed, it was only one room with a small iron stove, a little bed, a table and two chairs. A bucket of water, presumably for cooking or washing, stood in a corner. There were two windows, one at the side and one at the back.

'It's very primitive.' Blue gave her an unsympathetic look.

But Alice didn't care. She went over and lay on the bed. For a moment, she kept her eyes open, enjoying the gloom and stillness, knowing that as soon as she shut them she would fall asleep.

The scene was lit like an old master: an oil lamp stood on the table, giving Blue a diffuse halo. He was making himself a cheese sandwich. An open bottle of beer stood at his elbow. Alice had no idea how long she'd slept but felt revived. Her knee although it was stiff when she stretched it, hardly hurt at all and her head was clear.

Blue looked at her. 'Do you want a sandwich?' His tone was milder, she thought, his expression kinder.

'Thank you. I'll make it.' She went over to him, suddenly conscious, in the evening darkness, that her legs were still bare. 'Are my clothes around anywhere?'

'Yeah.' He indicated her backpack in a corner, and Alice put on her trousers. 'Pity, that. You looked better before.'

'I'm dressing for dinner.' Alice found herself smiling. She supposed she should have slapped his face. 'What time is it?'

'Ten o'clock.'

'No wonder it's dark.'

'It gets dark much earlier in London.'

'London has street-lights, car lights and house lights.'

Alice thought about London, about Richard's flat, Richard's bed, Richard's cupboard, from which Peter and Baz had taken suits. She thought about the balcony on to the street where she liked to stand, and the drifting white curtain, which had turned out to be her mother. I'm glad I'm not in London,' she said.

'Here.' He'd made her a sandwich and opened a second bottle of beer.

It seemed to be a peace overture so Alice sat down with him. The atmosphere was almost cosy. Further along the table, there was a large pair of powerful-looking binoculars. 'Do you watch birds?'

'Never.'

'I thought not. So, what are you doing here?'

'You really don't know?'

'I really don't know. Except that it's something between you and Brendan, and Guy's involved too.'

'I'll make a deal. You don't ask me questions now and I promise to tell you in the morning.'

Alice looked at his face, tired now and with none of the glow she had seen in her romantic dreams.

'It's a deal.' It was also, in some unexplained way, a relief. 'Do you think Terry will worry about me?'

'He won't do anything till morning.'

'I really don't believe I could walk back, although I feel incredibly much better.'

'You can stay here.' He indicated the bed. 'I often sleep outside on warm nights.'

Alice and Blue wandered slowly down to the sea. They had been drawn outside by the soft, warm night and the subtle night smells and sounds. Perhaps they would merely listen to the ripples breaking gently on the sand or perhaps they would take off their clothes and swim.

Blue went ahead, as if to make the point they were not together by choice but by circumstance, a night together that neither could avoid. A waning moon lay on the horizon, no longer the full harvest moon, with its glowing aureole, that Alice and Guy had watched on their Cornish beach. This light spread coolly over the dark sea, bright enough for Alice to see that Blue was paddling at the water's edge. She went up to him. He was looking down at the water. 'People find God in all sorts of strange things. Personally I'd go for phosphorescence in the sea. Silver tinsel in black water.'

Alice tried to see where he was looking but the only silver came from the reflection of the moon.

'The things you see when you go diving – the plants, the fish, colour, movement, a much more dramatic world than the one we inhabit – but still nothing moves me like simple phosphorescence on a summer's night.'

'I can't see any,' said Alice.

'A few years ago I was sailing across the Bay of Biscay. A hundred miles from Cape Finisterre I saw thirty or forty dolphins. Off the coast of Spain there were flying fish, great shoals. But at night the whole world was lit by phosphorescence, and the fish were like tinsel weaving through the water.'

'How magical it sounds.'

Blue turned a little her way. 'But I can't see any here either.' She could tell he was smiling. 'I was just thinking. It's all this being alone. Mind you, we might see some if we swam out.'

'Not tonight. Tonight I'm off duty.' Alice sat down. She was glad, nevertheless, that he had used the word 'we'. He came and sat beside her.

'You have family, don't you?'

'I arrived on this island because I was fleeing them.'

'Not in search of me, then?'

'Who knows?' Alice sighed.

He took her hand. He held her face and kissed her. 'For old times' sake?' His stubble was sharp against her skin. She thought of the grey hairs mixing with the gold. Of the peroxide blonde who'd come to him after her. But desire rose quickly, a bodily function keen to perform.

'Oh, Blue,' she murmured, meaning to say that once was fantasy – partly chemically induced, as it now turned out – but twice had to mean something more.

'Don't worry.' He undressed her deftly so that she was naked in a moment, the air fresh on her skin. She remembered how he had accused her of taking him last time, as if he'd had no right of refusal. This time the roles were reversed. He had rescued her from her rock and now claimed her as a trophy. It was a traditional romantic story in which she played the passive feminine role yet he needed to do so little to arouse her, as if their whole afternoon and evening had been leading up to this.

'I won't hurt your knee,' he murmured, astride her now, his body gilded by the moon, like a statue. His beauty was seducing her again, even though she had seen the tarnished reality. When he entered her, she cried out loudly. He seemed pleased by this, pressing his fingers round the curve of her mouth. But she felt sad enough for tears to overrun her eyes. Perhaps he knew this too. They lay side by side.

'I'll tell you something, you're a much better fuck than any hotel tart.'

'That's nice,' murmured Alice. She thought how tawdry it all was.

'You're still a bit of a romantic, aren't you?'

That's what he'd been shouting at her earlier, but his voice was gentle now, as if the act of sex had made her more acceptable. Alice felt far away and still sad. After a while he got up and left her.

Alice lay for a long time on the sand, until eventually she couldn't bear the sensation of damp grit on her naked back. The moon had changed position and the sea was crawling closer: a few more inches and it would reach her feet. Slowly, she sat up. There was another sensation to add to the wet sand, the cool air, the salty smell, the feeling of having just made love. Yes, she was bleeding.

Alice moved away and saw the dark patch in the sand. Even more slowly, she walked towards the sea and sat in its quiet incoming flow. She remembered how horrified she'd been at the possibility of pregnancy and tried to feel blessed by this modest draining. But somehow she couldn't stop tears dripping down to join the swelling sea.

'What are you doing?' Blue was swimming towards her.

'Trying to catch pneumonia.'

'That's not the effect I usually have on women.' He stood a foot or two away, shaking drops off his naked body.

'I guess I'm not a usual woman.'

Blue either ignored this or didn't hear it. 'I'm freezing!' His voice was happier than she'd ever heard it. Maybe he'd seen his phosphorous. 'I'll meet you at the hut.' He ran away from her, pounding up the shoreline.

Blue and Alice lay together in the narrow bed. When she'd warned him that she was bleeding, he'd merely commented, 'Women do,' in an uninterested way. He'd fallen asleep almost at once, but continued to hold her firmly.

Alice watched the moonlight through the window turn to darkness and then, almost imperceptibly, the square paled again. Eventually, she fell asleep.

Chapter Twenty-Five

A Fourth Tuesday

The beach was still in shadow, although another bright day was rising on the other side of the island. Terry stood beside a boat, pulled up on the sand. He was smoking a cigarette and looking out to sea. 'Here you are, then.'

His lack of interest in her movements over the last twenty-four hours reassured Alice. 'I saw the seals, you know,' she said brightly. 'After I hurt my knee.' She winced at the memory of the rock's crack and the morning's painful stiffness, as predicted by Blue. 'Where's Blue?' She looked round.

'Blue?' 'You mean the bird-watcher. He went off somewhere with his binoculars. They don't miss a moment, those twitchers. He could be anywhere.' Terry seemed to relish the idea of Blue's anywhereness, as if his island could make people appear and disappear in ways unimaginable to pathetic Londoners.

It was not as if Alice wanted Blue. He was no longer the father of her child or the ghost lover she had once desired. But he had promised to answer her question in the morning. Slowly she followed Terry to his boat.

Terry rowed slowly out to sea and then turned eastward. The moon hung like a white ghost in the sky and, despite the brightness of the rising sun, the night-time cool still clung to the clear water. Alice dangled her white fingertips over the tide and withdrew them hurriedly as cold water splashed past her wrist. But the feeling was good all the same. She put them back in, dabbling lightly in the surface of the waves.

Soon Terry tipped an outboard motor into the water and started it up with a great deal of smoke and noise. Alice sat back and felt the wind rush through her hair.

The tide was low as they approached the harbour so that the boat bobbed far down below the wall. An iron ladder, rusted and barnacled at its base, led upward. Alice climbed tentatively, afraid of banging her bad knee.

Terry waited patiently at the top. He gave her his arm. 'So, you found somewhere to stay last night? Demi was worried.'

'I banged my knee when I was swimming. On a rock.'

'So that twitcher said.' Once again they walked in silence.

'Look.' Alice pointed ahead across the field. 'There's a mushroom for our breakfast.'

Later, Alice went outside and found a plastic chair at the back of the house where she could sit with a view of the sea. Terry had given her a copy of yesterday's paper, her own, which she took for politeness' sake and laid unopened across her knee. After ten minutes or so she glanced down and saw Brendan smiling up at her. The photograph was not very large, but it captured his energy and big-bully charm. She picked up the paper to read the accompanying story. 'Sir Brendan Costa Taken In For Questioning.' He was being questioned on charges of fraud made by the Inland Revenue – or, rather, he had been questioned and released. The story was short but its prominence on the front page with the photograph suggested that the editor, the Master indeed, considered it was the start of something big.

Alice opened the paper, rifling through expertly to see if there was any more. She found only one piece, in the gossip column. There was another, larger picture of Brendan, this time with the odious Ivo Swayne. They were both wearing evening dress, held champagne glasses and smiled with a fat cat's look of drunken self-congratulation. The caption read, 'Sir Brendan Costa and Ivo Swayne, Minister for Prisons, celebrate at a government-organised party for the visiting Finnish Prime Minister.'

It wasn't much of a story, which made its presence all the more significant. Alice thought, Brendan is absolutely not my business, and wished very much that her mobile worked so that she could ring Guy and find out more. If he would tell her.

Restless now, she stood up and circled back, without much resolution, towards the harbour. She had changed into shorts on her arrival at the cottage and noted with interest the extraordinary colours decorating her knee and sliding down her leg, like purple, red, blue and green inks.

'That's quite a bruise.' Terry had come up behind her. He carried an empty crate and a large holdall. He seemed in a hurry and was already past her when he added, 'I'll be back with them about midday.'

This was clearly directed at her. 'Who?' she asked.

He turned briefly. 'Didn't Demi tell you? They rang my mum last night. Your family. They're coming for a visit.'

Alice found her knee suddenly hurt a lot. Couldn't she be left alone for a minute? She hobbled and skipped after Terry. 'I didn't invite them!' she cried.

'It's a free island, so I've heard.'

Alice continued to follow him down to the harbour, but by the time she arrived he'd already set off, taking the motorboat in which she'd come over. 'They won't all fit in that!' she shouted pointlessly, then gave up and sat on the edge of the harbour wall. Soon Pandora and Florrie *et al* would be speeding towards her. She imagined Pandora's lively, curious, old-young face

'My mother...' There, she'd said it out loud without being struck by lightning. She'd been right all along. Her mother had been out there waiting to come back. It had just taken longer than she'd expected. There was no point in crying for the child who'd given up hope. There was no point in blaming her father or anyone else. Pandora had come back and her hair had grown white in the interval, but she was still Alice's mother. As she thought this, an unusual sense of peace and hopefulness made her narrow her eyes to gaze across the sea. She felt a foolish smile on her lips.

She stood up hurriedly and set off, hardly hobbling at all, to the cottage to check that everything was ready for their arrival.

There was no sign of Demi. Keen for some coffee, Alice went to the kitchen, which was very clean and hot and smelt strongly of insect-killer. Alice was about to open the windows when she saw that the insects hadn't finished dying. A large bluebottle, like a garrulous drunk, reeled noisily around the window-ledge. Two smaller flies, on the floor, were making loud sizzling noises. To this was added the kettle's whistle. Alice made a mug of coffee and carried it out to the plastic chair. She sat down, and drank carefully.

Gradually, she heard far-off shoutings – more of jubilation, she felt, than disquiet. She raised her eyes from her mug and saw, out to sea, a small boat filled with wildly waving figures. Even though they were still distant, she could easily recognise them as her family.

She put down her coffee, jumped to her feet and waved her own arms excitedly. But why was the boat on this side of the island rather than heading for the harbour? The answer struck her when it had nearly disappeared from view. Of course, they must be heading for the beach where they could swim. She hurried up to her room for her backpack, hat and bikini.

The bright day was clouding slowly from the west. As Alice walked, taking the easier inland route, she watched the clouds, grey layer after grey layer, overlap, mass and move slowly towards her – where the sun still shone as strongly as ever. She supposed they were bringing rain, but the breeze was still light and their progress slow. Alice had lost her sense of urgency. If Florrie and Pandora had been eager to see her immediately, they could have come to the harbour and picked her up. She left the wide field of stubble and moved into the rougher ground where bracken and brambles had been allowed to grow, their green interrupted by brilliant yellow ragwort, spurting like fireworks.

She was the only moving thing to break the silence so she gasped when a pheasant clattered up from under her feet. Her heart pumped as if it had been far more threatening than a frightened bird. When she spotted a low, smooth stone to her right, she decided it was time to take a rest and some good deep breaths.

It was while Alice was resting that she heard some unlikely sounds. First a dog was barking but she had seen no dogs, except the tethered Gyp, on the island. This was followed by the roar of some very large engine, which cut out almost as soon as it started. There was a short pause, and then she caught a distant sound of men shouting angrily. These various noises were shocking in the context of the island, which had been so utterly peaceful. In her isolation, she entertained wild imaginings. She pictured the boat containing her waving family heading for some terrifying but unspecified danger. And where had Blue gone to, without waiting to say goodbye, without answering her questions?

Alice looked down at her knee: the virulent colours had spread even further down her leg and that, too, increased her sense of foreboding. It struck her that perhaps she was foolish to go forward, that she should turn round and head back to the cottage. The engine's roar rose again, then fell as quickly as before. This time, she could locate it much more clearly: it was ahead and to the right in a part of the island she hadn't explored, obscured from her by a rise in the ground

Curiosity being stronger than caution, Alice moved forward, ducking to make herself less visible. As she advanced to the top of the hill, the clouds, picking up speed, closed briskly over the sun so that the scene in front of her was dim rather than brightly lit. But there was no mistaking it: a helicopter was sitting in the middle of a smooth, grassy patch. Her first reaction was of relief: it was nothing sinister, just a helicopter. It must have flown in when she was making coffee in the noisy kitchen. She remembered what Demi had said about medical services arriving by helicopter.

She looked with more attention and saw no red cross or any other service-type feature. This was a commercial or private helicopter. Alice sat back reflectively. She'd guessed the answer before she heard the voice and recognised the man emerging from behind the tail of the aircraft. He was holding a mobile, which he threw to the ground in childish disgust. Alice smiled. Brendan would not enjoy being out of communication.

But her smile didn't reflect her mood. Brendan in a rage was not a pretty sight.

Alice wondered when she'd grasped that she was out of her depth with Brendan. Had it only been after they'd made love? A sense that, however pleasurable it had been, she'd become a counter in a game he was playing. One thing was clear: she didn't want her path to cross Brendan's again, certainly not on a remote island. Alice moved backwards until she was sheltered by the crest of the hill and sat down once more to consider her position. Overhead, the bulky clouds shifted a little and several large drops of rain landed around her; one targeted her bad knee and rolling like an outsize teardrop down her leg.

Alice looked up to the sky and again remembered the harvest moon she'd seen with Guy on the Cornish beach. She could picture exactly its aureole, the thick gold of it, with a shade of amber round the inner ring. She had talked about the afternoon of the eclipse when she'd lain on the roof of the church tower and Richard had stayed inside to watch television and she'd been happy. A few days later Richard had been dead.

Alice got up and walked, in a determined manner, in the direction of the bird-watchers' huts. At least she would have shelter from the rain and maybe her family would have pitched camp there. Or Blue had returned.

The heavy raindrops had thinned and turned into a continuous fine drizzle. Alice felt herself and the landscape through which she moved disguised in a delicate veil. Her footsteps and the rustling of the bracken were softened so that she felt less conspicuous and vulnerable. As she neared the path to go down, the day took on a dreamlike quality when the imagined becomes real or the real, already experienced, repeats itself. Yesterday she had descended the same path, swum, banged her knee on the rock and been rescued by Blue.

The sea in the bay was the colour of oyster satin. The rain shimmering on its surface was not heavy enough to break up its smooth texture and seemed more like mist or steam. Alice half slid down to the beach and found her footing on the scrubby edge of the sand.

Apart from a few birds on the cliff-tops at the mouth of the bay, there was absolute silence. No boat was pulled up on the beach or moored further out. Without a watch or the sun, it was hard to tell the time but she guessed it must be around three. She walked slowly up to the bird-watchers' huts.

She heard a man's presence before she saw him. He said, 'Ssh.' Her eyes grew accustomed to the dim light with no sun to pierce through the small windows, and made out a figure hunched over the table. He was turned away from her but she could tell he had his finger to his lips and that he was not Blue. He was too big, his hair was not bright enough and he wore glasses.

'Guy!'

'Ssh,' he hissed again, with even more intensity. Alice saw he wore earphones, which were attached to a machine on the table. It was clear he wasn't entertaining himself with a little light music. She came in and sat down on the bed.

After a couple of minutes, Guy took off the earphones and smiled. 'Sorry.'

Alice was glad of the smile. She was beginning to think she'd dropped into a Second World War spy movie and that at any minute the Gestapo would break down the door. 'What are you listening to?' It seemed the simplest question.

Guy came over and sat by her on the bed. He put his arm round her. 'Darling Alice.'

Alice found she would have been quite happy to sit with him in silence, question unanswered, but Guy said: 'Not what, who. I've listened in to Brendan. You might say I'm on duty as a newspaperman. This is a huge story, Alice. Huge. It's been building up for months and somehow I've got into the hot seat. I knew most, you see.' He took off his glasses and rubbed his face. 'It kind of landed in my lap because of Blue. And now you've got tangled up in it too. My fault. Sorry.'

'I'm on holiday,' said Alice. 'You sent me on holiday. I forgive you.'

'I never thought you'd come down as far as this island. I didn't think Blue would have to either.'

Alice reflected that chance and Pandora had propelled her further and further into the ocean. 'If it's serious—'

'It is serious.' Guy interrupted her.

'– why aren't the police involved?'

'They are involved. They've been involved for a long time.'

Alice examined this idea of 'a long time'. 'Do you mean the police knew Blue wasn't dead or even properly disappeared?'

'Blue was attacked on the boat. He was lucky not to die. He got back to St Mawes. I saw him there at the Smuggler's Cave.'

'Do you remember I thought I glimpsed him in Kensington Gardens?'

'He was never in London.'

'I imagined it then.'

Guy frowned. He took her hand. 'Do you understand what I'm saying? Blue was attacked by Brendan. Not personally, of course. Now he's become the minnow to catch the whale. It wasn't planned that way but that's the way it is.' He looked at her. 'You're soaking.'

Alice was not to be put off. 'Detective Constable Susan Paradise interviewed me three times. Do you mean that was all a charade?'

'I'm a newspaperman, not a policeman, remember? Maybe they

needed to check out what you knew. I told you Blue could have died – and, after all, you were close to Brendan.'

'So were you.'

'I set up the interview. That's true. I'm sorry about that too. Sorry for all kinds of reasons you couldn't imagine. I haven't given up hoping you will one day.' He squeezed her hand hard, then let it go.

Alice didn't try to understand his last comment. 'I feel like I've been set up at every stage.' She heard the bitterness in her voice. She felt as if she'd been set up at every stage in her life from when her mother had run away and her father had told her she'd died.

'Perhaps there were things you didn't want to know.'

Guy stood up. Even in the dim light, she could see he wasn't going to take responsibility for her problems. In fact, he looked as if he was thinking of something else. He walked over to the table and picked up the earphones.

Alice went to stand by the open door. The rain had changed its nature and become much heavier, arriving in sudden flurries and bursts as if driven by a wind. The sky was even darker than before. She wanted a beer but wasn't so keen if it meant getting even wetter than she was already. She came back into the hut and noticed a plastic cape. It was patterned with camouflage and must have been left behind by a bird-watcher. It was certainly not Blue's style – wherever he was, he was most probably soaked and hiding out somewhere. Unless, of course, he was off the island. Her one glimpse of Brendan had made him the predator, and who else would he be hunting but Blue? Guy's words had only confirmed what she'd instinctively guessed.

Alice brought in four bottles of beer and opened one each for herself and Guy. He took it without commenting. Restlessly, she walked round the cottage, taking a gulp, peering out at the rain or patting her now drying hair. It had grown fast over the last few weeks and she could feel its wildness and strength.

She was annoyed by Guy's lack of concern for her. However extraordinary the circumstances, he should know that she was under stress too.

'I'm going out!' she shouted in his ear.

Guy did a double-take, then grabbed her arm. 'Wait.' He took off the earphones. 'What are you talking about?'

'I've got to look for Florrie and Lily and Pandora. They were in a boat coming this way.' But, as she spoke, she knew that they would not have arrived on the island in this weather: they would have turned back as the sky darkened. Pandora, with her Mexican suntanned skin and flimsily flamboyant clothes, would have seen to that. She hardly needed to listen to Guy's rather distracted disclaimers.

'You're right,' she agreed eventually. 'I'm not anxious about them any more. Pandora will see they're all right. She's a survivor.'

'So please wait. It won't be for long now.'

What wouldn't be long now? Alice wondered, but Guy was back to his listening. She went to stand by the door again. As she watched, the sky was decorated by a small zigzag of lightning and, after she'd counted eight, there was a low roll of thunder. A real storm was blowing in from the west. Even though the rain had stopped, water still poured off the gutterless roof of the cottage in a thick curtain so she felt no urge to leave.

Alice went back to the bed and this time got right under the blanket that had covered Blue and her the night before.

Guy took off his earphones and came over to her. 'You look snug.' He moved nearer the door. 'Can you hear anything?'

'There was some thunder a moment ago.'

'Are you sure it was thunder?'

'Well, there was certainly lightning.'

'You asked me about the police. About their involvement. According to the Master, who's in touch with them, they should be on their way anytime. I thought the thunder might be them.'

'Can they land a helicopter in this weather?'

Guy looked gloomy. 'Brendan did.'

'The storm hadn't begun then.'

'Oh God!'

Alice wondered whether he was most worried about his story or whatever dangers must be out there for Blue. That was what all this watching and waiting were about, surely. Alice shivered and pulled the blanket up to her chin. She supposed that was what they were doing, watching and waiting. At least she had Guy. Guy, she noticed, hadn't touched his beer while she was ready for a second.

Clearly, it would be a serious setback if the police helicopter couldn't land. Alice started as a bright flash of lightning lit the hut, followed, after four counts, by a heavy roll of thunder. 'I don't expect it will last long,' she tried to console Guy.

'I don't know. I'm worried about Blue. And yet I can't believe Brendan would do anything really dreadful.'

'You can't?'

'No. I always felt the attack on Blue was only meant as a warning that got a bit out of control. Luckily, Blue's a superb sailor. The trouble is, things have changed now and Brendan may feel he's got nothing to lose. The police have probably got enough information to charge him. They've interviewed him already.'

'I saw the piece in yesterday's newspaper. But what's Blue's involvement in all this?'

'He's the original whistle-blower. The man who knows what happened to those gold bars they brought up out of the sea. And that's only the start of it. It's about millions, you know. And then about more millions if his company collapses. And that's leaving aside government involvement.'

'Ivo?'

'He'll be lucky to stay out of prison.'

'But he's prisons minister! And you arranged for me to interview him too.' Alice found herself laughing hysterically. Another flash and an even louder thunderclap sobered her a little.

'I wish I could laugh,' said Guy, when the noise had diminished. 'Brendan sounded absolutely manic, screaming and swearing at the men he's brought with him – there're four or five of them – and he's got dogs too.'

'I heard them. Not nice.'

'It's as if he's planning a manhunt. The point is, he absolutely hates and loathes Blue. He blames him for everything. That's why Blue had to disappear. In fact, it's more than just hatred – there's some kind of competitiveness in it, something in their past, long before the treasure-hunting. I don't know what. Blue's much younger than Brendan, of course. Perhaps it's just that they both started out from nothing.'

Alice remembered Brendan's seductive takeover of her body. Had he known about her love-making with Blue and, in masculine rivalry, wanted to claim her as his? She'd always felt that Brendan had used her in some way beyond simple physical pleasure and this would provide an explanation.

Guy was putting on a jacket.

'Where are you going?'

He pulled up the hood. 'I can't just abandon him. You see, I can guess where he'll be.' He had gone before Alice could say a word.

The thunder continued to roll, one clap merging into another, and the cottage was almost continually charged with blue-white electricity. Alice lay shivering under the bedclothes. At first she was angry with Guy for leaving her so abruptly, but then she admitted that she could hardly weigh her own convenience against whatever dangers Blue faced.

At last the storm was moving away. The thunder was quieter and sometimes several minutes passed in silence, apart from the rainwater dropping off the roof.

Alice got out of bed and went to the door. The air was several degrees colder, as if the heat of the last weeks had been doused and blown away by the storm. The sky in the west was brightening with a clean silver and, in fact, it was raining very little. The wild weather was moving off the island and towards the mainland.

Alice walked. It was raining again, and although the brightness in the west remained, it didn't seem to get any closer. Her biggest worry now was whether she could actually find Neolithic Billy, for she was sure that that was where Guy had gone to look for Blue. It was only yesterday afternoon that he'd shown her the place but the day had been so different, the sky clear before it transformed into a rich sunset, the greenery feathery and bright, the stones pale, almost white in the dry heat. Now the colours were muted and merged by the rain so that hillocks and boulders were no longer distinctive or recognisable.

She proceeded cautiously as the undergrowth thinned and the land rose. She believed she was going in the right general direction but it was taking longer than she remembered. Her knee had ached then and it ached now. She stopped to rest, looked up and saw, with a gasp of horror, five silhouetted figures on the skyline to her right. Before she could do more than fall into a crouch, they had gone. She took a deep breath and told herself she was pretty well camouflaged by the cape. On the other hand, perhaps she should have waited for the police. The wind had dropped and the rain wouldn't stop them.

Alice's knee was objecting strongly to her position. She'd just have to stand up again. She went forward deliberately, so keen to make no sound that she found she was holding her breath. Almost as soon as she had started, she thought she heard a dog yap.

She was now recognising the roll of the land. This was the same path Blue had led her along. It wasn't much further. The rain's quality had changed to sheets of water that doused her in regular waves. Alice could feel it trickling down her rats' tails' hair into the collar of her cape and from there all down her body so that she was, literally, soaked to the skin. She supposed she was bleeding, too, although the general wetness made it hard to tell.

In the end she almost stumbled over the stone man. In an absurd way, she found she was pleased to uncover the strange, broad-mouthed face. It felt like rediscovering a friend from the past who was, moreover, a friend of friends. But there was no sign of Guy or Blue. She cursed her stupidity: if their aim had been to avoid Brendan, they certainly wouldn't stay on this exposed headland, Billy or no. They might have met here, Blue might have lain at Billy's feet for a while, but by now he could be anywhere on the island, even back in the bird-watcher's hut.

She had just reached this conclusion when she heard voices coming rapidly closer. She pulled back the vegetation around the stone face and lowered herself carefully into the hole at its base. She drew across the curtain of sharp brambles, swathed in long grass, and found herself in a small room bathed in a trance-like green. As it brightened she realised the evening sun had come out and shrank down even further into the surprisingly dry earth.

'I'm giving you two more fucking hours and after that you're not getting a fucking penny out of me, whether you find him or not!'

It was Brendan, in an even fouler mood than when Alice had spotted him by the helicopter. By the sound of the voices that were replying to him in similarly angry tones, the whole lot of them had gathered only a few yards from where she lay. One was complaining that the island was like a maze in which a man could go round and round in the same circle. 'Look at the sun!' screamed Brendan. 'The sun will tell you where you fucking are.'

Another voice pointed out that until this moment they'd been searching in storms and rain, and if he hadn't sent the dogs back to the helicopter at least they'd have had a chance, which merely encouraged Brendan into a further orgy of invective. 'Those bloody dogs knew as much about sniffing out a man as I do. The only thing they knew was how to chase every fucking bird and make such a racket the whole island knew we were coming.'

'What we need is a boat,' suggested a weary third voice, 'or, better still, we should get back to the fucking helicopter. I'd vote for spotting from the air over this caper any day.'

There was a silence – presumably while Brendan considered his options. Curled up in her hiding-place, Alice prayed he would go for the helicopter. Which, eventually, he did. After a bit more bad-tempered planning, footsteps moved away. The only problem was that someone had remained. Every now and again he stamped his feet and the smell of an expensive cigar wafted through her lacy canopy. She had never seen Brendan smoke a cigar, but it seemed only too likely to be him. And he was not standing there to admire the view. Alice squirmed in her nest. It was all going on too long. One of her legs had cramped and she needed to move. Very gently, she eased an arm and then a leg.

The bullet cracked against the stone behind her head, then reversed its trajectory to spin back through the greenery.

Alice screamed, and a second bullet repeated the process but very near her left shoulder. Tearing her hands on the brambles, she burst outwards into the dazzling sunshine. 'What do you think you're doing?' The man facing her, backlit but easily recognisable as Brendan by his bulky, powerful shape, lowered his gun.

Alice continued to scream accusations: 'Have you gone quite crazy? You can't go round shooting guns at people! You might have killed me!' Her terror and rage had wiped out Guy's view that killing someone was exactly what Brendan most desired. The reality, the hard force as the bullet had hit the stone, the feeling that the stone might as likely have been her bones and flesh, had put everything else out of her mind.

'I thought you were a rabbit.' Brendan came up to her and put his hand on her shoulder. She stepped back quickly. She could hardly believe she had once found his touch comforting. Now it increased her trembling shock. 'What possessed you to hide in the undergrowth? There might have been a nasty accident.'

Alice tried to recover her wits. 'I was studying a Neolithic monument, which you've just fired at twice in an utterly reckless manner. That figure is millions of years old.' Just as she finished speaking, a horrible noise made her turn round – in time to see Billy break into two and the top half, eyes and flattened African nose, topple forwards on to the ground.

'Look what you've done!' She cast herself in front of the fragmented stone, where she burst into tears of shock and outrage.

'This is fucking ridiculous.' There was no pretence at calm or charm now. Brendan hauled Alice to her feet and shook her roughly. 'Where is he? Where's that disloyal cunt?'

'Let me go!'

'You can show me your lover-boy's hiding-place, can't you? Can't you?' He was pushing and shaking her at the same time.

Now that Brendan was on the verge of losing control – 'lover-boy', what a ridiculous term! – Alice found that her brain was working again. 'Stop it, Brendan. I'm not afraid, you know. You're just a bully. I've known an awful lot of bullies in my life and I'm just about fed up.' This felt good. 'If I do know where Blue is, give me one reason why I should tell you.'

Brendan didn't release her but he did stop the shaking. His voice became almost wheedling and, to Alice's disgust, his blue eyes welled with tears. 'I thought you were my friend. I trusted you. I told you about my childhood distress, the bombing, the deaths of so many of my family. I entertained you in my home. I looked after you. I took you into my confidence – and look how you've repaid me!'

Alice resisted the temptation to point out that she had repaid him by writing an extremely favourable interview, which she now deeply regretted. Without even mentioning other, more intimate favours.

'And I know what caused the change. You got entrapped by that convicted criminal who thinks he can make the world a fairer place by sticking a few failed drop-outs like he was into wetsuits and sending them into the ocean.' Now the bully was back. 'And, of course, he wants me to provide the money! He's just a common or garden blackmailer. He used to mug old ladies and now he's moved on to bigger things. But he's still the same lying, cheating, childish thug!'

It seemed sensible to keep quiet though this tirade. Perhaps letting him vent would help Brendan's state of mind.

'For thirty years I've been making money for other people – men have started their own businesses with the money I've made for them. He has himself, the disloyal arsehole. Who do you think gave him the money to turn his life round? Every day I carry this great weight around with me. I don't complain. I'm proud of it. And now some fucking little water rat wants to blow it all apart because he's got some bloody stupid scheme to rescue boys who've never had a chance like he did. No one was there to rescue me either! But I take a man's attitude to it. I do a man's job of work.' His little blue eyes fixed closely on Alice. 'You have shares in one of my companies. Did you know that? Bought by your late husband fifteen years ago. I checked you out. How will you feel when their value goes from a hundred and ten pence to fifty pence or twenty pence or five pence? You won't be too pleased, will you? So how do you think all my other shareholders are going to feel? Forty per cent of them are pensioners. You didn't know that either, did you? And all this pain and misery because a self-indulgent wanker thinks he can change the world. Let me tell you something, bringing me down will change the world for the fucking worse and you can tell that to Mr Golden Cunt and he can stuff it up his blue arse!'

At last Brendan had run out of steam. He was panting heavily and his sweating face had an unhealthy grey puffiness. Alice understood that he truly saw himself as a hero whose world was being torn apart, not because he had hung on illegally to an untold amount of millions but because of an act of revenge by someone he despised. Worse still, by someone he'd once helped. That was the final piece of puzzle in their relationship. Brendan had been the philanthropic businessman who had helped Blue on his road out of prison.

It struck Alice that, since she had no idea where Blue was, although she trusted he and Guy had found each other, there could be no harm in leading Brendan on what would certainly be a wild-goose chase. 'I've no special brief for Blue,' she said, as a preliminary.

'Blue!' Brendan exploded. 'Lionel Brian is his name. What a load of romantic bullshit!'

'Blue,' repeated Alice patiently, 'is his own master. I can't predict where he'll be but I could make a pretty fair guess.'

'You could?' Brendan's fingers dug into her shoulder painfully. 'And why would you do that?'

'You're hurting me.'

'That's enough reason?'

'Blue and I spent the night together, true enough, but the next morning, he kicked me out in preference for his girlfriend. You know what they say about a woman scorned . . .' Was this fantasy going to be enough for Brendan? It had the virtue of being true, if girlfriend was not quite accurate. At least, he *wanted* to believe.

He changed his grip to hold her arm. Alice remembered how his thick fingers had gripped his tennis racquet, smashing Ivo out of existence until he'd hurled his racquet to the ground in frustration. Brendan expected to win.

'So, which way?'

Alice led him off towards the furthest point of the island. At first the ground was open and broken up by smooth-topped rocks showing through the wet turf, but as they neared the cliffs above the sea a colony of gorse, yellow flowers drying in the warm sun and scenting the air, sprang up round them. As Brendan continued to hold Alice's arm, their progress was hampered by avoiding the sharp spikes between the flowers.

'Shit!' exclaimed Brendan, rubbing his free hand.

'I'm not going to run away, you know. Where would I run to?' They were nearing the cliff edge now and the sea, lurching still with the effects of the storm, unrolled in a wider and wider space below them.

'Where are you leading me?' asked Brendan, roughly.

'There's a path that goes down to a lower level of land, just a strip, really, before it drops vertically into the sea. At the back there's a cave.' Alice wondered at her powers of invention. She also wondered whether Brendan would shoot her if she ran away. She trusted that was a melodramatic idea.

'You go ahead.' Brendan let go of her arm and pushed her in front of him.

Alice stumbled a little, glanced down at her bruised knee, but any pain was wiped out by fear and excitement. Having invented this low-level spit of land with accompanying cave, she really did need the police helicopter to come sooner rather than later. How long could she keep Brendan in suspense, following this narrow path, slippery after the rain, which might easily circle the whole island without once dropping down? She looked north over the sea to the thin lines of the other bigger islands and saw that the sky was clearing, although the thick layer of purple blackness above the blue suggested that the storm was moving in the direction of the mainland. In a moment, she supposed, the other helicopter, Brendan's, would rise above their heads.

'How much further?'

'Any time now. We'll come on it quite suddenly.'

'I think I see something.' Brendan's panting breath came up closer. 'Something pale. Could be a fucking path.'

Alice looked but with her next step forward any identification became academic as the paleness rose off the path with a hideous squawking and shrieking and into their faces. It was what felt like hundreds of gulls, perhaps blown inland by the storm, but for whatever reason they had arrived, they were in no mood to put up with intruders. As Alice flailed her arms and then, frightened for her face, covered her head with them, she heard Brendan swearing furiously behind her. Suddenly there were two sharp shots and the whole screaming white mass of feathers and beaks rose into the air.

For a second it was a relief, until an even louder noise came deafeningly close. A helicopter, coming from the interior of the island and therefore definitely not the police, approached them, flying low enough that Alice could see the face of the pilot, peering intently down.

As Alice watched, aware that Brendan was doing the same – with the pistol in his hand – the helicopter began to jump and judder in the sky. It had flown straight into the great mass of seagulls.

'Oh, my God!' Alice ran slipping and sliding along the narrow path. It seemed certain to her that the helicopter must crash down on top of her. Behind her she heard Brendan shouting. Perhaps she should stop, explain that she was running to save her life not to escape him, but as she hesitated, there was a disgusting dead thump beside her, and then another. The blades of the helicopter were knocking the seagulls senseless and dumping them back to earth. Next moment there'd be blood raining down, chopped pieces of bird flesh everywhere. Another seagull hit the ground ahead of her, with blood round its eyes and a circle of loose feathers settling round it. Whatever happened, she must keep her legs pounding along.

'Alice!' Someone was yelling her name, but the overwhelming noise of the helicopter, the screaming gulls and her own deaf terror made it a thin, unrecognisable sound.

'Alice!' Her tired legs were slowing however hard she pushed them and her name was louder now. She looked up and saw, still at some distance, Guy standing in the path.

'Guy. Oh, Guy.' Why wasn't he coming closer? Behind him she could see another figure, presumably Blue. Of course, Brendan must be following her with that pistol in his hand.

As she slowed, she could hear the helicopter again so she knew the birds had not brought it down. She glanced backwards, and could see no sign of Brendan.

Now Guy and Blue began to run towards her. She stopped and bent double. She thought she might vomit. A spangled black veil seemed to be hanging between her and the rest of the world. Peculiarly, there was a sharp pain not only in her side but in her teeth.

She felt Guy's hand on her shoulder. She wanted to ask him where Brendan was, but found she couldn't speak. Vaguely, she heard the helicopter moving further into the distance. The seagulls were quiet now.

'Go and see if you can find him,' she heard Guy say to Blue. Then he sat her down gently. He crouched beside her and held her hand.

Gradually the veil lifted and the sickness passed. 'What happened?' she asked.

'We don't know. One minute he was on the path behind you and the next minute he'd gone. He might have lost his footing. You were both very near the edge and the storm might have softened it. We were terrified when you were running.'

'You mean he fell?'

'There were gulls landing all around him. Maybe he panicked.'

'I panicked. It was horrible. Disgusting.'

'Yes. Blue's gone to see.' He looked beyond her. 'I'm sorry I've got no water for you.'

'I'm OK. Just puffed.'

'Do you mind if I go and help Blue?'

She did mind, actually, but obviously mustn't say so. 'What about his men in the helicopter?'

'I don't expect they'll stick around long.'

'But they must have seen him fall. If he did fall. They could help rescue him!' Alice felt herself getting worked up again. However hateful Brendan, he was a human being, maybe suspended from some cliff edge by his fingertips.

'Alice.' Guy pulled her up so she had to look at him. 'Blue and I will see to Brendan. The police helicopter's on its way so Brendan's lot won't want to be caught on the island. What I mean to say is, they've done a bunk or they're doing a bunk. There's no danger to any of us any more. It's over.'

'Over,' repeated Alice. 'Gone with their dogs,' she added inconsequentially.

'Not very effective ones,' Guy detached his hand and stood up. 'We won't be too long.'

Alice lay back. There was a pillow of heather behind her. It was soaking wet, she supposed, but she didn't care about that. Her throat was sore, her teeth still hurt and she still felt rather sick. Even so, she only meant to rest a moment before she followed Guy. She sat up again: her knee had given a single throb of threatening intensity: the adrenaline of fear must be draining away. Alice decided to stand up before it went altogether.

There was no sign of either Guy or Blue on the path from which she'd come. Immediately anxious, she tried to recall the assured tones in which Guy had pronounced all dangers 'over'. But until she could see Brendan disarmed and pinioned, how could she be certain it was 'over'? It dawned on her that Blue and Guy must have somehow climbed over the cliff edge in their search for Brendan. To her left the sun, which had reappeared after the storm, was now sinking fast into the ocean. Her shadow was long and dark ahead of her. She realised how shaky she still was when her heart jerked horribly at the sound of an approaching helicopter before her head told her it belonged to the police.

'It's all going to be fine now,' she tried telling herself, speaking out loud for greater emphasis.

Almost immediately, she heard a furious man's voice shouting. She thought it was Brendan's. She stopped absolutely still, undecided whether to run towards it or away from it, but she was far too beat-up to run anywhere. She approached the direction of the shot slowly and warily. The path was still eerily empty but the noise of the helicopter, probably heading for the same spot where Brendan's had landed, was very loud.

At first it drowned any further shouting, but then she heard Guy's voice. Dreading what she would see, Alice neared the cliff edge and peered over. There was far more vegetation growing down the side of the rock face than she'd expected so at first she failed to read the meaning of what was in front of her.

'Guy!' shouted Alice, trying to focus beyond the sea pinks and sandspurry. Or was it samphire? 'Guy, where are you?'

'Alice?' His voice came back at once and now she could see him. He was on a ledge about two or three feet wide directly below her, probably only ten metres or so down. He was sitting with his back to the rocks. Further down, on a rather wider ledge, Blue and Brendan were standing facing each other, Brendan on the outer limit of the ledge. He was silhouetted against the rosy sunset so Alice could see that he still held a gun.

Guy had given up shouting, perhaps at Brendan's command, and Blue was still and silent. Only half consciously, she heard the helicopter landing in the middle of the island and gradually the noise of the engine decreased. If James Bond had been in charge, Alice thought distractedly, he would have flown right up to the cliff and resolved the situation.

She became aware that the angle of Brendan's face had altered and he was staring up at her. She felt unnerved as if she was no longer a member of the audience but a participator in the drama.

'Brendan! Please! Throw away your gun!' It was a ridiculous appeal and her voice was still hoarse from running so it hardly carried a few feet beyond her vantage-point. Near at hand she heard a guillemot's growling call, as if it were mocking her. What she should tell him, of course, was that the police were on the way. But surely he would have seen the helicopter for himself? She screwed up her eyes to see more clearly.

'Go on!' shouted Guy suddenly, his voice filled with derision. 'You're so big and bold with your gun in your hand. Think what you'll look like on the front pages of the national newspapers. Go on, Brendan. Shooting an unarmed man is just up your street. You're going to get a whacking long sentence already so why not get two for the price of one? I dare you.' Then he added, with hissed venom, 'You *loser!*'

The movement was so slight that Alice could have blinked and missed it, had it not been accompanied by a single shot. One second Brendan was poised firmly enough on the ledge and the next he'd vanished, like a conjuring trick. There was no scream, just the sound of tumbling stones and the sense of a sack-like object dragging itself all the way to the bottom of the cliff. Two or three birds flew away angrily.

Alice stared, mesmerised. Blue and Guy, crouching on their ledges, also stared.

Alice sat in Demi's stuffy kitchen. Even though she had returned from the cliff several hours ago, her legs and hands were still shaking. Her vision seemed altered too: everything was brighter than usual, but with a black outline. Guy, sitting across the table from her, was defined in this way.

'I thought they might take you with them.' Alice smiled at him gratefully. He had only just reappeared and she'd dreaded the police summoning him to the mainland. She thought, with a perceptible increase in her shuddering, that perhaps there would be no room in the helicopter after Brendan's body had been loaded in.

'I wanted very much to stay here,' said Guy. 'With you.' The warmth in the room had turned his face a solid brick red while Alice felt that all the blood had drained from her skin.

'Now, you get that into you.' Demi set a plate of sausages and mash in front of Guy and Alice saw the sickened look that she'd tried to suppress when she had been faced with food. Terry's large glass of medicinal whisky had been much more welcome. Terry had gone out again, she didn't know where. She didn't want to imagine anything that was happening on the island any more. This small cosy room was enough for her, with Demi who could be a very motherly sort of person when the chance arose. And now there was Guy.

'But Blue went with them?'

'No. Terry's taken him over. He didn't want to go with the police.'

'Brendan fell. He just fell. The ledge broke and he fell!' Her voice was overwrought, over-excited.

Guy looked at her sympathetically. 'He was threatening Blue with a gun. He might easily have killed him. He wanted to kill him, I have no doubt. It was just luck that he fell.'

'Luck.' Alice shuddered again.

'Lucky for Blue.'

'Yes. Yes. I've never been so close to someone dying. And in such a horrific way. How can you be so calm?'

'There are jobs to be done. Always jobs to be done. I've had a go at dictating a story to the Master.' He took a forkful of mash to illustrate, it seemed, the need to carry on. 'But it wasn't easy. And it wasn't very good either. I didn't like Brendan but I didn't want him to die. At least, I hope I didn't. Blue was trying help him off the cliff, you know.'

'What about Blue now?'

Guy gave her an odd look, as if he was trying to decided what was behind the question. 'I don't know. I'm just a sailing friend, remember? The police will give a press conference tonight probably. It's a front-page story.' Guy tried to chew a bit of sausage. 'Even without death and attempted murder. Brendan couldn't face it, of course. It wasn't just the gold-bullion tax business.'

'You think he jumped?'

'The police found the ledge had broken away a bit. Perhaps you're right and he fell. It comes to the same thing in the end.'

'What will happen?'

'There won't be much for Jago to inherit.'

For a moment Alice couldn't remember who Jago was – Brendan's son had been only briefly on her agenda. 'He was disinherited anyway, I think. They seemed to hate each other.' She watched Guy eating more mashed potato, then he pushed away his plate.

Demi poured them mugs of strong tea. She stood back respectfully. 'I'd never have thought such things could happen on this island.' Her tone was reverential, as if her opinion of the island had gone up. 'If you don't mind, I'll go next door.'

Alice guessed she had gone to watch television at her mother-in-law's and tried hard not to imagine what she would hear or see. Feeling distinctly worse about everything, she tried to remember if the holiday cottage she had rented for Florrie and herself had a television. She thought it was an extra she hadn't indulged in. But there would certainly be one in Pandora's hotel.

Demi closed the door carefully behind her.

'You don't look too good.' Guy came round to her.

'It's a nightmare.'

'Yes. Is there anywhere else we can sit? And how about locating Terry's whisky?'

Alice had never sat in the front room, an old-fashioned parlour, heavily furnished in fifties style with the exception of a tall lamp whose base was filled with a violent purple liquid that writhed around as if trying to escape its glass container. 'I suppose this is better,' she said doubtfully, 'but it's so cold.'

Guy was pouring them large slugs of whisky. 'Much better,' he said firmly. 'Those sausages stank of chickens' entrails.'

'I'll draw the curtains.' They were a stiff orange and brown stripe.

'Come and sit by me.'

They sat together on a small hard sofa.

'I just couldn't believe Brendan was so, so serious.'

'Even though I warned you, I never really thought so either. Otherwise I wouldn't have let Blue go to find him alone. Brendan was lying down when he got to him. He wanted Blue to think he was unconscious, badly injured.'

Alice didn't know if she wanted these new images. 'How can we know what was in Brendan's mind? If he thought he'd killed Blue that would be another reason to jump.'

They finished their whisky with a disappointed grimace.

'More?' suggested Guy, and poured lavishly.

Alice felt her blood warming and a pleasant distance created between herself on the sofa and the woman who'd lived through the afternoon's events. 'What do you think of that lamp?' she said, pointing at the purple monstrosity.

'What?' Evidently Guy had not noticed it.

Alice wondered if this was an illustration of the difference between a man and a woman: a man concentrated on the matter in hand, a woman spread herself about, her attention caught at so many different levels that her view was splintered and unclear. Just now, when she most wanted to feel close to Guy, her mind had flown to Pandora, their interview on the hotel terrace, her stated determination to join her life again with Bingo. My father, Bingo Featherstone, thought Alice. My mother, Pandora Featherstone. They sounded like something out of an Oscar Wilde play. 'Do you remember when I talked to you about my mother?'

'Your mother!' She could hardly blame him. 'A little,' he conceded.

'Until very recently I thought she didn't exist. She died when I was three – that's what my father taught me. I've told you before.'

'And a little girl believes her father.'

'She learns to disbelieve whatever she really believes. My mother came back once when I was about four – she said that to me a few days ago and I pretended not to know. But I did know. I saw her leaving our house and I knew she was my mother. It was wicked of my father to tell such a lie.' The whisky rose in Alice's blood like the purple genie in the lamp.

'I expect he thought he was doing the right thing. That generation believed in secrecy. Did your mother ever try to see you after that?'

'I don't think so. She's not a very motherly person, to say the least, and she went to live in Mexico. She's quite eccentric.' Alice found she was smiling at Pandora's eccentricities. 'I can't even remember if I told you it was she who kidnapped Lily. Although she says she was only taking her for a spin. And now she's planning to kidnap my miserable old father.'

'That sounds like a good idea. Make sure he doesn't have another stroke.'

Alice sighed. She put her glass on the floor and shifted along the sofa to put her head on Guy's shoulder. He let it rest there but didn't take her hand or put his arm round her. He had kissed her when they lay on the beach but it was no good thinking about that.

'You know I can't look after you, Alice.'

He said this in an unemotional tone, and through the muzzy waves of alcohol, Alice tried to work out what he meant. Had she asked him to look after her? She thought not. Was she the kind of helpless female who unconsciously put out signals for masculine protection? She hoped not. Guy must be feeling as overwhelmed and disoriented as she was. Perhaps he was merely referring to the police investigation, not something more personal.

'No. Of course not.' Her voice sounded mournful.

'You're very capable of looking after yourself. I've always thought so. And in the last few weeks I've seen it.'

So, it had been a personal pronouncement. But how strange that Guy should think she had shown self-reliance in the last few weeks when she had felt as if everything were falling apart. 'I didn't do very well as a journalist.'

'There were big forces out there. Blame me for putting you in touch with them. You had a lot to contend with.' Guy leant further back against the sofa so Alice's head was dislodged. He didn't notice. 'You played along as far as you could.'

Is that what she'd done? What did he mean? Was he talking about her interviewing technique, so kind and understanding as she'd been with Brendan, or was he talking more personally? His voice had been rougher, the slow pace of exhaustion quickened. Could he be referring to her night – or, more exactly, her couple of hours – in bed with Brendan? Or with Blue?

'I'm too tired,' she said, 'to understand what you mean.'

Guy stood suddenly. Alice blinked. Why was he doing this? She would not cry. Now he was collecting the bottle and glasses.

'We need to get some sleep. I'll leave a note for Terry. Will you join your family in the morning?'

'Yes. I suppose.' He was brusque. His back, as she followed him out of the room, was disapproving, cruel. Why had he changed so completely? Without analysing it, she had assumed he had stayed on the island to be her comfort or, at least, to be with her, and now he was separating himself with no explanation.

At the kitchen he dismissed her upstairs. 'I'll see you in the morning.' They had both been through a dreadful ordeal, she reminded herself, and also had finished off most of Terry's whisky. Guy was acting out of shock, and out of character. It would be all right in the morning.

'Goodnight.' Alice stumbled upstairs and fell fully clothed on to her bed.

Chapter Twenty-Six

A Fourth Wednesday

Three hours later, with her blood pulsing in her head, her throat raspingly dry and her heart filled with dread, Alice woke. It was unbearable to stay where she was. She had to have water to cool her inflamed blood although – she began shivering uncontrollably – her skin was icy cold. It was still dark when, without putting on a light and clinging to the banister, she staggered downstairs.

'Oh, my God!' The kitchen was glaringly bright. Guy stared at her. 'Why are you dressed?'

Dazed, Alice looked down at herself, then back at him. 'You're dressed too.'

'I never went to bed.'

Alice shuffled round to the sink and ran the water. 'I've got to have a drink.' She put her mouth to the tap. Water ran over her face and neck. She sighed, turned round and saw that Guy was making tea. 'What time is it?'

'Four thirty.'

'It'll be getting light fairly soon.' She wondered whether to tell him she'd lost her watch when she'd swum on the afternoon he'd shown her Blue's boat. He'd known then, she thought, that Blue was alive. What a charade.

'Someone's drilling a hole in my head.'

'Perhaps the whisky wasn't such a good idea.' He brought her tea.

He couldn't look after her but at least he brought her tea. 'It was that room, that lamp.'

'I'm waiting for the sun. Then I'm going outside.'

'I'll come with you.'

'I've been thinking about Brendan,' said Guy. They both sat

down, although not close. 'He was a thief on a huge scale, of course, but maybe it didn't have to end like this. The Inland Revenue might have done a deal; the government didn't want to be dragged into it. Ivo was there to help sort out something. It's even possible his companies were strong enough to pay back the pension money he'd siphoned off. That's only coming out now, of course.'

'But what about Blue?'

'Yes. There was Blue.'

'And the Master. The revered master of our revered paper. He'd never have let it go. It would have been wrong to let him off!' Alice spoke vehemently, encouraging the drill to go deeper. She put her hand to her forehead.

'I suppose I'm just trying to work out a way it could have been avoided.'

'Brendan's . . .' Alice hesitated '. . . Brendan's death, you mean.'

'Brendan grew up against a background of violence – e.g., the famously tragic bombing of his family, which you wrote about so movingly. You're right. It couldn't have been avoided. Once Blue had consented to confront him.'

'What do you mean, "consented"?'

Guy didn't answer but continued his own train of thought. 'No, I think it was inevitable for someone with Brendan's nature. He only understood violent resolutions.'

Unwanted images of Brendan making love to her forced Alice to acknowledge that he had a tender side. Yet even so she had been disgusted in the morning. Even then she'd known he was only using her.

'Do you remember how I helped you get away from him?'

Alice woke up a bit more. Why had he read her mind like this? Yet it seemed more of a reminiscence than a question.

'Of course, Blue had a violent background too.' Guy got up and went to the uncurtained window. He was clearly searching for light.

'Maybe the whole thing was between them and not much to do with the rest of us.' Alice heard the hopefulness in her voice.

'Tell that to the shareholders.' Guy spoke without turning round. 'It's a journalist's duty to get involved.'

Alice thought about this. 'Not truly involved.' It had not been her duty to sleep with Blue or Brendan.

'If you mean journalists are voyeurs, I won't argue. It goes with the territory. Like doctors are voyeurs.'

'But doctors change the course of events.'

'So can journalists. When you interviewed Blue, even though you only wrote that little piece, Brendan had realised his time was up.'

Alice stood up too. She felt restless as well as exhausted. 'Is there any light yet?'

'Yes. Yes. It's coming. Another ten minutes or so.'

Alice sat down again. 'I feel such a fool.'

'There're worse things to feel. Come on, let's go and watch the sun rise outside.' Suddenly his voice had become gentler. He found coats for them, belonging to Terry and Demi, and led her outside.

They sat on the plastic chairs, wet from the dew, but the coats were thick. There was already a smooth grey light, showing a streaky sky, still undecided whether to clear or cloud over.

Alice found herself complaining in a petulant tone, as if it were Guy's fault, 'We won't see the sun rise from here. It comes up behind the headland.'

Guy didn't trouble to argue. 'It may be cloudy anyway.'

Alice knew this was the time to speak. 'You probably knew I slept with Brendan.'

Guy didn't react or move his eyes from the sky.

'Of course you know because you helped me escape. You must think so little of me that I could . . .' What could she do? Sleep with Blue, too, and again only two days ago. Or maybe it was yesterday. The days and nights had become so muddled. She had a sneaking longing to sob, throw herself on his mercy, confess all and be forgiven. But she had more pride and good sense than that. They were working colleagues, with a friendship that had begun when she was a married woman with two teenage children. As he still said nothing, she, too, looked at the sky and thought things might improve if the sun came out. For all these weeks it had broiled and burned and caused her to do all sorts of unlikely things; now it must come to warm her heart. But the cloudy stripes were heavy, dark, forbidding bars.

'I found him attractive, that's the simple, tawdry, honest truth.'

At last Guy turned to her. 'You don't have to tell me this.'

'I don't want you to think . . . to think it *matters* to me.'

'I don't. I didn't then, and I don't now. You made a mistake. People do.' His voice was cold, objective, carefully expressionless.

'Anyway, I wanted to tell you and have it out of the way.'

'Out of the way.' Guy gave an ironic laugh. 'Brendan's certainly that.'

Alice couldn't think of any more to say. It was as if the whole conversation had a sub-plot that neither of them was willing to acknowledge. 'It's so confusing,' she muttered, looking down at her hands, which surprised her by their pallor. She supposed this strange pre-dawn light had drained out signs of the sunburn and scratches gained over the past days.

'Look!' Guy touched her arm. An orange flare was poking round the headland to the left. It seemed confident, a herald of something greater. It even made a reflection on the dark water.

'Have you had many deaths in your life?' It was a childish question, perhaps, but Alice wanted to know the answer.

'I told you once, I think. My parents died when I was quite young. I learnt to be self-sufficient early.'

That was what made him different. He wasn't looking for attention, he was self-sufficient. Should she ask him if that was why he hadn't married? No, not today. Just watch the sun, Alice told herself again, and don't think too much.

Guy and Alice walked to the harbour, with Demi, at her insistence, carrying Alice's bag. She had become her acolyte, following her around, regretting that she couldn't come over to see Lily. 'But someone has to keep things going on the island.' It seemed she was apologetic for their rancorous exchange in which she'd accused Alice of being 'winkled and cold and unloving'. Now she saw her as a heroine and very nearly a victim of all the dreadful happenings. She carried Alice's bag with chatty goodwill, exchanged complicit looks with an exhausted Terry, then waved them goodbye in hearty sweeps as Alice and Guy set off in the boat.

'I'm glad someone's happy,' murmured Alice.

Guy didn't ask her to explain. He turned his back to the island and faced ahead, basking, perhaps, in the sun's rays, which now shone boldly from a clear blue sky.

Alice was glad to be on the sea rather than looking at it from above as she had mostly for the last few days. The surface was smooth but she could see a strong swell underneath as if yesterday's storm had sunk to its depths but not entirely gone away. Occasionally, tresses of shiny seaweed floated by, torn from their moorings by the violence of the waves. Alice turned her head to look the way they were going. The idea passed through her mind that she had reached the furthest point and now her life was running in reverse.

Tresco got closer and bigger very quickly. Soon she could see Pandora, Florrie, Baz and Lily lined up on the harbour wall, just as they had been when she had departed. Perhaps they waved even more energetically. Then she could see the welcoming smiles on their faces.

'Quite a homecoming,' commented Guy. He hadn't met them before, Alice reminded herself. He couldn't appreciate the deranged untrustworthiness of Pandora, the self-absorbed irresponsibility of Florence, Baz's drop-out lethargy or Lily's disloyal insouciance – for her 'Mama' applied to everyone. I am a solitary widow, Alice tried telling herself, but the warmth of her family's greeting made such an analysis seem churlish. Besides, she could feel herself smiling too.

'This is Guy Vernon, a colleague from work.' She tried to introduce him, but several other families were embarking at the quayside and the smallish harbour was filled with loud English voices, children's shouts and the thumping of cases. Pandora and Florrie, meanwhile, were hanging round her shoulders, patting her back and generally making a fuss of her.

'If the weather hadn't been so frightful we'd all have been there to support you. You might have been killed! What a terrible experience! The news report said Sir Brendan Costa, or whatever he was called, went absolutely berserk before throwing himself off a cliff.' This was Florrie, as they walked from the harbour. She had passed over Lily to Alice as if possession of such a treasure would console her.

Pandora was walking behind with Guy, who was trying to field her detailed line of questioning. 'We understand he was trying to kill this man called Blue, a diver, is that right?'

'Did you get that from the news?' Alice heard Guy's calm voice. He had written up this story, she reminded herself.

'Some things we heard on the news, others from island talk.

Islanders are always good at drama. It's because their lives are generally so boring. I once lived on Crete, a brief period with my second unforgivable husband . . .'

Alice stopped listening as Lily made a determined grab at one of her earrings. She was amazed to find she'd put on jewellery that morning, then remembered she'd not taken it off the night before. 'No, darling. You don't want to hurt Granny, do you?'

'Of course, she doesn't.' Florrie laughed. Alice was amazed at her wonderful youthful energy. 'We all love you madly, Ma. And we've been most terribly worried.'

It was true – Alice could see it in her face. She hadn't looked more worried when Richard died. Baz, walking ahead, turned round and gave her what could only be described as a winning smile, clearly intended to show solidarity with Florrie's statement. Alice sighed. 'And I'm very glad to be with you all.'

Pandora, it turned out, was taking them, including Guy – she was the sort of woman who needed a man to hold her elbow, thought Alice – to lunch at her hotel.

'Dadada!' cried Lily, taking two fingers from her mouth and holding out her arms to Baz.

'So she's moved on too,' Alice commented to Baz, who smiled both proudly and sheepishly.

Pandora caught them up, and found time, as she negotiated the uneven path in three-inch heels, to whisper in a loud aside to Alice, 'He's most attractive, your friend.'

'He's not my friend in that way.'

'More's the pity.'

Alice couldn't help smiling at her. Her very bossiness had come to seem appealing, as if she had decided to take any amount of flak from Alice and not be put off.

When they got to the hotel it turned out that Pandora had arranged drinks and canapés on the terrace for a much larger group. Clearly, her approach to tragedy – if that was the right description of Brendan's death – was to throw a party. However, she took time off from terrorising the waiter to take Alice aside. 'We all think you should carry on with your holiday here.' She brought Baz into the conversation. 'I shall leave tomorrow but Baz and Florrie and her dear one will stay.'

'What day is it?'

'Wednesday.'

'You see, I lost my watch in Cornwall and once I stopped working and . . .' What was she trying to say? Two faces waited expectantly. 'I'm sorry, I'm not feeling too good. I think I'll sit inside for a while . . .' The sun, which she had wanted so much at the start of the day, was now bouncing off the sea and rooting into the top of her head.

Gallantly, Baz escorted her into a room behind the upper terrace, empty on such a fine day. He brought her a glass of water and promised to see she was undisturbed. 'Are you sure you don't want to go back to the cottage?'

'No. No,' Alice assured him. She liked the sound of the voices outside; she didn't want to be entirely on her own, just a little withdrawn, in the wings of a brightly lit stage.

There she sat for at least half an hour, by turns nursing the tenderness shown to her or contemplating slides of yesterday's horror. Some she had not seen but only imagined: Brendan tipping or possibly diving off the ledge, his fleshy but strong body smashed on the rocks below until it was retrieved and bagged up by the police. This slide passed and too soon, was replaced by another: Blue and she arguing across Billy's then immutable face. He had accused her of all sorts of cowardly, middle-class things – she could remember that but not the specifics. It struck her now that her reason for sleeping with him later had been to do with that quarrel. She had wanted to make it up, and what better way? They had lain together afterwards, his arm heavy on her body.

Alice might have sat for a long time in her quiet corner but she became aware of another occupant of the room. She hadn't noticed him entering but now he was at the far end reading a newspaper. He was completely absorbed, studying each page thoroughly. This was the way she'd scanned newsprint when she set out to be an interviewer. She had bought every paper and researched methodic- ally page by page. They were weighty, dirty objects that filled not only her time but her bags and her wastepaper baskets. Then they had not yet been on Internet or her self-imposed task would have been much easier and less physically arduous. Even Richard, who'd encouraged her on this trail, questioned the need to carry back quite so many Sunday papers from the newsagent. 'Get them delivered, Alice,' he'd advised. 'But I like to see how they feel,' she'd insisted. She became obsessed, addicted, and determined to succeed. At first she spent hours writing pieces that only she saw. Then she had shown a few carefully chosen ones to Mitzi, who was hardly helpful: she had pointed out that, these days, you needed a degree in journalism plus years of experience before anyone would look at your work. 'Of course you can write,' she added, glancing cursorily at Alice's neatly printed pieces, 'anyone can write, but to succeed you need the right background and push. Push is not your strong point.'

On reflection, this had been helpful because her determination became even more steely. Angrily, she reported Mitzi's view to Richard who'd actually laughed. 'She's quite wrong, of course. Probably doesn't want you competing in the career-woman stakes. What she should have told you is perfectly obvious: "It's not what you know but who you know." Now, let's consider our acquaintances in the world of journalism. I did defend that editor in a libel case, the one his hacks called "the Master" . . .' So it had been Richard who had eventually arranged an interview at the Daily——. By then she had enrolled in a journalism course and had also published several articles and interviews in her local London magazine so she hadn't presented herself as a complete amateur.

But the Master hadn't been impressed. He had given her ten minutes in his office, during which he recalled Richard's winning address to the judge while paying attention to her legs. He asked her only one question, which followed his invitation to file an interview with a film star of her choice and he'd print it if it was good enough. 'Is your hair naturally red?' he'd asked her, as if collecting useful information.

Alice had understood he was giving her a chance because of Richard and nothing else – although her legs hadn't been a disadvantage. This was the experience that later decided her to wear a skirt when interviewing men – who were all, as it turned out, she did interview. She had come out of the office bewildered, and grasped only slowly that she had got what she wanted.

'Well done,' a voice had said at her elbow. There had been a second man in the room with her but he hadn't spoken and the intensity of the interview had left her no time for observers.

'Thanks.' She'd glanced at him, noticing no more than a friendly face. 'Now I've got to find a subject. I can't say film stars are on my beat.'

'Oh, we'll find someone better than that. The Master likes a tease.'

They had walked down the corridor together, Alice looking for the lifts and the exit. It was nearly one o'clock and her companion was also heading out. At the glass doors he said, 'Want to bat round a few ideas over a sandwich?'

This had been Guy. That had been their relationship.

Alice looked across the dim room at the man immersed in his newspaper. 'Guy!'

He put down the paper at once – in fact, half crumpled it and threw it on to the floor. He jumped to his feet. 'Alice, I didn't see you there in the corner.'

'You're in the corner too.'

'There are four.' They smiled at each other.

'I thought you were outside, socialising with my family.'

'Couldn't quite make it.' They were talking across the room and now Guy took a step forward. 'Your family are great. It's just . . .' He looked down at the paper.

Alice saw what he'd been reading about. 'All over it, I suppose.'

'Yes.'

'Your story?'

'Much expanded. Plus four more pages, including the front page. The Master's gone to town.'

'And me. Us. Do we figure?' Alice asked the question without thinking through the implications.

'There's a pretty photograph of you.'

Pretty! Why had he said that? What did that matter? She watched Guy come over to her. A nasty new sensation was replacing her reliving of yesterday's horrors. That was the past. This was the present. Was her private life to be chortled over by a lascivious readership? 'Who've they interviewed?' Her voice was pathetic, so lacking in gumption.

'Basically, it's my story rewritten, a lot about the financial implications, a police statement and they've talked to Brendan's first wife who, I happen to know, wouldn't have had anything to report because they hadn't met for years.'

'Jago's mother. The potter,' murmured Alice.

'Yes. She's fairly spaced out.'

'I know it's feeble and unprofessional of me but I can't bear to read it. What about Blue? Has he been interviewed?'

'Why should you read anything? You're off duty.' She was grateful for his patience. 'I doubt if Blue will talk. It's not his style. I suppose Terry might or Demi, but they knew very little and these islanders are close.'

'That's not Pandora's view.' Alice managed to smile.

'Your mother's a one-off.' He paused, as if debating whether to say more about her, then apparently decided against it. 'Did you know the police mistook you for an islander? There's a strong red-haired strain on that island.'

'Perhaps I lived there in another life. I did love Billy. Poor Billy.'

'Billy's a survivor. A bit of glue and he'll be back in business.' Guy held out a hand. 'Let's go and join the party. We might even persuade Pandora that lunch is the next item on the agenda.'

Even after so many days without a watch, Alice glanced at the blank space on her wrist. She wondered if she was longing to buy a new one and bring time back into her life. She'd wait till she returned to London. As she followed Guy back into the sunlight, she pictured her flat, Richard's flat, Richard's widow's flat. The computer would be overflowing with email messages, the landline, too, and her mobile had already sprung into action, although she hadn't listened to it.

'The children want me to stay here, finish the holiday as planned.'

Guy was staring at the charming scene ahead. More hotel guests, presumably invited by Pandora and all wearing colourful summery clothes, had joined their group, turning it into a real party. Pandora had acquired a large pink hat, with purple pansies and red roses on the brim. Florrie and Lily were sitting on the ground, the baby's mouth opening like a bird's as Florrie spooned in orange-coloured mush.

'I should have said,' Guy turned back to Alice, 'you only figured in Brendan's story as the reporter who interviewed him most recently. Our paper was sure to give you a certain amount of prominence as one of our own writers. It was a very small photograph of you. The main one was of Brendan with Ivo. Ivo resigned this morning. The opposition are getting their teeth into the government. This story is about politics and money, about corruption.'

'You mean I'm nothing in it?'

'I mean you can stay here and enjoy your holiday.'

'But you'll go back?'

'Yes. I'm not on holiday. Cheer up, our livers should be able to cope with a glass of champagne by now.'

The shadow of the hotel building moved in a black line across the terraces. Out to sea the water and sky glistened in silvery brilliance. Lily went to sleep in the arms of Baz, who held her so sturdily that Alice could hardly believe she had once thought him Florrie's droopy appendage. Florrie wore a plaited scarlet belt hung about with little bells that tinkled as she moved. Every now and again she glanced towards Alice as if to check she was all right.

Pandora, clinging to Guy's arm with sinewy fingers, announced that they should go inside now because a table had been prepared for lunch.

Once again, Alice studied her watchless wrist. She felt at a point of nervous re-entry. 'Please sit beside me,' she whispered to Guy.

The room set aside for their lunch was as dark as a mausoleum. It was soothing to Alice, although she wished she hadn't likened it to a place of death. 'Can you really not stay for a day or two?' she asked Guy.

'The Master is shocked and appalled that I'm not back in the office already.'

'Oh, yes. He won't care how you're feeling or how you might be needed by someone else!'

'I'm going back in about an hour. Then I can catch the overnight train from Penzance. It's important I'm there. It's my job, Alice.'

'Your job? That makes all the difference.' Why was she picking a quarrel? She tried to laugh, determined not to say more. Before these last few weeks all the men in her life had used their jobs as a barricade to any proper intimacy. First her father, the doctor; from as far back as she could remember, he had shut her out of his life. Even at breakfast he'd be engrossed in some medical journal or in letters that he slit open with a paper knife as if it were a scalpel. Richard had been worse when she married him. Some mornings he hadn't addressed a word to her before he left for the office. She had been too young, too admiring, too malleable. Her father had trained her that way.

But the lunch was enjoyable, all the same. After she had said goodbye to Guy, she would go and lie down for an hour or so. Pandora had informed her that she'd booked her a room in the hotel because her dearest daughter needed peace and there would be no peace with a baby in a tiny cottage. Alice hadn't objected.

The room was at the back of the hotel with very little view. Alice closed the curtains thankfully. She'd had enough of views. She took off all of her clothes and crawled between the smooth sheets.

In what felt like a moment there was knock on the door. 'Who is it?' She struggled to remember where she was. She didn't open her eyes when she heard the door open because she'd remembered about the hotel and decided it must be the maid to turn down the bed. She'd go away again. Then she felt a weight on the bed. Still she couldn't find the energy to open her eyes. 'Florrie?'

'It's Blue. I knocked and the door was unlocked so I came in.'

'Blue.' Now she opened her eyes. It really was him, sitting on the end of the bed and watching her. There was not enough light in the room and she was still too sleepy to focus on his expression. 'Are you all right?' Slowly, she sat up. He'd been through a much worse ordeal than she had.

'The police wanted to know if I'd pushed him over.' His voice, with its slight Australian twang, didn't sound too disturbed.

Alice sat up, pulling the sheets round her naked breasts. 'Both Guy and I saw what happened. We told the police.'

'Yeah. It was OK. They probably didn't like the cut of my jib. They knew the story from before. My so-called disappearance. That sort of thing. Do you have a mini-bar?'

'I don't know. I only just got here. Have a look.'

He got up and wandered round the room. Eventually she heard him open a door and, from the sounds, assumed he'd taken out a bottle and a glass.

'Care to join me?'

'No, thanks. I had champagne at lunch.'

'Classy.'

'My mother bought it. She likes that sort of thing.'

He came back to the bed and sat down with his glass. She could smell whisky. 'So, how do you see my future?'

'What?' She was fully awake now but it didn't help. What did he want from her? Sex? Advice? Perhaps she should ask him.

'I like you. That's why I'm asking you. How should I go from here?'

She still didn't know what he wanted. Not her, it seemed, although even that wasn't certain. 'You mean now you can't get Brendan's money for your training school?'

'I suppose.' He was staring moodily into his glass, which was empty already. 'I might go to Australia. There's more openness there. Do you mind if I take another drink?'

'Be my guest.'

He went away, then returned again to the bed. In the meantime Alice recalled, almost nostalgically, what a god-like figure he'd been in that other hotel room in London.

'I could sign up for another trip.'

'What do you want to do?'

'Hey, that's funny, Alice, really funny.'

His tone now held a dangerous intensity. The suddenness of it bewildered Alice. She remembered how he had shouted at her when they stood beside Billy. Her nakedness was making her feel vulnerable. She realised she hadn't expected to see him ever again. 'I tell you what, Blue. Do you remember when you told me about phosphorescence?' He didn't answer but didn't interrupt either so she went on, not knowing what she was going to say but hoping she could calm him. 'That's what you care about most. That's what you told me. You said it almost made you believe in God. I think you said that. You love the sea, Blue. That's what matters to you.' That's what attracted me to you, she thought, the sense that you were part of something outside everyday life. You seemed to be the ultimate escape.

Just as she was wondering what more she could say, Blue stood up and, putting the glass on the bedside table, bent over and gave her a kiss on the mouth. His mouth was hard and his hand slid behind her hair. Alice felt herself tense but then he stood upright.

'You've got style. I'd get into bed with you for half a sixpence but I know you don't want that. Thanks for the whisky. I'll be off. I only dropped in to say goodbye.'

Blue . . .' began Alice, but she couldn't call him back. He was right, she didn't want him. 'I'll keep in touch.' But she wouldn't do that either.

'You're just a woman, after all. Women only think about happiness. They're programmed that way, something to do with wanting the best for their babies, although since they usually look to a poor weak male for satisfaction, they haven't a hope in hell of success. My mother was just the same when I managed to catch up with her. Her eyes were "deep wells of unfulfilled love". I read that somewhere.' He moved away from the bed. 'Goodbye, Alice. You were a lovely fuck, as I think I told you once before.'

'Thanks,' murmured Alice, weakly, as the door closed behind him.

Chapter Twenty-Seven

Alice waited for time to become recognisable again. She knew it couldn't while she remained on the island but she stayed there all the same, grateful for the privacy and the protection of her family. Peter and Jennie, worried about her, came to join them over the weekend. To her surprise, Peter appeared to take Pandora in his stride, as if returning grandmothers were to be expected. Pandora, it was true, made a great fuss of him, referring to him as 'the head of the family', or 'HF' since, as she put it, 'Your poor old granddad is well past anything but fun and laughter.' At first Alice continued to be amazed by her absurd bossiness – after all, she was a runaway, a deserter – but gradually she forgot to think like that and, instead of trying to fit Pandora into her childhood imaginings and unhappiness, she accepted her as someone new in her life. It was easier that way. Reproaches almost too deep to be put into words could be buried, and she could appreciate what Pandora had to offer. She could see that her mother had come back to give herself to the family she had left and, if her talk of priests and penitence was more fancy than truth, it nevertheless expressed a reality. Pandora had returned and was not going away again. Alice's responsibilities had lessened. It was a heady feeling.

Much to her relief, she was not asked to attend Brendan's inquest, which she'd been dreading. For five days she managed to avoid reading any newspapers, listening to the news or watching television. Of course, she couldn't avoid people talking and she overheard a teenage boy laughing about the 'Island of Death'. She felt upset for Demi and Terry, their little paradise despoiled, until an unusually chatty boatman, taking her, Florrie and Lily for a ride, boasted of sharing in Terry's good fortune. 'They've never had so many tourists. It's an ill wind that blows nobody any good. It's really put the place on the map. Demi's planning to make a little café out of one of those bird-watching huts. They've got more business than they can manage themselves. That's where I come in. Boat trips to the Cliff of Death . . .'

After that Alice shut him up. But it had made her more observant, and now she noticed how many small boats and larger launches passed by their island to visit the next. The point was that Sir Brendan Costa, fraudster and party donor, had become extremely famous. It was time she went back to London.

In the end, she couldn't get a booking with the others so she travelled alone on the sleeper from Penzance, as Guy had a week earlier. She felt a precarious sense of going back in time and slept hardly more than a few hours. It was still early when she arrived outside her flat. She paid off her taxi and looked up at the shadowy building.

If there had been any sun, it would have been hidden at this hour behind the building but, in fact, it was a dull grey day with clouds weighty enough for rain. The porter wasn't yet on duty so she let herself in through the outside doors and took the lift up.

The flat was warm and airless. She felt as if she'd been away for months or even years, rather than a couple of weeks. She'd bought milk at the station so she could make herself a cup of tea, but now she hesitated. What did she usually do when she came into her flat? Listen to messages on her landline, read her emails. Make communication. She had finally listened to as many of the messages on her mobile as she could bear – too many journalists wanting her point of view on Brendan's 'suicide', as it was generally described, but in the last couple of days they'd been tailing off.

Alice sat on the sofa in the living room. There wasn't the smallest draught to move the curtains – now white with an edge of dirty grey, she noticed. On the island she had spoken to Jonathan and Mitzi, to her father and Sister Mary Rose. She would simply wipe all the other messages and start afresh.

Alice made herself tea and, mug in hand, went round each room, throwing open windows. She had always disliked this flat, she reminded herself exultantly, and now she would put it on the market. In an hour or two she would go out to the estate agent on the corner, which Richard had visited to note the rise in value of his property, and wash her hands of it. She became aware that the telephone was ringing. 'Hello.'

'How are you? Are you OK? How was the journey?' It was Guy. He'd rung most days, always briefly, always to the point.

'I've decided to sell the flat. I feel wonderful.'

'That's good. About feeling wonderful, I mean. Have you opened any letters yet?'

'Not yet.' She had forgotten about letters. Usually the porters brought them up but she hadn't noticed any.

'You know what the Costa Goliath shares have fallen to?'

'No.'

'Five pence. The company may yet go into liquidation. More debts are being uncovered every day.'

'But I thought that at least Brendan was a good businessman!'

'You weren't the only one. But he was using the company money to hike up the shares. There might be enough worth saving to attract a buyer.'

'At five pence?' Five pence, she remembered, was the figure Brendan himself had predicted.

'Quite.'

'So it's lucky I'm selling the flat.' Alice had told Guy about her shares. She'd been shamed by not picking up the name Costa Goliath when she'd interviewed Brendan, but Richard had always managed the financial side of her life and after his death she'd allowed their solicitor and accountant to take over.

'Don't forget to give Pandora first refusal.'

'I had forgotten. Was she serious?' During that dim-lit, Tresco lunch, Pandora had announced that she hoped to buy Alice's flat, install Bingo in it with a nurse and make it a family home.

'Very serious, I'd say.'

'And she always gets what she wants.' Alice laughed.

'I guess so. I'll speak to you tomorrow.'

He was always abrupt like this in ringing off. She had wanted to ask him how far down the news the Costa scandal had dropped. Or whether the government's involvement kept it up there still. Brendan's name hadn't been in the headlines – she had noticed that while buying the milk. But she couldn't go on behaving like a ridiculous ostrich with her head in a bag. She might have been the only woman he allowed to interview him but she certainly wasn't the only one he had slept with. Today she would buy a watch and a paper, bring time and order back into her life.

Today was Thursday. She would do what she always did on Thursdays.

The grey clouds had thinned so a white light streamed over the sea, which would have been flat without the multitude of boats, skiers and swimmers breaking up its surface. This was Brighton, the sea as public service, hardly anything at all to do with the glossy waters swirling round the islands. Alice was glad of it. She walked briskly along the promenade, only stopping for a moment to consider the derelict, barbed-wire-fenced pier where Pandora had abandoned Bingo. Then she carried on at the same intent speed.

'Oh, Alice! You do look well.' Mary Rose, softer and bigger than Alice remembered, greeted her warmly. How surprising that she should look well after all that had happened. Yet it was true: she caught a glimpse of herself in the hallway mirror and saw a woman younger than she was, long hair bleached by the sun and caught back from her glowing face. She supposed she should have it cut. 'I'm afraid your father's out. You never usually come on a Friday.'

'Friday?' Of course. She had set out from Penzance on Thursday and not noticed, with her sleepless night, when one day had changed into another. Alice laughed. 'I'm so confused.'

Mary Rose assumed a sympathetic look, not wholly professional, Alice thought. 'I'm so sorry ... that you got caught up in such unpleasantness.'

'Yes. Thank you.' Alice liked the sound of 'unpleasantness'. It had such a normal ring. 'I'll go upstairs and wait for him.'

'Oh, I wouldn't do that.'

Alice looked at her enquiringly. Mary Rose wore an almost complacent expression. 'Your mother's taken him to her flat for lunch. She's a fast worker, your mother.' Her tone was admiring. 'She only rented it yesterday. Fully furnished. They won't be back till late. You must be so pleased by the way it's turned out, the kind of happy miracle that seldom happens in real life.'

Alice stared at the kind face in front of her. She was being told that her father was being looked after now and her weekly visits, previously essential to his well-being, or so she had always believed, were no longer needed. It felt too late to reproach her for keeping the secret.

'I'll give you the address, shall I? Now you've come all this way, you won't want to go away without seeing him.'

Alice walked back slowly the way she'd come. She hadn't dressed up for this visit and wore trainers, cotton trousers, a T-shirt and a light cotton jacket. A bag swung off her shoulder. It was lunchtime and the promenade was crowded with not only holidaymakers and tourists but workers from the city, come out of their shops and offices for air and a glimpse of the sea. Alice felt herself merge with these people. This was where she'd been born, where she'd grown up.

'Darling! What a perfect surprise!' Pandora called over her shoulder, 'Bingo, dearest, Alice is here. Alice is joining us.'

The hallway was dark but the room into which Pandora led her was flooded with light. Two chairs were set by the window. Against the back wall, a table was still laid with the remains of lunch. Alice noticed smoked fish and salads, the sort of things she'd always assumed Bingo hated and could neither masticate nor digest. He sat in a rather kingly way with a red rug across his knees and a jacket draped round his thin shoulders. He looked suspiciously towards the door and the darkness, evidently not quite able to see who was entering. Then he said, quite loudly, 'Alice, you say'. But Alice has had enough of me. Can't be Alice.'

Alice decided to ignore this, went over to him and kissed his cheek. She noticed that the texture and colour of his skin had changed: where before it had been pale, blotched and scaly, now it was smooth and ruddy. 'It *is* me,' she said. 'I would never desert you.'

'Ha!' He snorted.

'Be calm, my darling.' Pandora put her arms on both their shoulders – she wore a fine blouse with wide sleeves that draped over them like angel's wings. 'Desertion is not a good word in this family. We enjoy where we are, is that not better?' She turned to Alice. 'Have you eaten?'

Alice sat at the table and ate hungrily. She had known her father would have no more need of her. A truth so obvious that she couldn't think why she'd never understood it before it came to her quite suddenly: her father had never loved her. Perhaps he'd even hated her. She had reminded him of her mother, whom he had wanted and couldn't have. His lie about Pandora's death had indeed been an aggressive act of cruelty.

'He is your own father, however flawed and weak, decrepit in mind and body.' Pandora settled by Alice. She was smiling as if the image amused her.

'He's never cared about me,' said Alice, loudly enough to reach the window.

'But you will sell me your flat? Don't forget you're poor now.'

'If you like,' agreed Alice, negligently. 'I never thought of it as mine anyway. Richard bought it. Actually, he inherited it from his father.'

'That's good.' Pandora rose again. 'We women must never accept the unacceptable.'

At this Alice felt like repeating her father's derisive snort but contented herself with reaching for a strawberry. 'Does he eat strawberries?' she asked curiously.

'No. But the colour is cheering.'

Alice went back to her father. 'I hear you're coming up to London.'

He looked up at her, his red-rimmed eyes shrewd. 'You approve, do you?' His voice was stronger than she remembered, more focused at least, as if he believed in what he was saying.

'Of course,' said Alice. 'You have Pandora now. She calls the shots.'

He smiled at this and rubbed his hands together, then placed them back on his sharp knees.

'We're going out now.' Pandora stood by the window. Her loose blouse and floating skirt entwined with the long white curtains. 'Would you help with the chair, Alice?'

Alice did so and was glad to be reminded of her father's frailness, the hard work and awkwardness involved in moving him. She noted with approval that Pandora's forearms under the fluttering sleeves were strong – stronger than her own – and she remembered that the Mexican husband had needed care in the last years.

'I shall have twenty-four-hour care when we move to London,' whispered Pandora, as they emerged on to the pavement.

'Let's move, let's move,' grumbled Bingo.

'Say goodbye to Alice first. She's got better things to do than attend on two arguing antediluvians.'

Alice kissed her father, who pursed his lips vaguely, like a child, and her mother, whose skin, despite its leathery appearance, was soft and smelt of expensive creams. Then she watched them progress, with almost dangerous swiftness, down the pavement.

Just as she was about to turn away, the chair halted abruptly and Pandora darted back to her. She put her hand on Alice's arm. 'I have had one of my better ideas. We'll swap flats immediately. You have too many dark thoughts. You'll have my sun-filled rooms with this glorious view of the sea and I'll have your splendid red-brick building with its bribable porters and apparent respectability. I've a six-month rental so we must make it happen quickly and you won't miss a day.' Before Alice, bewildered, could respond, she'd dashed back up the pavement to where Bingo was waving his stick threateningly.

'I'll think about it!' shouted Alice, because she wanted the offer to be real. She began to walk almost at random, heading into the town away from the sea. Very soon, she found her attention drawn by a shop window filled with unusual objects, mostly coloured orange or turquoise. She looked closer and saw that some were made entirely of feathers, roundels or prisms, others were heavy stone carvings of squat humans or sturdy animals. In the middle, more striking than anything, was a mask, its surface decorated with turquoise mosaic and its wide eyes filled with black stone, which glittered as the light caught it. She stared for some time until the black eyes began to stare back at her. She was seized with a longing to buy it, and hurried into the shop.

'You've been attracted by our Aztec display. I saw you outside.'

'Aztec. Yes, of course.' Now that she was inside the shop Alice recognised it as the place of fortune-tellers and crystal balls where she and Mitzi had met the giant seer, whose name she couldn't remember. It was a woman who spoke to her now, in her fifties, with a strong, stern face, softened by looped Indian earrings.

'They're fine copies. The mask in particular.'

'Yes. I thought so. Is it for sale, then?'

'Of course, but you need to want it a lot. The craftsmanship and the materials make it a work of art in its own right.'

'I've never seen anything like it. A mask with seeing eyes.'

'Or are they blind?' The woman had been standing behind the counter laid out with tarot cards but now she came round. Alice thought she was going to extract the mask from the window but instead she passed her to drop the latch on the door, then returned. 'I don't think you're feeling too well.'

It was true. She could feel the blood draining away and a swaying sensation as if she might faint. Before the blackness spread, the woman grasped her arm and let her through a curtain to a small room. Dimly, Alice heard her say, 'I always keep tea in a Thermos,' then felt a mug being pushed into her hand. The hot liquid, laced with sugar and something spicy, raced into her blood vessels.

'I'm Becky,' the woman continued, 'and I can see you've been on a difficult journey.'

Alice smiled inwardly at such an absurd cliché but she was grateful to a stranger who had bothered to look after her. 'Yes,' she agreed.

'Most people think of the Aztecs as a brutal nation, whose idea of fun was watching a young man's heart cut out and, if you were lucky enough to be a priest, eating it. But, actually, they were very civilised – they loved flowers, gave kindly attention to cripples and had a highly developed moral code. For example, drunkenness and adultery were severely frowned upon.'

'They did sacrifice human beings.'

'One can't deny that, although they chose their victims from neighbouring tribes. I mean, you didn't knock off your mates. Life expectancy was not high then, anyway. Would you like some more tea?'

'Thank you.'

'No one can avoid death.'

Alice looked down at her mug. This was just a little too trite, she thought. Very few people plunge on to rocks a hundred feet below.

Becky seemed to sense her lack of empathy because she added, 'What I mean is, it doesn't have to be the most important thing in your life.' She stood. 'If you're feeling better, I should open the shop again but stay here for as long as you like.' She shook her head, in a friendly, horselike manner, and went through the curtain.

Alice wondered if she still wanted the mask. What was it that had attracted her to it so strongly? Was it only the association with death? Contrary to what Becky seemed to be implying, she was good at coping with death. Richard's had been shocking but it hadn't frightened her. Perhaps she should have explained that she had had to deal with her mother's death when she was three. Alice got up, planning to look at the mask again, and found herself thinking, almost idly, that sometimes it seemed as if she was the only person who wasn't wearing a mask.

'I really would like to buy it,' she told Becky, who was still alone in the shop.

'It's certainly very beautiful.' This time Becky went to the window and came back carefully holding the mask, which she laid almost reverentially on the counter.

It was smaller than Alice had thought, the face of a small person. Much too big for Becky, a little too big for her. There were leather straps threaded with a few coral beads, which were obviously there as ties. Alice touched it gingerly and the black eyes watched her knowingly.

'It costs two thousand four hundred pounds, I'm afraid,' said Becky, in the voice of someone who assumes the deal is off.

But the huge sum hardened Alice's determination. 'Can you wrap it so it's safe?'

'It's quite strong, actually. Do you mean you're going to buy it?' Her surprise made Alice smile.

'Certainly. I'm selling a home in London and renting a flat in Brighton. It'll look good there. Do you accept Mastercard?'

Chapter Twenty-Eight

The doorbell rang loudly. Alice wasn't used to the way it vibrated on the wall of the main room, although she'd been in the flat for ten days. She spoke into the intercom. 'Come up, Jonathan.'

She sat in a chair with her back to the sea. She knew its power and wanted to concentrate on her visitor.

'Dear Alice. How kind of you to let me visit. I gather this place is a bit of a secret.'

'Oh, no. Just small. Not much room for guests.' She kissed him and took his coat. It was September, the air cooler, trees in the Pavilion Gardens curling at the edges – although that might be the corroding effect of salt.

'You enjoy living by the sea, then?'

Alice was glad to see he was looking nervous. As it was Saturday he'd dressed in casual clothes, corduroys, an open-necked Viyella shirt, an expensive-looking jacket, probably cashmere. It struck her how seldom she'd seen him out of a suit. Soon she was going to make him more nervous.

'Tea?'

'Yes, please.'

When she came back he was studying at her mask. It stood on a plinth between the two windows. 'That's an amazing piece of work. It can't be genuine Aztec.'

'Just a copy.'

'It's very compelling.'

'It reminds me of all the masks people wear in this world.' Alice hadn't thought she would begin at once on the thing that mattered but she couldn't see any reason to delay.

'I miss our Wednesdays,' said Jonathan.

'Do you?'

They were both sitting now, Jonathan facing the mask to which his eyes slid unwillingly. 'Don't you get lonely? No work. No friends.'

'I may not stay long.' Alice leant forward, cupping her face in her hands.

'Ah, so then we can resume our . . . ?' His voice trailed away and his eyes slid upwards again.

'Tell me, Jonathan, why did you throw yourself at me, pretend you loved me?' She spoke gently, but Jonathan was already wriggling like a fish on a hook. 'The moment Richard died you were trying to fix yourself up with me. Wasn't it rather a humiliating thing to do? I mean, how did you expect me to take it? What's it all about? Why don't you tell me honestly?'

'Alice . . . I do love . . . Always . . . Richard was my oldest friend . . .' Away slid his eyes.

'It's not as if you aren't a dignified and successful person. I admired you so much in the Privy Council, in all your gear, doing good, saving lives. Guy and I came to watch. Do you remember?'

'Of course I remember. I . . .'

Suddenly Alice felt sickened with the game of it. If he had truly loved Richard he had suffered as much as she had, if not more. It seemed better to say the words standing up. 'You see, Jonathan, I know about you and Richard. I understand what you felt about each other. Understand enough, anyway. It makes sense of all sorts of things. But I can't help thinking you were both cowardly, so lacking in conviction. And I can't carry on with it any more. Particularly if you're trying to convince yourself that you're in love with me. You know it's nonsense and I know it's nonsense. You love me because I was Richard's wife. You both made a mistake, perhaps you agreed to make the mistake together. You both married. Perhaps it wasn't such a huge mistake. Times were different then, you'll tell me. But things are different now. So stop pretending and maybe, somewhere in the future, not now, you can become an old family friend again.'

Alice delivered all this hardly looking at him. He gradually bent further and further over so that she couldn't see his face. There was a silence that grew. Alice heard flurries of rain against the window. She felt quite calm, and when she saw Jonathan's shoulders shaking with what must have been sobs, she felt reasonably sympathetic, without regretting her words. 'I'm sorry I've upset you but that's the way, isn't it? I don't mind you crying at all. I'll take it as an apology. You cry and I'll make some fresh tea.'

Alice stayed some time in the little kitchen, gazing out of the window that also faced the sea. On the whole, she didn't think there was much Jonathan could say or that she wanted him to say. His tears were acknowledgement enough and she didn't want explanations.

When she went back into the room Jonathan was standing. He'd put on his coat and his handsome, usually pale face was patchily red and swollen. 'I'm sorry.'

'That's all right.' Alice heard her voice ridiculously cheerful, as if she'd forgiven him for spilling his tea. She had a wild urge to laugh but he would have thought it cruel. 'What I mean is, I'm all right. In fact, Richard gave me a lot of important things: the children, security, and then he encouraged me to find my job. I've a lot to be thankful for.'

'Yes. I'm glad.' He was edging towards the door and she was glad to let him go. She wasn't the one to help him, to tell him he could be happy.

'Goodbye, Jonathan. Good luck.'

'Yes. Thank you.' He was gone. Just the door closing quietly.

Chapter Twenty-Nine

'But I want you to see the flat, Guy. And my mask.'

'Ah, your mask. I'm looking forward to making its acquaintance. Unfortunately the Master keeps me tied to my desk.'

Alice knew this couldn't be true. The government had survived the scandal of Sir Brendan Costa. Everything had been exposed that could be exposed. Even the most indispensable of editors had free time. She hadn't seen Guy since he left the island, although they still spoke to each other most days. So much time had passed that the last vestiges of bruised colour had disappeared from her knee. She wanted to say to him, 'You're the only unsolved mystery.'

It had been cold that morning. She'd walked very early by the sea: the city was hardly awake, just a few buses, a few cars still with headlights on and a bunch of dozy-looking seagulls walking ahead of her along the beach. When she got back she had returned to bed then got up again and eaten a lot of hot buttered toast while waiting for Guy's call. He most often rang about nine – after his first meeting and before the day really fell in on him, as he had told her. But why wouldn't he meet her?

'I went to Brendan's funeral yesterday.'

'Oh, God.'

'Yes. There were surprisingly few mourners. As if people were afraid of being associated with him. But I spoke to Jago.'

'Jago hated him.'

'He was with his mother.'

'But she hated him too. Were there any press?'

'Some. Me.'

'So, it's over now.'

'Jago has a plan.'

'Has he?' Alice couldn't feel much curiosity.

'He's hoping to help Blue with this school he was planning. For young offenders.'

'Surely there's no money?'

'Don't tell the shareholders.' Guy laughed. He knew Alice had been badly hit by the collapse of Costa Goliath, but had never shown much sympathy. 'So you may yet write up that interview with Blue.'

'No, I won't. Not ever.' Alice wondered if Guy could hear the agitation in her voice. She'd been happily imagining Blue on some very distant sea.

'I see. Well, that sounds final.'

'It is. Blue's not part of my life.'

There was a long pause, as if Guy was assessing her statement. He changed the subject: 'How are you amusing yourself today? Taking an autumnal walk by the sea?'

'Done that.' But Alice heard in his voice that he was about to ring off. A week ago he'd hinted that the Master would like her to do an interview and she'd declined. Now she could use it to extend the conversation. 'Who was it the Master suggested I interviewed?'

'Oh, that. Someone else did it. Polly Omar, actually. She did it very well.'

Alice found herself filled with hatred for Polly Omar, whose conker-coloured hairless arms and bright, confident manner she could still picture. 'Is she doing a lot now?'

'Quite a bit. The Master's taken her up. You know how keen he is to be in touch with youth.'

This was much worse. In her solitary situation, she still hadn't recaptured the journalist's occupation of obsessively scanning the newspapers. She listened to the radio and that had been enough. What had started as a defence against reading about Brendan – and maybe herself – had become a habit. She was giving herself a break, but what if her place on the paper was no longer open to her?'

'I'm not planning to stay away for ever,' she said. 'I just needed time out to regroup.'

'I'm glad to hear it.' But his voice was cagey rather than enthusiastic. Another silence fell. He really would ring off this time.

'I saw Becky yesterday,' she said, a little desperately.

'The mask vendor.'

'She's longing to read my future in the cards but I'm too scared.'

'Quite right. Speak to you soon, darling.'

The phone was put down. But the 'darling' remained. Alice tried to imagine what his expression had been as he'd said it. Maybe the word had just slipped out, an automatic endearment for women he spoke to frequently. Alice became aware of the mask's eyes glittering critically in her direction. It had become a hard task-master, forcing her to admit any move in the direction of avoidance techniques. She would go and buy a bunch of papers and read them from cover to cover. Damn to hell Polly Omar.

The summer edged away slowly. Every time the air cooled and a crispness sharpened the line between shore and sea, sea and sky, a warm spell drifted back. Towards the end of October Alice even swam. She was watched by Becky, who had needlessly brought a huge towelling robe and a flask of brandy. They drank together sitting – almost basking – on the pebbles.

'Do you remember Luke Nestor?' asked Becky.

'I don't think so.' Contented after her swim, Alice didn't try too hard.

'My brother, the seer who comes once a week to my shop.'

Alice pictured the bearded prophet, who'd warned her of Pandora's existence.

'Luke admired you very much.'

Her meaning was clear but Alice pretended not to pick it up. 'My friend Mitzi, who was with me when we met him, is coming down next weekend.'

Becky didn't comment.

Previously Alice would have been happy for summer to extend itself indefinitely, but this year it unsettled her. She wanted it to end so she could begin again. Sometimes when she walked over the Downs, she looked in despair at the green swoops of grass. It all looked so unchanging. Not that she was living such a solitary existence as she had at first: two days a week she worked in Becky's shop – on days when her brother didn't appear – and one day she helped the Brighton Festival organisers. It was hardly serious work but it filled her time. Twice now she had gone to her cottage and stayed with Florrie. The second time Florrie had announced she and Baz needed a break from Lily and Alice had been left holding the baby. That had been exciting: Lily crawled now and much preferred standing to sitting, clinging precariously to any handhold of the right height. Alice arrived back in Brighton exhausted, and laughed at herself for ever believing she was young enough to give birth and have her own new baby.

As soon as Mitzi arrived off the train she announced that she was visiting Brighton to give Greg space to bond with his father.

'Are you really together again, Mitzi?' Alice was truly horrified that Mitzi could turn back the pages in this way. They were walking arm in arm from the station and she knew at once she'd said the wrong thing.

'Oh, yes.' Mitzi was haughty. 'No one can ever understand anything from the outside.' Alice admitted to herself that this was probably true. 'We're having a remarriage ceremony, if Greg can be brought round. You'll receive an invitation, of course.' But Alice could see that she, the recipient of all that was worst about Mitzi's husband, was not at the top of the welcome list.

As Alice made lunch, Mitzi walked round the flat, fulsomely praising the spacious brightness of the living room. She came into the kitchen and leant against a wall. 'Very nice place to have a breakdown, I'd say. When are you returning to the world?'

Alice was taken by surprise. 'I told you. I've sold my flat to Pandora and I'm not having a breakdown. In fact, it's quite the opposite, a kind of sticking-together.'

Mitzi gave her a sceptical look. 'Even judging by what you haven't told me about the summer and what I've read in the papers, you've a perfect right to have a complete collapse.'

'You always imagined I cared more about Brendan than I did. It was just a shock. How he died. On top of Pandora reappearing.'

'Now, that is a story. When am I going to meet her? I hope you're giving her a hard time.'

Alice smiled. Mitzi knew that she and her mother were on perfectly good terms. But it didn't seem worth arguing. Instead, when they'd returned to the table with their soup and bread, Alice told her about her discovery – or, rather, recognition – of the truth about Richard and Jonathan.

'But all men love each other more than their wives!' Mitzi wore an exasperated expression. Then she laughed. 'You don't think you're telling me something *new*! I think it's charming that Jonathan transferred his affection to you.'

Alice saw that it would take a while for Mitzi to forgive her for knowing so much about her ex-, soon-to-be-present husband's bad behaviour and decided to give up on any personal conversation.

Despite Mitzi's lack of sympathy – or perhaps because of it – Alice felt galvanised enough to get a commission out of Guy when he rang the following day.

He was co-operative: 'There's a golfing champion, who was accused of raping an under-age girl and got off on a technicality, looking for a sympathetic interviewer.'

'Oh, no.' Alice had hoped he might have divined her new attitude. 'I want to write about widows.'

'You want to write about yourself?' He sounded amazed.

'Why not?'

'No reason.' He suggested a 2500-word piece and gave her, understanding the power of a deadline, till the end of November. She bought a laptop, which sat on the table, invitingly open, its sea-green screen reminiscent of wide oceans. Words would seem puny on its endless expanse.

At last cold winds made the tall windows shiver in their frames.

Now and again Alice took Sister Mary Rose, whom she'd forgiven for keeping Pandora's identity secret, for an early supper at one of the hotels on the front. As they walked there, one late afternoon in November, passing the West Pier silhouetted against a dark red sunset, a mass of starlings whirled like a black catherine wheel into the sky. They were far enough away, hardly more than dots, to be unthreatening and yet, for an unpleasant moment, Alice was reminded of the gulls rising in front of Brendan and herself, then flying inexorably for the helicopter.

'What's the matter?' Mary Rose, ever vigilant, took her arm.

Over their meal, Alice talked about her summer. Mary Rose's eyes misted behind her glasses. When Alice had finished, she allowed a longish pause, then said softly, 'I suppose it's the price one pays for being a widow.'

It took Alice a second to understand that Mary Rose was including herself in this comment. 'I didn't know ...'

'We hadn't been married long. He was killed in a scaffolding accident. No children, of course. I left Ireland for England and had a stab at running wild, but then I found my old people.'

Although she was amused at the picture of the large, comfortable nurse 'running wild', Alice was also impressed.

'You have to find out how to live with perfect honesty,' Mary Rose continued, looking rather oracular. 'Otherwise the ever-ready forces of chaos move in.' She smiled, as if to modify her image.

'I am trying,' said Alice seriously.

Chapter Thirty

Alice walked up Oxford Street. She was amazed at the lavish brilliance of the Christmas decorations. In Brighton she had hardly noticed any. The day had been dark from its beginning and now, although it was still only half past two, the arched stars, garlands, Christmas trees and reindeer shone into a gloom nearly as black as night. Around her, the mass of shoppers moved in a unified bustle of energy, many padded out with bags, like packhorses.

One of Selfridges' windows illustrated the story of Little Red Riding Hood at the point where the wolf in Grandma's clothing smiles in what he imagines to be a friendly welcome, causing Little Red Riding Hood to shrink back in terror, crying out, 'But, Grandma, what big teeth you have!'

Alice stared at the scene for some time, thinking how lucky it was that the good woodcutter, seen poking his head through the window, had stopped by at the right time. Life seldom had such happy endings. Although she supposed, according to modern thinking, the little girl would never throw off the trauma of her experience, however fortuitous her saviour's appearance.

She'd come to London for lunch with her parents in the flat that had once been hers and had planned to spend the afternoon Christmas shopping, like everyone else. At five she had a meeting for tea at the Ritz. In the silent darkness of the early morning she had tried on every appropriate – and inappropriate – garment in her wardrobe. She had ended up entirely in black, apart from a necklace of crystal beads she'd bought from Becky's shop. She had never cut her hair and wore it knotted loosely at the back of her head. She'd rather lost touch with her appearance, with no one apart from herself to take an interest in it, but she hoped she was smart enough for the Ritz. She gave up the idea of shopping, and wandered in the direction of Piccadilly, turning off Oxford Street into Bond Street where the shoppers instantly looked more prosperous, with a less crowded air of quality-not-quantity. She could no longer afford to buy from the boutiques and designer emporiums, whose windows attracted their customers with, perhaps, a fur-lined coat swagged with pearls instead of the grisly tale of Little Red Riding Hood.

She had no money to spare for luxuries now. Her money from the paper had finally stopped coming in and she had divided most of the proceeds from the flat between Peter and Florrie.

This pavement walking suited her, though. At the end of Bond Street she made her way through pale columns to the Burlington Arcade, yet another step into luxury. She walked slowly down it, admiring richly coloured cashmere, and jewellery polished till every diamond sparkled, like a Christmas decoration.

Piccadilly was less magical, filled with four lanes of nearly stationary traffic. Disoriented, Alice looked both ways for the Ritz and found her attention caught by a row of red flags. On one, the letters A Z T E C were written large. For a moment they seemed merely an alphabetical jumble and then their meaning hit her: the Royal Academy was advertising its exhibition of Aztec art.

Hurrying now, with only an hour left before her meeting, Alice passed more heavy pillars and ornamental jets of water spurting from the ground like geysers.

The gallery was crowded but she was able to buy a ticket and press on up the wide stairs and into the dimly lit exhibition halls. Despite the number of people, there was a hushed, intense atmosphere. This was an audience aware of the cruel ways of a race, far off in every possible way, and expectant of seeing evidence of its horrors.

Alice remembered Becky's pleading for the Aztecs' civilised love of flowers and cripples, of elaborate traditions and festivals. But here was basalt stone, harshly carved with faces of once living people. Here were the threatening images of the feathered snake, the monumental effigies of gods with a niche for blood or a sacrificial heart.

She would inform Becky that although a cripple had been an honoured citizen, on a special day of worship they had become an honoured sacrifice to the gods.

The exhibition was large, room after room where nothing was less than fantastical and everything, whether a rabbit hunched and staring, or the god image of Xiuhtecuhtli, clothed in the flayed skin of a victim, was filled with virtuoso life and menace.

Alice wondered whether she could bear to complete the whole cycle of rooms. But just as she thought this she caught sight of her mask. It seemed identical, the glittering black eyes amid their skin of turquoise mosaic easily piercing its dim showcase. Alice came closer. It was far more frightening than hers, with real yellow teeth where hers had an open mouth. 'Mask of Tezcatipoca,' she read. 'Human skull, turquoise lignite, iron pyrites, marine shell, leather.' The eyes bulged horribly towards her. Trying to avoid its gaze, she saw beyond it to the huge figure of the Lord of Death. She had heard of him, but hadn't expected the horror of his more than life-size presence, his flayed skin – the liver hung out through the exposed ribs, as grisly and elegant as a lily – and the claw-like feet at the end of marionette limbs. He was leaning forward, hands with their long fingernails raised towards her, a grimace or smile on his face. He was brightly lit, although the other rooms had been dim and his long black shadow almost reached where she stood. She turned away and rushed, rather blindly, for the final room and exit.

'Alice!' A tall man stood just within the door, shadowy in the darkness of the display. Alice had the impression, nevertheless, of a substantial presence. He was carrying an overcoat over his arm. 'Don't you recognise me? It hasn't been that long.' She could see that he was smiling.

Alice recovered herself. 'Of course I know it's you, Guy. I was hurrying to meet you at the Ritz. In my imagination you were at the Ritz, not here among these ghouls.'

'I was early so I came to find your mask.'

'I found the original. Actually, I was running away from the Lord of Death. I think I've had enough of my mask too.'

'I'm not sorry to miss it. I think I know rather too much about Aztec habits already and I've only been here five minutes.'

'Are we meeting in the Ritz now?' Why had she asked him that? What would he think she meant? 'I mean, now that we've met already.' This sounded even odder.

He was still smiling. 'I've booked a table. We can't waste that.' They were outside the exhibition now, descending the staircase.

They crossed the courtyard, where the geysers were flourishing higher than ever, and moved out to the noisy jams of Piccadilly.

'Well,' said Guy, bending to kiss her cheek. She felt it fix on her like an imprint. 'I'm glad to see you at last. Kind of amazed, too.' He took her arm.

'It's been ages,' she agreed. She felt the Lord of Death's presence receding into the realms of old, forgotten bones. The pressure of Guy's arm against hers gave her a hot, breathless feeling. She didn't want to talk, or even look at him, in this busy place.

'I'm afraid we're stuck in a corner behind a pillar,' apologised Guy, as the Ritz waiter, elegant in black, led them through a cornucopia of flowers and gilt.

'It's perfect.' They sat side by side on a velvet-covered banquette, which had the advantage of continuing contact and the disadvantage that Alice couldn't properly see Guy's face. 'Everywhere's crowded,' she said. 'It's Christmas.' But she didn't want to talk about family holidays, about their movements, about the year past.

'Did you bring your piece?'

He had ordered a glass of champagne for each of them, jasmine tea and watercress sandwiches, and now he had sprung this on her. She had forgotten that this was the ostensible reason for their meeting. Should she scrabble in her bag, express amazement that she had forgotten it? 'No. I never wrote it.'

He turned sideways to look at her. Now she could see his face. His skin had lost the ruddy look of the summer but his hazel eyes were clear and concentrated. 'You're not wearing glasses,' she said. With great difficulty she stopped herself touching him.

'I don't really need them except for driving. So I've been told. You look different too.'

'I've let my hair grow.'

'Why are you dressed in black?'

'Black's fashionable. Didn't you know?' But she liked the proprietorial tone in his voice, as if he had the right to choose the way she presented herself. 'Particularly in London. No one's who's anyone wears anything but black in London.'

'But you live in Brighton?'

She heard the question mark. 'Just squatting.'

They were both silent as their order was elaborately laid out, filling every space on the little table.

'Cheers!' Guy lifted his glass.

'Cheers!' Alice tipped hers and drank as deeply as the bubbles would allow. She thought of real ale, glowing like an amber light. 'Why wouldn't you see me?'

He didn't pretend not to understand. 'I had to be sure.'

She didn't dare ask about what. She knew about what. 'You always run away from me.'

'Yes.'

She was surprised he admitted to it. But it was true. He had run away dramatically after Jonathan's performance in the Privy Council and he had run away from their harvest-moon beach. She knew there had been other occasions, which now she couldn't remember. And they hadn't met for nearly four months. 'But you're not dashing off anywhere now?'

'Only if you come with me.' They were sitting so close that she could feel his warmth all the way down one side of her. 'Tell me, Alice darling, how are declarations looked upon in fashionable London? Outlawed with red, yellow and turquoise?'

'Declarations are in, I'm told.'

'Are you sure?'

'Absolutely.'

'In that case, I'll summon the waiter.'

Alice watched, trying not to laugh as Guy explained to the bewildered but deferential waiter that his friend's grandmother had suddenly fallen ill and, if he would be so kind as to pack up their tea in a box and add an extra bottle of champagne, just a small one as the grandmother had an acid digestion problem, they would be most grateful.

Alice and Guy stood outside the Ritz while the doorman found them a taxi. A mist was rolling up from Westminster and the river. Billowing white clouds curled up to their feet.

'I love you,' said Guy, as if he couldn't wait another minute. 'I've always loved you. I've loved you for ten years seven months two weeks and four days. That was when you were first interviewed by the Master.'

'I bet you made that up.' She giggled weakly. But she must make her declaration too. 'I love you,' she said. 'I've always loved you too.'

They got into the taxi. Alice's words echoed in her ears. How extraordinary that such a thing should be the case. She had always loved him too, a burden so heavy she'd kept the secret even from herself.

The taxi ride was long. They kissed once but only briefly. They were in a hurry but, on the other hand, they had all the time in the world.

Guy's flat was in a brand new block, built on the river and facing St Paul's. 'I moved here in September,' said Guy. 'I'm the first person to live in my flat. Keep your coat on and I'll show you the view.'

The terrace ran the width of the flat, eight floors above the black water of the Thames. Alice wasn't sure about the river: water had been almost too strong a theme in her life recently, she thought. She stared instead at the comforting dome of St Paul's, at the pointed spires of churches, at the tall and small, wide and narrow buildings that clustered round the cathedral and the narrow pedestrian bridge that unrolled like a ribbon towards it. Behind her she heard Guy unpacking their box on to a table.

'It's spectacular, but won't we freeze?'

'Certainly not.'

Alice turned round and saw a swing seat with plumped-up cushions and substantial awnings set against a side wall. On either side two yucca trees stood sentinel. 'You planned it all!'

'I've waited so long.' Now they could kiss again, sip some champagne and kiss some more.

'Sit down.' The swing seat creaked and swung in the night air.

'I thought I'd have a chance when Richard died,' Guy said softly. 'I knew it was hopeless before. But you were like a sleepwalker, going through the motions of a dream. I didn't know how to wake you. I didn't dare. I didn't dare take the risk.'

'I love you, Guy.'

'Yes, I know.' The swing seat creaked and swung in the night air while the lights of the city flashed up and down and then became dim.

Guy separated himself a little. 'I suppose I should be grateful to Blue.'

Alice shivered. 'Why? What do you mean?' How could he want to talk about Blue now?

'For waking the Sleeping Beauty.'

What should she say? Did she have to say anything? Wasn't it enough that they were together now? 'So you knew?'

'Yes. Blue didn't exactly tell me, he wasn't like that, but I guessed.'

'You know he wasn't important to me.'

'I know.'

But did he know about the second time she'd slept with Blue on the island? She would never tell him about that. She was old enough to know that you don't have to tell everything. 'Don't let's think about it.'

'I'm not.'

Perhaps. 'I suppose you have a past too? All those hearty sailing girls in St Mawes.' But she didn't want to hear about his past. She willed him to keep silent.

He didn't even seem to have heard her question. 'Our coats are bothering me. It's like trying to make love to a Yeti.' He stood up and pulled Alice to her feet.

'What about the sandwiches?' She was like a blushing maiden, looking backwards.

'The night air will keep them fresh.' He seemed calm enough, leading her though the sparsely furnished living room into the bedroom, lit only by the faint glitter of the buildings beyond the river. The bed was a white mound in the middle of the room. 'I can't be less than serious about you.' Alice heard the tremor in his voice and felt the tremor in the hand that held hers.

Seriousness had been about being a widow, a mother, a grandmother, a working woman. Now it was about something else. 'I love you.' But had she the strength, after all, to start this brave new life? This was not an easy falling into bed. 'Kiss me.'

They wanted each other. That must be enough for now. He was undressing her. She was undressing him. They knew their bodies, but only to look at, not to touch, never naked. They were both romantics and wanted everything to be perfect, but they weren't young any more and knew it wasn't possible.

'We're only human,' murmured Alice, as his fingers moved over her body, carefully learning.

'Nonsense.'

'My darling.' She needed to touch him too.

Far below them on the river, a barge, passing slowly by, set up a wide wave that slapped loudly against the stone embankment. A pleasure boat, advancing from the opposite direction, gaudily lit and playing loud music, saw it and blew a high clarion. The barge answered, in a lower, mournful tone.

The two notes entered Alice's consciousness and, as she and Guy made love, they continued to sound the tired passing of the old and the optimism of the new.